The Devereaux Decision

Steve McEllistrem

CALUMET
EDITIONS
Minneapolis, Minnesota

SECOND EDITION DECEMBER 2022

THE DEVEREAUX DECISION.
Copyright © 2015 by Steve McEllistrem, All rights reserved.

ISBN: 978-1-959770-84-8

10 9 8 7 6 5 4 3 2

Author website: www.mcellistrem.com.
Book cover and design by Gary Lindberg

THE DEVEREAUX DECISION

STEVE MCELLISTREM

CALUMET EDITIONS

Minneapolis, Minnesota

Chapter 1

Sally23 longed to stay in the warm pub, but she'd already received one message from Sally2 ordering her to return to base. Seated at her table, Reg and Murph, her fellow graduate students, continued their good-natured argument over what the limits of science ought to be. As if it mattered anymore. As if their lives would not end soon. She didn't tell them that, however. They had to remain ignorant.

"I don't think you appreciate just how significant this development is," Murph said, "what this can do for the sick and dying."

"I understand perfectly, you gormless sod," Reg replied, a smile mitigating the insult as he gestured to the tablet between them on the table. "You're talkin' about playin' God. These people are messin' with things they shouldn't be messin' with."

Sally23 glanced down at the tablet, next to the basket that had held their deep-fried mushrooms and chips. She slid Reg's pint a few inches farther away from the tablet in case the argument heated up, as such arguments were wont to do. The tablet displayed a story about the upcoming transfer of a rat's mind from an animal on Earth to one on Mars. Playing God: that's what people did. She turned to look out the window at the smoke-laden sky. Here we are, a year after the Las-cannon attacks by the lunar terrorists, and the air still holds particles of toxic ash. That used to royally piss me off. Ah well, we won't have to worry about it much longer.

She wondered what death would be like. Part of her wanted to end it all right now. She knew she wasn't worthy of life. But then, nobody was. Worthless lives made her think of her father. Was he still alive? She glanced around the crowded pub, took in her fellow diners, all stretching their lunch breaks out a few more minutes, their self-indulgent conversations creating a din of blather.

There was a small part of her that still feared death. It lurked at the base of her consciousness, tamped down by a kind of indifference that came with sick understanding.

"Your ideas are antiquated, Reg," Murph spoke slowly and carefully. "Mind transfer opens limitless possibilities. If you could just expand your horizons a little—perhaps you could benefit from a transfer yourself, so you could see it doesn't change you. You'd still be the same frustrating you."

"That's insane," Reg said. "No different? You're talkin' about transplantin' a person's soul into another 'uman bein'."

"Who's talking about a soul? I'm talkin' about a mind. There's no such thing as a soul. That's an artificial construct created by man to appease a guilty conscience."

Another text arrived on Sally23's PlusPhone: where r u!!! She shook her head. Should she return to base and the rigid demands of Sally2 or just walk away and leave it all behind? Did they really need her? She'd already given them her life. Wasn't that enough? Besides, the bitch annoyed the hell out of her—worse than her mother.

"Can you believe this divvy, Bluebell?" Reg said, pulling Sally23's arm to get her attention. "Tell 'im 'e's wrong. Tell 'im 'e's goin' to 'ell."

"The only hell," Murph said, "is the one we've created right here on Earth. Have you looked outside today?"

Reg kissed Sally23's cheek. "Hey! Where's your mind been lately? You're so distracted. Tell 'im the destruction of the soul is murder."

Sally23 shook her head. Though she sided with Murph, she couldn't say that without hurting Reg's feelings. And she couldn't tell either of them the whole truth: that people were a pestilence upon this planet.

"Rats don't have souls," Murph said. He looked at Sally23. "Neither do people. You get that, don't you, Crimson?"

"You prat," Reg said. "Every 'uman bein' has a soul. Even a barmpot like you."

Sally23 stood, her eyes level with their Adam's apples. "My name isn't Bluebell or Crimson. And you're talking about a life," her voice whipped across them harshly. "Killing a rat is playing God. Experimenting on animals is playing God. It must all stop. And it will—soon enough."

Reg and Murph stared back. "Sienna, please," Reg said. "I just love your blue eyes, that's all."

"And I love your red hair," Murph said. And what's with all the Gaian talk? I thought you were done with that. I haven't seen you at the Earth Guardian meetings for months."

Because I got recruited by the Sallies and can no longer go back.

"Sienna," Reg said. He reached for her arm. "Honey?"

Stupid, Sally23 thought, to get involved in their tired argument. She pulled away from Reg's grip. "I'm running late for my tutoring session," she lied. "Somebody's got to teach our ignorant youth." She thumbed the seam of her long coat over her sweater and jeans, and headed for the door. She probably ought to stop seeing Reg. Although she liked the comfort of his body, she also felt ashamed by her physical desires. Sex was so damn complicated. Was her mother's frigidity a reaction to her father's interest in young girls? Her mother still believed that her father never would have touched her inappropriately. And she blamed Sally23's accusations for her husband's decision to abandon them.

It had taken years to detach her feelings about sex from her father, and she probably would never be able to fully distance herself from the guilt. Yet the alternative—abstinence—held no appeal. She enjoyed sex. Did that make her worse than other people? Glancing at the salon across the street, she wondered if she should become a blond for her last few months on Earth.

Using her thumbprint to start her electric scooter, Sally23 merged into the congested traffic and rolled along Oxford Street, through

London's West End, toward her meeting with Sally2. Despite the darkness of the late afternoon, the signs along the street were unlit, the businesses complying with the energy rationing imposed by the government—at least Londoners were good at rationing. The mass of commuters on this scooter-only route caused Sally23 to snort her disgust. At a crossing, where the rumble of the underground vibrated up her legs, she heard Arabic coming from the rider stopped on her left, Russian from the rider on her right, both chatting inanely on their PlusPhones, unaware that they would soon be dead.

She reached the end of Oxford Street at Marble Arch, accelerating away from Little Riyadh onto Bayswater Road, and worked her way toward Holland Park. Though she'd been born in London and was used to crowds, they seemed worse now. Was that because of her indoctrination into the Sally Sisterhood? When she spotted her destination, she veered toward the side of the road, braking in front of Sally2's temporary headquarters. The guy behind her honked as she cut in front of him; she ignored him and parked her scooter.

Peeling off her mask and goggles, Sally23 entered the building and nodded to Andre, the heavily muscled black man who ran the cell's visible security force and followed Sally2's orders with a zeal that led Sally23 to believe the two were lovers. Andre used to scare the hell out of her before she became one of the trusted and forfeited her life to the cause. He nodded back.

"Glory to Gaia," Andre said in his rough bass voice.

"Glory to Gaia," Sally23 echoed. You too, she thought. You're an infestation just like the rest of them—the rest of us. We're all a blight. We can only create perfection on this planet by purifying it of our murderous existence. Yet even as the thought crossed her mind, she shivered. Am I really ready to die? Does it matter? I've already committed to it. No stopping it now. I carry the virus.

She hung her coat on the rack, placing her backpack on the floor beneath it, then took a deep breath and used her palm print to open the metal door that provided the only access to the basement. As she descended the stairs, a man's mellifluous voice floated up to her:

"What can you possibly hope to gain with this outrageous plan? No matter how many you manage to kill, you won't be able to control it. You'll die just like the rest of us."

Sally23 reached the room—a laboratory with several machines running quietly and four Wallys working at tech stations. On a bench along the right wall, Sally17 and Sally8 sat together, whispering to each other. In the center of the room, Sally2—tall, dark and intimidating— stood facing the most beautiful man Sally23 had ever seen: brown curly hair and warm brown eyes, high cheekbones and a delicate nose atop full, sensual lips. He was secured to a metal chair, shirtless, his wrists and ankles bound tightly. Sally23 stopped in the entrance and stared at him, feeling an instantaneous connection as a tingly warmth spread up her torso. I want him. I want him to caress my body, cover me with kisses, take me on the bed, the couch, the floor.

"You're late, Twenty-three," Sally2 said.

Sally23 pulled her eyes away from the man, focused on Sally2. "Something about him looks slightly familiar, though I can't place where I might have seen him before."

"Take a seat," Sally2 said. "You'll have to catch up later."

"That's okay," the man said. "I can fill her in. My name's Trogan Brosk. I'm a CINTEP ghost."

"CINTEP?" Sally23 said. She sat next to Sally8, a tall Nigerian with a regal face and a multi-colored wrap, and nodded to Sally17, an Asian girl with a button nose, short black hair and a beauty mark just to the left of her lips. "The Center for International Economic Policy?"

"Ah," Brosk said, "you've done your homework."

Sally2 held up her hand to stop Brosk from continuing. "Up until the Las-cannon attacks," she said, "it was headed by a man named Elias Leach. Brosk worked for him as a field agent. His job was to seduce women. You can see that he was remarkably good at it."

Indeed, yes. Take me, baby. You can seduce me anytime. Sally23's eyes drifted from Brosk's lean chest to his face. A tear formed in his right eye and trickled down his cheek. He returned her gaze, as if he felt a connection to her alone. His face suggested disappointment, made her feel guilty for what was being done to him, even for what she felt about him. She thought of Reg—pleasant Reg; ordinary Reg—and looked away.

Sally17 giggled. Her short skirt hitched up a little higher, showing her dark muscular legs. "So gorgeous." She was the youngest of the trusted, having only recently taken over the 17 designation from a comrade who'd sacrificed herself releasing a new and extremely deadly batch of the Susquehanna Virus in Jakarta.

"I think I'm in love." Sally8 sighed as she leaned back and crossed her long legs, her black jeans immaculate under her orange, yellow and red wrap.

Sally23 trembled as she returned her attention to Brosk, who gazed upon all three women. He sat calmly, no trace of fear marring the beauty of his flawless face. His dark brown eyes offered the promise of a gentle lover. His plump lips invited caresses and kisses. He batted his thick lashes, and another tingle shot through Sally23's loins. She forced herself to watch Brosk only with her peripheral vision, as if he were the sun.

Meanwhile, Sally2, seemingly unaffected by his looks, began attaching a series of electrodes to his head. Sally2, in her late fifties or early sixties, carried herself with a kind of athletic arrogance—a product of her mental and physical enhancements. Yet she professed hatred for all muties. She seemed to hate everyone, herself most of all. But then, didn't everyone in the organization? Sally23 often wondered why Sally2 didn't volunteer for a dispersal mission herself, just to put an end to her miserable existence. Still, Sally2 was a critical component in the fight to save Earth. She was one of the Founding Three: one of the brains behind the Susquehanna Virus—though Sally23 knew almost as much about biochemistry as she did. And Sally23 knew a hell of a lot more about computers.

"You're enhanced," Brosk said to Sally2, his voice eminently calm and reasonable, deep and trustworthy, "and American, I think, though your accent is quite good. You almost sound British. Who are you? You remind me a little of this doctor I once knew—Leah Shafer—a genetic psychologist who did occasional work for CINTEP years ago and then just vanished one day. She helped me overcome a bout of fear a few years ago with advanced conditioning. Are you her?"

"No," Sally2 said.

"I think maybe you are," Brosk said. "You don't look the same, but then you could have easily changed your appearance. Whoever you are, I can sense your pain. I can read it in the way you hold yourself, the way you move. Who betrayed you? Who is it you can't forgive? A man, certainly. Your father? A lover? I'm sorry for what was done to you, and I forgive you for what you're doing to me."

Sally2 avoided eye contact with him. She clamped her jaw tightly as she pressed a hypo-pad to the back of his hand. Brosk looked at Sally23 again, at the Sallies beside her. "I forgive you too," he said, his voice trembling ever so slightly. "And I hope you forgive yourselves. You're all so damaged." Sally23 flushed. She suddenly recalled the vid-picture of her father that her mother kept on the sideboard. Brosk, though he looked nothing like her father, somehow reminded her of that. She felt excited and ashamed at the same time.

"He's probing for weaknesses," Sally2 said. "Ignore him."

"And you're trying to bend me to your cause," Brosk said, his voice quavering with sorrow. He studied Sally23, fixing her with the heat of his attention as if he'd determined that she was the weakest link. She spared him only brief glances. Even so, her breathing became shallow—almost panting. "Do you think it will work?" He appeared to be asking the question of Sally23. "Or is it just your way of feeling better about yourself?"

"This isn't about you," Sally2 answered him. "You're a tool, pure and simple. I'm going to use you as others before me have."

"I think you might have a touch of autism. Do you know if that's the case?"

Sally2 flushed and a muscle in her jaw twitched. She closed her eyes for a few seconds and when she opened them, she was back in control.

Brosk said, "What'd you give me, anyway, some sort of poison? I can feel it working."

"The Susquehanna Virus. And these," Sally2 touched one of the electrodes on the man's head, "are accelerating its dispersal through your body, into all your major organs. Heart, lungs, liver—even your brain."

"The virus doesn't work that way," Brosk said. "It hides in the immune system."

"It used to." Sally2 smiled briefly, a flash of teeth that made Sally23 shiver. The woman's an ice queen. "We've modified the virus," Sally2 explained. "There are now over forty-seven different varieties floating around. Some are self-mutating. Some we've altered here in the lab. Each new permutation attacks the body in a different way. All are fatal. Some just work more quickly than others."

"People have survived it though," Brosk said. "When it was first released in Rochester—"

Sally2 laughed harshly. "The first few versions were experimental— less potent. Some of the viruses we're putting out now are slow acting, but nobody completely recovers from them. And immunity to one version is not immunity to all. Eventually, one permutation or another will target every human and the entire race will disappear."

"So your Gaia movement is really humanicide?"

"You sound surprised."

"There've been many fanatics throughout the centuries," Brosk said, "with many different methods of killing. But I've never heard of one that wanted to wipe out the planet."

"No," Sally2 said. "Not the planet. That's where you're wrong. It's only humanity we wish to destroy."

"It's just a figure of speech," Brosk said.

"It's imprecise," Sally2 said.

"Don't you feel superior?" Brosk asked, his voice now hard, accusing. "Don't you seek an Eden where you can live in the bliss of perfect ignorance?"

Sally2 backed up a step.

"No one," Brosk continued, "ever gives up power completely, voluntarily."

"Until now," Sally2 said.

"And do all your followers, all Earth Guardians, share your viewpoint?"

Sally2 said, "The trusted do. And the Earth Guardians are fools, thinking they can alter the future with words."

Brosk looked directly at Sally23, his mouth curled in an ironic smile, as if he could read her thoughts, her doubts. A warmth spread through the center of her body. How could she want him so badly when she had Reg? On the other hand, Reg was so unremarkable, so safe. And she didn't love Reg even if she liked him. She broke eye contact.

"You think you can kill every human on the planet?"

"Our advances with the virus are so great that the annihilation of everyone will occur soon."

A brief tic developed at the corner of Brosk's mouth.

"I know what you're thinking," Sally2 said. "We're aware that two men have so far shown immunity to the virus. Two transgenic men. Pseudos. They call themselves Escala. They're unnatural freaks. So you hope that a cure may yet be found. And the great Walt Devereaux is working on it. But he will fail. The new versions of the virus are much deadlier than the old. Nothing will stop them. By the end of the month, Indonesia's population will be annihilated. By the end of next year, humanity will cease to be."

Sally23 shivered again. Was that excitement or fear?

"Why Indonesia?" Brosk asked.

"Because it's the most difficult area to infect," Sally2 answered. "All those islands. We want to prove that we can deliver our purification to the farthest reaches of the globe. After our work is done," Sally2 continued, in a more talkative mood than Sally23 had ever seen her, "the planet will become a vast wasteland to humans. Not even those pseudo freaks on Mars will be able to survive here."

"How will you know you've succeeded?" Brosk asked. "If you're dead too, how can you be sure? Unless you're planning to stay alive."

Brosk looked steadily at Sally23 now, understanding in his wonderfully expressive eyes. "That's it, isn't it? You don't really want to die. When it comes down to the end, you'll claw and scratch and fight for life, just like the rest of us."

Sally23 flushed as Brosk began to shudder, then groan. The four Wallys—techs who helped Sally2 build her versions of the virus—stopped what they were doing and observed him. Sally23 told herself she had no reason to feel guilty; she was committed to the movement. Yet Brosk wasn't evil. Somehow she knew that. *I'd bet my life on that—worthless as it may be.*

"Or perhaps," Brosk continued once he recovered his breath, "you've turned off the death genes in your bodies so you can live for hundreds of years."

"There is no antidote," Sally2 said. As Brosk's body spasmed, Sally2 reached out a hand briefly before pulling it back. *Was that real, or was a she playing game with the Sallies, trying to get them to care about him?* "And we're already all infected. But some strains of the virus are more painful than others. The virus infecting the trusted, for example, will simply cause us to fall asleep, drifting gently into eternal slumber."

Sally23 recognized the phrasing from when she'd been asked to join the trusted. It was exactly the kind of manipulation Sally2 delighted in. *Did the other Sallies notice the cliché? Did they have doubts too? Was that why they were here, to witness Brosk's painful death as some sort of warning?*

"The virus I gave you," Sally2 continued, "is agonizing—a result of its relatively fast-acting nature."

Brosk began to twitch, his jaw muscles working angrily as short grunts emerged from his throat.

"What a shame," Sally8 said. "Such a lovely man."

Sally17 giggled again. "He'll make a lovely corpse."

Sally23 shook her head as Brosk stared at her. *Why had he fixated on her?* His arms and legs fought the restraints, and his head moved from side to side. His grunts grew louder, until he began screaming. Sally23 jumped to her feet. She'd never heard a man scream before. It took her a moment to realize what she'd done. She stopped herself from walking over to him, forced herself to take her seat again, to put a neutral expression on her face. *Is that my heart breaking? Will I fight for life the way Brosk is?* She wanted to tell Sally2 to stop torturing the poor man. This wasn't what she'd signed up for. *Humanity has to go, yes—but not by the most painful means possible.*

Sally2 had been watching her. Now she turned to Brosk, her lips trembling ever so slightly.

Finally Brosk's head dropped to his chest. Sally2 gestured to the techs, who removed Brosk from the chair and carried him from the room.

Sally2 turned to her. "You have a problem with what I did?"

"Frankly, yes. You said you were going to use him as a tool. How do you plan to do that if he's dead?"

"You have feelings for him."

"Why does he need to be tortured?"

"Brosk isn't dead," Sally2 replied with a smile. "We're breaking him down, reconditioning him, programming him for one final mission. We'll bring him to the brink of death a few more times before we begin to rebuild him."

"And those electrodes?" Sally8 asked. "For modifying his behavior?"

Sally2 nodded. "We're going to re-wire his brain. He'll be difficult to crack. He's been so thoroughly programmed by CINTEP that the process may turn him into little more than a simpleton. But we only need him to perform one simple task. And one of you will accompany him to ensure that he succeeds. Still, that's a project for another day. Meanwhile," she pointed to the table by the side of the door, "we have deliveries to make, people to kill."

Sally23 followed Sally8 and Sally17 to the table and looked at the shopping bags from local stores that now held containers of the virus. She said, "What about those two men who are immune? What if there are others? What if Devereaux finds a cure in time?"

Sally2's eyes narrowed, boring into Sally23's. "You're troubled by much of what we do. Can we still trust you?"

"I don't know. Can you act honorably?"

Immediately Sally23 regretted her outburst. Sally2 could have her killed with a word, either to Andre or one of the Wallys.

But Sally2 just smiled. "I took you off communications because you question too much. That's also why I no longer allow you to assist me with my experiments."

Sally23 swallowed. "I'm not afraid of you. If you want to kill me, kill me."

Sally2 glared at her as Sally8 and Sally17 backed away. Then Sally2 laughed, though her cheeks reddened. She looked at Sally8 and Sally17. "Eight and Seventeen, grab your bags and go. Twenty-three, you'll remain behind to help turn Brosk. You'll accompany him on his mission. Glory to Gaia."

"Glory to Gaia," Sally8 and Sally17 responded as they hurried out the door.

Sally23 stood before Sally2, her stomach fluttering. She wanted Brosk; she wanted an exciting, extraordinary man. Even though Sally2 was manipulating her into creating a bond with him, she didn't care. She desired Brosk—partly for his looks, yes, but also because he represented what humanity might have become had it turned away from selfishness. Sally2, on the other hand, confirmed the evil inherent in the species. Sally23 saw that clearly. Despite her agreement that humans had to vanish, she despised the arrogance of Sally2.

So she'd play the game that Sally2 ordered her to play. The end result wasn't in question anyway. She'd already surrendered her life and she accepted that. She didn't really regret giving it away. But now she wanted to see Sally2 die before she went.

Chapter 2

Aspen wiped the environmental sensors and flicked the dust cloth, releasing fine red particles that drifted down Dunadan's knoll toward the airlock to Tunnel Two. Moving on to the communications array, she glanced back at the sealed-off tunnel entrance to the New Dawn Martian settlement, then over to the pods where the idiots from the MineStar colony resided: a few kilometers away. A rotating crew of around fifty worked on Mars at any given time. Their current number was forty-eight. And their health was fragile.

Aspen still didn't understand why the Escala had elected to settle nearby; she would have chosen the other side of the planet. The miners annoyed her. Supposedly self-sufficient—a ship came to offload ore and deliver a new crew every twenty-six months—they constantly intruded on the Escala for assistance: food, medicine, equipment and companionship. She wondered if it would bother her as much if the miners hadn't created a trash dump a kilometer away, always in sight when she was outdoors.

Beneath her feet, the vibration of the miners' big tunneling machines suddenly stopped. They'd agreed to cease digging during the experiment, so it must be starting soon. Aspen gazed up at the three inactive volcanoes that made up the Tharsis Montes. Then she stared out into space, across the darkness that separated her from Zora, toward the small white light of Earth.

Home.

Aspen remembered almost nothing about her early childhood. She recalled her parents only vaguely. But one clear memory stood out: the dock out in front of their home, and the vast lake that stretched for kilometers. The image of clear blue water and sky, interrupted only by the green pines on the far shore, left her feeling hollow as she surveyed the endless reddish sand beneath her feet.

She activated her powerscope until Earth appeared as a blue marble, streaked with white. It still looked impossibly small; her powerscope's settings only went so high. Above the Earth the Moon circled slowly. Aspen wished she were back there, on the Moon, with Zora and Rendela. But Rendela was dead, the lunar colony was in the process of rebuilding, and Zora, after sending Aspen and five other cadets to Mars with the Escala, and after promising to keep in touch, had virtually shut down.

On the rare occasion that Zora returned a message, she provided scant information and almost nothing of a personal nature, as if she wanted nothing to do with Aspen anymore. No doubt part of it was the constant pain she was in: the cost of the transfusion that had saved her life. The blood she received had been infected with the Susquehanna Virus and resulted in severe and incurable arthritis. Aspen wondered if that was the only reason Zora had withdrawn. Had Zora forgotten their days together in the Tong? Had she forgotten that she was supposed to be the cadets' leader? How badly damaged was she?

"Aspen?" Addam's voice came over her suit's comm unit. "You mind if I join you?"

Aspen sighed and told him to come on up. She knew what he wanted, what all the boys wanted. In the last few months she and her fellow cadets had become sexually active. On the Moon as eleven-year-olds, they had been given hormones and nanobots and had their DNA altered until their bodies became fully developed adult bodies, but their sex drives had been suppressed and altered to bring out fits of rage so they would comply with their programming and destroy select governments on Earth. Now they functioned, according to Dr. Wellon, in the normal range for twenty-year-olds. Did all twenty-year-old boys want sex as much as Addam did? To be honest, Aspen found it less than thrilling. Maybe if she loved Addam, she would enjoy it more; but the person she really loved had abandoned her, and Aspen had too many things on her mind to be able to simply relax and enjoy sex.

Recently she and Addam had become a more-or-less monogamous couple, as had Shiloh and Phan, Kammilee and Benn. Occasionally one of them would sleep with one of the massive Escala teenagers but those instances were becoming rarer. The Escala were happy on Mars; this was the planet they were built for, while Aspen and her fellow cadets had been created for . . . what—Earth? The Moon? Or had they simply been designed to die? At any rate, she wished for the home she barely remembered, though her fellow cadets didn't seem all that depressed by their exile.

"Hey," Addam said as he nudged the shoulder of her Mars suit, "you worried about Guffie?"

"They don't care about him," Aspen said. "He's just a rat to them."

"They're scientists," Addam said. "They remind me of all the doctors who used to prod and poke us on the Moon. Remember Hack'emup?"

"Dr. Hackett," Aspen said with a nod. "I think I hated him the most. He made every visit painful."

"Well, he can't bother you anymore," Addam said as he rubbed the back of Aspen's suit, confirming her guess as to his intentions.

Aspen shut off the powerscope. "You think Guffie might survive?"

"I don't know," Addam replied. "Quekri says there's a good chance the experiment will work."

"She doesn't know, though. It's never been done before. And Guffie, poor little Guffie . . ."

"He'll probably be fine. And if he doesn't make it, there are other animals up here, other rats."

"You don't understand either," Aspen said.

"He's just a rat," Addam said. "He's a nice rat but he's still just a rat. I think the only reason you like him so much is because you want to have babies."

"You're a stupid boy."

"I'm sorry," Addam said. He touched his helmet to hers, pinching his eyebrows together and pursing his lips in a plea. "Please don't be mad."

Aspen pulled away from him. "Why are you out here?"

"Quekri thought you'd want to be there when they start the experiment."

"I'll be there shortly."

"By the way," Addam said, "did you know Kammilee wants to get pregnant?"

Aspen nodded. "She told me. I think it's stupid. She only wants it because three Escala women managed to get pregnant."

"I still don't understand how that happened. I thought they were sterile."

"On Earth they were—even on the Moon. But their bodies continue to evolve. Dr. Wellon says all the Escala women will be able to get pregnant within the year. If you want, they might even let you father a child."

"I wouldn't mind sleeping with Zeriphi."

"She's already pregnant," Aspen said.

"Too bad. I'll do the visual scan on the ship if you want. Have you done it yet?"

Aspen handed him the powerscope and he put it up to his helmet, staring off toward Earth. Aspen looked at the distant planet again, now just a bright light, little different from all the others in the darkness. It wasn't even as large or luminous as Deimos, the smaller of Mars' two moons. Phobos, the bigger moon, had already set, due to rise again in seven hours.

"The ship's changed direction," Addam said. He sent the coordinates to the control center while Aspen finished cleaning the communications array. "It's no longer navigating off our comm-link. Maybe it's not really coming here."

Aspen shrugged. "Quekri said the trajectory is perfect and it'll be here in about a month. But the Chinese aren't saying anything." She glanced toward Earth again, but couldn't see the ship. "If it's just changed direction, then nobody really knows."

Addam lowered the powerscope and looked at her. "You think Curtik and Zora are okay? Curtik sounds all right when he answers my queries."

"Zora's in a lot of pain. She won't take the drugs they've offered."

"Why not? Curtik says they work great."

"I think it's because she's in love with Jeremiah Jones."

"That old guy? What's he got to do with it?"

Aspen shrugged. "He's in pain, so she wants to be in pain too."

"That's weird."

Aspen sighed. "I sort of understand. Anyway, it doesn't matter. We'll never see home again."

As they walked back to the Tunnel Two entrance, Addam said, "Zora might visit us."

"And leave her precious Jeremiah behind? I don't think so."

"Well," Addam said. "We should forget about Zora and Jeremiah Jones and Earth and the Susquehanna Virus and all that crap. We're on Mars now. We're part of the future of humanity. We're with the Escala."

As they reached the New Dawn airlock, Aspen gazed about her at the desolate landscape, no less barren than the Moon, except for the MineStar colony and the garbage dump. She said, "This place will never be home."

Entering the airlock, Addam right behind her, Aspen sealed it up and removed her Mars suit. She placed her suit beside Addam's and opened the inner lock to the tunnel. It stretched away in a curve, moving down and to the right, leading fifty meters underground, with dozens of small caves branching off for various rooms. It looked much like the tunnels on the Moon, though the rock surface shone red in the light of the glow globes that hovered near the ceiling. And like the tunnels on the Moon, this one held hundreds of small vines that climbed the walls, providing oxygen and, someday, berries. But the atmospheric pressure was lower, which gave her a headache. And the fine red dust was inescapable. Her throat always felt parched.

As they walked along the tunnel, Aspen recalled her time on the Moon. Everything was so different here, partly because gravity was thirty-eight percent Earth standard, while the Moon had been one-sixth. She felt more substantial and yet more lost. The sun, whenever she was outside, looked so small and shone with so little intensity in comparison to its size and brightness on the Moon that she despaired of ever feeling normal again—whatever that meant.

"I like it here," Addam said, reaching out to brush the leaves of a vine.

"Have you noticed how content Shiloh and Kammilee are?" Aspen asked. "And even Phan and Benn?"

Addam nodded slowly. "We've got it pretty good. Benn said he wouldn't mind having genetic surgery to become one of the Escala."

"What?"

"He and I have talked about it," Addam said.

"Well, you can't do it."

"Why not? We'd have an easier time on Mars if we had the surgery. And who made you the boss?"

"Zora did, remember?" Aspen reached the entryway to her room— her little cave—and swept the curtain aside. "Quekri would never allow it anyway. We're a separate race—not that many of us left. You and Benn can't change what you are. There's a chance we might return to Earth one day, if the old humans die off."

"You think the Susquehanna Virus will kill them?"

"Dr. Wellon says it's getting deadlier all the time. She says some of the newer varieties are extremely potent, killing within days."

"Serves them right for ruining the planet."

"I don't care about them," Aspen said. "I care about Zora."

"What about Curtik and the others?" Addam said.

Aspen shook her head as she entered her room. Without asking permission, Addam followed her inside. That irked her a little. This was her place, not his—her bed, her chest of possessions, her vid of Emerging Man on the wall. "Do you ever feel the rage anymore?" she said.

"No."

"Do you miss it?"

"Why would I?" Addam's voice rose in surprise. "It feels nice not to be angry all the time."

"I think when Dr. Wellon cured us, we lost some essential component of who we are."

"You have to admit that on the flight here, we were in pretty bad shape. If not for her, we might not have survived."

"True," Aspen said. She thought back to the four-month flight from the Moon to Mars, to the terrifying rage that overwhelmed her and her five companions, threatening them with complete devolution into unreasoning animals. "But for some reason, I feel like I'm not complete, like I'm missing a part of me."

"Didn't Dr. Wellon explain it to you?" Addam asked. "She said the whole point of the Lunar Cadet Program was to create super soldiers who would kill without hesitation, with maximum efficiency and speed. The rage was necessary because it clarified thought and allowed for quick, decisive action. That's probably what you miss."

Aspen shook her head. "Sometimes I wish I had a Las-cannon so I could demolish a city or even a whole country, purifying Earth of the crazies who run it. But no matter how many I managed to kill, more would sprout up to take their places. And those miners . . . sometimes I want to wipe them out before they ruin this place."

"Perhaps Susquehanna Sally, whoever or whatever she is, will change all that. She claims to have a new metric. Global cleansing. Maybe that's why that Chinese ship is on its way here." Addam's eyes glazed over for a second. "We'd better get to the lab."

"Go. Tell Quekri I'll be right there."

When Addam left, Aspen took a moment to decompress, to savor being alone. Perhaps that's why Zora never initiated contact with her. Maybe Zora was relishing her first taste of life without responsibilities. Possibly she was just being a kid. Aspen opened the chest and removed the vid-picture of Zora she'd made before leaving the Moon. It showed Zora breaking into laughter. "I miss you," she said. "I love you."

She stared at the vid-picture for a few seconds until her eyes began to blur, then put it back and headed to the lab—a well-lit cave further down the main tunnel, where Quekri, the Escala leader, stood before the equipment that would be transmitting Guffie's mind to Earth. A quick rush forward, a knife severing the spinal cord, would paralyze Quekri and allow Aspen the time to make another strike into Quekri's heart. Aspen told herself she didn't really want to kill Quekri; that image was just the residue of her rage.

"We couldn't wait any longer," Quekri said. "We started without you."

Her dark hair and skin reminded Aspen of a wild animal—huge and powerful. Was that just because Aspen was so pale and blond? She glanced over at Zeriphi, working at another station. Zeriphi—the prettiest Escala woman—had blond hair like Aspen, but darker skin. She stood six and a-half feet tall and weighed over two hundred Earth-pounds, yet she was actually a little shorter and thinner than Quekri. The male Escala were even bigger, nearly seven feet tall and three hundred Earth-pounds: more than a foot taller and twice the weight of the cadets. The cadets maybe moved faster, their transgenic nature granting them speed surpassing anything ordinary humans could achieve, but the Escala were nearly as fast and they had enormous strength.

Shiloh, working beside Zeriphi, looked like her true age of eleven. Aspen had to remind herself that Shiloh actually possessed the body and mind of an adult woman. Sometimes Aspen wished she could be a kid again. And then she would recall the physical and mental enhancements and all the things she could do and she would be glad they had accelerated her growth.

And according to Dr. Wellon, their minds had been enhanced to the point where they were almost as advanced as the Escala.

Addam stood before the DCD—the Stelzie-Hanson Digital Collector and Descrambler that was transferring Guffie's mind to Earth. On the far wall a holo-projection of the Earth rat—Hugh—was being projected to Mars, an image that was actually fifteen minutes in the past.

Aspen nodded as she approached Guffie, who lay motionless on the receptor plate, four small transmitters aimed at his skull, set to transport Hugh's mind into Guffie's brain. "It's okay, Guffie," Aspen said to him. She wanted to stroke him, comfort him, but she knew Guffie's mind was already gone. And Quekri insisted that no one touch him during the transfer. Even the tunneling machines had been shut down, a precaution against a particularly strong vibration that might throw off the calibrations of the DCD.

She studied the monitor above Guffie's body. So far, everything appeared to be working perfectly. The chemical and electrical signals of Guffie's neurons were compressed by the DCD and transmitted as electrical impulses to Earth, where they would enter the machine and reconstitute as chemical and electrical signals in the Earth rat's brain. A glance at the chrono showed that the transmission to Earth had begun thirteen minutes ago; the data Earth was transmitting back had begun at that instant.

Addam stepped back and gestured for Aspen to take his place at the DCD. He was a good guy, Aspen realized, even if she didn't love him. She smiled her thanks and went over the controls, confirming that the calibrations were perfectly aligned. Quekri gave her a nod as her eyes darted from system to system, checking the status of each one, as if she could do anything about it now. Why did Quekri consider this experiment so vital? Even if it worked, its practical applications were limited. She had to know that.

A small light came on above Guffie's head, indicating that Earth's transmission had finally arrived. The machine now dispersed Hugh's mind into Guffie's brain, which meant Guffie's mind was even now loading into Hugh's brain. When Aspen examined the scanner monitor, checking for brainwave activity in the appropriate regions, she found none.

"Nothing so far," she said.

"Give it time," Quekri said as she bent to examine the DCD more closely. "You can't expect it to absorb everything the other rat knew in a matter of seconds."

Aspen watched the scanner as the rat's brainwave activity began to register, just in bits and dashes at the moment, as Hugh's memories and knowledge transferred into Guffie's brain. Guffie's body, meanwhile, continued to perform all autonomic nervous system functions. If the experiment worked, Guffie's body would awaken with Hugh's conscious mind.

"Can you imagine the possibilities that arise from this?" Quekri asked.

"The ability to travel at the speed of light?" Addam said.

"Eventually, yes," Quekri replied. "But more importantly, if successful, this will open the door to potentialities only dreamed of. Combined with genetic manipulation, this will allow humans to evolve into many different subspecies, with special adaptations for survival in select environments. We'll be able to create humans who can breathe methane gas, for example, or people with gills who can breathe underwater."

Shiloh said, "I thought the mind-body connection was too strong to allow for such displacement."

"That's always been a problem with chimeras," Quekri acknowledged. "It's what created the rage in us. But if we're successful today, we might be able to avoid that kind of side effect in the future, in which case we'll be able to create as many permutations of transgenic species as we can imagine."

"We could also," Zeriphi spoke for the first time, "postpone death for many years."

"Like turning off the death gene?" Addam said. "A fountain of youth?"

"The technology could be used that way," Zeriphi said, "with robotic bodies."

"I wonder," Aspen said, "if Devereaux had all this in mind when he conceived his ladder of enlightenment."

"He knew it was possible," Quekri said. "But he cautioned against going down this path."

Zeriphi said, "Yet he knew there would be humans who would seek eternal life. Just as there were people who cloned themselves, there will be some who seek to live forever. And we're giving them the tools to do it."

"Sooner or later," Quekri said, "someone was going to experiment with mind transfer. Whether we succeed or not, someone will solve the problems eventually."

Zeriphi shrugged ever so slightly, acknowledging the truth of Quekri's statement. Aspen, glancing down at her monitor, saw that conscious brain activity had increased dramatically. She hoped without really believing that somehow Guffie's mind had returned to them. She tried to keep the excitement out of her voice: "Near normal levels of brain activity on the graph."

Guffie's legs started twitching. He lifted his head as his tail flicked back and forth. Come on, Guffie, Aspen thought. Rub your nose with your left paw. She bent down to look into Guffie's eyes. He ignored her.

"You have to reboot him now," Addam said.

"I know," Aspen replied. She picked Guffie up and placed him at the starting point of the maze.

"Did you notice that?" Quekri said. "He didn't rub his nose with his paw."

"I noticed," Aspen said, her stomach dropping. "And he didn't recognize me."

"Because he's not Guffie anymore. He's Hugh."

"So," Shiloh said, "this maze has been reconfigured to exactly match the one the scientists are using on Earth?"

"Correct," Quekri said. "If the mind transfer worked, Hugh should be able to navigate the maze."

Aspen glanced at the holo-projection. Hugh's body lay motionless, the transfer no doubt complete back on Earth, but the data stream lagging by fifteen minutes.

Shiloh said, "Can't we just scan his brain to see if the transfer worked?"

"We'll do that too," Quekri said. "But running a full analysis will take a couple days. And our experiments indicate he must be challenged mentally as soon as possible after the transfer to seat the mind properly in the new brain."

Hugh struggled to his feet and entered the maze. Aspen knew he ought to turn left, right, left if the transfer worked. If not, if this was somehow actually Guffie, he ought to turn right, left and right. As he made his way to the first T in the maze she found herself holding her breath. When the rat turned left, she exhaled, fighting the disappointment. She glanced at the holo-projection again, hoping Guffie was okay in Hugh's body on Earth.

"It worked!" Addam shouted.

"Patience," Quekri said.

But the rat turned right at the next intersection, then left. "He's doing it perfectly," Shiloh said. "No hesitation at all."

"Not yet," Quekri conceded. "But if there are problems, they're likely to appear later in the memorized sequence of turns."

Hugh made yet another turn correctly, scurrying along a straight run for several feet, then went left at a T halfway down the run. Aspen told herself she ought to be happy. Hugh was navigating the maze perfectly. At the sixth intersection he turned left. On the holo-projection, the light over Hugh's body came on, indicating the beginning of the transfer on Earth.

Aspen returned her attention to Hugh. He walked more slowly now, as if less sure of himself. Upon reaching the seventh intersection he stopped. His whiskers twitched as his head turned left, then right.

"Right," Shiloh whispered.

But Hugh moved in neither direction. He simply sat on his haunches and stared at the wall. He seemed to have lost all interest in continuing. A minute passed. Quekri strengthened the odor of peanut butter and even ran a slight electrical current into Hugh's backside but the animal refused to go any further. He began to tremble, lowering himself to his belly. Finally he fell over on his side, his breathing distressed.

Aspen felt a numbness overcoming her. Addam put his arm around her shoulders. On the holo-projection, Guffie awoke and rubbed his nose with his left paw, then was placed at the start of his maze.

"So close," Quekri said, picking up Hugh and holding him close to her face. She peered into his eyes as if she could see into his tiny brain.

"We'll have to run scans," Zeriphi said, "to see what went wrong. Clearly, given how fast he moved through the first few turns, the transfer was—at least in part—successful. There must be another problem."

"He's dying," Quekri said as she placed Hugh back on the receptor plate of the DCD. She looked at Aspen. "Let's get as much information as we can. Aspen. Aspen! You all right?"

Aspen nodded. She pulled away from Addam and set the scanner to run accelerated scans, providing less detail but more images, hopefully allowing for enough extrapolation to determine what aspect of the transfer had proven fatal. As the scans ran, she stared at Guffie back on Earth. He began navigating the maze tentatively.

"I realize this is tough for you," Quekri said, "but we brought these rats to Mars for a reason. They're doing what they're supposed to."

"I know," Aspen replied. "But I still don't see why this is such a big deal. Who would want to give up her body?"

"You're young," Quekri answered, "and enhanced. You may never need something like this. But there are millions who could benefit from this technology."

"I get that," Aspen said. "It's for old people. But what about the effects of age on the brain? What about the inevitable decline? Won't that just continue to worsen with each generation of host bodies? Even if you put a mind into a new brain, won't the old mind, with all its shortcomings, continue the degradation predicted by the Patterson formula?"

Quekri frowned. "What do you know about the Patterson formula?"

Aspen recalled the summary of the formula she'd stored in her implant. "It theorizes that no matter how one tries to revivify a mind, even to the point of transfer to an entirely new brain, the favored patterns of the old mind will result in a decrease in the efficiency of future growth that will eventually become a retardation."

"Very good," Quekri said. "And it's possible the Patterson formula applies. But until we achieve a successful mind transfer, we'll never know."

The scanner beeped, indicating that Hugh had died. Aspen glanced at the holo-projection, where Guffie continued to work his way through the maze, slowly, as if in pain. She shivered as she checked the scanner, saw that it had completed only eighty-eight percent of the rapid scans required to get a full picture of the brain. She took a deep, calming breath, remembering how Guffie used to run up her right arm, across her shoulders and down to her left hand, where she always had a peanut ready for him. She said, "We lost twelve percent."

Quekri sighed. "It will have to do." She stared at Aspen for a moment, raising her eyebrows. "I didn't realize you were such an expert on mind-body connectivity. Perhaps you should take the lead on this. Analyze the scans, run the projections, discover where we went wrong. I'll help as much as I'm able but running the colony takes a lot of my time. Can I count on you?"

Aspen longed to punch Quekri in the face, chop her fat throat, kick the side of her knee so she'd drop to the ground, where Aspen could pummel her. A sudden bout of nausea forced her to clamp her teeth together. She didn't really want to hurt Quekri, she realized. She just felt sad and angry. She took shallow breaths and thought about Guffie until the urge to vomit passed.

"You okay?" Quekri asked.

Aspen nodded. On the holo-projection, Guffie continued through the maze. He finally reached the end and began licking at the peanut butter there before falling over on his side. Was he dying too? With the fifteen-minute delay in transmissions he might already be dead, but he still lived on in the holo-projection. Aspen stared at it. A pair of hands picked Guffie up and placed him back in the Earth DCD, where the scanner began running.

"Just because our rat died doesn't mean theirs will," Zeriphi said.

But Aspen knew Guffie was doomed. No matter that Guffie had been a fighter. Guffie's decline almost exactly matched Hugh's. In moments Guffie would be dead.

Everyone in the cave stared at the screen now, waiting for the inevitable. No one spoke. Aspen found herself wishing for Guffie to live. She closed her eyes and begged whatever higher power there was to spare Guffie. She promised to obey all Quekri's orders without question.

"He's still hanging on," Addam said. Aspen opened her eyes, watched the holo-projection, where Guffie's legs twitched. That was different from what happened to Hugh. Hope flickered in Aspen's thoughts. Perhaps Guffie would make it after all.

"Aspen?" Quekri said.

Aspen looked at the Escala leader. "Yes?"

"Can you take the lead on this project?"

"Oh, sorry," Aspen replied. "Zora knows a lot more about this kind of thing than me. But yes, you can count on me." She turned back to the holo-projection, watching Guffie continue to make feeble movements with his legs. At least he was still alive.

Chapter 3

Doug Robinson heard a distant explosion as a plume of smoke rose in the direction of Freedom Park, where food riots had been reported earlier. Before he could pull up the vid of the commotion, Walt Devereaux's PlusPhone rang again. Gwendolyn Pryce-Jones was on the line. The calendar also chimed quietly with a reminder for one of Quark's radiation treatments. Doug sent a message to Quark as he answered the PlusPhone, "Hello, Madam Prime Minister."

"Dougie, how are you, lad?"

"Fine, thanks for asking. How are you?"

"Shocked. I just heard that before you went to work for Devereaux you were incarcerated for drugs and theft. Is that correct?"

Doug gritted his teeth. He hated having his past brought up. He felt like telling her it was none of her business, that his past didn't matter to Devereaux so it shouldn't matter to her, that he had been imprisoned because of prejudice in the system against those with darker skin, that whites still saw far less prison time than blacks and Hispanics, and if he'd been white he would have received a lesser sentence, maybe even a suspended sentence, and maybe the cops wouldn't have harassed him at all, but he knew that wasn't the complete truth, for he had broken the law. He said, "Yes, ma'am."

"I'll be damned. I never would have guessed. You clean up nicely. Obviously Devereaux knew about your past."

"Yes, ma'am. He said he saw potential in me and wanted to give me a chance. Not many people will hire a convicted felon who used to be an addict and thief."

"I also heard that he insisted you be given the job or he wouldn't work for the CDC."

"He what?" Devereaux, that greatest of men, rose even higher in Doug's estimation. Why hadn't anyone ever mentioned that to him? Because Devereaux would have told them not to. He probably didn't want Doug to know. How could Doug ever repay him? "How did you—"

"I'm the Prime Minister of Great Britain, Dougie. People tell me things. Don't worry, this doesn't change our relationship. Is the great man in?"

"He's working on the Susquehanna Virus at the moment. He told me he couldn't be disturbed."

"Now don't be an officious little bastard, Dougie. Is he aware of the havoc that's being caused by this bloody little rodent?"

"Yes, ma'am. But he believes the virus is almost out of control and he doesn't have time to worry about anything else at the moment."

"Riots in the streets don't matter?"

Doug could tell she was close to a fit. "Of course they matter, Madam Prime Minister."

"I realize that this isn't totally his fault, but his theories formed the foundation for this project. He and the Escala share in the responsibility for this backlash. I'm simply asking for any assistance he can provide. Perhaps a statement that this is not a further attempt to destroy religion or the status quo?"

"I will certainly ask him, ma'am," Doug said, "as soon as he gets a free moment."

"Thanks, Dougie. That's a good lad." Pryce-Jones disconnected.

Whoa, Doug thought. So intense. Glad I'm not married to her.

His eye drifted to the small vid-picture on the corner of his desk. It displayed a vid of his daughter, Celestia, who lived with her mother.

Although she was only fifteen months old, she was already talking like a two-year-old. Doug treasured the half-dozen vids he'd received from Zeriphi. She didn't have to do that for him, but he was grateful she had. In every one Celestia babbled on about some new thing she had seen or learned, causing Doug to marvel at the hollowness she could generate inside his chest. This tiny child who was born on the Moon and now resided on Mars held a power over him he wouldn't have believed possible two years ago. He wondered what it would feel like to hold her.

Three more calls came in on Devereaux's PlusPhone. He didn't recognize two of the senders, so he diverted them to the system's automated answering/screening service—probably more threats. The number of irate callers had grown exponentially since the Cambridge Experiment on the rats began. The program Devereaux had set up automatically diverted each threatening message to the FBI.

The third call, he saw, was from Dr. Chandrika Jaidev, the Secretary of Health and Human Services. This was the second time she'd called this morning and it wasn't yet seven o'clock. What was she so worked up about? She was another of those women Doug couldn't imagine being married to—pushy, self-righteous, humorless. He sent the call to Devereaux's personal answering system rather than speak with her again. What could he tell her that was different from last time?

These people treated Devereaux like their personal assistant, placing horrible demands on his time. Well, not today. Doug could repay his debt at least a little by restricting access to only those people Devereaux really wanted or needed to speak with. He would do the best job he could so that Devereaux's workload wouldn't be quite so dreadful.

Doug was just about to check on the plume of smoke in the distance when Quark entered the room. Seven feet tall and three hundred pounds, with black hair, a full beard and overly snug blue lab clothes, Quark looked a little like Cookie Monster, the character from the old Sesame Street shows, especially when he smiled. Quark was the sole remaining Escala on Earth. When his people left for Mars, Quark decided to stay behind with Devereaux. Despite his wild appearance, he was a gifted scientist—not in the same league as Devereaux, but brilliant all the same.

"You sent for me?"

"It's time for your radiation treatment," Doug said.

When Quark scowled, Doug added: "Devereaux insisted you follow the schedule. You know it's the only thing keepin' you healthy. Don't make me call him."

Quark held up his hands. "Okay, in a minute. What's the situation in Indonesia?"

"Thousands more dead this morning," Doug said. "Maybe tens of thousands. Reports are sketchy. So far the virus doesn't seem to have spread to the Philippines, though it's worked its way into Thailand, Malaysia and Borneo."

"It's in the Philippines too," Quark said. "It's all over the planet. It's just more concentrated in Indonesia right now.

"How is that possible? The whole country's a bunch of islands. Seems like it'd be the last place the virus would spread quickly. And a full quarantine's in effect."

"Clearly terrorists are spreading it. We don't yet know how— possibly as suicide infectors. We've identified over forty varieties to date. The most recent variations have apparently originated in Jakarta. Also, the symptoms appear to vary depending on the strain infecting the individual. Most start with a headache and joint pain, plus a light fever. Some escalate rapidly from there to heart attacks and strokes while others linger in the body for weeks. Those deaths are the beginning of a major outbreak."

"You mean it's gonna get worse?" Doug pointed toward the screen. "There's already reports of bodies in the streets."

"Devereaux thinks the terrorists are trying to prove that even the most remote locations can be targeted effectively. He believes we're days away from a massive outbreak."

"I can't believe people are doin' this on purpose. How's the cure comin'?"

Quark shrugged. "The virus is very hardy. And there are so many different strains that no single vaccine can be utilized."

As he spoke, Dr. Jaidev stormed through the open doorway, her shimmer cloth dress swirling about her with rainbow brightness, her forehead dark with anger. She wore a shiny gold interface on her right temple and touched it briefly as if to say, Look at me. I'm important.

She stopped two feet in front of Quark and tilted her head up at the Escala. "Where," she spoke slowly but forcefully, "is Walt Devereaux?"

"He's in the lab," Quark replied in his usual quiet manner, seemingly unaware of her anger, "working on a vaccine for the virus. We only have enough for several hundred people at the moment. And none of the vaccines work against all strains, especially the more recent varieties we've identified. They're more lethal than any of their predecessors."

"I've been trying to reach him. And this man," Dr. Jaidev indicated Doug with a flip of her wrist, "has been putting me off. I'm not happy about that."

"Well," Quark said, "he's good at his job. He's only doing what Devereaux asked him to do."

Doug felt a rush of warmth at Quark's kindness—another man he could never repay.

"There are riots on the streets," Dr. Jaidev said. "Do you know how upset people are by this Cambridge Experiment?"

Doug said, "They're also rioting over food and heat and health care and jobs."

Dr. Jaidev glared at him. "Those are not my concerns." She stopped herself, closed her eyes for a second, and said, "Of course I'm worried about that. The global winter brought on by the Las-cannon attacks is of great concern, but that will resolve itself over the next year or two. My concern at the moment is handling the riots over this rat transfer."

"We haven't been focused on that," Quark admitted.

"We've had to put Elite Ops troopers outside the building to keep the protesters away."

Doug shivered.

The Elite Ops terrified him.

He glanced up at Quark to see how the Escala was taking the news.

The Elite Ops had killed quite a few Escala over the years—many of Quark's closest friends. They'd tried to kill Quark too. But Quark showed no concern or even surprise at having his enemies protecting him now. How could he be so calm? Like Devereaux, he was a rock of stability. *I can be a rock too. If Quark, who lost so much, can do it, then so can I.* Doug took a deep breath and held himself a little more erect as he stared at Dr. Jaidev.

"I don't see what that has to do with the virus," Quark said.

"The virus is an urgent matter," Dr. Jaidev said. "No one has pressed harder than I for a solution to that problem. But we have civil unrest."

"That's why you have Elite Ops troopers," Quark said. "That's why the law was changed to allow the Army to help maintain order inside the borders of this country. Besides, what can Devereaux do to prevent further unrest? He's the one they're mad at."

"That's exactly why we need him," Dr. Jaidev said. "He's the one who started all this, trying to take religion away from the people."

"Here we go again," Quark replied. "He merely said we have to move beyond God if we wish to reach our full potential. Blaming him for the Cambridge Experiment is illogical."

"His research led to the creation of your people. Now scientists and your Escala have used his research to transfer a rat's mind. Next it'll be a human. The media keep harping on Devereaux's influence, on how if he was right about mind transfer, and right about transgenic creatures, perhaps he was right about there being no God. That's stirred up old trouble. People think this is somehow a precursor to the destruction of souls, condemning us all to hell. They want it stopped . . . now."

Quark held up his hands. "But Devereaux can't fix all that. They won't listen to him anymore."

Doug added, "He still receives hundreds of threats a day. How will a message from him help anything?"

Dr. Jaidev shrugged. "I don't know. But the President wants to speak to him. She's running out of patience. Now will one of you fetch him or shall I?"

While Quark went to retrieve Devereaux, Dr. Jaidev stepped in front of Doug and changed the wall screen to its vidphone setting so she could place a call. No, Doug thought, please don't ask my permission to take over my communications area. Feel free to just jump in and do as you please, you annoying bitch.

President Angelica Hope appeared on the monitor. Sitting at a desk before a blue curtain, she wore a shimmer cloth blazer that danced in the light, changing colors with every slight movement of her body, her blond hair framing her still-beautiful face as she stared at the camera. Doug wondered if she was in a bunker somewhere or in her temporary office at the FBI building. The White House, destroyed by an orbiting Las-cannon last year, had only been partially rebuilt. "Hello, Chandrika," the President said in her smoky voice, sounding every bit the movie star she had once been. "Is Devereaux there?"

"He's coming," Dr. Jaidev said.

"And who's that with you?" President Hope asked.

Dr. Jaidev nodded to Doug, who said, "Doug Robinson, ma'am. Walt Devereaux's communications liaison."

President Hope said, "Ah, the find of the century. I hear great things about you."

"Me, ma'am?"

"You're our greatest hope for the future, Doug. You and people like you—ordinary folks who have discovered how to improve themselves and inspire the people around them, how to work for a cause greater than themselves. Oh, we need people like Devereaux too. We can't survive without them. But we'll never be like them either. They're too different, too advanced. You and I, however, we ordinary humans, we are the future of humanity."

Doug felt heat suffusing his face. Her sincerity created that electric spark people talked about, the connection that made you believe she cared about you. "You're far too modest, Madam President. You're an extraordinary woman too."

"Only because people like Devereaux have inspired me, just like he inspired you. I may be extraordinary, but you are too. Perhaps you'd like to come work for me."

"Oh, Madam President," Doug answered, his stomach fluttering, "I could never leave Professor Devereaux."

"Loyalty. I like that. And did I hear you've taken up tennis?"

"I took some lessons, ma'am. But I haven't had much time to play lately, what with the world going to . . . I saw the highlight of your U.S. Open victory. You were amazing."

President Hope held up a hand and said, "That was a long time ago." But she smiled at him, a real smile that brought out the wrinkles around the corners of her blue eyes. God, he could love a woman like this! No chance of that.

At that moment, Devereaux and Quark entered the room. Devereaux looked more stooped each time Doug saw him. He nearly disappeared beside Quark's massive bulk. His blue lab clothes hung loosely on his skeletal frame and his face was gray with exhaustion. Doug wanted to grab him by the arm and lead him to a chair, offer him something to drink and remind him that he needed to slow down, but he knew Devereaux wouldn't follow his advice, might not even appreciate the effort. So Doug just smiled at Devereaux, who winked as he passed. The great man's eyes still shone brightly. "You wanted to see me?" Devereaux said to Dr. Jaidev. Then he spotted President Hope on the screen. "Madam President."

"What are we going to do about this mess?" President Hope asked.

"Are you asking me to put my research on hold?" Devereaux asked. "The future of humanity is at risk and you want me to make a speech?"

"I understand your reluctance," President Hope said. "But we must maintain order. Food supplies are dwindling. Already tens of thousands have died here, millions around the world, if not due to the virus, then to toxins in the air and water. Religious figures are calling it the beginning of the end—the apocalypse. Today, I reluctantly issued an order allowing

National Guard and Army units to use lethal force against the thousands of protesters and looters who keep growing by the day, mostly because of this Cambridge Experiment. I've appealed to the nation for calm. You've seen that it's had no effect. We need another solution. We need a miracle."

Devereaux closed his eyes for a moment. "As someone once said, 'I'm afraid I'm all out of miracles.'"

"As foolish as this may seem to you," President Hope continued, "it is absolutely imperative that we maintain the infrastructure necessary to deliver services to our citizens. If the forces of anarchy succeed, then even if we discover a vaccine, we won't have the means to efficiently inoculate the population."

"Okay." Devereaux held up his hands. "If you think it will help, I'll make a statement, urge my brothers and sisters to cooperate. But I fear we've reached a point where there simply aren't enough resources to support our population. Starving people will do what they must to survive. Have you released all the nation's stockpiled food supplies to alleviate the famine?"

"Most of them, yes," President Hope said. "Only extreme emergency rations have been withheld."

Devereaux shook his head. "Isn't this an extreme emergency?"

President Hope sighed. "What remains would feed very few. It's being kept in a secure location in the event the worst happens and the leadership of this country must retreat there."

Devereaux glanced over at Quark. The two men smiled briefly.

"In that eventuality," the President said, "we would of course request your presence in the bunker."

"Quark and I would prefer to go to Mars," Devereaux said, "if the Starfarer is ready to go, as promised."

"We can't send you to Mars at this time," President Hope said. "The Chinese and the Brazilians refuse to consent to the Starfarer's departure. They're both threatening to shoot it down if we attempt a launch. And the Chinese continue to withhold information about their Mars expedition, so we don't know what their plans are, if they're hostile or not. They may simply be sending their own manned mission. We can only hope they mean the Escala no harm."

Doug glanced at Quark, whose shoulders and chest seemed to expand, his eyes narrowing. Quark's companion Quekri led the Mars colony. What would Quark do if she were killed or injured?

Devereaux stared at Doug, a look of concern on his face. Though Devereaux had no family on Mars, he was the Escala's spiritual leader. He'd also held Celestia in his arms, an experience Doug envied. Would Doug ever meet his daughter in person? Probably not. And if the Mars colony were attacked by the Chinese, Celestia might be killed. The Escala were scientists, not fighters.

"We're willing to take the risk," Devereaux said. "If nothing else, we could go on the next MineStar ship. I think it's set to depart in six months."

"I'm afraid we can't allow that," President Hope answered. "We need you."

"I'm just one man."

"The most important man on Earth," President Hope replied.

A beep sounded on Doug's control board. In the small info-window came the message "Chaos in Jakarta." Doug reached down and activated the vidlink, compacting the President's image on the screen into a small window, while the bulk of the screen showed an external view of a train station labeled "Sudirman station: 7:14 p.m." Bodies lay strewn about on the sidewalk; buses drove past them without stopping. One truck ran over a fallen body and swerved around a vehicle parked in the middle of the street as it made its way to an intersection, where it turned right. Dozens of people ran away from the station, trying to escape the carnage. Sirens sounded in the distance.

"Are you seeing this, Madam President?" Devereaux asked.

"Yes, Walt."

Dr. Jaidev crowded close to the screen. Quark and Devereaux each took a step forward as well.

On the screen a woman wearing a long dress and a headscarf stumbled over a body. She managed to keep her balance, walked another few feet, then clutched at her chest and toppled to the ground. Doug's mouth went dry. He looked out the window at the plume of smoke in the distance. Soon the virus would be here and Atlanta would look like that—people dropping in the streets. Thankfully his daughter was safe on Mars. If only he could be with her, hold her just once before he died, he would feel fulfilled. He wondered how long he had before the virus reached Atlanta.

"My God!" Dr. Jaidev said.

Devereaux shook his head. "We just ran out of time in Indonesia."

Chapter 4

Ned Jefferson donned the sensory helmet and waited for the tech, Jenrie Roth, to adjust the settings so he could open a link with Hector Martinez. He said, "Are you sure this isn't going to fry my brain?"

Jenrie laughed. "I don't know. You may become a zombie. Woooo." She waved her hands in front of his face. "Don't worry. All the tests worked perfectly. Hector's implant will provide everything his brain captures, so you'll be able to see, hear and feel everything he experiences in almost real time—like you're in Hector's body in addition to your own. A couple of our testers found the sensation mildly disorienting. One found it thrilling." Jenrie gestured toward the lights. "We'll dim those and try to hold the sound to a minimum. Now lie back."

Ned complied, his head on a soft pillow, the mattress firm. "I can feel the ship moving."

"We're trying to hold it steady. I'd prefer to do this on land, but the Indonesian government has refused to grant permission for the Elite Ops to operate in Jakarta. We could have put you there with Hector, but we decided to keep you onboard in case there are any unforeseen problems."

"You mean like a heart attack or a stroke or something?"

"You'll be fine, Ned. It's just a precaution. As soon as we get confirmation that we've found a Sally cell, we'll send the Elite Ops out. As the old saying goes, better to ask forgiveness than permission."

"How long to get them into the city on a jet-copter?"

"Eight, ten minutes, tops."

"Okay. Connect me with Hector."

"Remember, I'll be right here beside you so if you need anything, let me know."

Jenrie made the connection. Ned immediately felt hot and sweaty. Every joint hurt. Through Martinez's eyes he saw the famous flea market of Jalan Surabaya. Superimposed over the ceiling of the darkened room, it made him feel as if he were standing rather than lying down. He took a moment to orient himself to the surroundings, noting the colorful awnings rising above the stalls, the thousands of people chattering in Indonesian as they passed him by, the smells of cooked fish and nuts infused with allspice and cardamom and ginger, and beyond that, deeper than that, the odor of decay and death. A few meters away, he spotted a corpse on the sidewalk. How could these people ignore it? How could Martinez?

"I'm live, Hector," Ned said.

"About time. She's still moving through the market, but I think she's getting ready to leave. Hey, Ned, what's it feel like to be connected to me? It must be the greatest thrill you've ever had."

Martinez chewed and swallowed a neo-dopamine pill and within a few seconds Ned felt the quick rush. "Weird," Ned replied. "Like I'm you and me at the same time."

"Lendra there too?"

"No, she's busy with important administrative details."

Martinez laughed. "I don't know what I was thinking."

"She's probably hooked up to London or Athens or Cairo or East Nowhereville. I'll send her a report if we find a Sally cell."

"Only ghost she ever cared about was Jeremiah."

"And look where that got him."

"Yeah," Martinez said. He paused, as if remembering Jeremiah's situation. "Yeah. I think I'll just slip out of the flow my way."

"Not today, Hector."

Martinez adjusted his heavy backpack and stepped into the crowd. Ned almost moved his arms and legs in sympathy. His head ached, his throat felt parched, his stomach twisted itself into little flips that threatened to erupt in vomit. Much of that was Martinez, but some was his own body reacting to the link. God, did Hector feel this bad all the time now?

Another corpse lay on the sidewalk. Martinez skirted it, his knees throbbing with every step. Damn this Susquehanna Virus. The poor man had days, at most, to live. Would Martinez really end it all today? Would Ned get in trouble for failing to inform Lendra that Martinez was suicidal? It didn't matter. He couldn't do it. And if he were in Hector's shoes, he wouldn't want Martinez doing it either.

"Where is she?" Ned asked. Though he was using Martinez's eyes, he couldn't see their target yet.

"Up ahead," Martinez said, "wearing the green and white sarong—long black hair." He stepped past another body as Ned spotted the young woman. She blended into the crowd as if she were a native. "I can't believe these crazy bastards," Martinez continued, "in complete denial, continuing to sell their merchandise while people drop in the streets."

"People have to eat, so they go about their business as if tomorrow and the next day will come, as if they aren't doomed. What else can they do?"

"Nothing, I guess," Martinez said. "Particularly when their government tells them the bodies aren't contagious, though I would think the stench would make them want to clear the streets a little quicker."

Ned tried to ignore the smell. His stomach felt queasy enough without the added odor of death.

In front of Martinez, a middle-aged man suddenly staggered. Ned flinched as if he might run into the man, who toppled over and hit the concrete with a thud. Is he dead? As Martinez glanced at him, Ned noted that the man's dark face was contorted in pain. His stomach fluttered. He used to be able to distance himself from the dead. But after his brother Dez died last year, never knowing that Ned was still alive, he could no longer separate himself from destruction, and he'd returned to CINTEP.

He counted twenty-six corpses as Martinez weaved his way toward the bus stop where the young woman waited. Martinez stumbled as he reached the young woman's side. Bumping into her, he deposited a small handful of dust on her short dark hair as he steadied himself. "Mengampuni," he said. "Forgive," he repeated in English, holding up his hand in apology before backing away. Ned noticed the woman's button nose and a small beauty mark to the left of her mouth. No doubt about it: Ivra Golonea—the one they were after.

She stared at Martinez as he retreated, her face scrunched up in a frown. Did she know they were on to her? And how did such an attractive young woman get involved in the Sally movement anyway? As Martinez reached the intersection, Ivra walked away from the bus stop.

"Damn," Martinez said. "She might have made me."

"No," Ned replied, "she's never seen you before. She's just very careful—almost paranoid. Find Santoso. He'll have a change of clothes for you."

"Right." Martinez hurried down the block until he reached Santoso, the CINTEP contractor serving as his Indonesian guide. Santoso waited for him on an Ojek—a motorcycle taxi—and held up a bag of clothes as Martinez approached.

"Getting a transmission from her?" Martinez asked.

"It's working perfectly," Ned replied. "Well done."

Martinez changed his shirt, just in case the young woman spotted him again. Then he activated his scanner/tracker and studied the screen. "She's taking an Ojek," Ned said, "instead of the bus." The target on the screen moved away from Martinez.

"Thanks, Ned."

"You need anything else?"

Martinez shrugged. "An antidote?"

Ned laughed, trying to sound chipper. "You want to live forever?"

"Well, another few years would be nice. I'd like to die between the legs of an Olympic gymnast."

Ned laughed again. "I'm sorry, Hector. I don't know why the vaccine didn't work for you."

Martinez said, "Tell that bastard Jeremiah he's worthless."

"I suspect he knows that already."

Martinez stepped to the Ojek and settled himself behind Santoso. It felt like Ned was pressed up against Santoso's body. Martinez gave Santoso the scanner/tracker and said to Ned, "If you see or hear anything that will help me . . ."

"I'll let you know," Ned said. "Good luck." What a stupid thing to say. Still, one had to observe the social protocols. "I've always admired your courage."

"You don't need to suck up to me," Martinez said. "I won't be around to reciprocate. Okay, Santoso."

Santoso hit the accelerator and sped off in the direction the target had taken, toward the Monas Monument in the center of the city. As they weaved their way through traffic, Santoso occasionally veered onto the sidewalk to get around a congested area. Ned's body shifted on the cot almost against his will, reacting to the movement of Martinez and the sensation that he was really moving through space. He could actually feel the hot breeze on his skin as Santoso drove him between crowded vehicles. Once Ned felt his shoulder brushing a bus. He smelled the acridity of burned fuel and human waste mingling with cooked food, heard the blare of horns and the growls of engines past the roar of Santoso's Ojek. He hoped he never had to do this again.

Martinez said, "What's the deal with the Elite Ops?"

"We can't bring them ashore yet," Ned replied. "Might cause an international incident. They're standing by, awaiting your signal. If you find the cell, we'll have them there in less than ten minutes."

"Okay. It's easier now, with the end in sight."

So. Martinez didn't plan to survive this mission. Ned kept his voice light. "Maybe it's just the joy at having me with you in spirit."

"No, it's not that. For sure it's not that, you demented old bastard." Martinez spoke into Santoso's ear: "Make sure we don't lose her."

Santoso snorted. "We're a block behind her."

"Good man." Martinez patted him on the shoulder, then reached into his pocket and removed another neo-dopamine pill, which he chewed and swallowed. Ned felt another little rush. An overdose of neo-dopamine would fry Martinez's brain, but he no doubt needed the energy boost. And it wasn't like he had to worry about long-term damage to his neurons—unless he found an antidote to the virus. That was still theoretically possible.

As Martinez passed by the Monas Monument—the 450-foot tall testament to Indonesia's independence, he looked up at the flame-shaped top. Ned was glad he was lying down. The view was disorienting. He'd always wanted to ride the elevator to the observation area and look out over the city. That probably wouldn't happen now. Maybe someday he'd take a balloon ride over Jakarta. Santoso kept the Ojek headed north toward the massive levees that kept out the sea. Even though global winter had begun rebuilding the polar ice caps temporarily, ocean levels were still high enough to make flooding a common event in Jakarta.

"Ned," Martinez said, "how the hell have you managed to stay uninfected?"

"Clean living. I never place myself between the legs of Olympic gymnasts."

"You know what I wish? I wish Lendra was here in my place."

"Yeah. There must be something about running CINTEP that turns you into an ass. You got Ivra in sight yet? She's less than a block away from your position."

Martinez relayed the information to Santoso, who kept the bike moving at the same pace through the heavy traffic.

Ivra, the young woman they were tracking, worked for Susquehanna Sally. Ned had been on her trail for months. Unfortunately, she had spotted him twice during the course of his surveillance, and he'd had to back off. Lendra then put Martinez on the case. If Martinez could confirm the location of Sally's Indonesian cell, they could send the Elite Ops in, political consequences be damned. But so far Ivra had only led them to a series of drops—never the same one twice. And no one ever came to a drop after she left it. All they'd ever found at any of them were empty containers. Her paranoia or radar was incredible. Today, though, Ned had a feeling she might return to the cell. That was part of her pattern—drive around for three days, then vanish. And today was the fourth day. That's why Ned had hooked himself up to Martinez.

Santoso and Martinez neared the north end of the city, where the flooding tended to be the worst and where warehouses and older office buildings stood.

Ned noticed an increase in the bodies lining the streets here. The smell reminded him of an abattoir. As Santoso pulled to the curb Ned saw Ivra stopped around the corner of the next intersection, rummaging through her bag.

He tried to read her lips and thought she said, "I don't see anything suspicious." A pause followed. Then she might have said, "Good idea. Where should I leave it?" After a few seconds, she hopped back on the Ojek.

"Any clue where they're headed?" Martinez asked. "I thought maybe we'd arrived at our destination."

"Probably another drop," Ned replied. "Or maybe she's just being paranoid. Frustrating. I thought for sure she'd return to the cell today. Stay with her. Be patient."

Martinez and Santoso followed her again, maintaining a one-block distance. The tracking transmitters in Ivra's hair continued to provide Ned with her location.

"She been to this neighborhood before?" Martinez asked.

"Not while I've been on her," Ned replied. "That's why I thought maybe she was returning to her base."

Ivra now backtracked toward the city center and Martinez let her build the gap between them a little more. Ned had been positive the cell was located in the northern part of the city, which had become rundown in recent years. Rent was cheap and scrutiny was lax. But so far, except for her brief excursion just now, Ivra hadn't ventured into the north end at all. *Where are you going, little girl? Why the hell won't you return to your people?*

Ivra stopped at a train station as Santoso closed the gap. If she tried to board a train, Ned might order Martinez to capture her, hope they could somehow get the cell location out of her before her comrades could disappear. When Martinez reached the station, Ned spotted her Ojek parked at the curb, the driver waiting for her to return.

"Should I follow her inside?" Martinez asked.

"Just take a quick look from the door," Ned answered. "If she boards a train, we'll track her and pick her up at the other end."

"We could lose her."

"It's a risk we have to take. She's a clever little thing. If she gets any whiff of you at all, she'll bolt."

Martinez hopped off the Ojek and slipped inside the station. He caught sight of Ivra by the locker area. She was placing her bag inside one of the medium-sized lockers.

Ned said, "Looks like another drop. We'll keep an eye on it. Get back to the Ojek. I think she might still be in play."

Martinez returned to Santoso, who drove half a block away and waited by the curb. For a minute Ivra's signal didn't move. Ned tried to ignore the incoming signals from Martinez, instead focusing on the darkened room around him: Jenrie monitoring his condition, the two technicians sitting quietly at their stations against the wall. Then Ivra was moving again, back to the north for a second time, toward the same neighborhood they'd just left. Ned felt a surge of adrenaline, or maybe it was the neo-dopamine boost. He sensed that Ivra was leading Martinez to the cell.

"I think this is it," he said. Turning his head to Jenrie, he added, "Tell the Elite Ops to suit up."

Ivra's Ojek stopped beside an open lot surrounded by onlookers. As her driver sped off, Ivra sidled to an opening in the crowd and stared through the chain-link fence at rows of corpses, where a group of city workers had parked a large incinerator truck that burned the bodies one at a time. Santoso pulled to the side of the road and Martinez disembarked, grabbing the scanner/tracker from Santoso as he did so.

"Thanks, muchacho," Martinez said. "You'd better grab that Ojek driver. He might be involved, or infected."

As Santoso followed the other Ojek driver, Martinez neared the lot, where another group of city workers wheeled in more bodies, unloading them respectfully, laying them in rows beside one another.

"Like Dante's Inferno," Martinez said.

"Awful," Ned agreed.

For a moment Ivra watched a worker cataloging information on the new corpses. After a few seconds, Martinez sat on a stone bench at the edge of the sidewalk. Ned's breaths came more raggedly, more painfully. Was that Martinez struggling to breathe? It had to be. Ned hadn't realized just how far gone Martinez was.

"She's not moving," Martinez said needlessly. "Like she's happy watching the horror she wrought."

"I think she's making sure she's alone."

And suddenly Ivra began moving again, heading toward a building across the street: a four-story office structure. Ned checked his Interactive Map to identify the building's inhabitants. He said, "It's called the Jakarta Coalition for Disease Prevention."

"The bastards have a sense of humor," Martinez said.

Ivra looked around briefly before entering the building but Martinez held his ground. Ivra's signature disappeared from the scanner/tracker, the building obviously protected by a dampening field.

"This has to be it," Martinez said.

"Copy," Ned answered. He gestured to Jenrie. "Elite Ops are on their way."

"I'm going in now."

"I think you should wait for the Elite Ops."

"Sorry, Ned. I'll try to take out their dampening field so we have some idea what the Elite Ops are walking into."

"Hector, they'll be there in less than ten minutes."

"Roger that." Martinez pulled his backpack off and armed the neuro-tingler bomb it held. Then he extracted two Las-pistols. Finally he removed another couple neo-dopamine pills from his pocket and bit down on them, chewing them into small pieces. Even so, he could barely swallow them.

"You don't have to go in alone, Hector," Ned said.

"You're a good man, Ned—no matter what they say." Martinez laughed.

Another rush of warmth and energy flooded Ned, even as he shivered with fear.

Martinez hoisted the backpack onto his shoulders once again. The load felt heavy. How much of that was Martinez and how much was his own trepidation at what would happen if Martinez detonated the neuro-tingler bomb? From what Ned understood, the device disrupted the body's cells with cascading electrical impulses that were excruciating and lethal. He'd never seen one used before, though he'd seen the results of a detonation on dogs and cats—their bodies contorted in agony.

"Hector," Ned said again, though he suspected Martinez wasn't listening anymore. He'd probably set the audio to one-way.

"Boosting transmitter power to maximum," Martinez said as he followed Ivra into the building. The signal weakened, breaking up occasionally, like watching an old vid with scratches and static. Ned almost felt like he was winking in and out of existence as Martinez glanced left and right across the lobby. By the time Ned realized that Martinez had spotted the security guard, Martinez had drawn his weapon and shot the man in the chest—a red laser pulse. The guard dropped.

Martinez checked his scanner/tracker again. Ned saw that Ivra had climbed up one flight. Adjusting the scanner/tracker, Martinez studied the bioelectrical signatures. Most of the energy output came from the second and third floors. There were at least a dozen people inside. The power signature of the field dampener appeared to emanate from the second floor. As Martinez climbed, Ned's legs twitched, as if he were climbing three or four steps at a time. The signal broke up more frequently now as the dampening field weakened the signal.

Martinez reached the second floor and broke into a painful run. He turned right, the sights and sounds flickering in and out, a strobe effect of sight and sound that would have knocked Ned to the floor if he'd been standing. Through the intermittent connection, it appeared that Martinez was following the trail Ivra had left. He went down a dark hallway—tenths of seconds dropping from each image. Ned struggled not to vomit. Finally Martinez reached an open doorway, where Ivra stood in a laboratory with a handful of other people, various machines on the counters. The people clustered before a screen, on which a woman spoke. Ned could make out only a few words: ". . . three . . . intense . . . dispersal—" The woman's voice broke off as she spotted Martinez.

Martinez fired the Las-pistols, blue stun pulses, as the six people in front of him tried to dive out of the way. An alarm sounded, no doubt triggered by the woman on the screen, who disappeared as the screen went black. Martinez kneeled beside a cabinet, firing pulse after pulse, using only the low-power setting. Good man, Ned thought, but didn't say. Take them alive if you can.

A young man in a white lab jacket, who had dropped behind a chair, fired a red laser pulse at Martinez, narrowly missing—at least Ned thought he missed. He couldn't sense any pain from Martinez. The connection vanished for a second. When it returned, Martinez fired a red pulse into the man's chest. Ned couldn't tell how many had been taken out. He thought four had been stunned and one was dead, but where was the sixth person?

Ned heard a small scraping sound to his left. A brown pant leg vanished behind a counter. Martinez ran forward, his knees nearly giving out, the image cutting out again. When it returned, Ned saw a blue stun pulse firing into the stomach of a dark-haired, middle-aged woman, who dropped to the floor unconscious. She looked vaguely like the computer-generated image of Susquehanna Sally. Could that really be her? Ned transmitted her image to CINTEP.

He felt light-headed, and at the same time he experienced a heavy pressure in his chest that made breathing difficult. Dr. Poole had told Ned that the stress of battle might accelerate the virus' progress. Martinez knew that. Was that why he chose to charge the cell without waiting for backup? Or did he want a chance to search for an antidote?

On the scanner, bioelectric signatures clumped together one floor above Martinez.

"Elite Ops will be there soon," Ned offered, in case Martinez could hear him.

Martinez lifted his head and then the image stopped for perhaps three seconds—three seconds that seemed like a minute. When the connection was restored, Ned saw nothing he could identify as a field dampener.

"The field dampener, Hector," Ned called out.

Taking several deep breaths, Martinez strode toward Ivra. Again the image dropped for a second or two. When it returned, Martinez had Ivra by the neck. He shook her, keeping an eye on the doorway from where the reinforcements would attack. While Martinez waited for her to waken, he studied the room, the shelves and the counters. What was he looking for?

As the image went black again, Ned began repeating himself over and over: "The field dampener, Hector, the field dampener."

Back came the image.

Martinez let Ivra's head fall to the floor, slapped her hard several times until she started to moan. Then he grabbed her by the neck again, keeping a Las-pistol lined up on the doorway, set to full power. When Ivra's eyes focused on his, he snarled, "Where's the antidote?"

"What?"

"The antidote, girlie," Martinez snarled.

"There's no antidote," she said.

"Liar! Where's the antidote?" Martinez punched her in the face. Ned reached for Martinez's arm to try to stop him, knowing even as he did so that it was idiotic—like trying to touch a holo-projection. To have these additional limbs and not be able to control them was infuriating.

As Ivra screamed, Martinez yelled, "Where is it?"

Ivra said, "There is none."

The signal cut out again. When it returned, Martinez broke the girl's middle finger and she screamed again. "Stupid bitch. What's your name?"

"Sally16."

"Cute. Well, Sally16, I'm going to torture you until you tell me the truth." He slammed her head into the floor. Ned winced. He knew she was a terrorist, a murderer, and yet he still struggled with the violence of Martinez's assault.

Finally Martinez grabbed his scanner/tracker. He adjusted the setting until he found what appeared to be the field dampener coming from four small speakers in the corners of the room. He fired four red pulses at the units and the field dampener winked out.

Now Ned was completely back inside Hector's body. He felt a powerful urge to vomit and managed to turn his head to the side before puking. Jenrie jumped out of the way. "ETA five minutes," she said.

Wiping his mouth, Ned said, "You did it, Hector. Well done."

"You getting this?" Martinez asked.

"I got you," Ned replied. "The Elite Ops will be there in five minutes."

Martinez didn't seem to hear him. He turned toward the doorway as several purple pulses—medium setting, probably to protect the lab as much as possible—fired at him from the darkness beyond. He took one to the stomach. A blistering, stabbing pain knocked him to the floor and caused Ned to cry out in pain. That should have knocked Martinez unconscious. It would have if he hadn't taken so much neo-dopamine.

Martinez found cover behind an island counter. He reached around it and fired his Las-pistols into the darkness.

The people in the room began to stir, groggily sitting up. More purple pulses flashed from the darkened doorway. Soon the reinforcements would set their Las-weapons on high and charge. Ned was surprised they hadn't done so already.

"Hang on, Hector," Ned begged.

Martinez leaned back against the counter, his body hot all over. He began to sweat profusely. His hands shook. He grew dizzy. The Susquehanna Virus would soon overwhelm him. He reached for the backpack.

"Hasta luego, Ned."

"Hector," Ned shouted.

Martinez fired at the doorway again. He missed, the red pulses from his weapons going through the walls and eliciting screams from the other side. He pulled the remaining supply of neo-dopamine out of his pocket and put the tablets in his mouth. Chewing and swallowing, he began to fade a little, though the pain diminished too.

Red pulses shot toward Martinez from the doorway. They began slicing through the counter over his head, pinning him down.

"You're going to die," Sally16 said. She sat up, blood trickling from the corner of her mouth.

As the reinforcements charged the room, Martinez detonated the neuro-tingler bomb. Despite the overdose of neo-dopamine and the slightly degraded signal from the transfer, Ned still felt the searing heat, the intense prickling agony of a million white-hot needles piercing every skin cell. His body felt like it was being ripped apart. He grunted, curling up in a ball as all around him the cell members screamed. Then the sensory link connection went dark.

Ned felt instantaneous relief, and at the same time an almost uncontrollable urge to cry as loneliness engulfed him. One second he was two people, bound together. The next, he was alone, and Hector Martinez was no more. He wanted to be angry with Hector. He wanted to rage at the injustice of it all. And yet if their places had been reversed, he might have done the same.

"It's over," he said to Jenrie as he removed the helmet. "Sorry about the mess."

Chapter 5

Lendra Riley, acting head of CINTEP—the Center for International Economic Policy, which purportedly worked to open free markets worldwide, but actually conducted espionage, anti-terrorism activities and the occasional assassination—sat in her office, fidgeting as she stared at the holo-projections being transmitted from Jakarta. On one of them, three Elite Ops troopers moved through the building Hector Martinez had found. They looked huge, seven-feet tall in their gray armor, their shields glowing ever so slightly as they searched the building for hidden terrorists. The neuro-tingler's energy had dissipated quickly.

Martinez, blessedly, had died almost instantaneously. Some of the terrorists, however, were still alive, screaming their throats raw. Lendra wished she didn't have to listen to their cries.

On another projection, three more Elite Ops troopers knelt over dying terrorists, using med-kits to try to keep them alive. Dr. Taditha Poole, CINTEP's chief medical officer, stood in the corner of Lendra's office next to Jay-Edgar, CINTEP's technology guru, and relayed instructions to the troopers.

Poor Hector, Lendra thought. For some reason, the antidote hadn't worked on him. A team of doctors was analyzing why—too late for him, of course. It should have worked. Jeremiah Jones was immune, and the antidote had been derived from his blood, so why didn't it work?

She found it difficult to think over the screaming of the terrorists and asked Jay-Edgar if he could do something about the noise. He silenced the audio feed.

"Thank you." Lendra sat back in her chair to collect her thoughts. She tried to ignore the cameras installed by the President, meant to monitor everything that occurred inside CINTEP: the price she paid for her predecessor's treachery in unleashing Curtik, Zora and the rest of the cadets on Earth last year. Damn Eli!

And damn Jeremiah for being so uncooperative. Yes, she'd used him, just as Eli had before her. And yes, she'd impregnated herself with his sperm and delivered a baby girl to ensure that his line continued. She'd do it again too. The problem now was that their daughter Sophie had been fighting a fever for days now, with no apparent cause.

Lendra struggled with how to handle that. Should she take time off work to be with Sophie, or did her responsibilities require her to put her daughter second? She wouldn't admit this to anyone, but she was far too driven to just stand aside during a time of crisis like this. And there was nothing she could do for Sophie anyway; she wasn't a doctor like Taditha.

She glanced at Dr. Poole, who looked darker than usual standing next to the pasty Jay-Edgar, and marveled that two women with African-American blood could be in such positions of power—though she didn't consider herself black. Her racial heritage included Polynesian and European blood. Still, quite an accomplishment. She might have been prouder of it if her job wasn't dependent on positive reports from Dr. Poole about her performance.

Damn Eli again!

How was she supposed to run CINTEP when Dr. Poole could have her removed at any time for psychological reasons? Or was she just annoyed because Dr. Poole had been a mere operative under Eli's regime, promoted by President Hope for the sole purpose of determining whether CINTEP should be disbanded, or subsumed into the CIA or NSA? What would she do if President Hope fired her? She had to stay on Dr. Poole's good side. She decided to check on Sophie.

Using the interface attached to her left temple, she called the nanny. Through the connections to her optic nerve, she saw Isabella standing in the nursery, worry in her dark eyes. Pale blue clouds and multi-colored hot-air balloons moved slowly across the pastel yellow wall behind her. Isabella held up Sophie, who was crying loudly, her face red and puffy, her dark curly hair plastered to her head. "Miss Riley," Isabella said. "She won't stop crying. And she's still running a fever of a hundred and three. Should I call Dr. Poole?"

"She's here with me," Lendra said. She activated the holo-projector in front of her desk so that Sophie could see her. "Hi, Sweetie," she cooed. "It's okay, Sweetie. Mommy's here." She waved at her daughter, whose crying tailed off for a moment. In the far corner of the nursery, Dr. Poole's infant son Jack, six weeks younger than Sophie and irritatingly healthy, played with a musical rattle.

Dr. Poole looked over from where she was giving instructions to the Elite Ops troopers and said, "Do you want to take some time off?"

"No," Lendra replied. She refused to give Dr. Poole any more power, any more leverage. She was a professional; the job came first. Dr. Poole would see that as a positive, wouldn't she?

Jay-Edgar interrupted: "She didn't make it."

"What?" Lendra asked. She glanced at the holo-projection, where an older woman in a lab coat lay on the floor in a pool of vomit.

"We need an ID on her ASAP," Lendra said.

Sophie began crying again.

"What should I do?" the nanny asked.

"Sophie, Sweetie," Lendra cooed again. "Don't cry, Sweetie. Isabella, take her to the infirmary, please. I'll get there as soon as I can."

Lendra disconnected. She knew she ought to be more concerned about Sophie, but she was fighting for her job, and she couldn't afford to be anything but focused. Besides, Sophie had Jeremiah's blood in her— blood from before he was infected with the Susquehanna Virus—how sick could she get?

Dr. Poole's voice trailed off. She shook her head. "Call it."

The Elite Ops troopers packed up their med-kits and stood, soon rejoining their comrades in the search for any clues about the Susquehanna Sally organization. All the data they collected went to CINTEP's Intelligence Gathering Unit, where CINTEP's computers analyzed it.

As they moved off, Lendra stared for a moment at the inert form of Hector Martinez. He lay in a contorted position, obviously in great pain at the time of his death. Too bad about that: Lendra now had only three CINTEP ghosts left to work with: Trogan Brosk, Ned Jefferson and Jeremiah Jones. Trogan Brosk, however, had disappeared last week while hunting down a terrorist cell in Rome. He had a history of stress-related erratic behavior and had only been reinstated to the ghost program three months ago, so Lendra didn't know if his vanishing act was due to the pressures of the job or something more sinister.

As for Jeremiah Jones—Sophie's father—he had retired, making it clear that he no longer wanted anything to do with CINTEP or Lendra. Not that he was worth much in the field anymore anyway. He could barely move due to the constant pain in his joints—a result of being infected with the Susquehanna Virus. He'd once been the best of the ghosts. Elias Leach, the former head of CINTEP, had transformed Jeremiah from a gifted operative into a superior being: a transgenic creature with both human and animal DNA. For a time, Jeremiah had been the unstoppable agent Eli had sought, with incredible power, speed and healing ability. But he continued to evolve and now his immune system attacked his joints constantly, as fast as his transgenic body could repair itself, leaving him a helpless cripple. Yet, she could use his mind if only he weren't so damned stubborn.

The bottom line: she only had Ned left.

"Major Payne has uploaded the last of the data files," Jay-Edgar interrupted her thoughts. "We're still analyzing them. They don't seem to contain much helpful information though. Nothing connecting them to any other cells."

"No surprise there," Lendra said. "We knew they were smart."

"It was clearly a production and distribution center for the virus," Jay-Edgar said. "From a brief examination of the strain they were working on, it looks to be a known variety, though we'll have to study it further. Major Payne wants to know if they can leave the building now."

Dr. Poole said, "I recommend you minimize their exposure to the virus."

"Have they completed their search?" Lendra said.

"The longer they stay there, the greater their chances of becoming infected. Besides, the Indonesian authorities may provide us with any information we missed."

"After we invaded their sovereign territory? I don't think so. But I agree that they shouldn't stay any longer than necessary. How soon before the police get there?"

"Perhaps ten minutes," Jay-Edgar replied. "The only reason they're not there yet is because their emergency call center is dealing with thousands of reports from across the city."

Lendra shook her head—so few weapons in her arsenal. "Keep them searching until the last minute. I want everything I can before they have to leave." *This is why we need to reinstate the ghost program.*

Dr. Poole said, "You're thinking of turning Curtik and Zora into ghosts again, aren't you?"

"How did you . . ."

"I've seen that look in your eyes before."

"They've already been infected and they're both fine. They're highly intelligent, superb physical specimens—both of them transgenic as well as having nano-tech enhancements. They're extremely adaptable. And they need something to do. Better to use them for what they're best at than train them for something beneath their unique skills."

"You've seen my reports. They're not ready."

"We don't have more time."

"Their conditioning on the Moon was strong. At times of stress, they'll want to lash out. And there's little in life more stressful than undercover operations. Brosk broke once before under the pressure. He might have again—unless he was taken."

"They're young," Lendra said, "and eager. At least Curtik is eager."

"That's what worries me. His psychometric analyses show little loyalty, little discretion, and poor impulse control. I think he sees becoming a ghost as getting a license to commit brutal acts of violence."

Lendra pointed toward the building on the holo-projection. "Isn't that what we need right now?"

"As long as the acts of violence are the acts we want them to commit."

"Are you sure you're not just prejudiced against him because he killed Jack Marschenko?"

Dr. Poole closed her eyes and Lendra wondered if she'd gone too far. After a moment, Dr. Poole opened her eyes. "I live with that every day. I'm as much to blame as he is because I created him. It's not that. No, I'm concerned that he's too unstable."

"What better means of determining their ability to act properly in those situations than training them?"

Without being consciously aware of it, Lendra reached up and grasped the small glass bulb that hung from her neck. Only when Poole stared at her did Lendra realize what she'd done. She pulled her hand away like it had been scorched. "I don't keep neo-dopamine there anymore," Lendra explained. "It's just a necklace."

"Just a necklace?"

"Perhaps a little more than that," Lendra admitted. "But it's none of your business."

"Oh, it's my business, Lendra. Everything you do is my business. I don't want to shut this place down, but I promised President Hope a full and accurate assessment and if I don't give her one, she'll shut us down anyway."

"I understand. Are you going to let me continue training Curtik and Zora?"

"For now." Dr. Poole stared ahead blankly for a moment and Lendra knew she was making notations to her interface. After a moment, Dr. Poole directed her attention to Lendra and said, "How are you holding up now that you've gotten what you wanted?"

"I didn't ask for this job," Lendra said.

"Don't play coy with me." Dr. Poole leaned forward. "We both know you wanted CINTEP. I studied your interviews with the President. I ran your psychometric analyses. I know the truth."

"My point is that I didn't ask for the job. The President gave it to me because she knows I'm the best person for it."

"You're under incredible stress. I need to know if you can handle that. We must stop Susquehanna Sally. And we must find a cure for the virus."

"So why are you questioning my use of Curtik and Zora?"

"Technically, they're still in protective custody. And even though they were exonerated because of their youth and the compulsions inside them, they're still dangerous. Can you imagine the harm they could cause if they went rogue? You've seen what they're capable of. Do you want everything riding on them?"

Lendra shook her head. "We have Ned. And perhaps you could talk to Jeremiah again."

Dr. Poole shook her head. "I've spoken with him. He won't help you. He doesn't trust you." Dr. Poole rubbed her eyes. Her cocoa face looked almost gray in this light, tension lines surrounded her eyes. No doubt she needed sleep. The same held true for Lendra. She wondered what she looked like, grateful that there were no mirrors in the office. Even living here in the CINTEP building in the apartment next to Dr. Poole, with a one-minute commute, she wasn't getting enough rest.

Dr. Poole stepped over to Lendra's desk, looked down at her and said, "How do you feel about that?"

Lendra almost smiled—such an obvious question.

"I understand why he's angry with me, but he knows how critical the global situation is. In addition to the virus, which may kill us all, we've now got dozens of countries eager to destroy America. Time is of the essence, yet he sits on his porch doing nothing."

"He's allowed us to take samples of his blood on many occasions. And Walt Devereaux is closer to finding a cure for the virus as a result."

Lendra shook her head. "Devereaux's overly optimistic. The virus keeps mutating. Or Susquehanna Sally and her organization keep modifying it. At any rate, the more the virus adapts, the more difficult it will be to eradicate."

"Devereaux will find a cure. Let's get back to Jeremiah. How do you feel about him?"

"I can work with Jeremiah. I can separate my personal feelings from my professional ones. That's all that really matters."

"Hmm." Dr. Poole again stared blankly ahead as she made more notations to her interface. "And how do you feel about CINTEP's reduced role in world affairs?"

"I've made that pretty clear," Lendra said. "I told the President we could be an enormous asset. She's chosen to limit our role to finding Susquehanna Sally. And she's forcing us to compete against every intelligence agency in the world to get to Sally first. That's . . ." She reconsidered her word choice. "I feel threatened and energized at the same time. Imagine if we succeed."

"Then you'll become the kingmaker and puppet master Eli once was."

Lendra clasped her hands together and placed them on the desk. "I want us to be relevant once again. I want America back atop the world. We're the best hope for the planet. Surely you don't disagree with that."

"Isn't that precisely the kind of attitude that got us into this mess?" Dr. Poole said. "That was Eli's vision too. Look how that turned out."

"I'm not Eli. I don't dream of running the world."

"Don't you?"

Jay-Edgar interrupted: "Major Payne says the local police are nearly there. He wants to leave."

"Get them out," Lendra said. "What did they learn?"

Jay-Edgar put up a picture of one of the terrorists, the young Asian woman Ned had followed from Rome about the same time Trogan Brosk had disappeared, the one who had led Martinez to the cell. "She was using the name Ivra Golonea," he said. "We don't think she was the ringleader."

Her image was replaced by one of the middle-aged woman in the lab coat. "This one was probably in charge. Definitely Eurasian. Using the name Elsa Lochstein—likely an alias. Maybe she was even Susquehanna Sally."

Lendra shook her head. "I doubt Susquehanna Sally is one person. From all the vids I've studied, I would say she's a conglomerate of several people. However, this woman might very well have been one of the brains behind the operation."

"The Elite Ops are on the move," Jay-Edgar said. "Major Payne wants to know what their next mission is."

Lendra took a deep breath. President Hope had lent CINTEP Major Payne's Elite Ops squad after Trogan Brosk disappeared. They'd been searching for him in Rome when Ned and the Intelligence Gathering Unit had found Ivra Golonea, and they'd been diverted to this assignment. She probably had to return them to General Horowitz now.

"Bring them home," Lendra finally replied. Damn Jeremiah anyway. His skills were much better suited to a search for Brosk. But Lendra could only use the tools at her disposal.

"What about Ned?" Dr. Poole asked.

"I've got another mission for him," Lendra said. "And I still think we might be able to convince Jeremiah to return. If we can't appeal to his sense of duty, then perhaps we can target his fondness for Ned, and even for Brosk. If he doesn't help, we could lose our last active ghosts."

Dr. Poole's eyes narrowed. "What are you planning? Did you deliberately set up Brosk to be taken?"

"Absolutely not." Lendra paused for a moment. "He was following a good lead. I had to decide whether to go in light or heavy. I chose to go in light. A heavier approach might have scared off the people he was watching."

"So you're trying to cover your ass."

"Perhaps a little," Lendra conceded. "I should have given Brosk backup. But I don't have the personnel for that. I can only work with what I have. That's why I need to get Curtik and Zora up to speed."

"I don't want you using Ned for bait."

"Of course not. Right now, he's our best chance of finding Susquehanna Sally. And I don't intend to use Jeremiah in the field. I'll keep him here in the office, where he can be protected night and day."

While Dr. Poole stared at her, Lendra felt increasingly uncomfortable, as if she'd said something wrong, something that might get CINTEP shut down. But Jeremiah, priceless commodity that he was because of his immunity to the virus, would be safe doing analysis down the hall.

"I still don't think he'll help us."

"He might if we tell him we're going to use Curtik and Zora too."

"Ah, there it is," Dr. Poole said. "That's the ruthlessness I've been waiting for."

Lendra's cheeks felt warm. She said, "He's the greatest asset we've got. I'm not just going to let him walk away if I can help it." She turned to Jay-Edgar. "Where's the greatest likelihood of a Sally home base?"

"London. Added to what Major Payne just learned, the greatest intersection of travel patterns, infections—"

Lendra stopped him with a wave of the hand. "You can summarize the data for me later, Jay-Edgar. I just want to know where to send Ned."

"It's possible," Jay-Edgar continued, "that the London indicators could be a statistical disparity."

"Or Susquehanna Sally could be trying to lure us into a trap," Dr. Poole said.

"One we might not be able to ignore," Lendra said.

"I would recommend notifying the British at once," Dr. Poole said. "They'll be much more cooperative than the Indonesians."

"No." Lendra said. "We'll run the operation from here."

"So this isn't just about finding Susquehanna Sally," Dr. Poole said. "You're not coordinating with the CIA, FBI or NSA. Now you want to withhold information from the British? They might be able to help us."

"You've seen our Intelligence Gathering Unit, Doctor. It's the best in the world. Do you really think the British can do better than IGU?"

"I think that two heads are better than one."

"If the President hadn't conditioned CINTEP's continued existence on our finding Sally first—"

"That's not what she said," Dr. Poole interrupted. "She may still shut us down. But she believes CINTEP can be useful if given a properly narrow agenda."

"Then we might as well become a branch of the CIA. Our successes have resulted largely from the fact that we're not a government agency."

"So have our failures."

"I'm not Eli," Lendra said. "I don't have some grand vision of a world living in iron-fisted peace. I accept that other nations have their own ideas about where humanity should be going. Look, America is struggling. Our population feels insecure. Civil unrest remains high. It's only going to get worse with these images from Indonesia. We're going to have to use the Elite Ops to maintain order."

Two messages buzzed inside Lendra's interface: one from Isabella, that Sophie was in the infirmary now; the other from President Angelica Hope's office, requesting an update on the search for Susquehanna Sally. She closed her eyes for a moment before sending a reply to Isabella, telling her to wait for the on-call doctor's report. "Get me the White House," she said to Jay-Edgar. She refused to feel guilty about spending so much time away from her daughter. She was doing what had to be done—for everyone, including Sophie.

Still, she longed for a taste of neo-dopamine.

Chapter 6

Curtik studied himself in the mirror. God, you are a handsome devil—dark hair, high cheekbones, a narrow nose, flawless skin and plump lips. He puckered up, blew himself a kiss. His brown eyes shone as he laughed. How could any woman resist you?

He thought about sending a message to Benn and Addam via his implant, but decided not to. They were on Mars, while the rest of the cadets—except for Zora, whose parents were dead—were back with their families being re-integrated into society, whatever the hell that meant.

Backing up a step, he did a twisting kick-punch. He was going to be a ghost! Just like dear old dad, only better. For a flash he felt sorry for Jeremiah. Then the familiar anger returned. He was no longer Joshua Jones, Jeremiah's son.

Tonight, he and Zora were going on a real mission, posing as a couple, getting out of this damn CINTEP tower and out into the streets of Washington, D.C. He'd only seen the city through the windows. Up until now, he'd either been stuck with Jeremiah in nowhere land or locked up here. Not tonight, though. Tonight, we dance. He reached up and ran his fingers through his hair. Then he caught sight of Zora in the mirror.

"Don't you knock?" he said as he turned to face her.

"You never knock," Zora said.

"Well, that is wrong of me. I sincerely apologize. Besides, I never see you naked."

"And you never will. Are you finished admiring yourself yet?"

"You're such a bitch." He looked Zora over. Slim, athletic, with liquid brown eyes, curly blond hair and skin the color of melted butter, she was dressed, like he was, in drab-looking clothes. Even so, her brown shirt and faded black pants clung to her lithe body, her pants fitting perfectly over her rounded ass. Curtik planned to kiss her tonight, in public somewhere, where she couldn't object. He wasn't in love with her, like she was with Jeremiah. Gag me! But he'd sure plow her.

He stepped closer to Zora and looked down at her face, her plump lips and high cheekbones and straight narrow nose. She could be his sister.

"Zora, honey," he said, "you look absolutely fab."

"Don't call me honey," she retorted.

"Oh, that's right. You only want Jeremiah to do that. Has he called you honey yet?"

Zora shook her head, then grimaced in obvious pain. "He's your father. You should show him some respect."

"Why?"

"You're so full of yourself. You're still just a ten-year-old boy. You don't care about anyone. You don't have empathy."

"Are you telling me to grow up?" Curtik grinned.

Zora snorted. Winced.

"This is never going to work," Curtik said. "You can barely move your head without flinching. How are you going to handle yourself in the field when you're in constant agony?"

Zora glared at him. "I'll manage."

"Look," Curtik said, "I know you're tough. And you think you're honoring my dad by suffering like he does. But he wouldn't want you to do this. More importantly, you can't concentrate on the mission if you're in pain. And I don't want your lack of focus to get us killed."

"I can handle it."

"Now who's being childish? What if we have to move quickly? What if we need to follow someone or defend ourselves?"

Curtik took a swing at Zora, a punch he held back on only a fraction. Zora parried the blow, twisting his arm behind him, but gasping as she did so. Curtik took advantage of her distracted state to spin around and kick her legs out from under her. She fell to the ground, a cry escaping her.

"See?" he said as he reached a hand down to help her.

She grabbed his hand and pulled herself up, gritting her teeth as she did so. At that moment, the door chimed. It slid open a second later and Dr. Poole stepped inside. Curtik turned to her. "Piscine," he said. "Maybe you can reason with her. Zora won't take her medication."

Dr. Poole studied Zora, who crossed her arms in front of her breasts and stared back.

Shaking her head, Dr. Poole said, "Jeremiah gave you a transfusion to save your life, Zora, not to cause you pain. How many times has he told you he doesn't want you to suffer?" Zora rolled her eyes. "We've talked it over, Lendra and I. We know you feel strongly about this. But Curtik is right. If you don't take the meds, the mission is off."

"Damn it, Zora," Curtik said. "If you blow this, I will beat you senseless."

"Jeremiah doesn't get to lessen his pain," Zora said.

"That's not the point," Dr. Poole said. "Besides, his agony is vastly greater than yours anyway. So you would have to take something to increase your pain to be at the crippling level he's at. Do you want that?"

Zora sighed. "Fine. Give me the damn medicine."

After Poole dosed her, Curtik said, "There. Don't we feel all adult now?"

"Okay," Zora said, "you're right. I was being childish."

Curtik smirked and did a little jig.

"Now who's being a child?" she said.

"You're both children," Dr. Poole said. "Sometimes we forget that because you look like you're in your twenties. And even though you've been enhanced and your physical and mental growth accelerated, you're still only ten."

Curtik sensed she was reconsidering sending them out.

"We can handle ourselves, Piscine."

"I've told you I don't like that nickname," Dr. Poole said.

"Sorry. Didn't mean it. I promise. We're ready for this assignment."

"Hmm," Dr. Poole said. "We'll see. Remember, these are probably low-level couriers. They're Earth Guardians—part of the vast group of Gaia devotees who've been recruited via the Internet. They may not even be connected with the Sally movement. We just want to try to make contact. Failing that, we want to track them. Just put a small quantity of the tracking dust on their hair or clothes and we'll be able to follow them."

"That's so cool," Curtik said. "Tracking dust. I love it. I tell you, Doctor, I'm so psyched."

"Remember, there are civilians in the bar. It's not just Gaians. And so far, we haven't seen any sign that Sally members frequent the place. So tonight, listen to Ndabi Okoye."

"I still don't like having to take orders from him. He's not a ghost."

"He's a trusted operative. He's survived in the field a long time. He knows what he's doing. He's careful and he's very good at reading people. If he tells you to back off, then that's what you do. And we'll figure out some other way to go after them."

"What about dear old dad?" Curtik asked. "Is he going to get off his fat ass and join us?"

Dr. Poole shook her head. "I called him and told him you'd be operating on your own. I asked him to help with monitoring. He refused."

"Poor us," Curtik said, pretending to rub his eyes with his fists. "All by our lonesomes. Now can we go already?"

Dr. Poole closed her eyes for a moment and took a deep breath. "Okoye's already in the bar. So are the targets. He'll monitor you from the front corner. He invited a few friends along to provide cover, but they're innocents. He's wearing an interface so you can communicate with him, but we don't want to involve his friends if we don't have to. This is a simple assignment. Get the tracking devices on the targets and only engage them if you think you can do it without blowing your cover. Think of it as a test."

"Test," Curtik said. "Got it. Listen to Okoye. Got it. Don't do anything rash. Got it. Can we go now?"

Dr. Poole sighed. "I just know I'm going to regret sending you on this assignment."

* * *

Curtik walked into Cole's Wall—a dark bar with a couple dozen tables and booths, every one of them occupied—his arm wrapped around Zora's waist, pulling her into his hip, his hand sliding down to her bottom, cupping her left cheek in his palm. He gave her a little pinch as the door closed behind them. Zora reached down and grabbed his hand, pulling it back up around her waist, twisting his thumb awkwardly. Through her implant she sent, *Tomorrow you'll pay during training.*

Bite me, he answered as he freed his thumb from her grasp.

The patrons all looked their way, the long and dark-paneled room becoming quieter as the mere mortals acknowledged the presence of gods. Glancing into a corner by the front window, Curtik spotted Okoye at a table with three other men, all four tracking Zora's progress through the bar. Okoye wore a silver interface. Acoustic guitars mixed with wooden flutes, playing a tune that sounded vaguely South American. Liquor bottles stood in rows behind the bar, lit by spotlights that reflected yellows, browns, reds and greens.

"You want something to drink?" Curtik asked Zora.

"Water," Zora answered in a clipped voice. She preceded him to the bar, head held high, weaving her way around tables.

The women in the room, Curtik was happy to note, stared at him openly, desire written on their faces. Perhaps he'd take one home with him. With his peripheral vision, he caught a glimpse of a pretty woman with dark wavy hair sitting across from a tall muscular man, who scowled at them, as if upset that he and his woman were no longer the prettiest people in the room.

Okoye sent a message via his interface: *The table against the back wall. The two couples locked in close conversation.*

Got it, Zora sent a reply as Curtik pulled Zora in tightly. He ordered a beer and a water, supplying his thumbprint to verify his age and pay for the drinks. The CINTEP identity worked like a charm. The bartender brought him his beer with an inviting smile. God, she was ancient! At least 40. Curtik, taking a long pull on the bottle, almost gagged at the bitter taste. He should have ordered a mixed drink. Maybe next time.

Zora's water came in a fancy glass with a twist of lime. She held up the glass as if in a toast, her way of telling him he should have ordered water too. He shook his head. This was an easy assignment—might as well get some benefit to it. He leaned over Zora to give her a kiss, but she stepped away from him, making for a support column near the back of the room.

Where the hell are you going? he sent. *We're supposed to be a couple.*

He grabbed his beer and followed her. When he caught up to her at the pillar, he pushed her back against it and kissed her. Her mouth tasted faintly of limes. Desire for her infused him as her breasts pressed against his chest.

Hey, Okoye sent, *subtle, remember. You're memorable enough without a public display of affection.*

Old fart, Curtik sent to Zora. Then he snaked his tongue between her lips. She bit it hard enough that he hurriedly pulled it back inside his mouth, barely managing not to yelp in pain.

The man across the table from the pretty woman saw Curtik pull back and grinned. Bastard! Curtik put on a smile, promising her through his implant that tomorrow's training session would be painful.

You told me to bite you, Zora sent back.

Bitch!

Zora laughed, a melodic and charming sound that caused the room to cease all conversation for a moment and look her way. For the next twenty minutes, they stood by the pillar nursing their drinks, chatting just loudly enough to be heard at the back table, discussing the panic caused by the virus in Jakarta. A dozen people looked at them with interest, searching for any sign that he or Zora would welcome an intrusion, but the two couples at the back table ignored them, continuing their whispered conversation, their heads close together. They never looked at Curtik or Zora.

We're getting nowhere, Curtik sent. *These dimwits don't even know we're here.*

They'll leave in an hour or so, Okoye sent. *Be patient.*

They're staying away from everyone, Zora sent. *I'll need a distraction. Fun.*

This isn't part of the plan, Okoye sent.

Zora handed him her glass, then reached into her pockets to coat her hands with tracking dust. When she pulled them out, Curtik glanced at them. Though he'd known he wouldn't see anything unusual, he was mildly surprised that her hands looked the same as always.

Zora walked toward the restroom, past where the two couples sat with their heads close together. The bar quieted again, conversation occurring only in hushed tones. The men followed Zora with their eyes while the women stared at Curtik. He winked at the pretty one with the dark wavy hair, giving her his full-on smile, causing her nostrils to flare and her face to color slightly as she smiled back at him. The muscle man across the table from her glared at Curtik and said, "Rebecca."

"Just looking, Tad," she replied.

Rebecca and Tad, Curtik thought, two physically beautiful people without a thought to share between them.

What the hell are you up to? Okoye sent.

We know what we're doing, Curtik replied.

This is not the right move, kids, Okoye sent.

Curtik walked over to the bar and put his half-empty bottle atop it, along with Zora's empty water glass. Then he walked over to Rebecca. As he reached her table, Tad got to his feet and said, "What do you want?"

"Just looking for a little fun, Tad," Curtik answered. "Before the world ends."

"We're trying to have a private conversation here."

Curtik sneered at him, assessing Tad's height, weight and age. He looked to be about six-two, two hundred pounds—taller and heavier than Curtik—in his early thirties, a little pale and soft, likely because he spent too much time on his ass.

"Why don't I start with you?" Curtik said.

"What?"

Curtik took an easy swing at Tad—a semi-serious punch that Tad ought to have been able to block. Instead his fist connected with Tad's jaw, knocking the bigger man backward a step. With his peripheral vision, Curtik saw Zora brush past the two people on one side of the table, touching each of them lightly on the back. Now Tad lunged at Curtik, throwing a heavy roundhouse punch that made Curtik laugh. Easily dodging out of the way, Curtik slapped Tad's face.

Are you crazy? Okoye sent.

Tad roared, then dove at Curtik, his arms reaching out to encircle Curtik's waist. Curtik jumped, spun and kicked all in one motion, knocking the bigger man into the table, where he landed with a satisfying crash. Several women screamed. Adrenaline, that lovely drug, pumped through Curtik's body, sending a surge of pleasure into every nerve. Zora worked her way around the table to the other side, as if frightened of what was happening. Now a couple of bouncers converged on Curtik. This was more like it.

"Stop it!" Zora yelled. *Go,* she sent. *Acquiring final two targets now.*

Curtik grinned at the bouncers as Zora's fingers lightly brushed against the other two people. "Come on, you fairies," he said. "Come and get me."

They rushed him from both sides. Again Curtik leapt in the air, kicking one in the face, punching the other in the eye. He tried not to hurt them too badly, allowing them to get to their feet before hitting them again, trying not to look enhanced, only a little faster than they were. But, damn, it was hard not to kill them. Big and strong as they were, they moved like they were trapped in molasses. In less than a minute, they were laid out on the floor, groaning. Neither of them had managed to touch him.

What the hell was that? Okoye sent.

Zora moved away from the table with the Gaians, putting her back to the pillar in a classic defensive maneuver and sent, *Mission accomplished.*

Get the hell out of here, Okoye sent.

"I called the police," the bartender said. "They'll be here any minute."

Half the room laughed. No one believed the police would arrive anytime soon. Curtik joined Zora at the column and put his arm around her shoulder.

"We're all gonna die in a few weeks anyway," he said. "If not the Susquehanna Virus, then nuclear war, or food or energy riots." The two couples in the back remained sitting at their table, not moving, not speaking.

"She might have been lying to us," Zora said.

Brilliant, he sent. "She claimed it was unstoppable." He spoke just loudly enough for his voice to reach the back table. "We're in the endgame. Humanity is doomed."

Get out now, Okoye sent. *They're totally freaked.*

Which means they'll head to their superiors, Zora sent. *Or they'll run. Either way, we get information from them.*

It was the right play, Curtik sent. *Trust us.*

The people at the back table said nothing, but the bartender said, "What the hell are you talking about, boy? What's this end of the world crap?"

Zora answered: "I heard that the virus passed the global tipping point last week. You all saw what happened in Indonesia. Well, it's coming here next. We'll all be dead inside a month, maybe two."

"The government said it was an isolated problem, that Jakarta was under a quarantine, that there was no way the virus could escape."

Curtik snorted. "The government? You gotta be kidding me. Whatever they say, you can pretty much believe the opposite is true." He smiled at the bartender. "Hell, they just told you the police were on the way, didn't they?"

The bartender shrugged.

"She's right," Curtik added as he pointed at Zora. "We're all gonna die. Soon. Might as well have some fun before—"

You're overplaying your hand, Okoye sent. *They're panicking. Who knows what they'll do now?*

Curtik glanced at the foursome in the back. They looked around the room as if searching for another exit.

Time to move, Zora sent.

Curtik and Zora made for the door.

I still don't like this, Okoye sent. *You two are reckless.*

Calm down, Curtik replied.

Let's see how they react, Zora added.

When they got outside, Zora shrugged out from under his arm.

Curtik said, "Now what?"

"Across the street." Zora darted off and Curtik followed her to a darkened doorway, where they pressed tightly into the walls. The night air felt chilly but Curtik barely noticed. He could still feel the adrenaline pumping. The nanobots and the animal DNA fueled his replay of the frenzied fight, combining to give him a rush of pleasure, almost like sex, only more intense, deeper—a whole-body orgasm of joy.

I contacted Lendra, Okoye sent, intruding on his thoughts. *She's got drones ready to follow the subjects when they leave the bar.*

We should follow them, Curtik sent. *We set it up.*

You've been burned, Okoye sent. *If they saw you, they'd rabbit.*

At that moment, Tad stepped out of the bar, his face looking green in the light of the sign. He held his jaw in one hand and leaned heavily on Rebecca. When he spotted Curtik across the street, he gave Curtik the finger. Chuckling, Curtik flipped him off with both fingers, over and over—an octuple flip-off.

Tad called out: "I'll see you soon."

"What?" Curtik called back. "You want some more?" He started forward, but Zora grabbed his arm as Tad scurried away, his arm around Rebecca as they vanished around the corner. Too bad Curtik never got a chance to show Rebecca what a real man could do.

Lendra wants you to wait outside, Okoye sent. *She's upset that you didn't stay with the plan.*

The plan sucked, Curtik sent.

Zora said, "When she debriefs us, she'll understand that we did the smart thing."

"I don't know why we don't just follow 'em," Curtik said. "Take 'em down when they get where they're going. If they don't tell us what we want, we fill 'em full of drugs, pump their brains dry and dump 'em where we get the maximum amount of terror from their deaths. How hard is that?"

Zora shook her head. "Lendra must have a reason why she hasn't picked them up so far. Poole said they're low-level messengers. Likely they don't know enough of the command structure to be able to give us more information. Lendra's probably hoping they'll lead us to someone who might know something—a person who might bolt if the wrong approach is made."

A black car pulled up to the curb, the rear door opening. Curtik tensed, preparing to leap into action, wishing Lendra had given him a weapon. He felt naked without a Las-pistol.

But it was only Dr. Poole. She looked at them and said, "Climb inside."

Curtik headed for the car door, while Zora stepped around to the other side. At that moment the bar exploded, bricks and glass flying in all directions. The concussive force knocked Curtik off his feet, slamming him into the wall behind him. Dazed, he lay there for a moment trying to assess whether he'd been hurt. His head felt like it had been struck with a sledgehammer. A burning pain knifed into the back of his neck. But when he tested his arms and legs, he realized he was okay and scrambled to his feet. He noted the CINTEP driver opening his door and stepping out of the car, a Las-pistol in his hand, while Dr. Poole sat dazed in the back seat. Across the street, a massive fireball rose where the building had once stood, flames reaching at least a hundred feet into the night sky. No doubt a gas line had ruptured. Rubble and body parts lay strewn about the street. For a few seconds Curtik heard nothing but a continuous roar in his ears. Then his implant adjusted for the concussive shock.

"Cool!" he exclaimed. "I love explosions. Did you see that, Zora? Zora?" He vaulted over the car, fear numbing his body.

Zora lay sprawled next to the car, her head twisted at an awkward angle, a small pool of blood growing beneath her neck. Curtik's gut tightened. His mouth went dry. He knelt beside her and checked for a pulse. Nothing.

"Doctor!" he yelled.

Dr. Poole came around the car, one hand braced against it to steady herself, the other holding a medical bag.

"It's Zora," he said. "I think she's dead."

"CPR," Dr. Poole commanded as she knelt on the other side of Zora and opened her bag. The CINTEP driver stood guard in the street, Las-pistol out, looking in both directions.

Curtik began chest compressions, pushing down repeatedly on Zora's sternum while Dr. Poole checked her med-scanner. She put the portable auto-breather in Zora's mouth and lifted Zora's head so she could apply a QuikHeal bandage to the wound. Then she indicated that Curtik should move aside and slapped a hypo-pad onto Zora's chest. She said, "I've got an ambulance coming."

"Is she gonna be okay?" Curtik asked.

"I don't know. Keep going."

Curtik continued chest compressions, while Dr. Poole checked her med-scanner and prepared another hypo-pad. *Live, you bitch. I won't have you dying on me. What would I tell Jeremiah?*

A rush of hot air swirled around them as the whoosh of a jet-copter sounded in Curtik's ears. Within a minute, the machine had landed in the middle of the street. Two paramedics jumped out and hurried over with a stretcher. As they loaded Zora onto it, Dr. Poole said, "What about Okoye? Any chance he got out?"

Curtik looked over at the fireball across the street. For the first time he noticed the intense heat. And he also realized that the explosion must have occurred because he and Zora pushed the action. He was responsible for Okoye's death—for all the innocent lives lost. "I'm sorry."

"Get in the jet-copter," Dr. Poole said as the paramedics loaded Zora. She put a hand on his back and directed him to the open doorway, helping him up and in. As soon as she climbed in after him the jet-copter accelerated away, the CINTEP driver staying behind, holstering his Las-pistol as emergency vehicles approached.

Chapter 7

Bundled in his jacket, sitting on his porch swing, Jeremiah Jones looked out over the trees at the Blue Ridge Mountains. Although the calendar said June, it felt like March and the air still carried a faintly burnt odor. He'd come outside to avoid the news, which Hannah Swenson, the live-in CINTEP security officer, had decided he needed to see. He could hear her stomping around like an angry daughter while the latest developments—reports of the Susquehanna Virus, the transfer of a rat's mind from Mars and the chaos of a world trapped temporarily in global winter—emanated from the TV. Of course, he knew why she insisted on blaring the news every day, but so far, at least, she hadn't pressured him into returning to CINTEP.

He tried not to listen. Every story served as a reminder of his failings, no matter how many times Dr. Poole told him the world's problems weren't his fault. He knew he shouldn't blame himself. He was no Walt Devereaux. How could he, one man, have stopped the carnage wrought by his son, Curtik, and the rest of Eli's cadets? That kind of arrogant thinking bordered on megalomania. Yet he still felt like a failure.

Over the sound of the television he heard the crunch of tires on the gravel drive. Gritting his teeth and steeling himself for the pain of movement, he got to his feet and leaned against the porch railing, his right hand resting inches away from his holstered Las-pistol.

Behind him the TV quieted, the door opened and Hannah stepped out onto the porch. She stood on the other side of the stairs, a tall Nordic blond with short hair, broad shoulders and muscular legs. She wore a beige interface on her left temple, a brown jacket over green pants—her standard uniform—and a Las-pistol and scanner on her belt. Guard or jailer: Jeremiah didn't know how to classify her. All he knew was that after two months, she still hadn't warmed to him. She frowned at Jeremiah. "You should go inside. Could be trouble."

Jeremiah laughed. "It's trouble, all right—though not the kind you're thinking of. It's probably Lendra. Maybe with Curtik."

"You don't know that." Hannah put her hand on her Las-pistol.

"It's a limo," Jeremiah said. "Right?" Hannah's eyelids rose slightly, confirming his deduction. She would have seen the vehicle on the security vid via her interface. Hell, she'd probably been in contact with Lendra several times today. "And it's moving at the wrong pace for an enemy. Not fast enough to be an attack. Not slow enough to be reconnaissance or stealth."

A few seconds later, a black limousine emerged from the trees.

"Wasted talent," Hannah muttered, shaking her head as the limo pulled to a stop beside the house. The back door opened and Curtik sprang out.

"Hey, Pappy." Curtik looked up at Jeremiah and gave him a mock salute. "You don't look like a ghost to me. I can't see through you at all."

Jeremiah's chest tightened as he stared down at his son. Curtik—born Joshua Jones—stood nearly as tall as Jeremiah, though he was slimmer. Dark of hair and skin, with delicate features that had been genetically altered so that he no longer looked like his father, Curtik bore only the slightest resemblance to his mother Catherine. He sported the same mocking grin he always wore around Jeremiah: either as a defense mechanism or because he truly didn't like his father.

"Curtik." Jeremiah nodded to his son. "How are you?"

"Exceptionally skull bangish today," Curtik said, moving to some beat Jeremiah couldn't hear—music from his implant.

"You're a long way from DC," Jeremiah said. "You coming back home?"

Curtik scoffed, then looked at the limo as Lendra stepped from the car, pulling out a car seat carrying her daughter, Sophie. The guard/driver stayed behind the wheel.

"I thought I told you not to bring that child here," Jeremiah said.

"She's your daughter," Lendra said. "I thought you should meet her."

"She's a product of your treachery—yours and Eli's. I trusted you. And—"

"Eli ordered me to impregnate myself with your child." Lendra held the car seat up so he could see the baby. "I didn't want her any more than you did—at first. But now that she's here—"

"You'll do to her what was done to Curtik."

Curtik interjected, "I'm happy with what they did to me, old man."

Jeremiah held up a hand, wincing at the movement. His shoulder felt like it had been stabbed with a thousand needles. "Kidnapping you from your mother and altering your genetic structure?"

Curtik's head bobbed up and down. "Hey, animal DNA and nanobots. The way of the future. I'm gonna be the greatest ghost ever."

He giggled, then winked at Hannah, who snorted, glaring at Curtik and shaking her head almost imperceptibly. Jeremiah knew Hannah blamed Curtik for this assignment. She probably thought she could return to CINTEP if only Curtik stayed behind. Jeremiah didn't bother to disabuse her of that belief.

"It's too bad you can't remember your childhood," Jeremiah said."

"I remember parts—getting an ice cream at the water park with Mom. And the big guy who took me away. Mouthy Man Marschenko. I kind of recall him. I especially remember wasting him. Good times. But I don't remember you at all."

Guilt flooded Jeremiah. And anger. He shivered. "How come you never mentioned that?"

"Why would I tell you?"

"Because I'm your father?"

"Operational security, old man. You never know when you might need an edge."

Jeremiah shook his head. "It's sad that you think you need to get an edge over me." He turned to Lendra. "You see why I don't want to have anything to do with your daughter? Look what Eli did to my boy."

"Love you too, Daddio," Curtik said.

Jeremiah closed his eyes for a moment, collecting himself. He hadn't meant to offend Curtik. When he opened them, he saw that Lendra had stepped to the foot of the stairs. Jeremiah could clearly see the baby's head now, her dark hair sticking out from beneath her cap and her hazel eyes: exactly like his. The baby looked up at him, her tiny face scrunched up in a frown. She made little noises of discomfort. Jeremiah had no idea what kind of enhancements she'd been given but he was pretty certain she'd received some. She would become a target one day too.

"I'm sorry, Curtik," Jeremiah said. "How's the pain?"

To save his son's life—and Zora's—Jeremiah had provided a transfusion of his blood—blood infected with the Susquehanna Virus that nevertheless had amazing healing powers. In Jeremiah's case, it continued to produce antibodies that attacked and repaired his joints many times a day. Now the two children suffered, to a lesser degree, the same kind of joint pain he did.

"Drugs, man," Curtik said, bopping his head up and down, side to side, his breath condensing in the chill air. "You gotta love 'em. Too bad they don't work for you." He sounded pleased at that, which again made Jeremiah angry. He lived every moment with the needle-sharp, grating agony that came with the slightest of movements. If only Curtik knew how painful his life was, would he still be so dismissive, so contemptuous?

"And your friend Zora?" Jeremiah asked.

"I wondered when you'd get to her," Curtik answered. "You always liked her more than me."

"Why wouldn't I?" Jeremiah knew he shouldn't speak but he couldn't help himself. "All I've ever wanted to be is your father. And all you do is make smarmy comments and insult me—pushing me away like an enemy. Your mother did that sometimes. Drove me crazy. I know it's not all your fault. I know they made you this way and you're probably doing it as some sort of defense mechanism, but it hurts. Yes, your attitude hurts me. You're smug and cruel and without any hint of empathy."

"Jeremiah," Lendra said.

"It's true. If you can't be civil around me, Curtik, then perhaps you shouldn't visit."

"Oh, ouch," Curtik replied. "A dagger to my heart." Curtik feigned stabbing himself in the chest, then wiped off the invisible blade with a flourish. "How awful to stay away from all this luxury." He made a sweeping gesture. "I'll send along the preferred Zora next time. I wouldn't have come today, but . . ."

"What? Is she still refusing to take the drugs? I can talk to her again."

Curtik glanced over at Lendra, who waited patiently at the foot of the stairs. Hannah, meanwhile, pulled her scanner off her belt and made a pretense of studying it. Without knowing why, Jeremiah immediately realized something terrible had happened to Zora.

"How badly is she hurt?" he asked.

"Who?" Lendra said.

"Don't play games. Zora."

Curtik laughed. "Man, how do you do that? That's freaky!"

"That's why you have to come back to CINTEP," Lendra said. "You're so good at intuiting truth from almost no data at all. We need you, not because of your enhanced skills, but because you're so good at reading people and situations."

Jeremiah looked his son in the eye. "Tell me what happened to Zora."

"She'll be fine," Curtik said. "She was only dead for a couple minutes."

It felt like a punch to the heart, all the wind knocked out of him, his nervous system stunned. Jeremiah determined not to let the hollowness show. He looked at Lendra. "Where is she?"

"The CINTEP medical center. She'll be back on her feet in a few days. No permanent damage. Do you want to visit her? I can arrange that." Lendra looked over at Hannah.

"I'll get the car," Hannah said.

Jeremiah held up a hand. "No."

Hannah frowned. The baby squirmed in her car seat. Lendra shifted the child from her right to her left arm.

"Lighten up," Curtik said. "Except for Zora getting kinda blown up, last night was wicked fun. Sorta reminded me of that mission you had in Rangoon, when the café you and Julianna were in exploded."

Jeremiah glared at Lendra. "He read my file?"

Curtik whistled. "I wanna do the things you and Julianna did. Me and Zora, once she's healed up, we'll be unstoppable. We'll be the best. 'Cuz Julianna, even though she was enhanced, she wasn't like us. She was human."

Jeremiah said, "Julianna was better than me."

Curtik shrugged. "You gotta say that. She was your lover." Curtik made kissing sounds.

"That was before your mother."

"Don't matter to me," Curtik said. "They're both dead."

Jeremiah's stomach flipped at Curtik's callousness. It's not his fault, Jeremiah reminded himself. He wondered for a moment whether the other surviving cadets were as hard as Curtik and how their families were putting up with their return. Not my problem.

"That must have been one hell of a battle the two of you had with the Elite Ops in Minnesota," Curtik continued, "rescuing Devereaux, saving the Escala. Didn't work out too well for Julianna though. And it's too bad your last mission was such a disaster."

"Curtik," Lendra said.

"What? I'm just saying, he didn't stop us from blasting all those cities with the Las-cannons."

Lendra shook her head. "You sound like you're proud of that."

"Whatever," Curtik said. "All I know is I need excitement. Without it, I might as well be him—sitting around waiting to die."

Hannah leaned forward, the rail creaking as she pressed against it, her face tightening into a frown as she glared at Curtik.

"What?" Curtik said. "You want to go a few rounds? I haven't had a good fight in days." He grinned at Hannah until she backed away.

Jeremiah felt the menace of his son—how close Curtik was to the precipice of madness. Or was Curtik playing a game at Lendra's behest? Had she encouraged Curtik to act crazy as a way of ensnaring him back into CINTEP? He couldn't know for certain. His heart sinking, Jeremiah looked at the baby again. She closed her eyes and yawned widely, then opened and closed her mouth several times.

Lendra cleared her throat and said, "Hector is dead."

"Martinez?"

Lendra nodded. Hannah breathed in sharply.

Jeremiah said, "The virus?"

"No. A neuro-tingler bomb. He detonated it in Jakarta."

"On the trail of Susquehanna Sally?" He regretted his words the moment he spoke them. He didn't want to get involved. He wasn't interested in that life anymore.

"He was infiltrating a cell by tracking a courier. Turns out Indonesia's where Sally introduced her most virulent version of the virus to date."

"So that leaves just Brosk."

"And Ned," Lendra said.

"I thought he retired."

"Last year." Lendra nodded. "But he agreed to return when Susquehanna Sally's attacks became more deadly. He put his needs aside for the sake of the world."

"Good old Ned."

"How can you watch that much suffering without wanting to do something about it? You have to know that even if Devereaux finds a cure, Susquehanna Sally won't just walk away. She'll release some other horrible disease on the world, or some awful weapon of mass destruction. The only way to give humanity a decent shot at long-term survival is to find her . . . him . . . them."

Jeremiah looked at the baby once again. Then he shook his head slowly, trying to minimize the pain, and said, "You're just like Eli. Every mission is end-of-the-world vital. Yet the world never changes. I don't believe you, or trust you. And I don't really care if humans die off. Humanicide seems inevitable. If not this crisis, then the next one. I don't think the planet will be much worse off for that."

"Curtik tells me you made him slave away in a garden," Lendra said.

Jeremiah, confused by the change in topic, blinked.

"Worst job I ever had," Curtik said. "Planting rutabagas or whatever the hell they were."

"Radishes," Jeremiah said, "and lettuce, peas, cabbage and potatoes."

"That was a good idea," Lendra said. "Trying to get Curtik to connect with the earth he tried to destroy. Are you listening, Curtik?"

"Yeah, yeah, yeah. Gardening, good. Exploding planet, bad."

Hannah tensed, growling so softly that Jeremiah almost didn't hear her. He hoped she'd control her temper. No matter how well trained she was, she'd be no match for Curtik.

"Didn't you have to work in your parents' garden when you were a child?" Lendra said to Jeremiah.

Jeremiah nodded. "My father grew up on a farm. He taught me a lot."

"And how are you managing without Curtik? Or does Hannah help?"

Hannah snorted again.

Jeremiah shrugged. "The pain's not as bad when I'm working in the garden."

"I want Curtik to show it to me," Lendra said. "You stay here and watch Sophie."

"No."

Lendra ignored him. She carried the car seat up the stairs and put it on the porch beside Jeremiah. The baby looked up at him, moving her tiny fists back and forth beneath her blanket. Lendra said, "We'll be back in a while. Keep an eye on her." Then she walked around the back of the house, Curtik right behind her.

"Well done," Hannah said.

"Excuse me?"

"Telling that obnoxious little bastard off. He needed that. Did you see the way he reacted? He stopped all his twitching and just listened to you. Maybe the message got through. Maybe he'll stop thinking he's so great."

"I didn't mean to blow up at him. He's just so damn frustrating at times."

The baby began crying. Jeremiah looked over at Hannah, who simply shrugged. "Lendra," he called.

No answer.

"Pick her up," Hannah said. "She wants to be held."

"You pick her up," Jeremiah retorted.

"She's not my baby."

"Oh, hell." Jeremiah took a deep breath. Even that hurt. Lowering himself to the porch swing, he reached for the car seat, undid the security belts and lifted the squirming Sophie. She was heavier than he'd thought she'd be, more substantial. He smelled her milky breath and the baby powder under her diaper. Holding her in the crook of his arm, he hummed quietly until she calmed. Hannah, he noticed, had backed up against the wall. The baby—his daughter—watched him, eyes bright and alert.

From the back of the house, he heard Curtik exclaim, "Hey, look. The radishes are coming up. So's the lettuce. And that's cabbage. And peas. Hunh. I didn't think the old man knew what he was doing."

The breeze freshened, yet Jeremiah felt oddly warmed. He bundled the blanket around his daughter more tightly, then looked into her eyes and spoke softly:

"I can't help you, kid. I guess I'm not much of a father."

"Better than my dad ever was," Hannah muttered, so softly he wasn't sure he heard her correctly.

"We've turned the world into a cesspool," he said, loudly enough for Hannah to overhear, "and no one knows how to fix it. The only way to spare you pain would be to wring your pretty little neck. But I can't do that. So here we sit. Waiting for some madman to put an end to our miserable existence."

As he talked to Sophie, Jeremiah realized that his pain was no longer debilitating. The mere act of holding his daughter lessened the agony. How could that be? He tried not to think about that, instead simply basked in the unexpected deliverance, chatting with Sophie as she tracked his eyes. He smiled at her, then frowned, then began to make faces at her as she stared at him, occasionally smiling. Soon he was making baby sounds, just to revel in her reaction, more for his benefit than hers.

Amazed at himself, he glanced at Hannah, who quickly looked away, her eyes glistening. She grabbed her scanner off her belt and checked it again, running another sweep of the area.

All too soon Lendra and Curtik returned, and Sophie was lifted, protesting, from Jeremiah's lap, leaving him cold and empty. He used to be able to seal himself away in a stone dungeon—a self-hypnotic trick that freed him from all feeling, all pain. From within that dungeon, he could endure almost anything. But the last time he'd tried it, he'd almost lost himself. So he accepted the chilled hollowness and put a calm expression on his face.

"That's a nice garden," Lendra said as she fastened Sophie to her car seat. "I'm surprised they're doing so well without a greenhouse."

"I divert heat from an underground pump," Jeremiah said. "And early on, I used the solar panels to add supplemental warmth. But we don't need them anymore. The ground's greening up nicely."

"I know you hate me, Jeremiah," Lendra said, changing the subject again, rocking the car seat to comfort Sophie. "And I can't blame you for feeling that way."

"I don't hate you," Jeremiah said. "I'm disappointed in you."

"What about me?" Curtik asked. "I hope you're disappointed in me too. Running away from home to join the ghosts."

"I still don't understand all that," Jeremiah said. "The courts say you aren't responsible for your actions on the Moon because you're a minor, under a compulsion, and then they legally emancipate you as an adult."

"It was a complicated ruling," Lendra said.

"Oh, it was twisted, certainly. You need him to reinstate your ghost program, so you make sure that he's absolved of his prior crimes while ensuring that he'll be available to commit new ones in the name of almighty CINTEP. I'm only surprised you didn't figure out a way to get all the cadets put under your authority."

"If you're so concerned, you could return to us. As our head of operations, you would have supervisory authority over him."

Curtik startled, as if he hadn't considered that possibility before.

"Of all the people I know," Lendra continued, "you're the one who might be able to save the world. You see things we don't. You make connections we can't. Are you going to withhold your gifts out of self-pity? Are you going to condemn your daughter to a life of misery out of selfishness?"

Curtik shook his head as he fidgeted from foot to foot, frowning.

"I have nothing left to give," Jeremiah said.

"You know where to find us," Lendra said. Carrying Sophie to the limo, she opened the door and secured the car seat. Curtik followed her. He looked back at Jeremiah before seating himself beside Lendra and closing the door.

His face carried a look of sadness that Jeremiah had never seen on it before. Tears welled up as the air seemed to remove itself from the world. *God, I'm a terrible father. My two children are leaving me and I won't do anything to stop it. I'll just let them go.*

The car door closed as Sophie cried out. Jeremiah wanted to run to her, hold her in his arms and tell her everything would be all right, even though he knew it wouldn't. He wanted to grab Curtik in a giant hug and say, *I believe in you, son. And I love you. Some day you'll understand that, I hope.*

Instead, the limo drove away. Jeremiah walked down the stairs, following it a short distance down the driveway, imagining he could still smell his daughter, welcoming the knife-like piercing in his joints that came with each movement—fair retribution for his sins. Hannah trailed him quietly.

She said, "I trained with him."

"Curtik?"

"Martinez. He was a good man."

"Yes, he was."

"What about you?"

"I can't bring him back."

"I saw you playing with your daughter. You can't pretend that didn't happen."

"What can I do?" Jeremiah said.

"Sitting out here in the cold? Nothing."

Steeling himself for the agony of movement, Jeremiah walked around the house to the garden, Hannah a step behind. He hadn't been back here for days, the pain of movement no longer seeming worth it after Curtik left for CINTEP. He saw that Curtik had been right; the garden looked good—the neat rows reaching skyward, the lettuce nearly ready to pick, although a haphazard pattern of weeds attacked them from the sides.

He knelt beside the radishes and began plucking weeds. "I suppose I should thank you for not trying harder to convince me to return to the old life."

"Would you have done anything besides shut me out if I had?"

"No." He pulled another few weeds. "Aren't you going to help me?"

"What's the point? They'll only grow back. You can't hold them back forever."

He laughed. "Well played."

"I'm not saying you're wrong to refuse them. I see the pain you're in. I get it. But they're not wrong in wanting you back, either. You have a gift and you're squandering it."

"Shut up and help me with this or you'll be out here all day."

Chapter 8

As Trogan Brosk stirred beside her, Sally23 nestled her head against his shoulder. He came awake with a quiet laugh. "Wow," he said. "Mmm," she replied, rubbing her hand across his naked chest.

"What did I do to deserve such happiness?" he asked.

"Not a thing," she answered. "You're a devil. You're a bad, bad boy." She lifted her head and twisted to look into his dark brown eyes, the pupils dilated by drugs. Even so, they looked upon her with warmth. She could melt in those eyes. "Are you ready to be bad again?"

He grinned as he pulled her on top of him. "I suppose I could manage another go."

As he kissed her, the bedroom door slammed open. Sally23, knowing who was behind her, tried to go numb in preparation for what was to come. She turned as Brosk stared at the intruder.

"Jeremiah!" Brosk exclaimed. "What are you doing here?"

"Trogan," the man replied with a nod. He stood inside the door, a dark-haired man with hazel eyes and a nose that had been broken at least once. He held a Las-pistol in his right hand, aimed at Brosk's face. "I heard you went over to the other side."

"No," Brosk said. "I'm infiltrating this cell." He giggled. "I've already infiltrated her several times."

The man fired his weapon, a red laser pulse hitting Brosk squarely in the face. Brosk screamed and passed out. Sally23, pressed up against Brosk's body, felt a surge of electricity run through her too, her body absorbing the residue from the simulated Las-pistol strike.

"Damn, that hurts," Sally23 said as the man with the gun winked out of existence, the holo-projection shutting off.

This whole project was starting to piss her off—being forced to have sex with Brosk over and over, watched the entire time by Sally2 and the Wallys—though she had to admit that she enjoyed Brosk's touch. He was a gifted lover. If only his attentions were real and not forced by drugs and conditioning. She could easily find herself falling for him. In the same moment, she recalled that seduction was Brosk's gift. It was what he did. So he undoubtedly had no emotional attachment to her. But wow: it felt real.

Aside from being used as a sex object, she shuddered every time she saw the holo-projection of Jeremiah Jones. He had an intensity about him, much like Sally2, that bespoke of single-mindedness: a man who would not be dissuaded from completing his mission, no matter the cost. Was he really that way, or had Sally2 created him like that?

A few seconds later Sally2 entered the room and looked at Brosk, shaking her head. "We're still not getting a fear response from him," she said, "though we're detecting an increase in the loyalty response toward you. We'll run it again, only this time we'll focus the threat on you. Let's try to reinforce that connection. Tell him you love him—whatever—just continue to build that bond. And when Jones fires at you, you scream and pretend to faint. With all the drugs pumped into him, Brosk won't be able to tell you're faking." Sally2's eyes narrowed. "You all right?"

Sally23 said, "I need a break. I'm not some porn star." She reached for her bathrobe, then climbed out of bed and walked slowly to the bathroom, turning on the fan and the faucet before sitting on the toilet. Her body began to shake. She knew this cruelty was necessary, part of the process of breaking Brosk down, reprogramming him. Yet he'd suffered at least a dozen of these simulated deaths already, maybe more outside of Sally23's presence, and she was beginning to feel panicky.

How could she have feelings for Brosk? He was a killer, a human, part of the long-term disease that infected Mother Earth. He had to be annihilated, just as every other human had to be destroyed. What would death be like? Would it be nothingness, or would she emerge into some other plane of existence? And was she really destined to die or would Sally2 save her?

A knock came at the door. "We're ready for you," Wally5 said.

Sally23 took a deep breath. When she emerged from the bathroom, she said to Sally2, "Can't you just simulate the sex? Make him think we just did it? Do we have to do it over and over again?"

Sally2 frowned. "You seemed to be enjoying yourself. And you know the simulation can't duplicate the intensity of the actual experience."

"I'm tired and sore. We've done it practically nonstop for three days."

"We've come up with a twist we think will be much more effective. Once more, then you can have a break, okay?"

"Fine." Sally23 took off her robe and climbed into bed beside Brosk, nestling herself into the crook of his shoulder and waiting for the technicians to bring him awake again.

He awoke laughing softly. He pulled her in tight and caressed her face. "You little minx," he said. "You've got me so I can barely think."

"Me too," she replied, trying to keep her voice light. "I never thought I'd feel this way about anyone."

"We'd make a great team. If you could figure out a way to break me out of here, I could keep you safe. We could get back to CINTEP, give them the location of this cell, and maybe figure out who your leader is. She doesn't look exactly like the doctor I remember from CINTEP, but she might have had surgery to make herself like an Escala. What do you really know about her?"

"Shh," Sally23 said. "It's dangerous to talk like that. And I can't get you out. Whenever I visit you like this, they lock me in. There are always two armed guards outside that door."

"Think, darling," Brosk said. "There must be a way. Meanwhile . . ."

He pulled her up on top of him again, drew her into a deep kiss that exhilarated and drained her at the same time. For a long time, he kissed and caressed her body. She fought the pleasure for a while, irked that everyone was watching. But eventually she surrendered to Brosk's attentions. He brought her to the edge of ecstasy, then backed off, teasing and tormenting her until she begged him to end it, which he finally did.

As they lay on their backs, breathing deeply, recovering, the bedroom door slammed open again. Brosk sat up. "Jeremiah? How did you get in here?"

"Trogan," the holo-projection of Jones replied with a nod. He aimed his Las-pistol at Sally23's face. "Get dressed. I'll take care of this slut."

"No," Brosk said. "She's not with them. She can help us."

Jones shook his head. "Sorry. I'm taking no chances." He fired the Las-pistol at Sally23, who felt the sizzling fire of an electrical current. She screamed as Brosk threw her off him and dove into the line of fire. He too screamed, then passed out.

"What the hell?" Sally23 asked, shivering, as the holo-projection winked out again.

Sally2 entered the room. "I decided to make it more realistic."

"You could have told me you were going to shock me."

"I wanted you to be surprised." Sally2 offered a smile that touched her lips, her eyes remaining cold. "Better reaction. It worked too. Got a good fear response from him that time."

"I'm not your puppet," Sally23 said, glaring at Sally2. "I'm not just some tool. I'm a computer expert. I used to help with the virus modification project. Now you're treating me like a stupid schoolgirl."

Sally2 tapped her foot on the floor. "You're bright. But you question too much. I sometimes wonder about your loyalties."

"Then maybe you should kill me and be done with it."

"We've all been tested many times. It isn't personal."

"It feels personal."

Sally2 rubbed her temple. "Brosk may not even be salvageable. We have to move slowly, break down the hypno-commands delicately or he could dissemble completely."

"I thought we were running out of time," Sally23 said. "After what happened to Sally6 in Jakarta—"

"Sally6 got careless," Sally2 interrupted. "Too many people knew the location of that cell. And Sally16 never should have been allowed near it. There was always the possibility that she was going to be followed."

"If she was, perhaps they know our location."

"We're preparing a new site. Meanwhile, no contact with anyone outside this cell, not even the trusted. From now on, we operate as our own unit. And I want minimal traffic out front—no one coming or going unless it's absolutely necessary."

"Are you saying I can't leave?" Sally23 asked.

Sally2's eyes narrowed. "Why do you need to go out?"

"You pimp me out and zap me full of electricity. You make me pretend I'm on Brosk's side. You want me to keep him calm. Well, I'm not calm. I'm already infected with the virus—"

"We all are."

"Maybe that's making me edgy. I need to relax. So I need to go out. Besides, how are we supposed to continue distributing the virus if we can't access any of our agents on the outside?"

"Let me worry about that."

"Well, it's absolutely necessary that I get out of here for a while," Sally23 said. "If you really don't trust me, then kill me. Let the Wallys help you with the virus, and let Wally2 handle communications. But you're wasting my talents and we both know it."

"Perhaps you're right." Sally2 smiled in that odd way she had, a slight lift of her lips that served only to distort her cold face. "You should go see your mum. You may not get another chance. We need to let Brosk recover for a while anyway."

Sally23 grabbed her robe and belted it around her waist, then walked out of the room. An hour later, dressed in jeans, a sweater and her heavy coat, she went upstairs and took her scooter from its place by the front door. Andre, Sally2's pet security guard, watched her as she wheeled it outside, but he made no effort to detain her. No doubt he'd been watching her have sex with Brosk too. Degenerate.

She made her way west toward Hammersmith, studying the mass of people with a weariness that bordered on depression. She recognized her fatigue as the cause of her dour mood but she wondered if the virus had something to do with it as well.

Almost before she realized where she was going, she reached Beryl Road, where Reg lived with Murph in a two-up, two-down flat, almost indistinguishable from the rest of the serried row houses. Why had she come here, instead of to her mother's? Why not? Her mother had never forgiven her. She drove past rundown flat after rundown flat until she spotted Murph's scooter. When she pulled up next to it, she just sat there for a moment, trying to decide whether to go inside. Perhaps Sally2 was right and she should visit her mother—one last time before the end.

"Hey, Crimson." Murph leaned out the upper-floor window, staring down at her. "You gonna sit there all day?"

Reg leaned out the window next to him. "You here for a little action, Bluebell?"

"What?"

Reg leered. "I can kick Murph out for a half-hour."

"You've got to be kidding me."

"Just a suggestion."

Sally23 shook her head. "I've had a bad day. I'll see you later."

"Bluebell," Reg said. "We don't have to do it."

"Or if you want to do it with me," Murph said. "I could kick Reg out for a half-hour."

"Cretins!" Sally23 turned her scooter around and headed off again, south and east across the Wandsworth Bridge towards her mother's slightly more upscale flat. As she drove, she found herself looking at places she used to frequent—pubs and eateries, a few stores—with something like nostalgia. It felt like a farewell tour. Sally2 hadn't said anything about the upcoming mission with Brosk, but it was likely to happen soon, without warning. And it was likely to be fatal. The fact that Sally2 hadn't told her what her assignment would be made her nervous. Would she have to kill Brosk? Or Jones? Or was she simply bait?

Did it really matter if she died a few days or weeks early? With the Susquehanna Virus increasing the death toll around the world, with Britain losing dozens every day, the end would come soon enough.

Sally23 parked her scooter outside her mother's flat. I can do this, she thought. He's not there anymore. And she has no power over me now. She made her way up the stairs and let herself in. "Hello?" she called. "Mum?"

Scheherezade, her mother's cat, meowed and ran over to her, rubbing her side against Sally23's leg. She reminded Sally23 of Muffin, her childhood dog, who died from some disease caused by a parasite that shouldn't have existed in England, but that had migrated north with climate change. Muffin, who her father shut away in a closet while he did things to her, had been the only one she could turn to back then. That's all over now. I'm past that.

"Mum?" Perhaps her mother had gone shopping. Sally23 should have called first. But something seemed off. All the windows were open a few inches. That was odd. Her mother rarely left the windows open. Sally23 glanced around the flat, taking in the pictures and bric-a-brac her mother had accumulated over the years. Walking to the mantle, she searched for the vid-picture of Muffin. Oddly, it wasn't there. Instead, she spotted it on the sideboard. Taking it down, Sally23 brought it back over to the mantle. She studied the vid-photo of Muffin wagging her tail as she stared up at the camera.

Sally23 set the vid-photo next to her university graduation vid-picture. On the screen, she and her mother waved to the camera, she in her cap and gown, her mother in her best blue dress, strained smiles on their faces.

Scheherezade meowed again.

"Okay, I hear you," Sally23 said. She walked down the hall, only then noticing the unpleasant odor emanating from the bedroom. She knew her mother was dead, even as she pushed open the door and caught the stench of excrement and saw her mother on the bed, fully clothed, her face contorted in pain, her milky eyes staring sightlessly at the ceiling.

She thought she might gag. She sank to the floor, unable to breathe. It felt as if her entire being had been removed from her body and all that remained was a vacuum—a null presence.

I no longer exist. How could Mum be dead? She couldn't catch the virus because she almost never leaves the flat. And even if she did, how could she die so quickly? Of course, Sally23 hadn't seen her in weeks, so maybe it hadn't been fast. But somehow, Sally23 doubted this was the virus. She recalled Sally2 telling her to visit her mother. Getting to her feet, she went to the windows and opened them wide. Then she stepped to the bed and reached out her hand, touching her mother's cold, hard cheek. It took her a while to realize she was crying. Why would she do that? She backed away, stumbled to the kitchen and put on a kettle to make tea. She wiped her eyes and pulled down the good cups and saucers, placed them on the serving tray, then put away the dishes sitting on the counter. As she waited for the tea, she filled Scheherezade's food bowl.

Her first instinct was to kill Sally2—find a weapon and exact revenge. Even though she'd known for quite some time that her mother had to die eventually, even though she'd wanted her mother to die many times, it wasn't supposed to happen this way. For Sally2 to accelerate the process, to murder her mother, or more likely have Andre do it, infuriated her. Did she think she was doing Sally23 a favor? Did she, in her twisted way, think that would somehow increase Sally23's loyalty by severing her ties to the world? Or was it simply a message that she had absolute control, that she could take Sally23's life at any time? Didn't she understand that at some point, when death became inevitable, you couldn't use it as leverage anymore?

When the tea was ready, she took it into her mother's room, set the serving tray on the bed and placed a cup and saucer on the nightstand. She poured tea for her mother and added two spoonfuls of sugar, stirring carefully so as not to spill. Faint tendrils of steam rose from her mother's cup. She poured a cup for herself, added in a spoonful of sugar and a splash of cream, and sat in the chair beside the bed, the numb emptiness inside somehow spreading even though she was already completely hollow.

She finished stirring the tea, put down the spoon, and powered up her PlusPhone to retrieve an old message from her mother.

"Hi, Sienna, it's your Mum. I'm worried about you. I know you've been angry lately. I know I never should have blamed you for your dad leaving. I still find it hard to believe he did what you claim. That wasn't the man I knew. But I am sorry. Please call me. I'm all alone. By the way, I looked up this Gaia Manifesto. These people are fanatics. Eliminate humanity from the face of the Earth? That's crazy! Please tell me those aren't the people you're involved with. I'm afraid . . . if you are . . . well, they don't care about you. They're just using you. Call me. Please."

Sally23 wiped her eyes again as Scheherezade entered from the hallway and rubbed against her legs.

She couldn't stay here. She couldn't run. She was already infected with the virus, and without medication she'd just die that much quicker, that much more painfully. So she really had no choice but to return. And if she looked at it in the right light, she could even say that Sally2 had done her a favor—shown her the truth. Like all leaders, Sally2 treated her people as cogs in a machine. Her actions demonstrated just how necessary it was that humans become extinct—at least most of them. And as long as the list included Sally2, Sally23 could accept her own death.

She finished her tea, noting that steam no longer rose from her mother's cup. Collecting the cup and saucer from the nightstand, she closed the bedroom door softly, took the tray back to the kitchen and rinsed out the dishes, setting them to dry. Then she took the vid-pictures of her graduation and Muffin and called Scheherezade. Placing the cat inside her coat, she took a last look around. She locked the door behind her and climbed onto her scooter.

It didn't take long to get back to Reg's place in Hammersmith. She let herself in, walked up the stairs and opened the door.

Reg and Murph sat on the sofa, the pungent aroma of marijuana filling the air, an empty pizza box on the coffee table.

"Hey, Crimson," Reg said.

Sally23 pointed at Murph. "He calls me Crimson. You call me Bluebell. Remember?"

"Sorry, got a mite confused by the baked Italian."

Murph said, "We added a special ingredient to the 'za. Extra mellow, no anchovies. I'll call you Bluebell if you want, or Watermelon or SnickBiscuit or PantDoodle—any nickname you want."

"Hey, DimTwaddle," Reg said, "that's my girl over there, or at least she's more my girl than yours. Right, Bluebell?"

Sally23 felt a laugh coming, but she was afraid to let it out. If she did, she might start crying again. he pulled Scheherezade from its warm confines of her coat and set her on the floor. "I brought you another cat."

"Cool," Murph said. "Indifference will be entirely apathetic."

At the sound of his name, Murph's cat Indifference got up, stretched, and sauntered over, touching noses with Scheherezade before turning and walking away. Scheherezade followed him.

"We can always use another cat," Reg said. "Taste like chicken."

Or greasy Spaniards," he and Murph said at the same time. They both started laughing. Sally23 watched them for a moment, pitying and envying them at the same time.

"What is it?" Reg asked, suddenly sobering.

"Yeah, what's wrong, Crimson?"

"I'm in trouble," Sally23 said. "We're all in trouble."

"That's exactly right," Murph said. "Which is why we've chosen to combat the problem with high doses of baked frivolity."

"I sense something more," Reg said.

"I believe you're right," Murph said. "Very perceptive for a Neanderthal. What is it, Crimson? Tell us. We can help."

Sally23 shook her head. "You'll only get yourselves killed."

Reg said, "As opposed to waiting around for this obnoxious sod to bore me to death with more prattle about hell on Earth and science as the only viable long-term solution to our woes?"

"Or this lunatic spouting blather about souls and other religious pabulum while the fabric of society rips into shreds?"

Sally23 stood for a moment, taking in the normalcy of the scene, the playfulness of Reg and Murph—two lovable idiots who had no idea what was about to happen to them—and realized she shouldn't have said anything. Though, in their current state, they probably wouldn't remember much of this tomorrow.

"Goodbye, Murph. Goodbye, Reg." She turned and walked out the door, hearing them struggle to their feet as she did so. By the time she reached her scooter, they were again leaning out their windows.

"We'd really like to help," Reg called down.

"Except for Indifference," Murph added. "He doesn't care what happens to us."

"Right," Reg said, "except for Indifference. We'll be around, Bluebell. Let us know if there's anything we can do to help."

Sally23 started her scooter, gave them a wave and drove off, back to Sally2, back to Trogan Brosk, back to her impending death.

Chapter 9

Aspen leaned against the wall near the main cave's entrance and swallowed two more pills. She found it difficult to focus. This damn headache wouldn't go away. Quekri, conducting the briefing from the center of the room, was explaining to a handful of miners that the Chinese ship had once again locked onto the New Dawn settlement's comm-link to navigate. Also, the Escala sensors were now picking up a high-energy weapon signature—possibly a Las-cannon.

Bilson, the balding, heavyset mine foreman who seemed marginally smarter than the rest of the miners, said, "So does that mean they're gonna attack us? We got weapons, explosives. We can fight."

"No," Quekri said. "We don't know what it means. They're steering straight for us at the moment, but that may simply be for convenience. And even if they stay on that course, we can't assume they mean to harm us. They may be planning to shoot a meteor or an asteroid or they may simply be running tests on their weapons system. We have no way of knowing because they're still not answering our hails. Aspen? You and the cadets have the most military experience. Do you want to share your thoughts?"

Aspen glanced over at Benn and Addam, sitting beside Krall, Oggie and Poon—the three big Escala teenagers they'd befriended. She'd been having nightmares for a week: the Chinese ship landing just outside the tunnel entrance, soldiers emerging with Las-rifles and particle beam cannons blasting, bodies flying, Escala and cadets blown apart into bloody arms or legs, a few decapitated, while she tried over and over to load her Las-rifle, the chem-pack refusing to seat itself properly even as she kept skipping between the tunnels and the outside, where she found herself without a Mars suit, struggling to breathe, lost on a wasteland of orange-red nothingness, without any idea where the tunnel entrance was.

She shrugged the nightmares aside and took another sip from her water bottle. The red dust settled everywhere. Her throat felt dry all the time and her headaches, probably caused by the lower atmospheric pressure, seemed to be getting worse. The pills didn't seem to be helping, either. Why didn't the other cadets have headaches?

"It's possible," she said, "that the sensors only picked up the weapons signature recently because the ship is now close enough for them to do so. However, it's also possible that the Chinese have hostile intentions. For our own safety, we have to assume that's the case. And we should stop trying to communicate with them. They may be trying to make us nervous by refusing to talk with us. So let's return the favor and go dark on them."

"But why would they attack us?" Zeriphi asked.

The miners turned to stare at the lovely Escala. Addam stared too. He and Benn and the three Escala teens sighed as they took in her statuesque beauty. I don't care, Aspen thought. I don't love Addam anyway. And Zora's gone forever now. She almost died and I didn't know about it until way too late, and even if I had, there was nothing I could do about it and now she doesn't have her implant anymore and pretty soon I'll never hear from her again. I've got to be strong. I've got to be a leader.

"It makes no sense," Zeriphi continued, as if unaware of her effect on the men in the cave. "The most recent news reports out of China say this is an exploratory mission."

Quekri laughed bitterly, almost a bark. "It makes perfect sense when you think about it. How many times have people and countries taken actions against their own best interests? Wars, overpopulation, depletion of scarce natural resources. My guess is that they're coming to ensure they can make a claim of sovereignty at some future time. After their skirmish with India last year and the ensuing sanctions by most of Earth's nations, they probably believe they'll be left out of decisions on Mars and its resources if they don't have a population base here."

Aspen took another drink. She wanted to close her eyes and rest for a while, but she knew her headache wouldn't allow her to sleep. She said, "I recommend that the miners make their weapons available to us."

"Not a chance," Bilson said, the four miners sitting beside him murmuring their agreement. "We heard about what you did on the Moon."

Aspen shrugged. "Then you'll have to take the point if it comes down to a fight."

"We ain't afraid of them. Hell, we've survived up here without becoming like you Escala."

Yes, Aspen thought. Forty of forty-eight miners still alive after fourteen months on Mars. The next MineStar ship would arrive in twelve months. How many would still be alive then?

Mining ships arrived every twenty-six months, when Mars and Earth were closest to each other, to drop off the new crew and return the old crew's survivors to Earth. The hazard pay was good, she'd been told, but was it worth dying for?

"We could always dig deeper," Bilson added, "in case we have to fight."

"Good idea," Quekri said as if she meant it, as if it would help against a Las-cannon attack.

Should we take their weapons? Addam sent via his implant.

Not yet, Aspen replied. *We can always get them later, if necessary. By the way, where's Phan?*

Plowing Shiloh and one of the Escala teens—Esbeth, I think. He's a sex machine.

Disgusting. I don't want to hear any more.

Quekri wrapped up the meeting and showed the miners out. As they left, Aspen kept an eye on them, making sure no one pilfered anything on the way. A number of tools had gone missing and she was sure at least one of the miners was a thief.

Zeriphi stopped beside Aspen on her way out of the meeting and said, "How is the mind transfer data progressing?"

"Pretty well. I'm running synaptic analyses at the moment. I should have a more complete picture in a couple hours."

"Good. Quekri and I will stop by to discuss it further. We'll want to have as much information as possible before we try again."

"Shouldn't we be worrying about this approaching ship?"

"What can we do? Most likely, they can eradicate us from orbit if they choose to. So why fret about it? Besides, you're the leader of the cadets. It'll go a long way toward calming everyone if you show them you're not concerned. At any rate, we may as well get on with our lives."

Aspen nodded, pretending agreement. "How are you feeling, with the pregnancy?"

"Fine. Much better than last time. It helps being on Mars. Our bodies are acclimating well. How are you doing? You don't look good. Maybe you should see Wellon."

Aspen took another sip of water. "I'll be okay. Just a dry throat."

"And the nightmares? The headaches? You still having them?"

Aspen glared at Addam, who shrugged.

"He's just trying to protect you," Zeriphi said. "Wellon said you're the only cadet who hasn't been to see her since we landed. Everyone else has allowed her to make genetic modifications, adjustments for the fact that we're now on a completely different world than you were designed for. Don't you think you ought to allow her to examine you, make sure you're okay?"

"I didn't think she had time. She's been so busy with the miners."

Zeriphi put her hand on Aspen's shoulder. "Wellon isn't Dr. Hackett. She's not going to subject you to painful experiments or try to induce rage and paranoia. You're safe here."

"I'll make an appointment, all right?"

"Good."

As Zeriphi walked away, Benn, Addam and the three Escala teenagers approached. They watched Zeriphi until she rounded a corner. Then Addam said, "What's our plan?"

Aspen looked from Krall to Poon and Oggie. She sent a message via her implant: *Why would you bring them in on this?*

Benn replied, *They're our friends.*

Addam sent, *We'll need everyone's help if it comes to a fight.*

If that happens, then we'll include them. But for now, let's keep things among ourselves. She said, "We wait, just like Quekri said."

Krall looked from Aspen to Benn and Addam, then said, "You were communicating by implant. What did you say?"

"Nothing," Aspen replied. "Now run along. We've all got work to do, and your mother wouldn't be happy if she knew you were just standing around."

"I won't tell Quekri what we're planning. I promise."

Aspen shook her head, indicating that the conversation was over.

"Forget her," Oggie said. "The bitch thinks she's too good for us. Let's get out of here." He strode away, Poon following and, after a moment, Krall joined them.

"What's his malfunction?" Benn asked when the three Escala were out of hearing range.

"Oggie's?" Aspen said. "He's mad because I won't sleep with him."

"Why not?"

"I don't want to. Okay?"

"I suppose."

Addam said, "She doesn't have to plow him if she doesn't want to."

Benn held up his hands.

"Do you want to sleep with Quekri?" Aspen asked Benn.

"Eew!"

"Well, there you go. Now, I want you two and Phan to look into making some Las-rifles. Quietly. The 3-D printers will do most of the work, but I want you to see if we have enough materials to create the chem-packs. We can always take the miners' weapons away from them, but I don't know how good they are. And we'll need more than they've got anyway if it comes down to a fight. Besides, if we let them keep their Las-rifles, we can use them as fodder for the enemy. Send them in first to draw the Chinese soldiers' fire."

"Nice."

"What about Kammilee and Shiloh?" Addam asked.

"Get Shiloh involved too. I don't know if we can trust Kammilee to keep a secret anymore."

"I'm sure she'll be fine," Benn said.

"That's your call," Aspen said. "You know her better than I do. But if she tells Quekri what we're doing and that interferes with our ability to defend ourselves, I'll hold you responsible."

"Just because Kammilee wants to get pregnant doesn't mean she's not still one of us."

"Perhaps."

"She knows that you're angry with her. She wonders if maybe you're starting to go a little crazy." Benn held up his hands again. "Don't be mad. She's just worried about you. These nightmares, and the headaches—you might be devolving. Or it might be a mental breakdown. This planet is so different from Earth, even the Moon. At least there we had similar atmospheric pressure, and Earth was close enough to feel like we were still attached to it. Now it's finally hitting us that we're never going back."

Addam touched her shoulder and said, "All the people who spent any length of time on Mars have incurred health problems—cancer and emphysema, auto-immune disorders and life-threatening allergies. And most of these miners have significant health problems as well. Wellon's had to do a fair amount of genetic modification just to keep a couple of them alive. Our concern is that something may be happening to you too."

"What's that got to do with my nightmares?"

"They might be a manifestation of a physical problem." Addam shuffled his feet and cleared his throat.

"Go ahead," Aspen said. "What else?"

"Well, we've researched mental health issues too. After all, we weren't made for Mars. We might not even have been made for Earth. At any rate, we haven't found much in the way of severe mental problems among miners or astronauts, but that might be because only the psychologically fit were chosen."

"So you think I'm cracking up?"

"No," Addam replied, "but I can tell you've got another headache right now. Don't try to deny it. I think you should see Dr. Wellon."

"I said I would."

"Yes, you did. You also told me you'd see her last week and you still haven't done it."

"Tomorrow," Aspen said. "I promise. Meanwhile, I have to get back to the lab, check on my results."

"We'll hold you to your promise. If you don't see Wellon tomorrow, we'll drag you there by your feet."

"Yeah, yeah, yeah. See you later."

Aspen left them standing at the cave entrance and returned to the lab. The first thing she did was swallow three more pills. Then she checked to make sure that Guffie was still alive on Earth. And he was, at least as of fifteen minutes ago. His motor coordination problems, however, lingered. Aspen examined the bio-scans the computers had run, trying to isolate why Guffie survived while Hugh died. Once again she compared the genomic sequences of the two rats, before and after the mind transfer. Finally, she programmed in a study of the scans of the two rats' minds after the transfer, even though she had only been able to capture eighty-eight percent of Hugh's post-transfer mind prior to his death.

She could make no sense of the discrepancies. But she knew she was missing something vital. If only she had Zora and Rendela here to help. But Zora had deserted her, Rendela had sacrificed herself for Zora, and Aspen was stuck on this dead planet with no one she cared about.

Enough. Concentrate. Focus.

She set aside her self-pity and returned to the data. Sifting through images and formulas, she fought to stay awake, the pills making her drowsy. She took a stimulant, knowing from past experience that it would likely turn her headache into a migraine within a couple hours. Despite the stimulant, as she was examining a complex equation, her eyes fluttered shut. She kept them closed for a moment, telling herself she wouldn't drop off into sleep. Some time later, seconds or perhaps minutes, an idea popped into her head. She opened her eyes, excited by the prospect of finding an answer, spent the next twenty minutes confirming her suspicions, and then called Quekri.

"What have you found?" Quekri asked when she walked into the lab, Zeriphi and Dr. Wellon behind her.

"I think it's here in the mind scans," Aspen said, laying out the data so they could examine it for themselves. "See how the myelin inside Guffie's new brain—Hugh's old brain—begins to break down in certain areas and build itself up in others? It seems to be reverting to the patterns of least resistance of Guffie's old brain here on Mars, as if the brain is trying to re-wire itself to the preferred circuitry that Guffie had up here. And then over here," Aspen pointed to a different set of data, "we see Hugh's new brain—Guffie's old one. See these favored synaptic pathways predominant with Hugh but not Guffie? There's a degradation of neuronal circuitry—as if both rats were struggling for control of the brain even though Guffie's mind should have been on Earth in Hugh's brain."

"That shouldn't be possible," Quekri said.

"I know," Aspen replied, "but it's the only solution that makes sense."

Dr. Wellon nodded slowly as she stared at the screens. "Interesting. Is there any way we can test that further? Maybe with the Earth rat? Or do we need to do another transfer to get sufficient data?"

"We'll need to do another transfer," Aspen said. "But I'm pretty sure the data will reflect this regression next time as well." She reached for a tablet and pulled up some figures. As Dr. Wellon studied them, Aspen said, "I'm still running various analyses, but all the data so far point to the same probable results."

"Then why didn't the Earth rat die?" Zeriphi asked.

"I believe it's got to do with dominant personality types," Aspen said. "The stronger the personality of the transferring mind, the greater chance it can exercise dominion over the receptive brain. And the stronger the mind from the receptive brain, the more likely that brain will reject the transferring mind. Guffie had a strong personality. That's why his body rejected the mind transplant from Hugh. And that's also why he was able to survive the transfer to Hugh's body."

"That's a pretty sweeping conclusion to draw from these numbers," Quekri said. "And what about the Patterson formula? This data seems to discount that theory."

"Well," Aspen replied, "I have to admit that I don't really know how the two tie together."

Quekri smiled. "Take a stab at it."

"Okay." Aspen took a deep breath, hoping the throbbing in her head would recede. "I think the Patterson formula might still apply over a longer period of time. So the favored patterns of the old mind still might result in a decrease in neuronal activity in the new brain. We'll probably see degeneration of myelin and synaptic pathways over time, but it's still early days. Plus, the two rats were about the same age, so we may not get any usable data on that aspect until we transfer the mind of an old rat into a young one. And Hugh died too quickly for us to get good readings on him. Perhaps if we do another scan on Guffie in a few weeks, we'll see a reversion occurring."

"Wellon?" Quekri turned to look at the big Escala doctor.

Dr. Wellon nodded. "Sound reasoning. Very well done."

"Thanks," Aspen said, an unexpected warmth stealing over her. In fact, she felt more than warm—almost hot.

"But it doesn't solve the larger problem," Zeriphi pointed out. "We still can't make the transfer work. And if Aspen's right, it creates an even bigger obstacle than we envisioned."

"True," Quekri said, "but understanding the problem . . ."

"Is the first step to finding a solution," Zeriphi finished with a grin.

"We'll have to test it," Dr. Wellon said, "with a dominant and a submissive mind as well as an old and young one. Let's transmit the data and Aspen's conclusions to Earth, see if they agree with the results. But first . . ."

She looked at Aspen.

"What?" Aspen looked up at the Escala surrounding her. Quekri, Dr. Wellon and Zeriphi all wavered before her eyes, as if an enormous heat wave separated them from her, its shimmering currents turning them into holo-projections, making them insubstantial.

"You're not well," Zeriphi said.

"How much medication have you taken?" Dr. Wellon asked.

"Just a few pain pills."

Dr. Wellon glared at her, as if looking right inside her brain, as if she could see the synaptic pathways and the pulsing pain, the electrical impulses darting from region to region. "How many?"

"In the last four hours? Seven pills and a stimulant," she replied as her knees began to buckle.

"Idiot," Quekri said as she scooped Aspen up in her strong arms.

Chapter 10

Doug Robinson sat in the back of the room at his communications console, out of the way, trying not to be pissed off. He didn't expect people to trust him, so he wasn't surprised that FBI Director Eric Sommersby had sought to have him excluded from the meeting. But Devereaux had insisted that Doug be present. Why? Just to let these power brokers know that Doug was a real person and not some cog in a bureaucratic machine? Or was it a message to Doug that he mattered, that he should pay attention and learn from what they were saying? At any rate, Doug was grateful.

Through the holo-projection, Vice President Miguel Rodriguez and HHS Secretary Dr. Chandrika Jaidev occasionally glared at him. The Vice President held a rosary that he continuously fingered. A pious man, a law-and-order former governor of Texas, he knew of Doug's criminal past and resented Doug's presence. In the center of the room the frail Walt Devereaux sat beside Quark, conferring with the big shots by holo-projection.

Also attending via holo-projection were Chairman of the Joint Chiefs Ralph Horowitz and President Angelica Hope. Those two, at least, didn't seem angry.

Devereaux looked so pale, so thin, so exhausted, that he ought to be in a hospital bed rather than subjecting himself to yet another stressful meeting, at which nothing was likely to be resolved. These damn politicians could talk all day.

The final person at the meeting was Dr. Mittrandur Ecuponte, the Surgeon General, who sat beside Dr. Jaidev and rattled off the rising statistics of dead and dying in Indonesia, Thailand, Burma and the Philippines while images from Jakarta continued to run on the screen behind him. No longer were government workers collecting bodies for disposal. Corpses were now piled up on the sidewalks. Fires burned, unmoving vehicles clogged the streets. Occasionally Doug spotted groups of young men running from building to building.

As Dr. Ecuponte's voice droned on, President Hope tapped her fingers on her desk. After a while she began to roll her eyes. Finally, she interrupted him.

"I can see it's terrible. I can see it's getting worse," she said. "What's the bottom line? How long before it hits here?"

"Here?" Doug said without thinking. When everyone turned to stare at him, he mumbled an apology.

"Did you have something to say?" Director Sommersby asked, his eyes narrowing.

Doug shook his head.

Devereaux actually smiled, which made him look a little less skeletal. "I believe Doug was thinking that it's typical of politicians to worry only about America, forgetting the rest of the world." He reached up with a shaking hand and dabbed at his left eye with a handkerchief. Couldn't these people see that they were killing him? Slowly, a small piece at a time, they were wearing him down to nothing.

"I'm not just concerned with America," President Hope said. "But my sphere of influence does not exceed this nation's borders. I'm worried about the whole world. But I can only control what I can control. Understand?"

Doug nodded.

"What I meant was, how long before the situation gets as bad here as it is in Indonesia?"

Director Sommersby glared at Doug.

Devereaux gave Doug a wink before turning back to the holo-projection images. He took a deep breath, as if gathering his energy, and said, "The projections vary depending on the models we run. Some have the virus raging out of control as early as next month. Others show it holding off for as much as a year. It depends on how quickly Susquehanna Sally decides to hit us. For some reason, she seems to be attacking Asia first. All indications are that China is having a major problem with the virus too, though their media haven't been as open about the numbers of deaths and infections."

"And a cure?"

"I can't guarantee one," Devereaux said, "until we acquire all the versions of the virus out there. Even then I don't know if I could eliminate it completely. But what I can say is that each new version released by Susquehanna Sally makes the probability of eliminating the virus that much more unlikely."

"We can't keep working like this," Quark said. "Professor Devereaux is exhausted. He's working far too hard. And don't forget that he's been infected with the virus too. Even though he's got some of Jeremiah's blood in him, he may not have full immunity."

Devereaux put his hand on Quark's arm. "I'm fine. Just a little tired."

He looked more than a little tired to Doug. He looked three inches from death. His hours in the lab had cost him whatever extra weight he'd been carrying. And he hadn't been a heavy man to begin with. Doug wished he could somehow cut everyone off—sever the connection and relieve some of the burden on the great man but he knew if he did it, Devereaux would disapprove.

"I still don't understand," Vice President Rodriguez interjected, scowling, "how the virus is continuing to slip past our security. How come we can't figure out a way to stop these people?"

Although Doug didn't care much for the Vice President, he'd been wondering about that too. These people claimed they were leading the greatest country in the world. Yet they couldn't find the terrorists who were spreading the virus.

Dr. Jaidev said, "The delivery mechanism keeps changing. We've seen the virus dispersed through the water supply, through food products."

Director Sommersby added, "A few times it's been delivered via air vents in public places. We found empty canisters last month in air ducts at the King of Prussia Mall and the South Coast Plaza. It took us nearly three weeks to discover them because no one got sick right away."

"The virus in those cases was a slow-acting version, designed for maximum dispersal before the manifestation of symptomology," Dr. Ecuponte said.

"I get that," Rodriguez said, waving his rosary-filled hand. "What I want to know is why the hell our law enforcement agencies, our spies and informants, can't find these people? What are they doing? Sitting on their asses while the world falls apart?"

Director Sommersby jumped to his feet, his face turning red. He pointed at the Vice President. "We're doing everything we can within the limitations of the Constitution. Why don't you come over here and see if you can do any better, you sanctimonious little prick?"

"Eric," President Hope said.

Sommersby sat down, his face still flushed with anger.

"And we've got rioting in the streets," Rodriguez continued, seemingly unfazed. "Our military can't keep the peace."

"Our military," General Horowitz said, his voice clipped, "is doing a tremendous job. Our men and women are working their tails off. And the Elite Ops have done everything we've asked of them and more."

"The streets aren't safer," Rodriguez said. "These problems are getting worse. His speech," Rodriguez pointed at Devereaux, his rosary cross swinging beneath his hand, "did nothing."

President Hope said, "What are you suggesting, Miguel?"

"The Apocalypse is upon us. This is the time of Revelations. We should all be praying for our salvation, repenting our sins." He glared at Devereaux as he spoke. Sommersby and Horowitz rolled their eyes. Dr. Jaidev and Dr. Ecuponte smiled briefly. President Hope reached up and pinched the bridge of her nose. "We should call together every American," Rodriguez continued, "to join us in one coordinated effort to speak to God. He will hear our voices if they are united in—"

"If you want to pray, Miguel," President Hope interrupted him. "By all means, pray. But we can't wait for God to solve our problems."

"That man," Rodriguez said, clearly meaning Devereaux, "is not going to be able to save us."

"Enough," President Hope said. "If you have something constructive to contribute, please stay. If you wish to pray your way out of this, then I suggest you leave now, find a church and let us get on with our jobs."

Rodriguez's face darkened as his lips clamped together. Doug bit his tongue to keep from grinning. Everyone knew the Vice President detested Devereaux because of his atheism. His hatred made Dr. Jaidev's dislike of Devereaux seem like mere indifference.

"This man cannot be trusted," Rodriguez said. "How long has he been working on this virus? And we're no closer now than before. I wonder where his priorities truly lie. A great many people believe he's only concerned about the Escala." Rodriguez spat the word out like some kind of profanity.

"Enough, Miguel," President Hope said.

"No, it's not enough. God-fearing Americans don't trust him—and for good reason. Everything we stand for as a nation he rejects."

Doug wished he hadn't attended the meeting now. He knew Rodriguez would drone on for minutes. The Vice President was a dangerous man. Yes, he had delivered Texas and enough southern votes to get President Hope elected. And he was certainly well respected by conservative and moderate governors as a tough enforcer of laws. But as Devereaux had pointed out, he tended to view everything through a narrow prism. Doug hoped nothing ever happened to President Hope. If Rodriguez were to replace her, one of his first actions would probably be to have Devereaux arrested.

As Rodriguez ramped up his rhetoric, Doug looked down at his communications board. He saw a message from Mars, from Zeriphi. His stomach fluttered with hope and fear. A quick glance at Devereaux and Quark, who were trying to stay engaged in their discussion with the big shots, and then Doug tuned them out, activated the privacy field and opened the message.

An image of Zeriphi appeared on his screen. The Escala woman looked as beautiful as ever, her long blond hair dropping around her muscular shoulders. Her face looked a bit heavier than the last time Doug had seen her. The indicator to the side of the screen showed that the last message he'd received from her had been nearly a month ago.

"Greetings from Mars," Zeriphi began like she always did. "I hope you are well. I'm glad you're with Quark and Devereaux. Take care of them, please." She took a deep breath, paused for a moment. "I'm calling today for two reasons. First, Celestia wanted to send you a message. I'll show you that in a moment. Second, I'm pregnant."

Doug's gut contracted, twisting into a knot. Zeriphi pregnant? Of course she was. She was by far the most attractive of the Escala. Why wouldn't she be pregnant? It felt like Quark was sitting on his chest.

"I thought I should let you know now," Zeriphi said, "before you found out from someone else. I hope this doesn't hurt you, Doug. Even though we were never together, I know you held out hope that we might become something more. But in my heart I was always Zod's wife . . . and I always will be."

And in my heart, Doug thought, you'll always be mine. Even though you never gave me a chance. Even though no one's ever given me a chance—except Devereaux. Love for that man filled him with lightness.

"I still thank you every day for your gift," Zeriphi continued. "Without you, I wouldn't have Celestia. But I've moved on. I've finally accepted Zod's death." Zeriphi's eyes glistened with moisture as she paused again. "Anyway, I hope you'll understand. Things were never going to work out between us. But Celestia will always be your daughter. Now here she is."

Celestia's face filled the screen. Her dark curly hair had grown out since he'd seen her last. Her brown eyes gleamed with intelligence. She looked twice her age. Probably that was her Escala nature.

"Hi, Daddy," she said. "I found this rock." The camera pulled back, revealing her extended arms. In her hands, she held a rock shaped like a cartoon heart. "I wanna send it to you but Mommy said I have to give it lots of hugs and kisses first." She pulled it back and kissed it, then held it tightly to her bosom. A hollow pain emptied Doug—an ache that left him without words. Her face became a blur and Doug realized his eyes were full of water. "Mommy says when it's full of love I can send it to you. So I'm gonna hurry and fill it. I love you, Daddy."

Doug paused the message for a moment until he could get his emotions in check. When he finally opened the rest of the message, the screen dissolved into an image of Zeriphi's face. "She's talking very well, don't you think?" Zeriphi asked. Doug found himself nodding, even though Zeriphi couldn't see him. "She's extremely bright. Inquisitive and well behaved. Thank you again. Doug, I remember you."

The screen shifted to an image of Celestia. Zeriphi ended all her messages that way, with the ritual Escala goodbye over Celestia's face. "Zeriphi," Doug whispered, "I remember you. Celestia, I remember you."

With his peripheral vision, he noticed that Vice President Rodriguez had finally given up his rant and was now sitting back with his arms crossed, fingering the beads on his rosary. Devereaux had reached up and begun massaging his temple, something Doug recognized as a sign of stress. He deactivated the privacy field and returned his attention to the discussion. If only he could get Devereaux out of this meeting without adding to the great man's responsibilities.

". . . put more bodies on the ground," President Hope was saying, "in Indonesia and the Philippines. I want more contacts with the intelligence communities across Asia. And try to engage China more heavily. Perhaps, Eric," she looked at Sommersby, "you should consider a visit. And Ralph," she turned to General Horowitz, "you might send a few Elite Ops to China and Indonesia as well in a sort of cultural exchange. Any other ideas?"

"Singapore," Sommersby said, "has a good intelligence community."

"Good. What else?"

General Horowitz said, "We're not seeing much activity in Africa. I wonder why that is."

Director Sommersby said, "We've already looked into that—haven't found much of anything."

"Keep at it," President Hope said.

"What about the riots?" General Horowitz asked. "My soldiers can handle the problem with force, up to a point. But I'd prefer not to have to do so. The situation is becoming increasingly desperate."

"Perhaps another speech by Mr. Devereaux," President Hope said.

"No!" Rodriguez shouted. "Absolutely not. He does not speak for us."

"I think your personal bias . . ." President Hope began. Then she stopped and looked at Devereaux. "Are you all right?"

Devereaux suddenly slumped in his chair. As Doug jumped to his feet, Quark grabbed Devereaux, lifting the older man as if he weighed no more than a child. "Code blue," Quark said. "Handle things here," he said to Doug. Then he carried Devereaux from the room.

Doug, his throat dry, his palms sweating, relayed the medical emergency to all personnel. Then he stood in the center of the room. What now? He wanted so badly to help, but he knew nothing about medicine and he'd only be in the way if he followed them. Besides, Quark had told him to handle things here, so that's what he'd do.

"What's happening?" President Hope asked.

Doug looked up at the holo-projection, wondering why she was asking him, and then realized she wasn't. She was looking at Dr. Ecuponte and Dr. Jaidev.

"It looks like a stroke," Dr. Ecuponte said.

"Or a heart attack," Dr. Jaidev added.

Dr. Ecuponte said, "He's wired with nanobots. We ought to be receiving telemetry now." He reached for a small monitor at his side, pulled it close and studied it, manipulating the screen to access

Devereaux's medical information. He tilted the monitor so Dr. Jaidev could see it as well. For a few seconds their faces showed only intense concentration. Then their eyes widened. Dr. Jaidev whispered something Doug couldn't hear. He knew instantly that it was something terrible.

"Why didn't we see it coming?" President Hope asked.

"A sudden onset stroke and heart attack," Dr. Jaidev said. "Absolutely no warning. It's got to be the virus."

"Running an analysis now," Dr. Ecuponte said. "Causative factors should be coming in any moment."

Doug gawked at the people in the holo-projection. Director Sommersby and General Horowitz looked shocked. President Hope, her face pale with worry, focused on the two doctors at the table with her, the fingers of her left hand drumming nervously on the tabletop. Vice President Rodriguez, sitting off to the side, had his lips clamped together as he tried to suppress a smile.

"You bastard!" Doug shouted.

"Calm down," President Hope said. "Anger won't solve anything."

Doug held up his hands in surrender. Then he switched the comm system to auto-answer and linked to the emergency room camera, which showed Devereaux on an operating table, tubes running from several machines through three small incisions in his chest. Four doctors stood there, monitoring the machines that manipulated microscopic, robotic tools inside Devereaux's chest and head in an effort to keep the great man alive. Standing by himself off to the side was Quark. Stuffed into surgical blues, his intense eyes visible above his mask, the giant looked fierce as he peered over the heads of the doctors at Devereaux's face.

Quark appeared to be shaking—or was that Doug? He had to stay under control.

He turned back to the holo-projection, where Dr. Jaidev and Dr. Ecuponte were whispering back and forth. Doug enhanced the audio feed until he could hear what they were saying:

"Clearly the Susquehanna Virus," Dr. Ecuponte said.

"It looks like multiple strains," Dr. Jaidev added, "hitting him all at once."

"The blood vessels are falling apart as fast as they're being repaired."

"I've never seen anything like it."

"Doctors," President Hope interjected, her voice booming in Doug's ears. He quickly lowered the volume. "What's the prognosis?"

Dr. Ecuponte grimaced. Dr. Jaidev lowered her head.

"Does he have any chance at all?" President Hope asked.

"There's always a chance," Dr. Jaidev said, shaking her head as if disputing her own words.

President Hope took a deep breath. "And the virus? What about our research into a cure?"

"We still have dozens of teams working on it," Dr. Ecuponte said. "We're making significant progress every day."

"But not fast enough," Rodriguez said.

"Do you have a suggestion, Miguel?" President Hope asked.

"I think we should begin the process of evacuating to the bunker," Rodriguez said. "We need to keep our command structure intact."

President Hope brought her hands together, resting her elbows on the tabletop. "You're right, Miguel," she said. "Why don't you put together a transition team, just in case? You're welcome to ask any of my undersecretaries to join you. My cabinet members and I will remain on the surface."

"But Madam President," Rodriguez said. "You're the one who needs to be kept safe."

"No, Miguel, my place is here, at the head of the government. We will fight this crisis with every bit of cunning and strength we can muster. And if we fail, only if we fail, then it will be your time, and your responsibility will be to lead this nation into the future." President Hope now looked at Doug. She nodded almost imperceptibly. "Please keep me informed of his condition. Thank you."

She signed off, the holo-projection going dark.

On the screen, where the doctors continued their efforts, and Quark maintained his vigilance, Devereaux lay on the operating table, eyes closed, face pale, oblivious to it all. A numbness crept over Doug—the loss of hope. No Devereaux. No Zeriphi. No Celestia.

This was his fault. He'd taken his eye off the ball and now Devereaux was going to die. He'd known he should be paying better attention. He should have figured out a way to get Devereaux free of these petty politicians. But because he'd been bored by Rodriguez's ranting, he'd neglected his duty. And now Devereaux was dying. Maybe he would have collapsed anyway, but maybe not. Stupid, stupid, stupid, Doug thought. All my fault.

Chapter 11

Lendra stood before the elevator doors, flanked by Dr. Poole, Curtik and Zora, waiting for Jeremiah. She resisted the urge to reach up and grab her glass bulb necklace. It no longer contained neo-dopamine. She'd kicked that habit almost a year ago, yet only in the last few weeks had she managed to make it through the night without the stomach cramps and migraines of withdrawal. She was proud of having kicked her habit, though she felt a little less sharp without the drug.

The doors opened and Jeremiah exited, his face gray, his movements painfully slow. Lendra hated to see this magnificent, athletic, vital man—this man she still loved—reduced to arthritic uselessness. Hannah slid out behind him, followed by two muscular but unarmored Elite Ops troopers, who immediately stepped to the side of the doors, their backs against the wall. They looked similar—short hair, serious faces.

"Do we need them here?" Lendra asked.

"President's orders," one of them said. "I'm Finn. He's Gil."

"We're the fish team," Gil said. "The best in the business. And we ought to be doing important work."

Protecting Jeremiah must seem punishment to these men, who still harbored ill will toward him for his exploits in Minnesota.

Dr. Poole smiled, making Lendra recall that she had a thing for big, muscular men—Elite Ops troopers like Jack Marschenko.

Lendra noticed that Hannah wore a broad grin too. Probably she was delighted to be back at CINTEP, thinking she was done babysitting Jeremiah. Little did she know: Lendra intended to keep her at Jeremiah's side—partly because Hannah's profile indicated she was perfect for bodyguard detail and partly because she wasn't Jeremiah's type. Also, Hannah, so deprived of attention by her own father, would transfer Jeremiah to a fatherly role.

Curtik, unable to stand still for more than a few seconds, began to dance beside Lendra. With her peripheral vision she could see him shuffling his feet and bopping his head to some hidden music. He avoided making eye contact with Jeremiah. To Curtik's left, Zora stared at Jeremiah, her mouth slightly open. She looked healthy, her coppery skin glowing. Her curly blond hair cascaded around her shoulders and her brown eyes appeared almost liquid in the hallway lighting. When Jeremiah smiled at her, she blushed. Lendra found her annoyingly perfect. She'd have to find a job for Zora far away from here.

"So," Lendra said to Jeremiah, "it takes Devereaux going down to get you involved?" She smiled as she said it.

Jeremiah shrugged, in obvious pain. Did the drugs really not work for him? How was he able to function when even the slightest movement brought such agony?

"Bad joke," she added.

"Ha!" Curtik roared with fake laughter. He slapped himself on the thigh and chuckled. "That's a good one. I didn't catch it at first, but now, whew, that's a doozie."

Jeremiah said, "I told you I was done. The only reason I'm here is because Devereaux is in a coma."

Lendra forced a smile. "It's good to see you again."

Jeremiah looked from Curtik to Zora and said, "Good morning, Curtik, Zora."

"The savior returns," Curtik said, finally looking at Jeremiah. "All our problems are over. The sun is brighter. The birds are happier. We might as well pack up and go home."

Jeremiah shook his head slowly. "How are you feeling, Zora?"

"Better, thanks," she answered. "Though my implant had to be removed."

"And the pain? Are you finally letting them manage that for you?"

Zora's eyes glistened. "Yes."

"Good. No point in suffering if you don't have to. You're smarter than that."

"Smart enough to know the truth," Zora replied. "Why don't you tell them what's really going on?"

Lendra frowned. She noticed that Zora kept her focus on Jeremiah, ignoring everyone around her. Was that because she was in love with him, or was something else going on? Lendra said, "What do you mean by that?"

Zora continued to stare at Jeremiah, as if expecting him to answer. Instead he turned to Dr. Poole and said, "Good morning."

Dr. Poole nodded. "Jeremiah."

"How is he doing?"

"He's got the finest surgeons in the world," Dr. Poole said, shaking her head slowly, "but the virus just keeps eating away at him."

"And a cure?"

Dr. Poole held up her hands. "We don't seem to be making much progress. The only commonality to the virus is that every known version attacks via the body's immune system. Otherwise, it individuates to each victim, which makes any vaccine only somewhat helpful. With Devereaux's assistance, we've created numerous vaccines. But each is effective, if at all, for only a single strain. And we don't have vaccines for every strain. Even when we combine the vaccines, they're only effective across the specific strains and not against the broad spectrum of the disease."

"Are we still seeing new variants?"

Dr. Poole nodded. "But only one in the past two weeks. Apparently, there are only so many variations that can be created with the lethality Sally wants."

Jeremiah looked off to his left. Lendra followed his eyes and spotted a young CINTEP agent approaching—Hannah's partner, Wilson Adler, who was now stuck in Analytical while Hannah was on this assignment with Jeremiah. He wore a fashionable bright red interface and smiled broadly at Hannah. "You're back."

"Only temporarily, Adler," Lendra said. "She's on assignment with Jeremiah. I'm afraid we still need you in Analytical."

"Oh." Adler managed to convey his disappointment in that single syllable. He glanced at Jeremiah with a mixture of awe and resentment. "Well," he said to Hannah, "I hope your assignment ends soon. I can't wait to get back in the field."

He moved on past them, turning back briefly to glance at Hannah.

They all waited for Adler to turn the corner.

Then Curtik said to Lendra, "Papster will solve the problem before you've got time to get back to your office. It'll be something brilliant, something no one's ever thought of before and at the same time so simple we'll be shocked we didn't see it. Right?"

"Relax, Curtik," Jeremiah said. "We're on the same team."

"Yeah, but Auntie Lendra has made me the second string."

Lendra sighed. How was she to deal with this impertinent buck? So unlike his father: no respect, no gravitas. "Enough, Curtik. Jeremiah, we've got your old office ready."

"That was fast."

Jeremiah glanced at Hannah.

"I only called this morning," Hannah said.

"We set it aside some time ago," Lendra explained, "on the off-chance you'd come around."

"Do I get full access to information?"

"Everything we have on the virus and Sally."

"Not good enough," Jeremiah said. "I want full access to the CINTEP database. I don't want to be slowed down making a request for information that some computer or analyst determined wasn't relevant."

Curtik stamped his foot. "How dare you interfere with the savior!"

Lendra took a deep breath. "Curtik, I'm warning you."

"What are you going to do, put me in storage? Can't be any worse than sitting around waiting for El Daddio to rescue us all. Right, Zora?"

Zora shook her head. "As usual, you don't know what you're talking about."

Lendra sighed. "Very well. I'll arrange full access."

"Don't worry," Jeremiah said. "You'll still be able to eavesdrop on me and track all my progress. Eli had the place completely wired. I'm assuming you haven't taken the bugs and cameras out." Jeremiah stared at Lendra with an intensity she found disturbing. "By the way," he added, "where's Ned?"

Lendra almost felt as if he could read her thoughts. She glanced at Dr. Poole and then replied, "We're sending him to London."

Jeremiah nodded slowly. "Perhaps Curtik and Zora should accompany him."

"Really?" Curtik asked. He began to bounce up and down, a broad grin creasing his face. Zora bit her lip as she stared at Jeremiah.

"You're not serious," Lendra said.

"They can help Ned and learn from him at the same time."

"I'm not certain it's safe," Dr. Poole said.

"None of us is safe anymore, Doctor. What do you want to save them for, the task of rebuilding the population when we're all gone?"

"I just don't know if they're ready."

"Don't worry," Jeremiah said. "They're not."

Lendra said, "There is something to be said for keeping them in reserve, in case we fail."

Curtik opened his mouth but closed it again comically when Jeremiah shot him a warning glare.

"I'm sure governments around the world are already creating more of the Escala as a hedge against our failure," Jeremiah said. "Hoping they come up with some combination of human and animal DNA that's immune to the virus."

Behind Jeremiah, the two Elite Ops troopers stiffened briefly. Lendra knew they still carried a residual hatred for the Escala, whom they called pseudos. She wondered if they would really protect Jeremiah in case of a threat, or if they would allow him to be attacked, or worse, join in against him. She pulled herself back to the present and said, "What makes you think that?"

Jeremiah laughed, cutting it short with a sharp intake of breath. Zora took a half step forward but Jeremiah held up a hand to let her know he was okay.

"No matter how religious they claim to be," Jeremiah said, "no matter how adamant they are that we retain our pure humanity, they know that the Escala—at least so far—have shown immunity. I wouldn't be surprised if half the leaders of the world have plans in place to become Escala themselves."

Dr. Poole said, "We don't know that the Escala are immune. They may only have immunity to one or two strains. For all we know, you're not immune either. You've only been infected with one or two variants."

"Actually," Zora said, "He's been infected with a lot more than that."

Dr. Poole said, "What?"

"Tell them," Zora commanded Jeremiah. "Or I will."

Jeremiah held up his hands, wincing as he did so. "Walt Devereaux sent me multiple versions of the virus. Asked me to infect myself with them, then ship him samples of my blood." He paused for a moment.

A tingling warmth stole over Lendra and her eyes began to well up. Once again this man had surprised her, letting himself be used as a guinea pig, knowing his decision required him to live in unspeakable agony. How she loved him. She blinked back the moisture and turned to Zora. "How did you know?"

"It wasn't hard to figure out. The drugs work on us. But Jeremiah wouldn't take them. And Devereaux made a comment a while back about using a pure research subject, unaltered by vaccines or antidotes. The only person that could be was Jeremiah—sacrificing himself for us."

Curtik snorted. "Crazy old bastard!" He looked at Lendra. "And you're worried about what I might do?"

Dr. Poole said, "How many strains have you been subjected to?"

Jeremiah shrugged. "Eighteen."

Eighteen!

The two Elite Ops troopers stared at Jeremiah before glancing at each other and shaking their heads.

Fool! Imbecile! Brave, crazy idiot! Lendra had to have this man back in her life. Their child needed him. And it wasn't just Sophie. Lendra needed him too. She'd felt an attraction to Colonel Truman while on the Moon last year, because he had comforted her after Jeremiah's rejection, but she'd never felt that indescribable spark with anyone but Jeremiah.

Hannah shook her head, her jaw quivering slightly. "I told you I couldn't look after him. He's impossible."

"Why would you do such a foolish thing?" Dr. Poole asked, echoing Lendra's thoughts. "You could have been killed." She stared at him, understanding coming to her eyes. "That's why you've refused all medical treatment for the past six months. You didn't want me to find out. Have you any idea how dangerous that was?"

Jeremiah said, "Devereaux monitored my condition, which remained essentially unchanged despite the introduction of the new strains."

"Apart from the increased pain that came with each new infection," Zora said. "Right? Right?"

Jeremiah nodded.

Dr. Poole shook her head slowly. "That's why he was making such swift progress with vaccines. He was using what he found from your blood."

Zora stepped forward and looked up at Jeremiah, her face tense with anger. "I knew you couldn't resist acting the hero," she said, wounded betrayal in her voice. "You tell me not to suffer needlessly, then you go and do this." Her eyes glistening, she put her hand on his chest and pushed against him. But because she weighed so much less, all she accomplished was to push herself away. He reached over and grabbed her shoulder, pulling her in close, and held her in his strong arms. Lucky girl. After a moment she managed to push free of him. Lendra never could have made herself do that. Zora turned away and ran down the hall to her room, slamming the door behind her.

Dr. Poole smiled sadly and said, "Poor kid."

"Yeah," Curtik said. "Very sad. So . . . London?"

Lendra spread her hands in defeat. "Very well. You and Zora will accompany Ned to London. But you will obey Ned completely or you'll be sent back here. Understand?"

Curtik stood at attention, saluting smartly, a broad grin on his face. He managed to suppress the glee for a second before the grin reappeared. "I'll go tell Zora."

He bounded down the hall to Zora's room—an excited puppy chasing a ball.

"At least now we can give you some pain relief," Dr. Poole said.

"Yes, do that," Lendra said. She gestured toward the infirmary. Dr. Poole reached a hand toward Jeremiah, then quickly pulled it back. What? Was even Taditha falling for him?

Jeremiah said, "Could you find Ned? I'd like to talk to him before he leaves."

"Sure," Lendra said.

"Where should I go?" Hannah asked.

"You're staying with Jeremiah," Lendra said. "You'll be assisting him—whatever he needs. I want you by his side 24/7."

"Yes, ma'am," Hannah replied, a catch in her voice.

As Jeremiah followed Dr. Poole down the hall, the two Elite Ops troopers stepped in behind him, moving slowly, solicitously, their hands down and slightly forward, preparing to catch him should he fall, as if all their hostility toward him had vanished in that moment of revelation, understanding finally that his sacrifice was intended to save them too.

Hannah looked at Jeremiah, something akin to awe on her face, and Lendra realized that she was now completely devoted to him; she would do anything to keep him alive. Sending a message to Ned to join them in the infirmary, Lendra joined the procession.

The two Elite Ops guards waited outside the infirmary door, while Hannah stood silently with her back to the far wall, arms crossed in front of her. Dr. Poole settled Jeremiah into a reclining chair, then placed a hypo-pad to the back of his hand, giving him a combination of drugs. They had an immediate effect. The pinched look on Jeremiah's face vanished and the tension in his neck and shoulders dissipated. What had it been like to struggle against such agony every moment of every day?

Dr. Poole said, "I want to monitor you for a while to see what the optimum blend of drugs will be for treating the pain. Just sit back and relax."

A knock on the doorframe made Lendra turn.

Ned Jefferson entered the room, nodding to Hannah, Lendra and Dr. Poole. He said, "Greetings, Jeremiah."

Ned looked so much different than Jeremiah, so much different even than his brother, Colonel Dez Truman. Short and wiry, bald on top, with salt and pepper hair around the sides of his head, he wore a white goatee and an ingratiating smile.

"Ah, Ned," Jeremiah said. "Come in. Do you know Hannah?"

"Of course. We all know Hannah. Heard she was working with you. Lucky you."

Hannah blushed.

Jeremiah smiled. He looked at Hannah, his gaze staying there a moment longer than necessary. Good God, was he noticing her now? No, it couldn't be. Everything in his profile suggested that she wasn't his type. She was too physically imposing; her psychological wounds weren't sufficiently grave.

Ned stepped over to Jeremiah and offered his hand. As they shook, Lendra watched closely. She noticed how their hands twisted slightly and recalled that this was the way ghosts warned each other to be careful. "I was sorry to hear about your brother. He was a good man."

"So I've heard. You probably knew him better than I did. At least he didn't suffer. And he died helping others."

"Your brother?" Hannah said.

Ned turned to face Hannah. "My brother was Colonel Dez Truman. I hadn't seen him for fifteen years. Officially, I disappeared during a mission in South America."

"They wouldn't even let you tell your brother you were alive?" She glanced briefly at Lendra.

Ned shrugged. "It's . . . complicated."

Hannah shook her head. "No ghost can have a connection that can be compromised—one of Eli's insane rules." Again she glanced at Lendra, as if suddenly realizing that Lendra now made CINTEP's rules.

"Is that why he wouldn't make you a ghost?" Ned asked.

Lendra caught Jeremiah staring at Hannah, his eyes widening slightly. So he hadn't guessed that earlier. If he hadn't been in such pain, he would have realized that Hannah had wanted to enter the ghost program. Perhaps now he knew why Hannah had been so angry stuck on bodyguard detail, annoyed that Jeremiah had walked away from what she most desired.

Hannah surprised Lendra by saying, "I don't want it anymore, not after seeing what you two went through—the sacrifices you've made."

Ned smiled at her. "Wise girl. I wish I'd been that smart." Turning back to Jeremiah, he said, "Would you like fries with that?"

Hannah frowned as Jeremiah laughed. Lendra knew they were preparing to speak in the private code of the ghosts. Did they suspect that she knew their code? She glanced at Dr. Poole, who shook her head slightly as she studied Jeremiah's reaction to the pain medication.

Jeremiah nodded toward Lendra and said, "Has she told you you'll be taking Curtik and Zora to London?"

"Yes, she mentioned it."

"A peanut butter solution," Jeremiah said.

You're probably walking into a trap.

Hannah frowned.

"With chocolate sauce." Ned replied.

We're both walking into traps.

"Taking your cat?" Jeremiah asked.

Will there be backup?

"She doesn't travel well anymore," Ned answered.

A purely covert mission: no backup other than Curtik and Zora.

"I've got a friend to look after her," Ned continued. "He'll take good care of her."

I promise to look after Curtik and Zora.

"Well," Jeremiah said, "she's an old cat."

Dr. Poole laughed. What did that mean again? Lendra glanced at Ned, who had raised an eyebrow.

"As I recall," Jeremiah said, "she likes to run in the alleys at night."

Ah, don't treat Curtik and Zora any differently than any other new recruits. Use them like any other assets.

Ned shrugged, acknowledging the request. "She does get into her share of scrapes."

"While you're gone," Jeremiah said, "I'll be looking into the data from this end, giving it a fresh set of eyes. I'll contact you if I can add anything to what you know."

Ned smiled. "If you can add anything at all, you'll be increasing my knowledge exponentially."

"So it's a numbers scenario?"

Ned nodded. "Another statistical deviation pattern or some such thing." He looked at Lendra. "Right?"

Lendra said, "Our analyses put the likelihood that a cell is in London at better than sixty percent. But we have no solid information on where in London the cell might be located."

"For now," Ned said, "my strategy is going to be to stand in the middle of Trafalgar Square, a pint of ale in my hand, and ask passersby if they know where I can find Susquehanna Sally."

"I'd check pizza parlors and pastry shops as well."

Was this code? Lendra didn't recognize it.

"Excellent idea," Ned rubbed his hands together. "And fish and chip stands."

"Oh, and pubs," Jeremiah added. "Don't forget pubs!"

"You don't need to remind me of that."

"Very thorough." Jeremiah smiled. "Commendable."

"You staying in the office for a while?"

"Until Tuesday," Jeremiah replied.

"Thursday it is." Ned winked. "I'll let you get some rest."

As he walked out the door, Lendra realized she had no idea what they'd just said.

Hannah said, "What was that? Your private code?"

"Code?" Jeremiah said. "Just having a bit of fun."

Lendra wondered if that was true. God, Jeremiah could infuriate her, even as he made her knees weak and her palms sweat. She looked at Hannah, then at Jeremiah. Did she have anything to worry about there? No. Hannah saw him as a father substitute. And Jeremiah, if he was in love with anyone, was in love with Zora. But he would never act on that. Still, Lendra was glad Zora would be traveling to London.

Chapter 12

Sally23 snuggled into the warmth of Trogan Brosk, her body tingling. Brosk's humming had awakened her. He matched the tune coming from the room's speakers—something with the Polynesian influence that was so fashionable these days: perhaps because of the devastation in Indonesia.

Brosk caressed her arm with his fingers. When she looked up at him, he smiled at her and she settled her hand on his chest.

"There you are," Brosk said. "How long will you stay this time?" He arched an eyebrow and she wondered what kind of game he was playing. Did he know that they were conditioning him to love her? And was he actually falling for her or was she simply falling for him? Perhaps Sally2's experiment had backfired.

"You've been distant since you returned," Brosk explained, "as if you're not fully here." He rubbed her arm gently. "Not that I mind the extra work it took to bring you into the present."

He glanced at the cameras before settling his gaze on her. What message was he sending? Did he know that she hated Sally2? Did he somehow glean that she was no longer a devotee? Maybe he was warning her to be careful.

Perhaps, even though he no longer seemed to be resisting the controls, he still had some fight left in him. Sally23 hoped so. He radiated a calm assurance, a core of goodness and light so much better than human.

Ultimately, it didn't matter that she had developed feelings for him. After all, they would both be dead soon. On the muted screen, images of Indonesia and other parts of Southeast Asia played across the screen. Pakistan had become a haven for the virus, its porous borders making it easy prey. Brosk glanced at the monitor only occasionally, as if the world held little interest.

"The programming of Brosk's mind," Sally2 spoke into Sally23's ear bud, causing Sally23 to startle slightly, "has reached a critical juncture. We need to test a few commands."

"You okay?" Brosk asked her. "You're a little jumpy."

"I'm fine," Sally23 answered. "I just felt a shiver run up my spine." She knew Sally2 couldn't read her thoughts through the ear bud, but she wondered whether Sally2 had any idea just how much she hated her. Sally2 could monitor her pulse, blood pressure, even her emotions, but could she tell that Sally23's rage was directed at her?

"It's getting cold in here. Perhaps we should get dressed." Brosk slid out from the covers and quickly pulled on his shirt and pants. "Think we could go for a walk?"

"Say yes," Sally2 commanded.

"All right," Sally23 answered.

"Do you think we could walk outside?" Brosk asked. "With all the controls they've implanted in my head, it would be impossible for me to run. And they can monitor everything I say just as well from outside as in here. Plus, I know your techs have figured out a way to nullify the CCTV surveillance system."

Sally23 smiled as she put on her slacks. Of course he would have intuited that. "They'll tell me in a moment."

"It's been so long since I've seen the sun." Brosk bent down to put on his socks and shoes. When he straightened, he said, "The virus is bad in London too. Isn't it?"

Sally23 nodded as she thumbed the seam of her shirt.

"When will we die?" Brosk asked, his voice carrying about as much emotion as if he were asking when dinner would be served.

"I don't know," Sally23 answered.

"Will it be painful?"

"Probably." Sally23 took Brosk's hand and led him from the room.

"Take him to Holland Park," Sally2 spoke into her ear bud again. "Not the Orangery. Try the sculpture gardens."

"Okay," Sally23 said as she led Brosk up empty stairs to the main level, which was also empty. "I just got permission to go outside. Let's walk to the park." She handed Brosk a jacket from a hook by the side of the door and let him help her on with her coat.

When Brosk opened the door and they stepped outside, she took Brosk by the arm and said, "Let's head toward Holland Park."

They walked along the quiet street. Many people kept indoors these days. And when they went out, they wore filtration masks. Two people up ahead spotted them and crossed to the other side of the street, no doubt hoping not to be contaminated. If not for the Las-cannon chill in the air, and the virus sucking the life out of every human on the planet, she might find it a pleasant day.

"Why do you think they let us out?" Brosk asked.

She looked up at his delicate face, into his eyes, immeasurably sad at the moment, and she felt a twinge of guilt. "It's too late now," she answered. "Even if we wanted to stop the virus, we probably couldn't."

"So there's really no antidote?"

"Not that I know of. I take medication that delays the onset of the virus and keeps me alive, but it won't work for much longer—a few more weeks or months at most before the virus overwhelms it."

"I find it hard to believe Sally2 hasn't come up with one."

"You don't believe we're serious about wanting to rid the planet of people?"

"I believe Sally2 wants most people dead—and all the men. But I don't believe she wants to die." Brosk stopped and stared into her eyes. "And I know you don't."

Sally23 smiled. Then she tilted her head in the direction of the park and they walked on. "That's the beauty of the virus," she said. "We knew we'd have second thoughts about all this. We knew we might be weak—that when the final throes reached us, we might fight for life. But intellectually, we know what we're doing is right. The planet needs us gone."

"So you set up an irreversible system, where death is inevitable?"

"We didn't do it lightly. But you've seen what humans have done to the planet. Extinctions. Pollution. Radiation. Earth is a toxic waste dump."

"If we're all going to die anyway," Brosk said, "why shouldn't I kill you now?"

Sally23 caught the hint of an ironic smile. So there was some fight left in Brosk after all. "You know they're following us too, not just listening to everything we say."

"Of course," Brosk replied, his voice now as chilled as the air. "But they couldn't stop me from killing you."

He gripped Sally23's arm tightly and her stomach twisted in fear. Was this part of Sally2's plan, to see if Brosk would kill her and try to escape?

Brosk laughed as he let go of her arm. "Don't worry, munchkin. I recognize the futility of action. All I could do is hasten my death. Whatever Sally2 has planned for me, I think I'll wait to see it. Unlike you people, I have no desire for the grand gesture of mass suicide. I'm not going to push the envelope."

"Thank you," Sally23 said.

"Besides, you've been hurt enough. How many people abused you? Was it just your father or were there others?"

"How did you . . ."

"It's obvious . . . well, it is to me." Brosk smiled sadly. "People are terrible. They do awful things to one another. They always have. But they're also great. Selfless. The man you want to kill, for example—Jeremiah Jones. He's a good man. He's done many bad things and yet he's still a good man."

They reached the park. Brosk stared up at the security camera by the entrance as they passed. Sally23 saw it as well. It should have been pointing away from them. Was that a mistake, or did Sally2 want their images captured? They began to stroll along a walking trail, past flowers that had shriveled in the cool air, their blooms faded, but not yet gone entirely.

"It's a losing battle, you know," Brosk said, his voice calm.

"What?"

"Trying to eliminate humanity from the planet."

"How so?"

"Life always finds a way. And we're long past the age of the dinosaurs—creatures that didn't know how to avoid extinction. Your Sally2 knows the truth, though she perhaps hides it from you."

"What truth is that?"

"That some humans will live. Sally2 intends to be one of them. She's been enhanced. You knew that, right?"

"You said that before."

"Trust me," Brosk said. "She's one of the Escala she rails against. She's got animal DNA mingled with her own, making her immune to the virus."

"He's lying," Sally2 spoke into Sally23's ear bud. "He's trying to manipulate you."

Sally23 shook her head, a reflex action, though she suspected Brosk was telling the truth.

"He's trying to divide and conquer." Sally2's voice carried an emotional strain that Sally23 had never heard before. She looked up into Brosk's face, noted his utter sincerity as he gazed upon her.

"You couldn't possibly know that," Sally23 said to Brosk.

"I was trained to spot small signs, inconsistencies, indicators of truth and falsehood," Brosk replied. "I admit I have no definitive proof. But it fits. Sally2, whatever else she is, is still human. She wants to live. She'll have built a safeguard into the system, something to insure that she survives, along with her friends. I think she might be that doctor I knew about back in Washington.

"Have you ever wondered how she ensures such a fanatical level of devotion and commitment to the movement? How many of you have been programmed to believe this is a good solution to our problems? Did she mess with your mind too?"

She recalled early meetings with Sally2, when she'd been hooked up to a polygraph and questioned for several hours. Had that been more than a lie detector? Had Sally2 begun to condition her mind even then, to program her to want to die along with the rest of humanity? And if so, why was she questioning it now?

"I can see your doubt," Brosk said. "That's honest. That's real. So maybe she hasn't conditioned you after all. But those other girls, and those techs, they believe everything she tells them. They've been engineered, just like those kids on the Moon last year. They don't have any say in what they believe. You do. You get to choose. Think about that. You still have free will."

Sally2's voice came stridently through the ear bud: "This experiment is over."

Sally23 stiffened and Brosk noticed. "She's ordering you to go back now," he said, "because she doesn't want the truth out. I'm sorry to tell you this, because it puts you at risk now too. She may have to kill you sooner than she planned. Or she may force you to undergo conditioning. But you should know what's really going on."

"Return to base," Sally2 said.

Brosk stopped moving. His eyes glazed over. He would have fallen if Sally23 hadn't grabbed his arm. Sally2 must have remotely activated a block of Brosk's motor functions.

"They'll be coming for us soon," Brosk said, his face contorting in pain.

Her ear bud crackled slightly, then went silent. Her legs wobbled. She spotted a bench and tugged Brosk over to it, somehow managing to keep him from toppling over. Settling him onto the seat and slumping down beside him, she drew her jacket in close against the cold.

"Munchkin," Brosk said, "she'll try to convince you I've lied. Or she may kill you. I'm sorry. I didn't lie. I just want you to know that."

They came from every direction—eight of them—all carrying disguised weapons down by their sides, none of them wearing masks. Andre, the head of security, walked at the point. He looked almost crazed, his eyes bugged out, his chest heaving. He'd brought his entire security team—Jarrod, Ron, Marcus, Sinda, Paul, David and Heather. The husband and wife team of Marcus and Sinda smiled at her. They'd always been friendly. The two new recruits, David and Heather, brought up the rear. Jarrod, Ron and Paul—similar-looking hard cases with crew cuts, angular faces and multiple tattoos on their thick necks—glared at her as if daring her to run. She made no effort to move. Neither did Brosk.

Where was there to run to?

Sally23 beckoned them over, her mind racing. If Sally2 had in fact programmed her and ordered her to succumb to the conditioning again, would she acquiesce? Or would she just force Sally2 to kill her?

As the guards reached them, Andre put out his free hand and lifted an unresisting Brosk to his feet, saying, "That's enough exercise for now."

No one spoke on the way back. Andre pulled Brosk along, the CINTEP agent's legs stiff, his arms rigid against his sides. Sally23 walked beside Brosk. She held his arm—to steady him or herself?—but he no longer seemed to know she was there.

When they reached base, Sally2 stood inside the door, arms folded across her chest, her foot tapping against the floor. She glared at Sally23. "Why didn't you return to base?"

Sally23 let go of Brosk's arm. "What was I supposed to do, drag him back? Besides, I'm not your slave," she said, anger bubbling up inside. "You preach that we're all equals in the Sally Movement, that the chain of command is just for efficiency's sake." She studied Sally2, noted the way she stood, the tension in her body, the stillness—almost animalistic. Or was that simply Sally23 projecting onto her? She said, "Did Brosk speak the truth?"

Sally2 maintained eye contact. "Of course not."

"So you're not one of those pseudos?"

Sally2's eyes shivered. She shook her head. "I can see why Brosk is so dangerous," she said, leaning forward, her hands clenching. "You don't trust me, do you?"

"I've never trusted you," Sally23 answered, "or any human being. That's why we need to go."

Sally2 relaxed slightly.

"And if you conditioned me somehow, I won't let you do it again. You'll have to accept me as I am."

Sally2 nodded. "Of course." She gestured off to the side and led Sally23 away from the others.

"You're not like the rest of these people. I need you thinking clearly. I know you're angry with me, but that's okay."

Sally23 said, "Things aren't progressing the way you promised they would. Indonesia hasn't been completely destroyed. Jakarta still has millions left alive. It doesn't seem like the virus has hit any country that hard yet."

"We're approaching the tipping point," Sally2 said. "Have you seen the news lately? There's been a fourfold increase in the numbers of deaths in Europe and Asia, and almost as much growth in the death rate in North America. Only South America and Africa are lagging behind at the moment. Patience. We're almost there." She called over to Andre. "Take Brosk to my lab." Then she returned her gaze to Sally23.

Sally23 stared back. She felt no fear. On the walk back, she realized that Brosk had used the only weapon left in his arsenal—his words, his truth. And she now realized the only means she had to carry out any resistance was to be Sally23 on the surface, no matter what her thoughts. She smiled.

A small frown of confusion crossed Sally2's face. "Get packed. Be ready to leave at a moment's notice. I'm expecting company before the end of the day."

"CINTEP?"

Sally2 bowed her head, acknowledging Sally23's guess.

"When I saw the security camera at the park," Sally23 said, "I realized what you were doing. CINTEP will spot the vid of Brosk."

"And they'll send Jeremiah Jones to check it out."

"What if they send the Army instead?"

Sally2 smiled. "You don't know these people like I do. They'll send Jones. They still think they can win."

Perhaps they can, Sally23 thought as she turned away. And then another thought hit her. Could Brosk have threatened to kill her as a way of protecting her? She didn't trust Sally2, but with Brosk it was all a bit unclear. He may have been trying to sow discontent, but he may also have been trying to help her. It was too bad she couldn't get him alone somewhere to talk, to find out if he could help her in some way, if he was even willing to help her. The only thing she knew for certain was that she was now completely alone. Whatever she did, she couldn't rely on anyone's help.

Chapter 13

Curtik fidgeted in his seat as the purple-haired bio-technician carefully fitted the neo-skin mask over his face. He listened to the Crystal Skull Bangers via his implant. Here at the edge of space he could see the Moon out the window. He wished he were back there. For a moment he felt fear. Strange how he hadn't been afraid when he was piloting the LTV to Earth through a horde of missiles, when Rendela had sacrificed herself and her shipmates to save him—well, to save Zora.

"Sit still," the technician said.

"How much longer?" he asked, shifting again to try to get comfortable. His hips and back ached.

She sighed. "Your bone structure is the same as your father's, so it will only take a few more minutes."

"No, I meant how long till we get to London?"

"Half an hour," Zora answered as she and Ned Jefferson came into view from behind him.

Curtik stared at her. She looked like an old woman, with dark chocolate skin and heavy wrinkles. She could be Jefferson's wife . . . or mother. He laughed at her, stopping almost immediately as his chest tightened up on him. "God," he said, "it even hurts to laugh without the painkillers."

"Jeremiah has it a lot worse," Zora answered. "We only got infected with one strain. And we have nanobots to assist with healing."

Jefferson shook his head. "You didn't have to stop taking the pain meds."

"If he could do it," Curtik said, "I can do it. Besides, I have to see what it's like so I can act like I'm in pain during the operation. I've never experienced anything like this before. I don't think I like it. Hey, after we're done with the operation, can we go see the Crystal Skull Bangers?"

"What are they, a British band?"

"Oh, they're wicked, Neddy. The best."

"We've got more important things to worry about," Jefferson replied. "You want me to give you a pain pad now?"

"In a minute. Just gimme a little longer to get acclimated to what it's like."

"Okay. Let me know. Meanwhile, Lendra will be calling soon and we still don't have a plan."

"Who needs a plan?" Curtik threw out his hands, accidentally swatting the technician's breast. "Oops." He thought about apologizing but couldn't remember the technician's name. Zora glanced at Curtik as if grasping his dilemma. She said, "He's sorry, Bonnie."

Bonnie, that's right. Curtik nodded slightly to thank Zora and said, "Sorry, Bonster."

Jefferson shook his head. "Focus, people. I've spoken with Major Somers of Britain's Combined Intelligence Service. They're the ones who spotted the vid of Brosk entering Holland Park. He said they've examined all the CCTV feeds from the area at around that time, but somebody had hacked into the system and there's no further footage of Brosk. And we won't even be able to use a trace scanner to pick up his signature because it's been too long since Brosk left and too many other people have been through that area."

"We'll think of something," Curtik said. "Won't we, Zora? Oh, before I forget, Neddy, can I use a particle beam cannon?"

"The Brits won't let us bring in heavy weaponry. Besides, we're not trying to blow up the neighborhood. This is a rescue operation and surgical strike. Think precision."

"Precision. Got it." Curtik quick-drew his plas-glass knife from its hidden flap in his combat fatigues, wincing at the sudden movement. "Okay, that's enough of that. I'll take a pain pad now," he said as he slid the knife back inside the flap.

Bonnie said, "You're done."

She held up a mirror and Curtik studied himself in it. The man staring back at him looked familiar and yet bizarrely different. Curtik suddenly felt as though he'd become his father. The wrinkles and pain lines around the eyes looked overly done. Did his old man really look that bad, that ancient? He turned to Zora, who stood immobile, staring at him.

Although she'd yet to have a new implant installed, she again read his mind. "Except for the eyes," she said, "your face looks exactly like his."

"Feels weird," Curtik said.

"It'll fool them," Jefferson said as he opened a hypo-pad and pressed it against the back of Curtik's hand. "Hell, if I didn't know who you were, I'd believe you were him."

"Thanks, Bonster," Curtik said as he took the mirror from her. She departed toward the back of the plane and he studied his reflection. As the pain receded, the muscles of his neo-skin face relaxed, making some of the lines vanish. He opened his mouth wide, then frowned and finally smiled. The face that looked back at him was so serious, so sad—even with the smile. Good God, old man, can't you just be happy for a minute?

"Don't dwell on it," Zora said. "You're still you."

"Am I?"

"Of course. You'll never be him."

"I know you mean it as an insult, but thanks."

Jefferson pressed an icon on his PlusPhone and the wall in front of Curtik became a screen.

A British news feed showed vids from Mexico City, Tokyo, Kolkata and Rome, which had disproportionate numbers of the dead and dying. New York City was rapidly catching up, as was Rio de Janeiro. Jakarta looked like a war zone, bodies littering the streets, the crews employed to pick up the corpses no longer doing their job. The news anchor speculated that it was probably a combination of the enormity of the task and the fact that there were few able workers left to perform it.

In somber tones, the anchor discussed the urgency and the seeming impossibility of finding a cure in time to prevent the disease from spreading to every village, hamlet and tiny township across the globe.

The anchor now turned to a doctor, who explained for those listeners who hadn't gotten it the previous 734 times, that viruses consist merely of DNA or RNA surrounded by a protein shell and that when they're not in contact with a host cell, they remain dormant—nothing more than static organic particles. Only when they attach themselves to cells do they become active. And because the Susquehanna Virus apparently could stay dormant for years in harsh conditions, scientists might never know if it had been completely eliminated. Adding to that complication was the fact that over forty variations had been identified to date.

The wall-screen then shifted to New York City, where bands of young men roamed across Times Square, crowbars and other crude weapons in their hands. They broke into stores, smashing windows and lighting fires. Riot police moved in to disperse them, a squad of Elite Ops troopers standing by in case they failed. The anchor noted that similar scenes were playing out around the world, not just in America, as frustrated citizens fought for food and medicine that didn't yet exist. Some of these anarchists were well organized, staying ahead of efforts to track them electronically.

Lendra's face replaced the image on the wall-screen. She said, "I've spoken with Major Somers of the CIS. He'll meet you upon landing. They've agreed to allow you to accompany them to Holland Park since they feel it's likely the cell is still in the area. The best place to hide is in the bustle of the city, so the enemy will still be around."

"So they agree it's a trap?" Zora asked.

Lendra nodded. "It's pretty clear they want Jeremiah and are unlikely to show themselves unless he appears. Of course they insist on taking the lead, so you'll be permitted to accompany them on the condition that when the action starts, you let them take over."

"Screw that," Curtik said. He started to play an air-drum solo to the beat of Death to the Mob, the Crystal Skull Bangers' best song, then realized he should have kept his mouth shut.

"We'll behave," Zora said.

"Curtik's right," Lendra said.

"Whoa, I am?"

"We do whatever it takes. If we piss off the Brits, we'll apologize after the fact. I want that cell taken, and I want Brosk rescued if at all possible. Good luck."

She signed off.

As the plane descended beneath the low cloud deck and into the light rain, Curtik could make out the craggy Scottish fingers extending into the Atlantic Ocean, looking like a fungus-covered hand floating on the surface, the rest of the corpse submerged under water.

"Next stop, merry old England," he said.

"Fifteen minutes," Zora said, glancing at the arrival info on the monitor above the cabin door.

Jefferson's PlusPhone buzzed. He looked at it and said, "Message from Major Somers. He's waiting at the airport. Expects us to cooperate fully."

As they flew over the hilly countryside, Glasgow appeared, a sprawling city growing out of the greenery, bisected by a wide river. Continuing along, Jefferson pointed out Manchester, then Birmingham and finally London. Curtik perused the massive city the Crystal Skull Bangers called home: Tower Bridge, the London Eye and the winding river Thames, where a destroyer was docked and several smaller naval vessels cruised.

"Looks like they're ready for war," Zora said.

"This is war," Jefferson replied.

"What are we going to do about Major Somers?"

Jefferson shrugged. "Play along. Pump him for information. Even with the economic crises the Brits have faced in the past few years, they've still got decent anti-terrorist operations."

"I almost blew up this place last year," Curtik said. "That would have been a shame."

"Take your seats and fasten your seatbelts," the pilot announced. "We'll be on the ground in a few minutes."

As Jefferson and Zora strapped themselves in, Curtik continued to study his reflection. It looked odd: his eyes trapped in his father's face. Was this what he would look like when he got old? Would he become his father? He sure as hell hoped not.

He almost didn't notice when the plane touched down. It taxied to a small hangar and by the time Jefferson and Zora had gotten their carry-ons and returned to Curtik's seat, the door opened and a thin Indian man of middle age entered. He wore a gray mustache under black hair, his eyes were a disconcerting blue.

"Major Somers of Britain's Combined Intelligence Service," he said. "Nice to meet you, Ned. I've heard a lot about you."

"A pleasure," Jefferson said. He introduced Zora and Curtik. Somers glanced at Zora with something like contempt before staring at Curtik's Jeremiah mask.

"Too bad the real Jeremiah couldn't come," he said.

Curtik grinned. "I'm way prettier and way more lethal."

"Yes, you're quite good at violence," Somers said. "I saw your handiwork at Stratford-upon-Avon."

"That's in the past," Jefferson said. "What can you tell us so far?"

"I was going to ask you the same question, but very well. I'll start. First of all, my government is furious that you've withheld information about this Sally cell. Granted, we knew about it. And although the information Ms. Riley provided gave us nothing new, common courtesy dictated that you inform us of everything you found."

"Bureaucrats," Jefferson said, shaking his head. "If it's any consolation, the three of us didn't learn about this cell until we boarded the plane."

Curtik managed not to laugh.

Major Somers smiled as if acknowledging how well Jefferson lied. "At any rate, your man will enter the park as bait." He made the word "man" sound like an obscenity. "My people will be stationed close by, ready to move in. The cell can't be more than five minutes away."

"As long as your people are out of sight," Jefferson said. "Any hint that Curtik has backup and the Sally wackos are liable to stay away."

"Agreed. Don't worry. I've been in the field. I know what I'm doing."

"I'm curious," Jefferson said. "CIS is one of the best intelligence agencies in the world. How come you don't know exactly where they are?"

"These bloody budget cuts," Major Somers said, his fists tightening at his sides. "The Metropolitan police get all the funding now. Riot prevention and all that. We're close. We'd likely find them in the next couple of days now that we've seen the vid of Brosk and the woman."

"I'm sure you would," Jefferson replied. "But you may as well take advantage of this opportunity. Zora and I will enter the park to provide immediate backup. I'll be wearing a hat and a filtration mask. No way they'll recognize me."

"I assume if I don't agree to that, you won't allow this man to act as bait." He glared at Curtik for a moment.

Jefferson nodded, ignoring the major's hostility. "You've been in the field. You know the drill. Foreign country—not allowed to go in alone."

"Of course." Major Somers gestured for them to precede him off the plane. "Shall we go? We'll handle customs on the way there, and you can fill me in on what you know, or what you're allowed to tell me, anyway."

Curtik bounded forward, barely noticing the discomfort in his joints. Finally some action!

Chapter 14

Sally23 waited beside Trogan Brosk, looking out the darkened windows to the sidewalk, where pedestrians hurried home from work, filtration masks on almost every face. Though the masks were largely ineffective against the virus, she supposed they provided some measure of comfort. Low gray clouds drizzled misty, ash-filled rain that dirtied sidewalks and streets, bringing a November feel to the June air. The screens on the wall captured news reports of Susquehanna Virus deaths, updating every few minutes with increasing numbers of victims.

Sally2 gave instructions to Andre and his security team—Jarrod, Ron, Marcus, Sinda and Paulo. The two newest recruits, David and Heather, had already gone on ahead, pleased to have a starring role in this operation. Their mission: approach Jones. Did they know, beneath their conditioning, that Sally2 expected them to die? Sally 23 had brought them into the fold back when she still believed in the cause. Now they would die because of her.

Marcus and Sinda stood close together. Jarrod, Ron and Paulo, hard cases with crew cuts and tattoos, caressed their three-bladed knives—plas-glass weapons that would be necessary if Jones was shielded against Las-weapons—as they received their final orders. Andre, as always, wore a look of intense concentration, brows furrowed on his chocolate face.

Almost everybody else had already left. Only the four Wally technicians remained behind: Wallys 2, 3, 5 and 6. Wally2, tall and lanky with curly brown hair, carried a flexible tablet linked to Brosk, able to monitor and, if necessary, control Brosk's movements. The other three Wallys, all short and slim Indians, carried Las-pistols. They looked uncomfortable, as if they only wished to dispense death from a distance, via discreet methods, perhaps from a joystick. Had they been conditioned too or did they just want to die? Or maybe they thought they'd survive.

Finally Sally2 finished giving instructions. She reached over and touched Andre's arm, and he smiled at her briefly before leading his team out the door. Marcus and Sinda took up positions at the rear, waving to Sally23 as they marched out; she waved back, wondering if she'd ever see them again. Brosk had repeatedly told her Jones would defeat Sally2's security team and he spoke with such quiet confidence it was hard not to believe him.

"I just got word," Sally2 said as she returned to the small group, "that Jones' plane landed an hour ago. He'll be here shortly."

Sally23 leaned into Brosk. He hugged her reassuringly as he spoke to Sally2: "I'm glad you're prepared to die because you're about to."

Sally2 looked from Brosk to Sally23, arching an eyebrow and causing Sally23 to pull away from Brosk's embrace. "I've considered that possibility," Sally2 said. "That's why we're relocating. We'll only be using this building to house Jones."

Then Sally2 nodded to Wally6, who changed the picture on the two large screens. They showed Holland Park in the rain, the famous Orangery, and the well-lit sculptures and walking trails. David and Heather were just now reaching the Orangery. They disappeared inside the building to stay dry, waiting for Sally2's signal.

***

Curtik walked stiffly along the trails of Holland Park, pretending his joints ached. Off to his left he spotted two young couples: one approaching, the other moving away. Neither looked like a threat. Neither wore protective masks. Curtik kept his hands in his pockets, the Las-pistol grips comforting as he shuffled ahead. He resisted the impulse to reach up and feel his neo-skin face. The proximity sensor in his implant showed only seven people in the immediate area—and he knew Zora and Jefferson were the other two—but the sensor displayed an odd feedback pulse.

See anything? he sent via his implant.

"Only the people you see," Zora whispered, keeping her voice low in case the enemy had sensitive microphones listening in. Since she no longer had her implant, she was using a conventional ear bud and a tiny microphone attached to the tip of her nose, both set to his implant's frequency. "But we're getting strange energy dispersal readings on our scanners, so they're around here somewhere. Probably using scatterers. You might want to activate your shield."

No, Curtik sent. *I want them confident.*

"My people are all in place," Major Somers said from his mobile unit. "They can be here in three minutes."

"Excellent," Jefferson answered. "Zora and I are entering the park now."

Curtik spotted them—an old black couple tottering along, their canes clicking on the path. The sculpture garden, lit with chem-lights, gave a warm orange glow to the dusk. A topiary lion looked ready to charge. Curtik stopped before it, pretending to examine it while he studied the two young couples on the path. One vanished behind a cluster of trees. The other approached. They giggled as their foreheads touched and they stared into each other's eyes. The man had his right arm around the woman's back, his hand in her right pocket. Curtik almost envied them. They looked happy, as if unaware of the deadly virus being manufactured nearby.

"Careful," Zora whispered. "Stay alert."

Yeah, yeah, Curtik sent. He stood at the side of the path, his body tensing, preparing to lash out. He focused on his Las-pistol grips, double-checked the power settings with his thumbs, making certain they were set on low.

The couple almost bumped into him, stopping at the last moment. "I beg your pardon," the young man said. "I didn't see you."

He looked only a little older than Curtik, not particularly handsome, with dark hair and a medium build, and he spoke accented English that sounded eastern European. The young woman was slightly overweight, or perhaps that was just the bulkiness of her jacket, and her plump face displayed a mole on the chin and heavy eyebrows. But she had a shy smile that Curtik found attractive.

"It's okay," Curtik said.

"Say, could you take our picture in front of the lion?" the young man asked.

"This is it," Zora whispered into his implant.

Well, duh, Curtik sent.

"Activate your shield," Zora whispered.

Not yet. If I do, they might run off.

"It's too dangerous. Activate your shield."

The young man held up his PlusPhone, waving it slightly, as if to say, "Here, use this."

Whoever they are, they're amateurs, Curtik sent. "Sorry," he said to the young man.

"It's just a picture," the young man said. "We're on our honeymoon. Please, mister?"

Curtik pulled his right hand out of his pocket to wave the young man off, keeping his left hand on the other Las-pistol.

"Catch," The young man tossed the PlusPhone at Curtik and dropped to the ground. The girl flopped beside him.

Curtik put up his right hand defensively as he activated the shield with his implant. The PlusPhone exploded.

***

Brosk inhaled sharply, squeezing Sally23's arm tightly as Jones fell to the ground. Was it going to be that easy? She'd thought Jones would have his shield engaged. Yet he hadn't done so until the booby-trapped PlusPhone had knocked him over and possibly destroyed his hand.

She felt a hollowness in her gut. Was that anxiety or relief? On the one hand, she didn't want her friends Marcus and Sinda to get hurt. On the other, she'd been silently rooting for Jones to succeed, to somehow rescue her.

Wally6 zoomed in on Jones, who lay on his back, his right arm raised above his head. He stared at the mangled hand in what looked like disbelief that slowly transformed into fury. Then almost faster than Sally23's eye could follow, he sprang to his feet, deactivated his shield and shot David—a deadly red laser pulse. As Heather got to her feet, Jones shot her in the back. She pitched forward. This was the Jones Sally23 had been expecting.

The elderly black couple at the edge of the sculpture area backed away toward the protection of a large tree. Probably not Jones's backup: more likely just trying to get out of the way. Sally23 hoped they wouldn't get hurt.

"Where's Andre's team?" Sally23 asked.

"Any second now," Sally2 replied.

Jones raised his head and howled. His yell turned into laughter. "You think that can stop me?" he called to the night. He stepped over to David and kicked his head, which flopped to the side.

"Come on!" he roared. "Is that all you've got?"

Now Andre's team emerged from behind the sculptures, wearing shields that formed pale yellow halos around their bodies. Jones again activated his shield, which displayed an iridescent glow around him.

"Well," Brosk said to the room, "you wanted to die. Now you get to."

"What are you talking about?" Wally5 said. "It's six against one."

"End game, Jones," Jarrod called as he approached. "You have to shut down your shield to fire, whereas one of us can fire at you at all times."

Jones snorted. "You're telling me about shields? Stupid son of a bitch!" Jones dropped his shield for a split second to fire a quick red burst at Jarrod. His shot bounced off Jarrod's shield and sailed into the night. Ron and Paulo began firing at him from a ninety-degree angle, long red strikes that engaged his shield continuously, turning it a bright yellow, giving him no opening to attack.

"Your people will be dead in seconds," Brosk said, his lips twisting in a smirk.

"Shut him up," Sally2 said, her eyes locked onto the left screen, which showed Andre and Jarrod advancing cautiously.

Wally2 touched the pad on his tablet and Brosk stiffened.

Sally23 glanced at Brosk's face. He stood rigidly, staring at the screens. This whole thing felt wrong. Even as that thought crossed her mind, the two old people hiding behind the tree lifted their canes and fired their disguised Las-weapons at Marcus and Sinda, who had just dropped their shields to fire at Jones. The purple laser strikes from the two old people hit Marcus and Sinda, who cried out and fell to the ground. Sally23 cringed. She squeezed Brosk's hand reassuringly and thought she detected a slight increase in pressure.

Now Jones walked toward Ron, absorbing multiple laser strikes with his shield, which began to glow a yellow-orange. Pocketing his Las-pistol, he pulled a knife and began to sing a familiar tune, though Sally23 couldn't remember where she'd heard it before:

"We're gonna kill 'em all,
The giant and the small.
The reckless and the brave
Are headed for the grave."

Ron dropped his Las-rifle and pulled out his three-bladed knife, held down low. He flicked it back and forth as Paulo approached Jones from behind, his plas-glass knife slicing through the air. The blades spun so fast that Sally23 could discern only a blur through their shields. On the adjacent screen Andre and Jarrod turned to fire upon the old black couple, whose shields glowed faintly as they advanced.

Jones chuckled. "Come on, boys," he said, "let's have some fun." He beckoned them closer with his knife.

Ron pounced.

Jones easily parried the blow and sliced Ron's belly open. He spun as Paulo came at him from behind, twirling faster than Sally23 would have believed possible, his knife sweeping across Paulo's face. Ducking Paulo's thrust, Jones slid sideways, kicking Paulo in the groin. As Paulo screamed, Jones sidestepped, lunging at Ron, planting the knife under Ron's chin, driving it up into the brain. Then he pulled the knife out, swung back to Paulo and thrust the knife into Paulo's chest, up to the hilt with a thud. Neither man's blades had touched him.

Andre and Jarrod exchanged fire with the old black couple. Somehow between bursts of laser fire Andre managed to toss a grenade at Jones' feet.

"Run!" the old woman yelled as she and the old man neared Andre and Jarrod.

Jones sprinted away. The grenade exploded before he'd gone ten feet and he flew through the air, his arms and legs flung out by the explosion. Sally23 heard the bang first on the vid connection and then the echo a half-second later as the sound waves from the park reached their headquarters.

Sally2's eyes were fixated on the screen, following Andre as he closed on the small black man.

"We must evacuate now," Sally23 said.

Wally2 and Wally3 looked at her nervously. Wally5 grabbed his bag, while Wally6 zoomed in on Andre and the old black man, who began grappling with each other. On another screen the old woman reached Jarrod, who grinned.

"Come on, you bitch," Jarrod said, his knife dangling so the plastic blades shimmered in the glow of his shield.

Andre was having trouble with the little old man, who appeared to be getting the better of him. Sally2 stepped towards the screen, settling next to Brosk.

Brosk glanced to his side. He managed to wiggle a couple fingers of his left hand but wasn't able to reach out to grab Sally2, who had carelessly placed herself next to him. Sally23 wished she could somehow disable the controls on Brosk and allow him to kill Sally2. Patience, she told herself.

She contemplated running for a moment—taking Brosk and heading for the tube, disappearing in the heart of London. But Wally2 still held the computer that controlled Brosk's movements. And running was a death sentence anyway. She raised her eyebrows at Wally3, who activated the dispersal scatterer that would mask their retreat from a trace scanner.

Sally2's lips parted slightly as she watched Andre and the old man fighting. It should have been over quickly, but the little old man was surprisingly strong. And fast. No doubt enhanced.

The old black woman closed with Jarrod as sirens sounded in the distance. The old woman's shield merged with Jarrod's. He lunged forward, his blades scything downward viciously at her neck, but she was no longer there. Faster than Jones even, almost faster than Sally23's eye could follow, she slid beneath the swiping blades, and plunged a plas-glass spike into Jarrod's neck, thrusting it up into his brain. He toppled over instantly.

"We have to go now," Sally23 said. She gestured to Wally5, who took Sally2 by the arm and pulled her toward the door.

"Right," Sally2 said, awakening from her trance. "Let's go." She turned to Sally23, her eyes glistening. "Thanks."

***

As Major Somers' people arrived, the sirens dying away, Zora glanced at Curtik, who lay on his back, staring at his mangled right hand, a look of utter confusion on his face. She felt like laughing and crying at the same time. Ned, she saw, was using a form of judo against their attackers' leader. He contorted his body, twisting and turning as the larger man tried to hit him. And though it seemed like Ned wasn't getting many blows in himself, his attacker was clearly tiring. She moved closer, preparing to step in.

The man grabbed Ned, who fell backwards, pulling the attacker with him, twisting in the air so that he landed on the man's chest. He poked the man's eyes and landed a punch to the guy's throat even as the attacker hit him hard on the side of the face. "Go check on Curtik," Ned managed to say.

"You sure?"

"I'm fine." Ned held his open palm against the bigger man's throat and a sizzling sound mingled with the man's screaming. Major Somers rushed forward from one of the vehicles, a Las-weapon in his hands. He directed the officers to spread out and check the bodies of their attackers but Zora was pretty sure they were all dead.

She left them to their work and found Curtik staring at his mangled hand, his jaw quivering with fury. She remembered waking up after the explosion that killed her for a few minutes—the confusion and pain. Was it better to have no warning?

"I told you to activate your shield," she said.

"I'm gonna kill 'em all," Curtik said. "I'm gonna torture 'em and keep on torturing 'em until the agony makes 'em beg for death."

Zora grabbed his arm and helped him to his feet. "We're going to have to get you a new hand. Good thing you're wearing combat fatigues. The tourniquet and the anesthetic seem to be working. Does it hurt?"

Curtik shook his head. "Completely numb. Looks cool, like something out of a horror vid."

Zora examined Curtik's ring finger and pinkie, the only two digits still attached to the hand. They were nearly stripped to the bone and Curtik's palm had lost almost all its muscle; it was just a bloody mass of tissue. She pulled out a QuikHeal bandage and placed it over the wound, wrapping it around the entire hand.

"Thanks," Curtik said.

As they walked toward Ned and Major Somers, the attacker now completely subdued, Zora tried to distract Curtik. "What were you singing?"

STEVE MCELLISTREM

158

"The refrain from Death to the Mob."

"Let me guess—the Crystal Skull Bangers."

Curtik nodded. "Their best song. I'm gonna sing it when I kill those bastards."

Ned had planted his right foot on the chest of the large black man, who was squirming as he whimpered. Major Somers stood beside Ned, a smile on his face. He gestured to a disk barely visible beneath Ned's foot. "Neuro-stimulator?"

"Just happened across it," Ned replied.

"What's it do?" Zora asked.

"Combines painful electrical impulses with drug dispersion to suppress will. Quick and reliable." Ned glanced at Curtik. "You okay?"

"Could be worse." Curtik held up his mangled hand. "Just a flesh wound."

"Where's your base?" Ned asked the man. "Tell me and the pain stops."

Sobbing now, the man murmured softly. Ned leaned down and listened for a moment, then straightened. He twisted the disk and the man went silent. Then he removed the disk from the man's chest.

"Why didn't we get neuro-stimulators?" Zora said, elbowing Curtik.

"Yeah!" Curtik said. "Where's our neuro-stimulators, Neddy?"

Ned shook his head. He gave Major Somers an address and the two men started off at a run. Major Somers spoke into his PlusPhone, calling for a tech squad. As Zora began to follow, she noticed that Curtik had stayed behind. He unsheathed his knife, knelt down and stabbed the unconscious attacker in the groin.

"Curtik," Ned yelled, "what are you doing?"

"Just cleaning my knife," Curtik replied. He got to his feet stiffly.

"Happy?" Zora asked.

"I'd be happier if I could clean it a few more times."

"Come on." Zora grabbed his jacket and pulled him away as more police vehicles arrived. When they exited the park, a large police van followed them. They caught up with Ned and Major Somers at a darkened commercial building two blocks away. Zora's scanner showed no bio-signs inside.

"We go in carefully," Ned cautioned. "The place might be loaded with booby traps."

The police van stopped, discharging a handful of tech officers, each suited in biohazard gear and carrying a scanner. They handed around masks, which everyone put on. As Zora helped Curtik seat his mask over his neo-skin face, Major Somers fired a red pulse at the door, destroying the lock. He pushed the door open, leading the techies inside. Ned, Curtik and Zora followed, weapons drawn.

A few boxes littered the lobby floor. On the wall to the right two large screens showed the scene at Holland Park. Officers strolled the perimeter searching the ground while more techies knelt over bodies. Medics worked on the large black man, who lay immobile on his back. A small crowd of citizens had now appeared, drawn by the police presence.

The techies in the lobby moved to the stairways—three went up, two down. Ned pointed at the disappearing feet of the three. "Follow them. Be careful. See if you can spot anything that might help us figure out where they've gone."

Upstairs, while the techies studied scanners and opened doors, Curtik and Zora entered a room lined with empty countertops and open cabinets. A machine sat abandoned in one corner. Zora realized it was a chemical mixer.

"Another manufacturing cell," she said.

A small explosion sounded down the hall, causing her to jump. She glanced down the hallway as one of the techies emerged from another room.

"Sorry," he called out. "Triggered a booby trap. Some sort of white powder. You'd better get out of here just to be on the safe side."

"Come on," Zora said to Curtik.

He stood inside the doorway, looking up into the far corner, where a small camera covered the room, a tiny red light blinking off and on.

Curtik held up his wounded hand and smiled at the camera as Zora dragged him toward the stairs. "Be seeing you soon," he called.

Zora opened a channel to Ned and said, "Anything on your end?"

"Nothing," he replied. "They're gone. And they used a scatterer, so we can't track them."

"We've got a camera up here," Zora said. "Maybe we can track the signal if they're watching us."

"Good idea. We'll put someone on it right away."

Chapter 15

Lendra sat behind her desk, her face in her hands, trying not to worry about her daughter, who had suddenly become critically ill. The President would be calling soon. How she wished she could just grab Sophie and Jeremiah and drive away from here, from all the headaches surrounding this damned virus. But Sophie needed the doctors and Curtik had lost his hand and she just knew Jeremiah blamed her for that even though his face had shown nothing when she told him. Let it go, she thought. There's work to do.

Across the room, Jay-Edgar ran compilations of broadcasts of the EuroNews Network and the 24-Hour Real News Network—both programs devoting their time to the virus and its increasing death toll.

Dr. Poole sat beside Jay-Edgar, analyzing statistical data, searching for patterns that might identify the remaining cells of the Susquehanna Sally movement. She occasionally asked Jay-Edgar to display an image or run a scenario based on input she culled from her interface. The holo-projections would change for a moment while she studied the results, after which she would nod and Jay-Edgar would return to the compilations.

Lendra forced herself to look away, instead returning to the task of analyzing the Gaia Manifesto, studying it for the thousandth time, trying to discern any tiny clue it might divulge about Susquehanna Sally.

God, it was difficult to concentrate on the job at hand. Sophie had caught a staph infection called TEM1 from the nanny Isabella. One of a new breed of superbugs resistant to current antibiotics, it had mutated from an earlier version after exposure to some of the new drugs used to treat the symptoms of the Susquehanna Virus. Now she apparently had beaten back the virus, but was still carrying a high fever.

The hell with it!

Lendra got up and headed for the door, gesturing to Dr. Poole as she left the office. Making her way to the infirmary, she passed Hannah waiting in the hall, so she knew Jeremiah was inside. She nodded at Hannah, a little surprised that the two Elite Ops troopers weren't standing guard with her. He must have sent them away; they would never have left him voluntarily.

Lendra entered the infirmary and stopped at the window to the quarantine area, where Sophie and her nanny Isabella now resided. Behind the glass, Jeremiah held their daughter, wearing neither biohazard suit nor mask, while Sophie clutched his finger in her tiny fist. Sophie stared up at Jeremiah as he spoke with Isabella, putting the nanny at ease. How did he make it seem so effortless?

As Lendra stood watching, they spotted her. Jeremiah walked Sophie to the window so she could see Lendra. When Sophie noticed her, she reached out with her free hand, keeping hold of Jeremiah's finger, trying to grasp both her parents at the same time. Lendra felt her knees weaken. She reached out and touched the window, partly to get closer to her daughter and partly to prevent herself from toppling over. Jeremiah held up Sophie's hand and waved it at her until Lendra waved back.

Lendra turned on the intercom.

"...isn't that right, Sophie?" Jeremiah was saying. "Soon you'll be all better and Mommy can hold you again and sing you songs and play with you. And you still have Isabella here to watch over you. Aren't you lucky? I wish I could stay here with you for hours, but I have to go back to work." He looked at Lendra. "I'll be out in a minute."

"No, that's not necessary," she replied as he handed Sophie off to Isabella. Sophie wailed as he headed for the sterilization showers.

"It's okay, honey," Lendra called through the intercom. "Mommy will be back to visit you soon." She began singing *Children's Moon* to Sophie, an old song that Jeremiah had sung to his son Joshua before the boy was abducted and turned into Curtik.

Gradually Sophie quieted in Isabella's arms. Lendra's voice died away as Sophie settled into a troubled sleep. Isabella put her down for a nap as Jeremiah emerged from the quarantine area.

Lendra shut off the intercom. "You're wonderful with her," she said. "Thank you."

"She's my daughter too. What's up?"

"Nothing. I just needed to see her."

Jeremiah nodded, but he didn't leave. Instead he looked at her, assessing. She felt as if he were testing her, as if the slightest wrong move would drive him away. How she wished she could reach out and touch his face once again—kiss him and hold him and breathe in his comforting scent.

"Well, I'd better get back to work," he said as he turned toward the door.

She wanted to ask him to stay with her a while, but her interface signaled that the President was calling, so she followed him out. He and Hannah went left toward his office; Lendra went right. She told Jay-Edgar to put the President through as she walked into her office and took a seat beside Dr. Poole.

The news reports vanished. In their place, Jay-Edgar projected a hologram of President Angelica Hope, the pompous Dr. Chandrika Jaidev by her side. The Secretary of Health and Human Services sat stiffly, wearing the ghost of a smile tainted by the dark circles under her eyes. She tapped her gold interface with a finger, manually disconnecting from some data flow—a showoff move. The President sat with her elbows on her desk, emphasizing her muscular shoulders. She looked out at them calmly, her face only a little pinched and pale.

"Madam President," Lendra said.

"Lendra, Dr. Poole," President Hope replied. "Have you got any more information about these Susquehanna Sally cells?"

"Not much, ma'am," Lendra replied. "We know that the London cell was a manufacturing base, as was the Jakarta cell. We believe there are one or two more. Almost certainly one is in the United States. Another might be in Brazil or China."

"And how are the efforts at a cure coming along?"

Lendra glanced over at Dr. Poole, who answered for her: "We're still working on a number of possibilities. Quark has been most helpful at coordinating the efforts now that Devereaux is in a coma. The CDC and Johns Hopkins have taken the lead, using samples Jeremiah Jones provided to Devereaux earlier. I'm sure Dr. Jaidev knows more about our progress than I do."

President Hope nodded toward Dr. Jaidev, who smirked and sat up a tiny bit straighter. "I've given the President my report. But progress has slowed since Devereaux fell ill. I can think of one way to speed up a cure."

Lendra's mouth went dry. She sat back in her chair, stunned. "Are you asking me to infect Jeremiah with new strains of the virus?"

Dr. Poole gasped.

"We must consider every strategy that can possibly save us," Dr. Jaidev replied, "no matter how painful."

President Hope held up her hands. "I couldn't ask you to re-infect Jeremiah at this time. I still find it hard to believe he voluntarily exposed himself to eighteen variants of the virus. To endure that much agony for us," President Hope spread her hands and shook her head slowly, "well, I honor him for that sacrifice."

"Still . . ." Dr. Jaidev said.

Lendra felt her heart pounding.

Dr. Poole shook her head and said, "Any further exposure might kill Jeremiah. He's not invincible. And as his doctor, I cannot condone such action."

"Don't you think that's his decision?" Dr. Jaidev asked.

"We both know that if the President asks, he'll agree to it," Dr. Poole said. "But we still have a long way to go in analyzing the samples he's already provided. There's no reason to expose him further." Her eyes jumped between Lendra and the holo-projection. "At least not yet."

Lendra looked the President in the eye and said, "He's currently assisting us in tracking down these terrorists. Running analyses, looking for patterns that might help identify their locations. He's the best we have. I'd hate to lose his skills."

"Why can't he do both?" Dr. Jaidev asked. "We need all the data we can get on the way this virus works."

"Do you know how hard it is to concentrate when you're in unbearable agony?" Dr. Poole said. "When all you can think about is the torture your body is enduring?"

"If I could help by doing what he did, I would. But my blood isn't—"

"I could make it work," Dr. Poole interrupted. "I could give you a transfusion of Jeremiah's blood. Then you'd be able to help exactly as he did. You'd be in excruciating pain, but we could infect you with the virus, see how you react to it and use those results in our efforts to find a cure. Would you like me to ask Jeremiah for a liter of blood?"

Dr. Jaidev sent a glare of hatred through the holo-projection, forcing Lendra to bite her lip to avoid laughing.

"As I said," President Hope smiled briefly, "for now I'm asking nothing. I'm merely suggesting that we might be forced into such an alternative if the death toll keeps increasing and we're unable to come up with a solution."

"What about using genetic surgery," Lendra suggested, "to create more Escala?"

"That has been discussed," President Hope acknowledged.

"Of course it would be impossible to save more than a few thousand people," Dr. Poole pointed out. "Most of us wouldn't be good candidates for the surgery. But some could certainly be saved."

"Have you been tested, Madam President?" Lendra asked. "To see if you could benefit from the surgery?"

"The President's medical condition is classified," Dr. Jaidev answered, her face scrunched up in a fierce frown, her plump cheeks darkening.

"We've decided to make genetic surgery a strategy of last resort," the President offered. "Any other ideas?"

"We do have one," Lendra said. "It's rather far-fetched, but . . . we discussed the possibility of transferring Devereaux's mind to a computer."

"You mean like the transfer of that rat's mind from Mars to Earth?" Dr. Jaidev asked.

"Except that we wouldn't be transferring the mind into another human," Lendra clarified. "We'd simply be transferring it to an organic computer inside a robot so that he'd have the ability to act and we'd have continued access to his ideas. Later—if his body recovers—we could transfer his mind back into his brain. Or if his body succumbs to the virus, we might be able to transfer him into another human brain, from a clone, for example—though the risks are quite high."

"Is that legal?" President Hope asked. "Is it ethical?"

"It can't be done," Dr. Jaidev said. "There's too much degradation of memory during thought transfer. The last time it was attempted . . ."

President Hope held up her hand and Dr. Jaidev went silent.

Lendra answered the President: "We don't know about the legality because to my knowledge it's never been done before—at least not successfully—though an argument could be made that it's legal for national security reasons. After all, Devereaux has made significantly more progress than anybody else with the virus. Without him, we probably won't find a cure for months, perhaps years. And I doubt we're going to have that kind of time. With respect to the morality of it, that's a question that could be debated for years."

She turned to Dr. Poole, who addressed Dr. Jaidev: "As for the likelihood of success, well, I wouldn't put it at greater than twenty percent unless we have the assistance of the Escala on Mars. As you know, they've put a great deal more time into researching this area. If we combine their results with the data we've received from Cambridge, it might boost the odds of success to around fifty percent."

"Can we check with them now?" President Hope asked.

"Certainly," Lendra answered, "but there's a long delay between transmissions."

President Hope lowered her head, closed her eyes and massaged her temples for a few seconds. "That's right. I forgot how long it takes for a message to get there. Fifteen minutes, is it?"

"Sixteen at the moment. Plus another sixteen minutes for the return message to arrive," Lendra added. Perhaps it would be best if you put together a vid asking for their assistance. We can broadcast that when we contact them."

President Hope looked at her watch. "How long to make all this happen?"

"A couple of days, at least," Lendra said. "They may not even be willing to help us. They'll only cooperate if they believe doing so is in Devereaux's best interest. I happen to believe that's the case. But will they think so?"

"I'm sure they'll help," the President said. "Their fondness for Devereaux will make them want to ensure his survival. Let me know what they have to say. Prepare as if it's a go. I'll give you the final word after checking with my people."

As the holo-projection faded to nothing, Lendra and Dr. Poole began to laugh. Even Jay-Edgar chuckled.

"Did you see the look on Dr. Jaidev's face?" Dr. Poole said. "I thought she was going to have a heart attack."

Lendra smiled. "That was fantastic. Is what you told her true? Could you use Jeremiah's blood on her to obtain testing samples?"

Dr. Poole shrugged. "I don't know. But I'd be willing to try. That arrogant bitch is only concerned with political fallout."

"Well, we'd better contact Mars at once, see if they're willing to help us. Without Devereaux, I'm afraid we've got very little chance of beating this thing."

She suddenly remembered Sophie in the infirmary and felt guilty for feeling happy for a moment. She had no right to be anything other than miserable.

"Don't worry," Dr. Poole said, as if reading her mind. "She'll be fine. I'm monitoring her continuously. And Dr. Hassan is brilliant."

But Lendra flashed on Devereaux, who had also been monitored all the time, and who had nevertheless succumbed to the virus. If Sophie died, how could she go on?

Chapter 16

Aspen stood next to Addam atop Dunadan's knoll. Dusk brought a blue tint to the brownish Martian sky. Through the dusty haze, the setting sun appeared as a small, pale sphere. Its sharp angle made the distant graveyard markers shine brightly—twenty-eight pinpoints of light. She was glad for Addam's company.

Dr. Wellon had made a number of genetic modifications after Aspen collapsed in the lab. For some reason, that made her angry. Why? Was she just tired of other people fixing her? She conceded that the headaches had gone away, but they might have stopped anyway.

Opening her powerscope, she focused on the approaching Chinese spaceship, letting the scope's computer do the vector calculations to determine the craft's orbital ETA. The ship looked huge through the powerscope. Its charged Las-cannon glowed—a yellow light near the nose that spun with the vessel.

Her nightmares hadn't gone away. She still dreamed that a landing party of Chinese soldiers, bigger than the Elite Ops, bigger than the Escala, would penetrate into the caves below, Las-weapons and particle beam cannons obliterating everyone inside, limbs flying, the complex crashing down on them while she tried to reach them, never getting close enough to help.

Quekri refused to build Las-weapons to defend the colony, while Bilson naively maintained that the miners could protect everyone, so

Aspen had ordered the cadets to construct a hidden cave in case the Chinese crew's intentions were hostile. *If we can't fight*, she thought, *we'll hide until we can*. Quekri's son Krall, seeing what appeared to be an exciting adventure, had volunteered himself, Poon and Oggie to assist in the project. They were now digging a cave at the end of the deepest tunnel that would hide the cadets and a few Escala. They couldn't try to hide everyone because the Chinese knew they were here, but if only a few people went missing, the Chinese might not notice.

She hadn't seen Benn and Phan for days. The two cadets spent almost all their time with the Escala teens, working on the hidey-hole, returning to their quarters only at night. Aspen suspected they wouldn't even do that if not for the fact that Shiloh and Kammilee were sleeping with them.

"Two days to orbit," Aspen said.

"Unless they decide to come straight in," Addam replied. Quekri had given him responsibility for the approaching ship, asked him to search for transmissions and other clues about its intentions. So far, the vessel had been completely silent except for the telemetry it broadcast back to Earth. Aspen found that silence chilling. It was the kind of ploy someone like Curtik would use to maximize terror in his victims. But for some reason, it didn't appear to be working with the Escala, nor with her fellow cadets. Was she the only one who saw danger in its stealthy approach?

"Course changes?" Addam asked.

"None," she replied. "What do you think about its silence?"

"Could be any number of things," Addam responded. "Transmitter troubles, a drone scientific vessel not programmed to answer hails, a military mission . . ."

"So," Aspen lowered the powerscope and stared at Addam, "they could be soldiers."

"Of course."

"How come nobody acknowledges that?"

"They've been fixated on this Devereaux thing," Addam said. "I thought you would be too, what with your experiments on the rats."

Aspen handed the powerscope to Addam and reached for the sensor-cleaning kit. "Quekri and Zeriphi and Dr. Wellon are handling the conversations with Earth, determining whether we should assist them. What do you think about transferring Devereaux's mind to a computer?"

Addam shrugged inside his Mars suit. "It seems logical to preserve his life, his abilities. Why throw that away just because the shell of his body is failing? If his mind can be saved, why not do it?"

"Because it's more complicated than transferring a rat's mind. It's even more complicated than transferring an ordinary human's mind. This is Devereaux, after all. And if we save him, we might at the same time be condemning him to some sort of limbo. We don't even know if the mind transfer will work. There are indications that Guffie's mind isn't completely restored. And although we'd be transferring Devereaux's mind to a computer inside a robot, rather than to another person's brain, there might be memory degradation or neural-pattern dispersal problems. What if we get just part of him?"

"It's still better than dying."

Aspen shook her head as she started cleaning the sensor array. "I'm not sure. Especially not with someone like Devereaux. His mind is his most important feature, and it's hugely influenced by its connection with his body. It's one thing to transfer a rat's mind to another rat, but the complexity of the human body is exponentially harder because our mind-body connection is so much more symbiotic. What happens when that connection is broken? Is he still the same person?"

"Well, at least you don't have to make the decision."

"But that's the thing," Aspen countered. "I should be in on the decision-making. I lead the cadets up here. And I probably know as much about this stuff as Dr. Wellon and Zeriphi and Keelar. It's all I've been doing for the past few weeks."

"If they decide to go ahead with it, they'll use you. I know they often think of us as just kids but they're smart enough to know we have areas of expertise they don't. Look at me with that approaching ship. Once I pointed out to Quekri my education in rocketry and missile systems, she put me in charge of it."

"I just . . ." Aspen sighed. "Sometimes I feel truly useless. With everything happening on Earth, I feel like I ought to be part of that somehow. I haven't heard from Zora in forever, not since she lost her implant."

"Yeah, Curtik doesn't contact us much anymore either."

"He called you yesterday to tell you he was getting a new hand."

"True," Addam conceded. "But before that, he hadn't contacted us in about a week. I think he's moving on with his life, just like we should be. That's why you should let Benn have the genetic surgery to become Escala."

"Is that why you followed me out here?"

"Benn asked me to talk to you. He said Dr. Wellon won't operate without your permission. Neither will Keelar."

"What if we want to go back to Earth some day?" Aspen asked. "What will Benn do then? He wouldn't be able to survive very long if he becomes Escala."

"He already said he intends to stay here. Kammilee agrees with him. They don't want to go back even if we can. She and Benn have talked about starting a family, moving over to the Escala side of the caves. In fact . . ."

Aspen paused in her cleaning, waiting for Addam to continue. She closed her eyes for a moment. When he remained silent she said, "They're children. They have no business—"

"We're not children anymore. We may not be adults yet, but we're not children either. We're something in the middle. And even though you're technically in charge, your authority only stretches so far. This isn't the Moon anymore. You can't tell us how to run our personal lives."

Aspen fought a surge of rage. She was grateful for the Mars suit, which hid her emotions, though she suspected Addam knew he'd angered her. Every decision she'd made had been with the cadets' best interests in mind. She'd acted as peacemaker and arbiter countless times. On difficult occasions she'd asked herself what Zora would do and tried to emulate her. And now her people were abandoning her. She kept her voice even: "Do Phan and Shiloh feel the same way?"

"You've done a great job," Addam said. "We all agree on that. But we're on Mars now. There's no going back. This is our future. We need to join the Escala. If we become Escala, some day we might be able to survive outside without our suits."

"The Escala need suits too. The atmospheric pressure here is less than one percent what it is on Earth, and the air is almost entirely made up of carbon dioxide—not to mention the radiation exposure. No, that's unlikely ever to happen."

"Sometimes I feel like taking off my suit and just walking around like we did on Earth. I sort of remember that. Don't you?"

Aspen's implant beeped. Quekri, always polite, letting her know that a message was coming through: "We've nearly reached a decision on Devereaux. Please come to the main cavern when you've completed cleaning the sensor array."

Aspen turned to Addam, who said, "I got the message too. Let me help you." He reached for a cloth and began wiping sensors in earnest.

***

It took Aspen ten minutes to remove and stow her Mars suit, prepping it for the next trip to the surface by plugging the powerpack into the recharger and topping off the oxygen tanks. She felt uncomfortable unless the suit was ready for a quick exit. One never knew when a hasty retreat might be necessary. She forced Addam to prepare his suit for the next outdoor expedition as well, waiting for him to finish before making her way to the main cavern.

When she got there, Aspen paused for a moment at the tunnel mouth, entranced by the cave's rugged beauty. The Escala had completed the lighting display a few days ago, and the cavern now sparkled with rainbow colors. Multi-spectral spotlights emanated from behind boulders set at the four delineated compass points, arcing upwards to the vaulted red ceiling forty feet above their heads, sending out prisms of light that warmed the air and sparkled off the sides and roof of the cave. Vines clung to the walls, most of them fruit bearing: blueberry, raspberry and plumberry. The special hybrids gave off double the oxygen of their Earthly cousins and a fruity scent floated through the air. The cave felt cool, but the Escala, with their extra bulk, were always warm. They maintained every room a few degrees too chilly for Aspen's taste. A dozen glow globes floated above as many tables, emitting a soft white light.

As she started inside, she noticed that every Escala looked to be present, as well as all the cadets—nearly eighty people strong. For the most part they sat quietly, wearing frowns as they looked at Quekri, who stood before the central dining table, Krall seated in front of her. Dr. Wellon sat on Quekri's right, her hand on Poon's shoulder. It took Aspen a half-second to remember that Poon was Dr. Wellon's son—the wild Poon nothing like his mother. And there was Keelar, the gray-haired Escala's hand on her son Oggie's shoulder. Another weird pairing—Keelar sensitive and thoughtful, Oggie impetuous and emotional. Zeriphi stood off to the side, shuffling slowly, her baby Celestia on her hip.

Aspen had never before noticed what a female-centric society this was. No doubt it had to do with, at least in part, the large number of males who had been killed on Earth. Was that why her fellow cadets were so enamored of the Escala way? Did it remind them of their forgotten mothers, ripped from them in their early years? She herself could conjure only the ghost of a memory: a tall woman with fair skin and golden hair; she couldn't remember her father at all.

Addam guided her to the table where Benn and Kammilee, Phan and Shiloh sat. All four cadets glared at her as she took a seat. She'd expected the first three to be angry with her but apparently even Shiloh wanted concessions she could not give.

Quekri nodded to Aspen. "Good. We're all here. Let's get started."

No miners present, Aspen thought. Interesting. So Quekri doesn't include them in everything.

"Devereaux," Quekri said, "is likely to die soon. However, total mind transfer entails enormous risks and Devereaux never gave us a clear directive as to his wishes should he find himself in this situation."

"Excuse me," Zeriphi said, "but we do know that Devereaux opposes extending life beyond its natural expectancy."

Murmurs filled the cave as the Escala considered this.

"True," Dr. Wellon conceded, "but this virus isn't natural. And I think Devereaux would want to be revived so he can continue to work for a cure."

"He talked often about the corruption of immortality," Zeriphi said.

"What does that mean?" Addam asked.

"It means," Zeriphi replied, "that those who become immortal are much more likely to engage in depravity. Power corrupts. Life is power. Immortal life breeds boredom, which ultimately births cruelty."

More murmurs: which quieted down when Keelar cleared her throat loudly.

"Devereaux," she said, "is first and foremost a humanitarian. Everything he's done has been with the purpose of aiding humanity. And this action, if taken, would not guarantee Devereaux immortality, nor would it preclude a later transfer either back into his own body, should it survive, or into another donor or cloned body for purposes of living out a natural life. As much as Devereaux has discussed the danger of power associated with eternal life, he has also by his actions demonstrated an unsurpassed devotion to his fellow creatures, an altruistic love that transcends our shoddy attempts to emulate it. And though many of you are not believers, there is also the issue of the soul. For those of us who still believe, we wonder what will happen to his soul."

Quekri said, "You're right to question all that. As for the soul, I can't speak to that, nor can any of us. Only God, if there is a God, knows the answer to what will happen. But if there is a soul, I would think it would move with the mind and consciousness of Devereaux rather than stay with his body—just as in death, the soul leaves the body to ascend to another plane of existence."

Murmurs arose among the gathered crowd. Quekri raised her hands until they quieted. "I know many of you feel strongly about this, one way or the other. But we cannot answer the religious question with any certainty, so I'm asking you not to take that into consideration for now. We are scientists. We must examine this issue through the scientific lens."

She looked at Aspen, raising an eyebrow. The other Escala turned to face her as well.

They want my opinion, Aspen thought. She was at once flattered and angry: flattered that Quekri should value her ideas, angry that she hadn't been consulted earlier. She said, "I know nothing about religion, so I'll speak only to the science. The transfer of the majority of Devereaux's mind would proceed relatively smoothly. The bulk of his personality would meld into the computer's organic software. However, there might be some loss of detail, some loss of essential mental processes—the unique complexity that makes Devereaux's mind so special. We also have to consider that the body plays an enormously important role in the development and functioning of the mind."

Paddon, an Escala technician who'd been wounded on Earth and still walked with a limp, spoke up in his soft voice. "Are you saying that without his body, the Devereaux we save might not be the Devereaux he used to be?"

"That's exactly what I'm saying."

"So he might not have a soul?"

The buzz of conversation grew louder.

"Please," Quekri said, and the room quieted once again. "Aspen wasn't talking about a soul. Were you?"

"No. I meant that his personality and his will might be different. You might call that a soul—I don't know. But whether it's the soul or something else, the point is, he might not be exactly the same. For example, he might not have a sex drive any longer, or hunger pangs."

Dr. Wellon said, "From a purely scientific standpoint, any personality discrepancy should be suppressible with sufficient willpower. And we all know that Devereaux has exceptional mental discipline. I'm not going to lie about the risks. Aspen is right. They're huge. But I fear that if we don't assist them, they may try to do this without us, and Devereaux might die . . . or worse."

Escala and cadets turned back to Aspen, looking for her counter-argument or assent. Even Quekri stared at her. Aspen felt an enormous pressure in her chest, making it difficult to breathe. Her stomach fluttered, a churning knot. She'd never asked to lead the cadets. Why was Quekri pushing her? Whatever the colony ultimately decided, Quekri's opinion would carry the most weight. So why ask her at all? Aspen couldn't even unite her cadets. Finally she said, "What does Zora think? Has anyone checked with her?"

"And what does Quark think?" Paddon asked.

"And Jeremiah," Krall contributed, shooting a glance at his mother. "What does Jeremiah Jones think?"

"Quark," Quekri answered, "believes we should save Devereaux's mind. And he's been closer to Devereaux than any of us."

"He's also an atheist," Keelar said.

"True," Quekri conceded. "As for Jeremiah Jones, I don't believe he has been consulted. Apart from us, I don't think anyone cares what he thinks. And Zora," Quekri looked at Aspen, "well, she trusted you to make the hard decisions."

"I don't think it's a decision I can make for someone else," Aspen said. "Bad things may result, whatever we decide."

More murmurs came from the Escala, while the cadets, except for Addam, glared at her. Aspen returned their stares, challenging them to come up with their own ideas if they didn't like hers.

Addam said, "Wait a minute. We're not actually deciding whether the mind transfer takes place, are we?"

"No," Quekri answered. "The President of the United States will likely make the decision. No one else has the authority. Perhaps she doesn't either, but certainly no one else can decide. And Devereaux is in her government's custody."

Aspen said, "And if we refuse to give them our data?"

"Dr. Wellon and I believe they'll go ahead with it anyway," Quekri answered, "which is one of the reasons I didn't waste your time with discussion. They're going to do what they want regardless of our concerns."

"Then why are we even having this meeting?"

"First, to make everyone aware of what's happening. Second, to ask that all our information on mind transfer be collected into a file we can transmit to Earth, so they'll have the best chance of bringing Devereaux through the procedure unharmed. And third, to discuss the approaching vessel from China."

"Finally," Aspen said. "I wondered if you were ever going to acknowledge its existence."

"I thought the ship would eventually contact us and that we'd have time to make a decision."

"We could have been building Las-weapons," Aspen said.

"We're not soldiers," Quekri said. "We don't wish to fight with anyone. Mars is plenty big for another scientific expedition. And it's an internationally recognized neutral zone. They have as much right to land on Mars as we did, or the miners.

"Where are the miners?" Keelar asked. "Shouldn't they be here for this meeting too?"

More murmurs.

"Please," Quekri said, lifting her hands again until the room quieted once more. "They're here for purely commercial reasons. Their goals are not our goals."

"All they care about is ore," Fazzerel, an older Escala with a thick, gray beard offered.

"They steal our tools," Garthod, the heavyset chief Escala engineer, said.

"They don't live here permanently," Quekri added. "They rotate out every time a new ship picks up ore."

"Some of them," Keelar said, "have done pretty well. Bilson, for example, has no major health problems."

"I've treated him half a dozen times already," Dr. Wellon said. "Granted, for small medical issues, but he hasn't been as healthy as you might think. And seven of them have died since they arrived. That's not a great success rate."

Quekri said, "We'll bring them in when necessary. For now we ought to get back to the Chinese ship. They've been sending telemetry back to Earth, so I hoped they were on a peaceful mission."

Aspen said, "What if they've come to attack us?"

"Indeed. It seems like a long way to travel just to kill a few pseudos." Quekri emphasized the hated term others used to describe the Escala, and for an instant Aspen saw a gleam of anger in her eyes. "But," Quekri continued, "you're right. We must consider that possibility. Quark reminded me that you are a valuable addition to this expedition. It would be foolish not to take advantage of your experience with battle strategy. And while it seems unlikely they've come to attack us, it wouldn't be prudent to ignore the potential threat entirely. So I'm asking you and your cadets to help us design a weapons system that can be used should their intentions prove hostile."

"Cool," Benn and Phan said at the same time.

"I still think we should include the miners," Keelar said.

"You may tell them what we've decided after the meeting," Quekri said.

"They should have some input," Keelar said.

"I'll entertain any suggestions they have later," Quekri said. "Any thoughts on weapons?"

"We should build a Las-cannon," Shiloh said. "Or a particle beam cannon."

Kammilee sighed. "I'm with Keelar. We should include the miners. They have Las-weapons, and they've said they're willing to defend us. Plus, if we build a Las-cannon or a particle beam cannon, we might provoke the Chinese."

"Kammilee's right," Keelar said. "We're here to learn, not to kill, not to commit atrocities like the ones still being committed on Earth. Let the miners defend us."

A loud buzz sounded from the Escala. But Paddon spoke up: "Look what our pacifism bought us on Earth. The Elite Ops attacked us. They would have wiped us out if not for Jeremiah and Devereaux. I say we build whatever weapons we can. We don't have to use them if it's not necessary. If we wait, it might be too late to defend ourselves."

"Perhaps we can study the issue for a few days," Fazzerel said. "Prepare our shuttle to intercept them in orbit and see what they're thinking."

Garthod said, "The shuttle would take three days to charge and provision."

"We only have a few days," Addam reminded them. "They'll be in orbit in two days unless they make straight for the surface. My guess is that they'll orbit a few times to verify potential landing sites and determine if we present any threat before they descend."

"We'll build Las-rifles," Aspen said. "The chem-fuel is nowhere near as complicated as it is for a Las-cannon. And a particle beam cannon is far too complicated. We can probably construct two Las-rifles a day. We could have six or maybe eight weapons ready by the time they land."

Quekri shrugged. "I hope it's for nothing. I hope they've just had problems with their communications system."

Dr. Wellon said, "What about shields? Can we build a few before they get here? And if they've got shields, which seems likely, our Las-rifles won't work against them."

Garthod said, "Shields are more complicated than Las-rifles. I doubt we'd have time to put together the materials we'd need to make an effective shield."

"Shields won't save us," Aspen said. "We'll use a dampening field to keep the hideout cave safe from their scanners. But the cave will only hold a dozen of us at most. We'll save that for Kammilee, Addam, Shiloh and a few Escala to help them build weapons—people like Garthod. The rest of us will use whatever weapons we can make or take from the colonists to defend the colony."

"I should help with defense," Addam said. "Put Phan in the hidey-hole."

"I want to fight," Phan said.

"We can't all fight," Benn said. "Addam, you're our best engineer. If it comes down to a fight, you'll have to go into the cave with Kammilee and Shiloh to build Las-rifles and prepare a counter-attack. The rest of us will hold them off as long as we can. Perhaps we can bring down the main tunnel on top of them as they advance, propping up a few mini-caves with grav-suspensors."

"Multiple explosions!" Phan jumped to his feet, bopping his head up and down. "We've got tons of rock we can use as shrapnel."

Now Shiloh rose to her feet as well. "The ideal detonation," she said, her voice trembling with excitement, "would produce dozens of shards per boulder. Properly directed, they'd form a lethal shower."

Kammilee stayed seated, shaking her head as she wrapped her arms around her stomach.

Quekri nodded to Aspen. "I'll leave the details to you. Tell us what you need. But remember, this is all just precautionary. We won't be the aggressors. All right, people. We've got a lot of work to do in the next few days. Let's collect every bit of information we have on mind transfer. Whatever else we do, we must save Devereaux."

Chapter 17

Inside the quarantine bubble, Jeremiah held Sophie against his chest, savoring the milk and talcum powder smell of her as she fidgeted. Perhaps the nurses' preparations clued her in that her next painful treatment was due. He glanced out the window at Hannah and the two Elite Ops troopers watching and no doubt listening. Mustering up his courage, he began to sing *Children's Moon*. He sang badly, his voice hoarse, his throat hurting, but Sophie appeared to enjoy the song. She quieted in his arms and grabbed his index finger in her tiny fist. When her eyes met his, he no longer cared if he looked silly. He was determined to do whatever it took to bring her through this illness, even though all he could do at the moment was comfort her.

Before the song ended, Sophie drifted off to sleep. Jeremiah continued to shuffle around the room. Despite the painkillers, he still felt some discomfort with every movement except when he held Sophie; she seemed to derive as much pleasure from their sessions as he did. And Dr. Poole had told him that the more time he spent with Sophie, the better she progressed. So he treasured this time, even though he felt guilty when away from his desk.

He'd reached an impasse in his search for the Sally cells, one that he doubted he could overcome by himself. He'd examined all the Intel CINTEP's analysts had provided, all their summaries and estimates as to numbers of Sally cells and probable future targets. It all made sense when looked at chronologically—the gradual buildup of the organization into a global network—but Jeremiah sensed something off about it. The pattern felt too flawed, the locations of known attacks too well spaced. The whole thing lacked the randomness a computer would have brought to the opponents' strategy. Why was Sally not using a computer to choose her targets?

It was good news for him because it meant that a human might be able to find this Sally organization. Maybe he couldn't do it himself, but he knew one man who might be able to help: Elias Leach, the former head of CINTEP and the man who'd ordered Jeremiah's son abducted. When it came to tactics, no one was as well versed as Eli.

And no one was as cruel.

Eli had done what he thought necessary, creating a threat that would unite the world. He was still alive, Jeremiah knew, hidden away somewhere. But Eli wouldn't run far. He needed to be near the power center—his drug of choice. So for the past few days Jeremiah had been focused on finding Eli.

But he still had no idea where Eli was. Even Lendra's searches had come up empty. How could that be? Someone powerful had to be hiding him, but who?

Over the past year, Jeremiah had deliberately chosen not to search for Eli, afraid that if he found the former head of CINTEP, he'd murder him—rip out Eli's beating heart and crush it in his fingers: squeeze the little man's neck until his head popped off. Not just for turning Joshua into Curtik, who murdered millions in the Las-cannon attacks last year, but also for indirectly causing Catherine's suicide.

To steady himself, Jeremiah held Sophie up to his face and inhaled her scent. She squeezed his finger tighter, as if even in sleep she could sense his anger. Somehow Jeremiah's rage toward Eli decreased, mitigated by Sophie's life force.

If only Devereaux were able to help. But he was in a coma and Quark didn't think he would live much longer. So Jeremiah was going to have to find Eli himself.

He flashed on Jay-Edgar.

So far, Jay-Edgar had been above suspicion, for he had assisted in every search and even offered suggestions to make them more effective, but he'd always been loyal to Eli too. He was one of the few people with the expertise to manipulate the feeds so as to create the illusion that Eli had vanished. Could he be involved? Jeremiah recalled that Jay-Edgar had supplied the best analytical work pertaining to the Sally cells. Perhaps he'd gotten that information from Eli.

And Mrs. Harris: might she be assisting Eli as well?

Jeremiah knew that Eli craved the emotional bonds he formed with his favored few. He himself had been among those favored few, back before Eli betrayed him. Mrs. Harris was another. The old cleaning woman seemed an incongruous choice until he remembered that she and Eli had been lovers years ago. Was it possible they were still involved?

Jeremiah thought back to all the times he'd seen her in Eli's office over the years. He had spoken with her on many occasions when they were both in the office late—he searching for his missing son, she cleaning up Eli's office after everyone else had gone home.

She hadn't told him much, but she intrigued him enough that he had conducted a little research, and learned that she had worked at the hospice center as a doctor, caring for Eli's dying wife Emerra. She and Eli had begun a relationship, and she eventually assisted Eli in euthanizing Emerra. When the center discovered the act, Dr. Harris lost her license and served two years in prison. Eli offered to get her license reinstated, but she refused, choosing instead to work as a cleaning woman, like her mother.

She insulted Eli often and he denigrated her as well. Was that foreplay for them? Their relationship might be ongoing. Jay-Edgar would know the truth.

He'd had his suspicions about Mrs. Harris in the past and he had lately examined surveillance footage that captured her movements coming to and leaving CINTEP. He'd pored over surveillance footage going back weeks, tracking the elderly cleaning woman as she followed the same route to and from work. But the footage hadn't shown him anything out of the ordinary. Could Jay-Edgar have manipulated that as well?

Sophie awoke, startled or in pain, and began to cry. Jeremiah started on another song: The Rumble-Tumble Belly Flop Stomp. He put a lot of effort into it, bouncing and stomping around the room until Sophie's tears stopped. Soon she giggled in delight. As Jeremiah finished up the song, he glanced at one of the nurses, who signaled that it was time for Sophie's next treatment. She eased over and held out her hands for the baby. When Sophie spotted the biohazard suit, she started crying again.

"It's okay," Jeremiah tried to console her as he handed her over, Sophie clinging to his index finger with her tiny fist, her face reddening as she howled in protest. She stared into his eyes with a ferocity that seemed highly intelligent: a reprimand to her protector for abandoning her. "It's all right, Sophie. I know it hurts, but we have to make you well." He gently disengaged his finger from her hand and turned to the decontamination area, a hollow ache emptying his chest, his heart breaking once again.

Hannah and the two unarmored Elite Ops troopers, Gil and Finn, waited outside the decontamination area. All three looked slightly off. Hannah's eyes were red, as if she'd been crying. Gil was overly solicitous, holding out Jeremiah's jacket and helping him on with it, while Finn handed over Jeremiah's PlusPhone, keeping his hand on Jeremiah's for just that extra half-second. He wondered at their odd behavior, but he had more important things to think about right now.

"I need to see Jay-Edgar," he said.

Hannah grabbed his arm.

"I think you need to call Curtik in London first," she said as she steered him toward his office. "They're fitting his new prosthetic hand tomorrow. It would do you both good to talk."

"You're right, thanks." Entering his office, Jeremiah glanced out the window. The nearly empty street below felt spooky. Everyone in the city feared contagion after Dr. Jaidev broadcast a warning that people should stay home unless they absolutely needed to work: police officers and firefighters, doctors and nurses, those who delivered food and medicine. Wind swirled beneath gray clouds, driving debris into the gutter as a man tightened the collar on his dark jacket, looking furtively about before crossing in the middle of the block.

Jeremiah felt the weight of Hannah's stare as he hefted his PlusPhone. Even Gil and Finn had squeezed into the office, as if fearful of an attack here in the heart of CINTEP. Ridiculous. But they were causing no harm, so he let them stay.

He called Curtik. Hannah stood to the side of his desk, her back against the wall while the two Elite Ops troopers maintained their wasteful vigil.

Curtik answered his PlusPhone, looking pale, his dark hair disheveled. "Hi."

"How are you?"

Curtik held up his bandaged hand briefly. "I'm fine, okay? I deserved to have my hand blown up."

"Anyone can make a mistake." Jeremiah tried to keep his tone light. Why should he be afraid to talk to his own son? He dreaded the possibility that Curtik might some day refuse to take his calls. "Tomorrow's the big day, right? The new hand?"

Curtik nodded. "A robotic one. Later a replacement grown from my own tissue."

"You did well, Son," Jeremiah said, meaning it. "The first mission's always the toughest."

"Yeah," Curtik replied, his voice sounding flat as he stared blankly at the PlusPhone camera.

"I think you're going to like the new hand." Jeremiah smiled. "So much power. You might not even want to go to a replacement."

"Maybe."

"How long will you be in the hospital?"

"I gotta go," Curtik said, "It's time for my pre-surgical exam."

Curtik disconnected before Jeremiah could say goodbye or wish him luck. At least he hadn't shut down completely. The lines of communication between them, however strained, remained open.

Next Jeremiah called Zora, whose face brightened into a smile as she made the connection. Her blond curls dangled to her shoulders and her brown eyes looked large and bright on the PlusPhone's screen. "Jeremiah, I'm so glad you called."

"How's Curtik doing?" Jeremiah asked.

"He's angry," Zora answered, her smile fading. "And depressed. I don't think he expected the opposition to lay a finger on him. Now he's isolating. And I don't know how to draw him out."

"You have to be patient," Jeremiah said. "He'll come around, especially once you get another assignment. The London Sally cell is still around. Lendra has finally released all our data to Britain's Combined Intelligence Service, so Major Somers will continue as your liaison. From now on all orders will come from him. Okay?"

"Right."

"You follow Ned's instructions and you'll be fine."

"I will," Zora replied. "And how are you doing?" Zora studied him through the PlusPhone connection. "You look tired. Are you still on your pain medication? Are you taking it easy?"

"Yes, Mommy," Jeremiah replied. "I'm fine."

Zora's face fell, her eyes glistening with moisture, and Jeremiah realized he'd offended her. "Sorry," he continued. "A bad joke."

"I know you think I'm a child," Zora's voice sounded raspy, as if she'd come down with a cold. "But I'm not. I know what I want. And I also know how you overwork yourself, how you sacrifice for everyone else."

Jeremiah didn't know how to answer that. He knew Zora worshipped him, leading her to ascribe to him qualities he didn't have. He wanted to tell her he wasn't worth her adulation but he feared she would take that truth as noble humility and only increase her affection for him.

"I talked with Lendra," Zora continued. "She thinks you're close to finding another Sally cell. And I think if you do, you'll go running off to take care of it by yourself. I'm asking you not to."

"I'll take Hannah with me to check out any leads."

"It's just that . . . I don't . . ." Her voice quavered before trailing off.

"Don't worry," he said. "I'll be careful. You be careful too. You and Curtik have both been injured now. You're not invincible, either one of you. Follow Ned's advice. He's survived in this business a long time. That's no accident."

"So you really do care about me?"

"Of course I do."

"You just don't love me?" Zora's voice sounded plaintive, breaking ever so slightly. She blushed as she said it, but her eyes locked on his with the intensity of expectation. Jeremiah glanced at Hannah, who stared straight ahead, her jaw clamped shut. "Is Hannah there?" Zora asked.

"Yes," Jeremiah answered. "She's always here. So are Gil and Finn— the fish team. Lendra won't let me have a moment alone. Like you, she thinks I'll go running off on my own if I locate a cell."

Zora's blush darkened, but her eyes never left his.

He found it astonishing that with the world on the brink of destruction, all humanity poised to die off, Zora was thinking about her feelings. Or perhaps it wasn't so strange. Wasn't he doing the same in his own way? Perhaps when death surrounded you, the desire to connect with a loved one was normal. So he could only give one answer.

"I do love you, Zora."

"But not the way I want you to."

"I'm afraid I still see you as a child, no matter what the courts say. I'm sorry if that hurts you. You have an adult's body, an adult's intellect, a wonderful personality and a caring heart, but emotionally you're not ready for love. Not with any man, and certainly not with me."

Zora's eyes glistened again. She reached up to wipe them dry. "I guess I just wanted you to know how I feel," she said, "that I'll always love you. In case something should happen, I wanted you to know."

"You'll be fine, Zora. Ned will look out for you."

Zora looked at him then with a sadness he couldn't comprehend, her face crumpling. Before he could say any more, she disconnected, leaving him with the image of her sorrow in that last moment, the tears just beginning to leak from her eyes. Was she afraid for herself, or for him?

His hand itched to hit the redial icon.

"Not a word," he warned Hannah, who stood rigidly, staring straight ahead, as if the opposite wall were the most interesting thing she'd ever seen.

"I didn't say anything."

"She's confused. She only thinks she loves me. If she knew the real me, she'd run away."

Hannah glared at him. "Stop doing that."

"What?"

"Just stop it."

Jeremiah shrugged and then called Ned. "I'm sorry about this, sticking you with two teenagers, neither one of whom is thinking very clearly at the moment."

"They performed all right," Ned replied, "all things considered. They just need a little seasoning. Frankly, the biggest disappointment of the mission was that the Sallies wanted you and not me." Ned grinned, exposing his white, even teeth.

"After this," Jeremiah told him, "you'll be on their list. Don't worry. I'm sure they want you dead."

"I hope so," Ned replied. "Especially after I smoked 'em out in Indonesia. I'm tired of you getting all the glory."

Jeremiah laughed, then cleared his throat. "Listen, Ned. I'm worried about Zora. She's extremely vulnerable right now. She's got some damn fool crush on me."

Ned rubbed his chin as he gave the problem due consideration.

After a wait of several seconds, Jeremiah said. "Well, out with it. What are you thinking?"

"It is confusing," Ned replied. "Frankly, I can't understand why she's not in love with me. Not that I want her to be, but I'm so much more handsome and intelligent."

Ned waited until Jeremiah smiled and then said, "She's lost her father, so my guess is you've taken his place."

"How do I get her to stop loving me?"

"Just be yourself." Ned grinned.

Jeremiah shook his head. "Can you be serious?"

"I am serious. Listen, Jeremiah. There's nothing wrong with a little hero worship. She'll grow out of it eventually, find a nice boy, and you'll just be a warm memory. In the meantime, be her friend. Don't pull her feathers before she can fly."

Jeremiah nodded. "Thanks, Ned. You always know what to say."

"That's because I'm a genius. Tell Lendra I deserve a raise."

"You're paid way too much already. Because of your exorbitant salary, I had to drink a domestic beer last night."

"Good Lord! Did you manage to keep it down?"

"Barely."

"The sacrifices you office types put up with. I commend you. Don't worry." Ned winked. "I'll keep you in the loop." He disconnected.

Jeremiah wished he could call Devereaux too, though that bond was probably forever broken now. He felt lucky to have people like Ned in his life. And Zora. And Curtik. Which made Jeremiah think of Sophie. He wondered how her treatment was going, decided it was too early to call Dr. Poole and ask. He could feel the electric buzz of pain lurking beneath the anesthetic as the virus attacked his joints, eager for the drugs to wear off. His hands shook with tension.

When Hannah put a hand on his shoulder he almost jumped. "Very well done," she said. "You're not such a grouch after all."

Jeremiah looked up at her and noticed the softness in her eyes, the slightly parted lips, her head tilted to one side. He knew that look. He dreaded it. The last thing he needed was another admirer.

"Time to visit Jay-Edgar," he said.

Gil said, "We can bring him here if you'd prefer."

"No. I want Lendra in on this as well."

When he got to his feet, he felt a deep twinge of pain in his knees and winced. Finn and Hannah both reached for him, stopping when he glared at them. "What's gotten into you all of a sudden? I'm not a cripple. Let's go."

He entered Lendra's office without knocking, Hannah and the two Elite Ops troopers behind him. Lendra was sitting at her desk, staring ahead blankly in that way she had when accessing her interface, while Jay-Edgar was examining footage from numerous sources.

"What's going on?" Lendra asked.

Jeremiah looked at Jay-Edgar. "We've got a problem."

Jay-Edgar shrank in his chair. He said, "I've been watching you, waiting for you. Just now, I saw you with Sophie—and with Curtik and Zora and Ned. And I realized that I put my trust in the wrong man."

"You're not going to deny it?"

Jay-Edgar shook his head.

Lendra said, "Would someone tell me what's going on?"

Jeremiah said, "Jay-Edgar knows where Eli is hiding. In fact, he's been manipulating the CCTV and surveillance feeds to ensure that we don't find Eli."

Lendra looked at Jay-Edgar, then nodded slowly. "Why?"

Jay-Edgar put his head in his hands.

Jeremiah said, "He thought he was doing the right thing. He rationalized his actions. Everyone does it, Lendra—you, me, President Hope, every nation on Earth and every person in every nation. We all cheat the rest of the world every day in little ways. We explain away our selfish behavior by saying that the world isn't our responsibility or that other people don't get to tell us how to live our lives. We make our choices and let others worry about the world. But not this time, right, Jay-Edgar? This time, if we fail, humanity goes away."

Jay-Edgar dropped his hands and said, "I'm sorry."

"I know you are," Jeremiah replied.

"He told me it was necessary—that he couldn't help us if he was in prison."

"Of course he did. I understand."

Lendra said, "Well, I sure as hell don't. You're a damn traitor."

"Is he?" Jeremiah said. "Any more than you? You failed to give the Brits all the Intel you had on the London Sally cell until after Curtik was hurt. You thought that holding a little something back wouldn't hurt anyone and might give you an advantage at some future time. Does that make you a traitor?"

Lendra held up her hands. "That's different."

Jeremiah shrugged. "It always is."

"So what do we do now?"

"We get Eli, bring him back here and see what he knows."

Lendra turned to Jay-Edgar. "Where is he?"

"In an apartment on 91st Avenue, near Hobart Street."

Jeremiah said, "Give Hannah the details. Gil and Finn, suit up. And bring a couple friends to cover the exits. I don't think Eli's dangerous. Probably no bombs or booby-traps. That's not his style. I just want you to form a perimeter and detain anyone who comes out. We leave in twenty minutes."

Hannah frowned, while Gil and Finn eased toward the door.

"Let me guess," Jeremiah said. "You were expecting me to run off on my own, slip away from my protectors and do that macho 'man alone' thing."

"Actually," Hannah replied, "yes."

"In the old days I would have. Not any more."

"What about me?" Jay-Edgar said. "Should I find someone to man the comm desk? Should I turn myself in?"

Lendra looked at Jeremiah.

"We'll discuss it later," Jeremiah said. "For now, I want Eli to think that you're still on his side. Keep him in the dark until I give you the word. Then warn him that we're on our way."

Chapter 18

Inside his basement apartment, Elias Leach faced the wall and its six screens showing various feeds from around the world. Yet he found it difficult to pay attention. He felt trapped here. Every day he was confronted with the same small table and two chairs in the kitchenette, the countertop and bank of cabinets next to the stove and refrigerator, the sofa that converted to a bed beneath the sole window, a reinforced plas-glass unit darkened for privacy, the shabby dresser and the single, large armchair where he now sat. He felt tiny and insignificant.

Why should that be?

He'd essentially confined himself to a similar space at CINTEP. But there, he'd been in control. Was that the only difference or was he feeling loneliness for human companionship?

He turned to where Manyara Harris was unpacking groceries, then reached up and scratched at his face, aggravating the ragged furrows that marked the many times he'd clawed it in the past. A trickle of blood seeped out as he raked his fingernails across his cheeks.

"Your face is pretty ugly already," Manyara said. "But you go ahead and gouge it some more. You can't make it any worse."

Elias turned from the screens, where he had been following the news closely. The two middle screens played the EuroNews Network and the 24-Hour Real News Network, which currently focused on the Greek threat to invade Turkey over fears that illegal immigration was spreading the Susquehanna Virus. Bulgaria and Romania offered support to Greece, Syria was sending troops to Turkey, and continuing hostilities between India and China after terrorists detonated a nuclear weapon in Mumbai last year threatened to escalate the conflict worldwide.

The screen to the right displayed images of the White House's reconstruction and other rebuilding efforts in the various cities that had been destroyed by the Las-cannons. The two screens on the left provided updates on the virus, sent to him via quantum flux link from Jay-Edgar: recent outbreaks and movements of suspected Sally terrorists. The final screen on the right showed images taken from the building's eight surveillance cameras.

"If you'd give me my medicine, I wouldn't have to scratch myself," he replied.

"All you had to do was ask."

"Where the hell is Jeremiah?" Elias said.

"You want him to catch you?"

"Of course not. But he's been back with CINTEP long enough that he should have found me by now, no matter what Jay-Edgar is doing to hide me."

"So?"

"He doesn't care enough to hunt me down. I'm irrelevant. I can understand him wanting to kill me, but how can he think I'm not worth the effort?"

"You're a strange, strange man."

Elias got to his feet as Manyara prepared his hypo-pad. He took a moment to study the street outside. Did Jeremiah really think he no longer mattered, or was he ignoring Elias as a form of torture? Every time Manyara visited he expected Jeremiah to follow her; every time, the street was empty. He felt an almost unbearable hollowness in his chest, a dryness in the mouth. Was that fear of Jeremiah finding him or fear that Jeremiah had moved past the hatred?

One of the reasons he hadn't run was because if Jeremiah wanted to find him, he would. No hiding place offered a safe refuge when Jeremiah was on the hunt. And no country wanted him anyway after what he'd done. But he refused to apologize for that. He'd done what he had to do. It hadn't worked out the way he intended. But that was largely due to the escalating threat from the Susquehanna Virus. So now he fed helpful information to Jay-Edgar and waited.

And waited.

"Nobody followed me," Manyara said. "Why do you always look for him?"

Elias looked at her for a moment before returning his attention to the screens. "He'll come."

"You're pathetic."

Elias laughed in spite of himself. He got to his feet and made his way to her side. "I know," he said.

Elias reached Manyara and winced as she slapped the hypo-pad to the back of his hand with more force than necessary. The neo-dopamine compound was necessary to keep him from scratching his face. Almost from the first moment he'd been injected with nanobots to save his life, he'd been convinced he could feel them moving about inside his skin. If he didn't receive a dose of neo-dopamine twice a week, his face began to itch uncontrollably, forcing him to claw at it, gouging out deep furrows in his cheeks.

Manyara had told him that it was a common reaction among people with a Frankenstein complex—a fear of artificial humans. The term had been coined during the twentieth century by Isaac Asimov and accurately reflected Elias' phobia toward the Elite Ops and nanotechnology, although Elias thought the fear was perfectly logical.

The Elite Ops had nano-computers swimming in their bloodstreams, communicating with cerebral monitors implanted behind their foreheads. They were part human, part machine: terrifying.

And now he had some of those same nanobots in his system. Repair nanobots, to be sure, but nanobots just the same. He'd told himself many times that his fear was nothing more than an emotional weakness. Yet he'd been unable to eliminate the phobia through traditional psychological methods. And he'd always been afraid of pumping medication into his body, wary of harming his magnificent brain.

After he'd found himself exiled and hiding, clawing himself bloody for hours each day, Manyara had finally brought him neo-dopamine. He'd been concerned that the drug would cloud his mind. Surprisingly, however, it had a clarifying effect. He could see now why Lendra had once been addicted to it. It enhanced thought processes if taken in moderate doses.

Manyara said, "Your scraggly face gets uglier every day."

Elias laughed. "You are a pure delight—all sunshine and roses. You know, I find you extremely attractive." He reached for her, but she knocked his hand away. "Come on, Darling. How about joining me on the bed for a spell?"

"I can't." Manyara patted his cheek. "I'm running late."

She started to turn away, but he grabbed her wrist. "Please," he said. "Stay with me a while?"

Manyara wrapped her arms around him. "They'll be expecting me to show up for my shift soon. I can't stay long."

"Just an hour."

"I have to go," Manyara said. But she continued to hold him.

"I swear you're driving me crazy on purpose," Elias said. "Come on. Give me a little love."

"Next time," Manyara said.

"That's what you said last time."

"They're going to get suspicious," Manyara said as she released him. She grabbed her heavy bag, checked the peephole and stepped outside. Elias followed her progress on the surveillance cameras as she made her way to the street. By the time she reached the end of the walkway, he had managed to return his attention to the job at hand. He needed to find Susquehanna Sally. If he wanted to have any hope of returning to CINTEP, he had to bring in Sally himself. Part of him knew that was never going to happen; Lendra had ensconced herself too deeply. But part of him would never give it up. CINTEP was in his soul.

A warning sounded from Jay-Edgar, followed by a brief message: "On their way. Just found out about it."

Elias's stomach fluttered. So Jeremiah was finally here. Glancing at the far right screen, Elias saw Manyara stop suddenly, her body stiffening. An Elite Ops trooper, fully armored, Las-rifle extended in one hand, approached her and took her by the arm. When he holstered his Las-rifle and wrenched her bag away from her, she turned to one of the cameras and mouthed what sounded like "I'm sorry."

Breath quickening, pulse pounding, Elias stared at the gigantic, robotic creature. Sweat beaded on his brow. His mouth dried up.

A bolthole existed at the far end of the apartment, through the closet door into a tunnel leading to the next building over. Jeremiah might not know of it, but he probably had more than one Elite Ops trooper working with him. Yes, Elias could make out three other Elite Ops troopers angling in toward the building, no doubt checking their scanners for bio signs. Running wouldn't save him. Nothing would save him now.

On the counter in the kitchenette he saw a chef's knife on a butcher block. He smiled as he thought of attacking Jeremiah with it. All he'd manage to do would be to anger Jeremiah more. He was surprised he wasn't more afraid. Part of him was glad that Jeremiah had finally deemed him worthy of pursuing.

What form would the retribution take? A quick death? Or would the Elite Ops torture him first?

For a long time the building's camera views showed only the Elite Ops troopers. Elias fought to maintain his composure, forcing himself to breathe evenly. Where the hell was Jeremiah? Had he sent the Elite Ops to do his dirty work for him? Did he think Elias wasn't worth the effort? No. There he was, exiting a vehicle and striding up the sidewalk toward the building, Hannah Swenson, a young CINTEP agent, at his side. She held a Las-pistol in her hand; Jeremiah carried no weapon. He needed none. He could break Elias' neck with one blow.

Elias wondered if the neo-dopamine had any impact on how he felt. He probably should be terrified. Even though he'd always known Jeremiah would come, and even though he expected to die, it was a relief in some ways to finally have it all end, to have Jeremiah acknowledge his importance. He was no longer tormented by the potentiality of Jeremiah's vengeance; it had arrived. As Hannah disabled the security system, Elias found himself timing her. Occasionally he glanced at Jeremiah, standing behind Hannah, looking around as if expecting Elias to run. Behind Jeremiah, the Elite Ops trooper gripped Manyara's arm.

Fifty seconds after she began, Hannah succeeded in bypassing the lock and alarms. She and Jeremiah entered the building, followed by the Elite Ops trooper and Manyara.

It took them less than another minute to reach Elias' apartment and broach the lock. Elias stood, trembling slightly, and placed his hand on the back of his chair, facing the door. When Jeremiah entered the room, Hannah dodged to the side behind him, her Las-pistol aimed squarely at Elias's chest.

Elias nodded. "Jeremiah," he said as the big Elite Ops trooper guided Manyara inside. "I wondered what was keeping you."

Elias forced himself to look away from the trooper and at Jeremiah instead. For a moment no one spoke or moved. Jeremiah stood still, his face frowning in concentration. Was he listening for danger?

Elias felt inexplicably happy seeing Jeremiah again, as if his long-lost son had returned. But he was shocked at the pain lines on Jeremiah's face.

He said, "No booby traps here." He gestured toward Manyara. "You can ask Manyara, if you like. And I'd appreciate it if you let her go. All she did was help me. She doesn't know anything. She's just a friend."

Jeremiah waved a hand at the trooper and Manyara pulled her arm free. She rubbed slowly where the trooper had grabbed her as she made her way to the sofa. When she sat, she stared at Elias, her eyebrows raised in query.

Elias closed his eyes in apology for a moment, then said, "How are you, Jeremiah? I heard about your reckless exploits, infecting yourself with the virus. You make me very proud."

Jeremiah took two steps forward before stopping, his hands unclenching as he glared at Elias. Then the intensity left his eyes and he spoke in a calm, unhurried voice: "You remember Hannah Swenson?"

"Of course," Elias replied. "A promising agent. How are you?"

"Fine," Hannah blurted out. She stared at Jeremiah as if uncertain of her role.

"I'd offer you something to drink," Elias said, "but I'm guessing you would refuse."

Hannah looked from Jeremiah to Elias and back, finally deciding no immediate danger presented itself and lowering her Las-pistol to her side.

"I won't apologize, Jeremiah," Elias said. "I did what needed to be done. We all had to make sacrifices for the greater good."

Jeremiah stared at him—no hatred, no rage, only a frown. How he wished Jeremiah would smile at him, just once more.

"The plan should have worked," Elias found himself saying. "And for a time, it did. But this virus trumped everything."

"You've been looking for Susquehanna Sally," Jeremiah finally said.

Elias nodded.

"Have you found anything of value?"

"As I'm sure you know," Elias said, "everything I put together I gave to Jay-Edgar."

"Not holding anything back?"

"No."

"So is there any reason I shouldn't kill you now?"

Elias felt his heart thump. "A good many," he said. "But perhaps none that override your need for vengeance."

Jeremiah tensed. He looked like he was coiling for an attack—legs bent slightly, shoulders forward, hands outstretched. Elias, having seen him take this kind of stance during training simulations just before pouncing, shivered. At least he could take comfort from knowing Jeremiah cared enough to dispatch him personally.

"I know I can help if you give me a chance," Elias said. He heard the quaver in his voice, detested it. "I'm close. I just need a few more days."

"I doubt you're that close."

Elias tilted his head in concession. "We'd have a much better chance of finding her together than we do separately."

Jeremiah closed his eyes for a moment and Elias felt his stomach fluttering with something akin to hope.

"A lot of people want you dead," Jeremiah said.

"I understand. But—"

"Spare me your rationalizations," Jeremiah said. "You'll be coming back with us. It took me a while to figure out that Jay-Edgar was manipulating the feeds."

"Is he okay?"

"As far as I know."

"I know you think I'm a monster, Jeremiah. But if you look deep inside yourself, you'll see that I'm a visionary. I act boldly. I'm willing to accept short-term disasters for the sake of larger goals. Our leaders fear the consequences of brutally necessary action and therefore move cautiously, increasing the risk of greater catastrophe in the future."

"I'm sorry. I didn't bring along any medals to bestow upon you."

Elias smiled briefly. "I'm just saying. You're a brilliant analyst. But you tend to think logically and with a utilitarian bent. I'm not encumbered by that weakness. Together we'll find Sally. I know we will."

"You'd better hope we do. Because if we fail, I'll kill you."

Elias shivered. He'd hoped that when Jeremiah found him, there would be some acknowledgement of the past, some residue of good feeling that might mitigate the anger. But Jeremiah gave off only cold disdain, and that struck him worse than he could have imagined.

Chapter 19

A few blocks north of Bayswater Road and Hyde Park, Sally23 looked out the darkened plas-glass window of the flat she and her fellow conspirators now occupied. She refused to cry; she refused to let them see how desperate she'd become. Across the street, stone owls and chimneys stood atop almost every roof. She'd rarely noticed them before, even though they were ubiquitous in London. Only now, as death encroached, did she observe such detail. How many other little things have I neglected to see?

"Watch it!" Wally5 said.

She turned as a metallic clatter sounded. Wally3, Wally5 and Wally6 stood before a canopy of protective plastic, filling canisters with the newest strain of the virus.

"Oops," Wally3 said.

"You scared the hell out of me," Wally6 said.

"It's just a cover," Wally3 said.

"You almost gave me a heart attack," Wally5 said. He caught Sally23's eye and winked. "Don't worry. We're fine over here."

He returned his attention to his fellow Asians, short and thin and nerdy. They seemed cheerful. Why were they doing this? Had they originally volunteered? She suspected they were under some sort of compulsion now because of their total unconcern over the future.

This new version of the virus, Sally2 claimed, would be the most potent yet. Sally23 had only caught a glimpse at the molecular structure before being shooed away, but it looked extremely lethal. She replayed the schematic of the modified virus in her head as she watched the Wallys, their gloved hands placed through the gasket-sealed openings to the materials on the counter, carefully measure the various ingredients that made up each aerosol bomb. Yes, this virus was more powerful. But if her recall was accurate, it also had a flaw. She said nothing. If only she could get another look at it to be sure. Not that there was anything she could do about it anyway, but it would be nice to know if she was right. And she couldn't ask Sally2 to see it without raising suspicions. Sally2 was already on the verge of irrationality over the loss of Andre.

On the south wall, the lanky Wally2 sat before a series of screens he'd set up. He fed incoming data to one of the screens while Sally2 looked over his shoulder like a vulture, dark and menacing. She had the muscular look of an Escala. No wonder Brosk had thought she might be one. And perhaps she was. Perhaps she wanted to live.

Wally2 said, "That's an awfully long message."

Sally2 said, "The message will be considerably shorter. Twenty-three, can you come over here and help with the decoding?"

Sally23 stepped beside Wally2 and glanced at the long series of letters and numbers. She opened her PlusPhone's UNCRYPT program and began changing parameters as the program queried various nonsensical clusters.

"A message from Sally1 is rare," Sally2 said. "It's essential that we get this decoded as quickly as possible."

"So why am I here?" Wally2 asked. "Sally23 handles these."

"Sally23 needs to complete her assignment with Brosk. She may not be here to help you in the future. So you need to learn as much as you can about how she decrypts messages."

Sally23 felt her heart beating faster than normal. How soon was Sally2 planning to kill her? Soon, apparently.

"Things are falling apart out there." Sally2 gestured toward the other screens, which showed the Indian Army mobilizing along its borders with Bangladesh, Pakistan and China in an attempt to prevent virus-infected immigrants from reaching its populace. Meanwhile, China was also mobilizing troops along its borders. A few skirmishes had already occurred. "Look at all that destruction. Paranoia. Nations attacking each other for no reason. We already have a Sally cell in China. It's too late for them."

Sally2 turned to Sally23. "You saw what Jones did. And those other two, especially the black woman—all three were enhanced. That's what humans will become someday if we don't stop them. Can you imagine a planet of super-humans waging war on each other? What would wars be like if people like Jones and Brosk were fighting them?"

Or you? Sally23 wondered. She shrugged, trying to maintain a calm demeanor, emulating Brosk's control. It was important that she seem completely on board with the plan. "You're preaching to the choir," she said as she continued finessing the UNCRYPT program. She glanced toward the wall screen that showed Trogan on a cot, drugs keeping him docile. She could recall no instance where he had acted anything other than honorably. His real crime was that he was nano- and genetically enhanced. If all humans were like him, perhaps the Sally movement wouldn't have become necessary.

Sally2 began to pace. "Hurry up," she said. "We must learn what Sally1 wants."

Sally23 said, "The program can only go so fast. Do you want me to check on Brosk while we're waiting?"

"No. I'll do it." Sally2 made her way to Brosk's room and stepped inside. She closed the door behind her, but Sally23 watched the screen. Brosk looked to be asleep. Sally2 bent over him, checking the IV drip, which was almost empty. She changed it out with another packet. Sally23 wondered what she was giving him and why she was using an IV. It couldn't be the virus; she'd already infected him with that.

It felt strange suddenly, being under a death sentence. Before, when she felt so certain of what she was doing, when living felt so hard, death had felt distant and unimportant. Now, however, with the feelings she had developed for Trogan, and with the likelihood that the two of them would be sacrificed soon, she struggled to avoid panic.

Sally2 emerged from Brosk's room just as the program finished its decryption.

"Decoding complete," Sally23 said as Sally2 crossed over to her side. She read aloud the text on the screen: "Jones in DC, not London. Other CINTEP agents your position. Use all means available to isolate and eliminate agents and Brosk."

Kill Brosk?

Sally23 felt her heart thumping in her chest. Her throat constricted as a warm flush came over her face. Would Sally2 kill him immediately? She could feel her pulse racing and wondered for a moment if she was having a heart attack. Was the virus finally asserting itself?

"You okay?" Wally2 asked.

"This is a mistake," Sally23 replied.

Sally2 smiled. "I'll enjoy killing him."

"Not yet," Sally23 said. She took a deep breath, her thoughts fleeing in myriad directions. She collected herself as much as she could. "We need to use Brosk to attract the CINTEP agents. If we kill him now, how will we lure them in to eliminate them?"

Sally2 frowned for a moment, then shook her head as she sighed. "I know what you're up to."

Sally23 wondered if Sally2 could read the fear in her face. "We're all going to die. We've all been infected. Why kill Brosk now when he can still be of value to us?"

"Because Sally1 wants him dead."

"I thought this organization prized independent thinking, not blind adherence to orders that make no sense."

Wally2 stared at her, his mouth slightly open. The other Wallys stopped what they were doing too. They turned to watch her and Sally2, their eyes shifting between the two of them.

Sally2 glared at her, small spots of red appearing on her cheeks. "We don't question Sally1."

"She's human, like us. She can make mistakes. And this is one of them. Killing Brosk now means we won't be able to eliminate the other CINTEP agents. Our security team's gone. Our dispersal Sallies are out in the field. We're," Sally23 gestured to the room, "all that's left. We're not warriors. The Wallys are techs. Who does that leave to eliminate the CINTEP agents? You and me? How are we supposed to do that? The only way we can succeed is by luring them in again. And for that we need Brosk. We're supposed to be a separate cell. Let's act like one."

"I have other resources at my command. You think these few people," Sally2 gestured toward the Wallys, "are all there is?"

Sally23 heard something in Sally2's voice—a small catch, a pause, indecision—and she immediately understood that this small group in fact constituted the entirety of Sally2's team. Sally2 had always been a bit paranoid, reluctant to bring new recruits into the group. Her dispersal team consisted of only three other Sallies now that Sally16 had been killed in Indonesia. And she'd relied too heavily on Andre for security matters. So now that the CINTEP agents had destroyed Andre's squad, no one remained to carry out security tasks but the Wallys.

"Omigod." Sally23 shook her head. "We're the last remnants of this cell, aren't we? Jakarta was more than four times our size. I just assumed there were other squads I wasn't familiar with, but we're it. We're all that's left to carry out the mission."

Sally2's face colored. She spoke mechanically, as if she hadn't heard Sally23: "Sally8 returns today. Sally17 arrives tomorrow morning. And Sally18 will be back tomorrow night. It's essential that we continue providing canisters for them. We must have the deathblow ready for London. The Wallys will take care of that."

"Which still leaves the CINTEP agents," Sally23 said. She struggled to keep the hope out of her voice.

"You're right," Sally2 said. "We can use Brosk to destroy them. In fact, I've already implanted nano-explosives in his body."

The Wallys gasped.

Sally23 said, "Nano-explosives are notoriously unstable. They could blow up any time."

At least now she knew what the IV drips contained.

Sally2 said, "The nano-explosives will interface with the nanobots in his system, making him a walking time bomb. We'll also dress him in linked metallic clothing to maximize the detonation and spread of the virus. I want you to accompany him to Hyde Park and wait for the CINTEP agents to show."

"Hyde Park?"

"There's a concert scheduled for tomorrow. It will be packed."

"If it doesn't rain."

Sally2 waved her arms in dismissal. "When the agents arrive, you will retreat to a safe distance and detonate the charges in Brosk's body, killing him and the agents, after which you will disappear into the city. Most likely your cover has been blown, so you can't return to us and you can't leave the country. If you like, you can accelerate the progression of the virus in your system with a pill I will provide. Death will be quick and painless."

Sally23 stared at Sally2, feeling as if someone had just kicked her in the stomach. So this was how she was supposed to die, blown apart in an explosion alongside Brosk. Sally2 knew, of course, that there would be no escaping the CINTEP agents. She would also be controlling the detonator, only pretending to give that power to Sally23.

"And one more thing," Sally2 said. "I understand you may feel some temptation to run. It's a natural human impulse. But if you run, you'll just die that much sooner. And without the pill I provide, your death will be painful.

"Also, Brosk is infected by multiple strains of the virus. And he's been rigged to explode in less than forty-eight hours. Plus, I programmed him to believe that you were the one who infected him. I tweaked his anger response. So you'll have to maintain perfect control with the box. If you try to take him with you, you'll have to give him freedom of movement and he'll kill you. Understand?"

"Perfectly." Sally23 shrugged. She felt like throwing herself at Sally2, gouging out the older woman's eyes and beating her to death. No. Remember Brosk. Stay in control. "Any more surprises?"

Sally2 held up a small controller, her thumb on the button. "With this remote detonator, I can blow up Brosk anytime before the explosives in his body reach critical mass."

"You're making another mistake sending us to Hyde Park," Sally23 said. She found herself thinking rapidly, logically, piecing together the most efficient way to die. "We should change our modus operandi if you want to lure the CINTEP agents in. They'll know it's a trap if we go to a park again. Better to head for Heathrow or Gatwick—make it look like we're trying to get out of the country."

"You'd never get past security."

"We wouldn't try. We'd just get close. Or maybe we should try for King's Cross or Piccadilly—some well-populated area with lots of commuters. I could park Brosk on a bench and wait for the CINTEP agents to approach. When they get near him, I'd trigger the explosion. Of course, I'd probably have to stay with him. An unresponsive man on a bench might draw the police before CINTEP could arrive. But it would be an instantaneous death—no suffering."

Sally2 frowned slightly, her nose scrunching up as her eyes turned inward with thought. No doubt she was puzzling out why Sally23 would be so helpful in arranging her own murder. How marvelous the human brain, Sally23 thought, when even a non-enhanced human like me can read the signs of another person thinking. I'll take you down yet, you bitch.

"You might be right," Sally2 finally said. "But you couldn't even get on the tube with Brosk. Security's too tight in the underground. Anyway, my controller hasn't the range to reach that far. It has to be Hyde Park."

"Now who doesn't trust whom? Perhaps Brosk was right. Perhaps you don't intend to die, if you think that we all want to live so badly."

Sally23 stared at Sally2, meeting the taller woman's eyes with a challenge. She felt no fear in this moment. Death came inevitably.

Whether Sally2 killed her now or in Hyde Park, whether Brosk killed her or the virus did, whether she escaped to live another ten or twenty disease-ravaged years, death would eventually catch her. She no longer felt like running from it. Death or life: it made no difference.

Sally2 turned and walked away, disappearing into Brosk's room. Sally23 noticed Wally2 studying her. He sat back, his eyes widening slightly before he looked away. The Wallys along the wall continued to stare at her.

"What?" she asked, flinging out her arms.

"Nothing." The Asian Wallys jumped in unison before returning to their tasks, while Wally2 kept his head down as if fascinated by the incoming data stream. Standing beside him, Sally23 suddenly remembered the biometric equipment in Brosk's room. Sally2 was probably looking over the recorded data from Sally23's implant, checking her blood pressure, pulse and emotional responses, seeking any sign of deception. Good luck with that, you bitch. I'm serious. I don't care anymore. We're all going to die—and especially you. I'll make sure of that—somehow.

Chapter 20

The Spook Hotel, so-called because it was where Britain's Combined Intelligence Service housed its visitors, struck Zora as an eerie place. Located in the old Scotland Yard building, it gave off an intimidating vibe. Its windows had been replaced with screens showing images of London landmarks like Big Ben, Westminster Bridge and the London Eye. But she knew they were false, like the "windows" on the Moon.

Last night, while studying the files on mind transference in preparation for Devereaux's procedure today, she'd heard a couple having loud sex in the room next door. The screaming and moaning had led her to fantasize about Jeremiah, despite her efforts to stay focused on her task. She wanted him to touch her, caress her, pleasure her the way the man next door was doing to his partner. But even the fantasy died as the logical part of her brain told her it would never happen, that Jeremiah was too noble and principled to make love to a woman he deemed a girl.

She walked into the lobby, having gotten less than an hour of sleep, her neck stiff, and spotted the two Eastern European massage therapists who flirted with her every time she passed. Handsome men with dark hair and tattoos all over their muscular arms, they played cards night and day. As usual, one of them called out to her: "We give good massage.

Loosen muscles. You relax." He spoke in an accent that reminded her of Crazy Vigg, who had given his life on the Moon so that others might live.

She stopped and shrugged. "Okay."

"Okay?" They jumped to their feet. "You not regret. We fix you up good."

They led her to a small room off the lobby with two massage tables and a screen she disrobed behind. When she emerged wearing only a towel, they gestured to one of the tables—no flirting now. They radiated calm. Music came from hidden speakers, soft and low and probably embedded with subliminal messages of relaxation. Already she felt better. She climbed onto the table and they oiled up their hands. Sliding her towel off, one of them began working her lower body, while the other concentrated on her neck and back. Again she thought of Jeremiah. How would it feel to have his hands on her body?

Then she thought of Devereaux and felt ashamed. What would it be like to be imprisoned in a robot? Would Devereaux still be himself? The mind-body connection is incredibly strong. How would being separated from his body affect Devereaux's mind?

Plus, caution dictated that they copy his mind rather than wipe it and transfer it to the organic computer. That way, if something went wrong, they would still have the original mind of Walt Devereaux so they could try again. And it was an easier procedure—less chance of a cascading system failure. But if they did that, how would Devereaux react to being two different entities, with a consciousness in each? Frankly, the whole thing scared her.

The masseur working her legs moved up to her rump, causing her to tense.

"Relax," he said as he kneaded her muscles. "I not hurt you."

But she couldn't. No matter how she tried, she couldn't trust him enough. If Jeremiah were doing the massaging, that would be different, but these men—she knew nothing about them.

"Sorry," she said. "That's enough. I have to go."

"You sure?"

"Positive. Thank you."

As she dressed behind the screen, Major Somers' voice came through her earpiece: "Conference starts in ten minutes."

She tipped the masseurs on her way out, then made for the conference room they'd used yesterday. Ned stood inside the door. Curtik and Major Somers were already there: Curtik on one side of the large table, Major Somers sitting stiffly on the other. Curtik manipulated some sort of plastic assembly with his mechanical hand while Major Somers barely glanced at her.

Ned gestured to a spot at the head of the table, which she took. On the far wall, holo-projections emerged with the images of Lendra and Dr. Poole sitting in Lendra's office. Dr. Poole waved to Zora and she waved back. Beside them, in a holo-projection coming from Atlanta, Walt Devereaux lay on an operating table, his head cut open. Zora could see his folded cerebral cortex swelling outside his skull, making his head look lopsided and alien.

Was he conscious? Was he in pain? It looked like he was sedated. Looming above him, the gigantic and shaggy Quark wore hospital scrubs and a mask, but she could sense the rage in his glare. Three surgeon-technicians stood beside Devereaux, monitoring the machines that kept him alive. In the corner of the room, behind Quark, Zora saw a humanoid robot standing motionless. This was no doubt where they hoped to house Devereaux's mind. Finally, sitting beside Devereaux and holding his hand was a thin black man Zora didn't know. He too wore surgical scrubs and a mask. Occasionally he glanced at the camera, his eyes blinking rapidly as he fought back tears.

Lendra engaged the audio connection from her end and said, "That's Doug Robinson." Her voice sounded slightly husky, as if she were having difficulty controlling her emotions. "He's Devereaux's communications liaison."

"And our friend," Quark added.

Zora nodded to him and he lifted a tentative hand, the other still firmly gripping Devereaux's.

In a third holo-projection space beside Devereaux, the Cambridge University team of scientists huddled together, perusing each other's tablets and whispering urgently, ignoring the holo-projection cameras. A fourth holo-projection showed an image of a cave, from which Quekri, Zeriphi, Dr. Wellon and Aspen looked out at the cameras with tight smiles. Zora waved to Aspen, knowing it would be sixteen minutes before the image arrived on Mars.

Without making eye contact, Major Somers slid two tablet computers across the table—one for Zora, one for Curtik.

Curtik said, "I really don't know anything about mind transfer."

Major Somers snorted. "Pretty good with murder though."

Ned held up his hands. "Hey, we're all on the same side here."

Zora turned to Curtik. "None of us knows much about mind transfer. That's why it's called the Cambridge Experiment."

Curtik said, "You're the genius at computer systems and data transfer."

"I need your help. Devereaux needs your help."

"I should be leaving with Ned to track down leads."

Major Somers said, "You're not allowed to leave. Be thankful we don't arrest you for trying to blow up half the world."

Zora said, "We're sorry. We were under a compulsion."

Major Somers shook his head. "I don't care what kind of programming they put into you. You still killed millions. He pointed to the tablets, which were linked to the holo-projections. "Your controls are there. If you want to disconnect from the conversation at any time, you just—right, you're geniuses. You'll figure it out."

Zora fought the urge to beat him senseless.

His face went pale and his eyes widened as he sat back in his chair. He looked at Ned, who had quietly stepped up behind Zora and put his hand on her shoulder. Zora unclenched her fists and forced herself to breathe normally. She refused to pummel him, no matter how good it would feel. Surprisingly, Curtik seemed unbothered by the major's words. Zora would have thought he would take offense, or maybe he was flattered.

Ned spoke quietly, "Everyone's a little tense. Just try to relax."

"Do your jobs," Major Somers said. "Be professional."

Ned backed away. "Right. I'll leave you to it, then."

Zora engaged the audio connection. As soon as the channel was open, Dr. Poole said, "Hello, Zora, Curtik, how are you?"

"Fine," Zora said. She pointed to the robot behind Devereaux. "Is that the Asimov Assembly?"

"Yes," Dr. Poole replied, "an organic mobile computer."

"I still don't understand why you need me," Curtik said. "You've got all the Cambridge Experiment scientists there."

"Yes, but we're not perfect. We might have missed something. I want you and Zora to look at the sequence we've projected. Study the pattern and see if there's anything that looks off to you. This is similar to what you were doing on the Moon."

"Yes, and Zora was really good at it—pattern analysis and infiltration. It'll take me hours to get up to speed."

"Don't sell yourself short, Curtik," Lendra said. "You may be able to offer some helpful insights."

"We'll be proceeding slowly," Dr. Poole said, "with the Mars Project scientists taking the lead. Transmissions each way take sixteen minutes and twenty-two seconds, so we'll have plenty of time to answer any questions you might have. I suggest you begin with the first three processes, make sure they're okay, then work your way forward from there. That way we can get started more quickly."

Zora said, "I assume we're doing a copy and not a wipe?"

"That's correct," Lendra replied. "However, we may only get the opportunity to do this once."

"Devereaux's body has begun to shut down." Dr. Poole pointed to the next holo-projection, where Quark and the surgeon-technicians now slid Devereaux's shoulders to the side and shifted his head so it rested on a white pad. Zora glanced down at her computerized model of the machine—a Stelzie-Hanson Digital Collector and Descrambler or DCD. Devereaux's head rested atop a receptor plate.

Dr. Poole continued: "He might not last the night. If we don't move now, we could lose his entire mind."

One of the Cambridge scientists turned to the cameras and said, "Dr. Tanaka here. We're initializing receptor series two-one-eight-alpha—preparing for digitized transfer. But we'll need him fully awake and the anesthetic removed."

The surgeon-technicians surrounding Devereaux adjusted the machines keeping him alive as Quark stepped forward and gently took hold of Devereaux's head. Doug began rubbing Devereaux's hand. Everyone in the holo-projections, except for those on Mars, went still, staring at Devereaux. His eyelids began to flutter; his mouth opened and closed. When his eyes finally opened, he stared about him, confusion on his face until he spotted Doug and Quark.

"It's okay," Quark said. "We're going to copy your mind into an Asimov Assembly."

Devereaux's head moved slowly back and forth against Quark's massive hands. He said, "I'm not sure about this."

"We discussed it," Quark said. "You told me to make sure you went through with it. You said I shouldn't let you change your mind."

"So I'm dying?"

"No!" Doug said. "You're not gonna die."

Quark touched Devereaux's cheek with the back of his hand. "We don't know."

"Terrible pain," Devereaux said as he winced. "Blinding."

Why should there be pain? That made no sense. The brain has no pain receptors—unless the virus was killing him more quickly than they knew.

"I'm sorry," Quark said, his voice quavering slightly. "We have to save your mind."

"I don't want to live forever, not even as a clone." Devereaux shuddered, either from fear or pain. "And I'd rather be dead than have people read my mind."

How horrible that would be, Zora thought, to have your private thoughts available to everyone. What terrible secrets was Devereaux hiding? How would she feel if people could read her thoughts about Jeremiah? She felt her face grow hot and sank a little in her chair.

"We don't know if that will even be possible," Dr. Tanaka said.

"No one will be able to access your thoughts," Quark reassured him. "I'll make certain of it."

Devereaux grimaced. "You won't be able to stop them."

He might be right, Zora realized. People like Lendra would do whatever they felt necessary to save themselves, even if it meant destroying Devereaux's privacy. They would likely justify it by saying that the robot wasn't Devereaux, but only a clone and therefore it had no rights.

"We still need you," Doug pleaded. "Only you can save us."

"Without you," Lendra added, "we have no chance of finding a cure for the virus."

"So this will be my afterlife?" Devereaux asked. Sadness entered his voice. "Stuck inside a robot?"

"You're not gonna die," Doug said, his voice breaking, his head dropping to settle on Devereaux's shoulder. "This is just a precaution."

"Of course," Devereaux said. He pulled his hand free from Doug's grasp and ran it across the top of Doug's tightly shaved head. Devereaux's face paled. He clenched his teeth as if trying not to scream.

Even now, knowing he was dying, Devereaux was looking out for others. Zora wanted to shout out to everyone to leave him alone, to just let him die. Her breathing came faster; her palms began sweating.

"We can begin now," Dr. Tanaka said. "There should be a tingling sensation on the right side of your head."

"I feel it. More like scraping away part of my brain." Devereaux twisted his head to look at the empty robot behind him, then up at Quark's face. "Can I trust you?"

"Absolutely," Quark said. "You don't even have to ask."

"If I were to ask you to stop?" Devereaux said. "To just let me die in peace, without pain?"

"We need your help," Lendra said. "We can't take the chance that we'll lose your mind forever. Please don't make me choose."

Zora shivered. They were essentially forcing him to do this. And if he died soon, his cloned mind would continue inside that robotic body. How would they treat it? As property? Would Devereaux exist only as a computer after this? Would they be able to compel him to work against his will? She glanced at Lendra and Dr. Poole, then at the Cambridge scientists. At least they looked uncomfortable, squirming as they prepared to disregard his wishes. Were they really saving him?

One of the surgeon-technicians said, "Think of your parents—a happy day—Christmas or a picnic." She looked at a screen and said, "Good. Wait, I'm seeing an increase in pain levels."

Quark leaned over Devereaux, tears running onto his mask, and said, "I've got you. Trust me."

Zora stared at the massive Escala. He looked to be in almost as much pain as Devereaux.

"Zora," Dr. Poole said. "Zora!"

Zora looked at her.

"You and Curtik let us know if you find anything that seems off. Anything at all."

Zora nodded. She watched Quark caressing Devereaux's face as the old man began moaning, then screaming. Doug and Quark cried openly. Even Curtik looked uncomfortable. Lendra wore a stoic expression— no surprise there; she cared about no one but herself—while Dr. Poole looked nauseated. Zora felt an overwhelming urge to help. And yet nothing she did would save him. They were going to transfer his mind no matter what. Quark had obviously reached the same decision. As Devereaux thrashed about on the gurney, Quark stroked his face gently, a deep moan rumbling from his throat, while Doug continued to hold Devereaux's hand. The great man's mind belonged to people like Lendra now. Fighting that would only get Zora exiled. Very well. She would do her best to make sure the procedure was a success.

Suddenly the sound stopped.

Curtik said, "I couldn't take that anymore."

"Thanks," Zora replied.

"He's dying, you know. That's the only explanation for the increase in pain."

Zora nodded. "Let's get to work, at least do what we can. How awful would it be if only part of his mind made it through?"

Curtik said, "I thought I was cruel. But Lendra . . ."

Zora turned to the tablet in front of her. As she studied the process, her message chime sounded. Zora activated the holo-projection's audio and looked up at Aspen, who said: "Zora, I've been so worried about you. I'm glad you're looking well." Aspen wrung her hands together. "I told them you were better at this sort of thing than me, which is why they've asked you to help." Aspen smiled hesitantly. "When are you getting a new implant? It would be nice to hear from you once in a while." Now Aspen looked off camera for a moment. "We're still not certain whether the Patterson Formula applies, and whether the favored patterns of Devereaux's mind will conflict with the organic computer, resulting in a decrease in the efficacy of future growth that will eventually become a retardation. Check the latest data on Guffie, the Earth rat, and perhaps you'll see something I'm missing. I hope you're taking care of yourself." Aspen's voice dropped slightly. "I miss you, immensely."

Major Somers snorted softly, but when Curtik cleared his throat, Somers held up his hands and quieted.

Zora sighed. She liked Aspen. But they'd always been somewhat different—Aspen harsher and more judgmental than either Zora or Rendela—and their days of cuddling for comfort on the Moon were long over. Plus, every contact with her reminded Zora of Rendela, who sacrificed herself so that Zora might live.

She took a few moments to compose a message in her head: We're on different worlds now, with different challenges and responsibilities. I put you in charge because I know you can handle the problems you'll encounter. I have great faith in you. Please take care of the others, and yourself.

But she simply said: "Aspen, I miss you too."

She glanced at Curtik as she sent the message, but he kept his head down. Major Somers looked at the floor.

Zora went back to work on her tablet, pulling up the latest data on the rat named Guffie, comparing the scans to those previously conducted on Mars. She tried to immerse herself in the statistics, go into a kind of trance, where nothing from outside intruded. She used to be able to focus this way, poring over the smallest details, memorizing and integrating them into a larger pattern, spotting those weak points that indicated a wrongness or a possible avenue of attack. She'd attempted that last night, but the sounds coming from the room next door had distracted her too much.

They kept the volume muted so they wouldn't hear Devereaux's screams of pain. But every time Zora looked up at the holo-projection, she saw him writhing on the table, Doug and Quark doing their best to comfort him.

Concentrate, Zora told herself. Ignore everything but the data. It showed certain vulnerabilities—decaying memory and corruption of mental processes in human-to-computer transfer projections. But that made no sense. With a newly initialized organic computer, the mind transfer ought not to result in a decline in cognitive acuity or agility. Something felt wrong. Zora couldn't identify the problem specifically. She just knew that a step was missing. Perhaps this was what all the other scientists sensed too: something beyond the scientific: that the end result would likely achieve a sum less than the total of its parts.

She closed her eyes, finally managing to place herself into a full hypnotic trance, letting her eidetic memory take over as she re-examined the data. What kept coming back to her was the disconnect in the pattern itself—the disparate ways brains and computers function—with brains leaping intuitively in directions often chosen for purely emotional reasons, while computers followed a perfectly logical one-zero paradigm. As difficult as it might be to transfer a mind to another person's brain, the challenges involved in housing a mind inside a computer for long periods of time presented another order of magnitude altogether.

Still, if she ignored that problem for the moment, what idiosyncrasies remained?

She submerged herself in the details, delving deeper into the mathematics and physics, letting herself drift in the trance, examining each step in the mind-transfer procedure for any tiny flaw. She sensed time passing abstractly, as if she were unaffected by its current. She felt a kind of joy at her apartness—a rock in the stream of time, breaking down processes and sub-processes and sub-sub-processes, getting ever closer to the ultimate truth, working almost like a computer herself, one problem at a time, experiencing something like delight.

As the possibilities began to narrow, the solution approaching from a distant point, she felt a nudge on her shoulder. She ignored it, concentrating only on eliminating impossibilities, while the pleasure that came with rightness intensified. Then she felt a slap on her cheek. Although it annoyed her, she maintained her trance, furiously discarding wrongnesses. Just as the answer began to dawn on her, she felt a pressure tapping her on the forehead: a cold, blunt object that repeated itself in a series of impacts—dot, dot, dot, dash, dash, dash, dot, dot, dot. Over and over she felt the irritating tapping: an emergency code that distracted her sufficiently that she finally opened her eyes and saw Curtik's face before her. His frown of concern faded as he stopped tapping her forehead with a mechanical finger. Behind him, Major Somers exhaled heavily.

"Thank goodness," Major Somers said.

"What the hell are you doing?" Zora asked.

Curtik pointed to the holo-projections. "You were out for over an hour. Major Somers tried to wake you. He even slapped your face." Zora noted the tingling of her left cheek and stared at Major Somers.

"Dr. Poole insisted I wake you," Major Somers said, holding up his hands.

"There was a lot in that slap," Curtik said with a shrug. "I thought he deserved the opportunity to hit you. You were in one of your deep trances. Almost into brain lock. And without your implant to revive you, you might have been stuck there until you passed out, or . . . ."

Zora reached up and rubbed her cheek. "Thanks, I guess. But you woke me too early. I almost had the answer. I still might have gotten enough . . ."

Dr. Poole said, "Are you all right, Zora?"

"I think so." She turned to the Cambridge scientists and said, "What kind of filter are you using for the mind transfer?"

"A Roth algorithmic diffuser," Dr. Tanaka answered.

"Why do you ask, Zora?" Lendra interjected.

"I think it needs to be modified with a series of electro-magnetic pulses to realign the stabilization vectors as the indicators approach point-three-seven. If you look at the mind transfer between the two rats—Hugh and Guffie—you can see what might be an increased resistance to the inflow of data at that point in the procedure. But it only manifests itself later. In the earlier experiment, it was at eight minutes for the Mars rat and fourteen for the rat on Earth. If we extrapolate that out to a human brain, we see that a similar resistance to data flow will occur at approximately four hours and thirty-five minutes, with a seismic schism resulting in a declination of function by nearly twelve percent."

"Twelve percent?" Dr. Tanaka said. "That's too much. That could be enough to ruin the upload completely."

"Will we lose a specific part of the mind?" Lendra asked. "Memories? Logical thinking skills? Or will there just be a general decline of function?"

"I don't know," Zora answered. She noted that Devereaux's pain had lessened. He lay mostly quiet, his face still pinched and pale, Doug holding his hand and feeding him an occasional ice chip. Was that a good sign or did it mean Devereaux was now beyond recovery?

"But we'll lose part of Devereaux's mind in the process of copying it," Quark answered in his deep voice. "And perhaps we'll lose the best part."

"Check with Aspen and Dr. Wellon," Zora said. "When they receive this transmission, I think they'll be able to verify what I'm saying."

Devereaux suddenly spasmed on the gurney. Quark bent over him as two of the surgeon-technicians began manipulating the life-support machines.

"We're losing him," the third surgeon-technician said. "His heart's going into full arrest and his blood vessels are starting to rupture."

"Keep him alive," Lendra said. "Whatever it takes."

Whatever it takes. Zora looked at Curtik, recalling that kind of fanaticism from last year, when a programmed compulsion directed them to attack Earth. Curtik shook his head with a sad smile. She wanted to hate Lendra, for lots of reasons. In fact, she was pretty sure she did. But she wasn't sure Lendra was wrong about this. It was just so unfair. Devereaux and Jeremiah were always being asked to give more than everyone else.

"We can't continue the process without knowing if we should modify the filter," Dr. Tanaka said. "Or how. If we're wrong, or if we don't use the proper series of electro-magnetic pulses, we might effectively abort the procedure, leaving a series of disjointed memories adrift in a directionless mind."

"Look at the screen," the surgeon-technician said, pointing to a rapidly oscillating graph. "We have to continue. He's losing mental function with each passing minute."

Lendra rubbed her face, then looked at Dr. Poole, who studied Zora's face for a moment. Finally Dr. Poole nodded. Lendra turned to Quark. He sighed and shrugged.

"Do it," Lendra said. "Make the modifications. Calculate the necessary electro-magnetic pulses for the filter as quickly as you can. But complete the upload as quickly as possible."

Dr. Poole nodded to Zora. "Good catch, Zora. That was amazing."

"I'm still not sure about this. You woke me too soon."

"We have no choice but to press on. You did what was needed."

Major Somers put a hand on her shoulder. "Well done, Lass."

She glared up at him. "Now you're my friend?"

He pulled his hand away. His eyes began to glisten. "My nephew was stationed in Singapore last year. During your Las-cannon attacks."

"Sorry," Zora said. A hollowness hit her stomach. Curtik, she noticed, had backed up a couple paces. She didn't point out that Curtik had been the one who fired on Singapore, against her orders. After all, she'd been in charge. She bore the responsibility for his actions.

Curtik spoke up: "We did what they programmed us to do, Major. I'm not gonna apologize for that. But I'm sorry about your nephew."

"Thank you, Zora," Lendra said through the holo-projection. Zora had forgotten Lendra and the others were still connected. "You too, Curtik and Major Somers. We're most grateful."

And with that, the connection broke, Dr. Poole and Lendra vanishing into the wall. For long seconds Quark looked up into the camera at Zora. Then he nodded once, slowly, before his connection too faded away. Zora took in the tableau of Aspen and the Mars Project astronauts, still unaware of what had transpired here on Earth. She held up one hand in a wave of goodbye, then reached over and cut the final connection, leaving only a blank wall on the other side of the room.

Chapter 21

The transfer of Devereaux's mind made Dr. Poole feel dirty, as if she had contributed to something horrible. Despite Devereaux's agony, the process continued, the surgeon-technicians asking him questions that lit up certain areas of his brain at a time, copying thoughts and memories, ideas and desires, imagination and insight.

Had Devereaux freely agreed to the procedure? Had he understood completely what was being asked of him? Poole wondered.

Her eyes were drawn to Quark. Studying the Escala's body language, she realized that although he loathed what he was doing, he couldn't help himself. He loved Devereaux too deeply to allow the great man to die.

"Are we certain this is the right thing to do?" she asked yet again.

"No," Lendra replied. "But it's not as if we're killing him. If he manages to pull through, we can destroy the copy of his mind in the robot. And if he dies, his cloned mind can help us find a cure for the virus. After that, we'll let him decide if he wants his consciousness erased."

"Do you really think they'll let him die if that's what he decides?"

Lendra shook her head. "We're not planning to enslave him, Taditha. Even though he'll be a clone inside a robot, we won't force him to do anything he doesn't want to do."

Poole refused to watch anymore. Instead, she examined footage that Jay-Edgar had retrieved from the 24-Hour Real News Network and placed on the secondary screens adjacent to the holo-projection of Devereaux's mind transfer. For the moment, Lendra had decided to let Jay-Edgar continue his duties, though every move he made was now monitored.

Jay-Edgar flashed another virus update on the screen, this time concerning an outbreak in Texas. Dallas, Houston and San Antonio all reported hundreds of new cases. Possibly they'd come from Central America, where the virus now progressed at a rapid pace. The streets of the cities looked deserted, San Antonio's famed Riverwalk closed up. She spotted two men on the screen, standing beside one another in front of a business, wearing masks, staring off into the distance and shaking their heads, a table and two empty chairs before them.

If the virus kept spreading like this, these might well be the last days of humans on Earth. Perhaps that was why she hadn't been sleeping well lately: her subconscious knowing all along just how deadly this thing was.

Her interface buzzed—a message from Jeremiah, asking for a moment of her time. No rush. See Jack first. Thank you, she whispered to herself.

"Jeremiah's asking for my assistance," she said to Lendra as she got to her feet. Lendra waved her out and she headed to the infirmary to check on her son.

Little Jack Marschenko Poole, although six weeks younger than Lendra's daughter Sophie, generally had a much stronger constitution. He rarely got sick. But he was sick now. At least he hadn't contracted the same staph infection Sophie had. The on-call infirmary doctor told her it was just a flu virus, but she still worried. What if it was some new strain of the Susquehanna Virus that the scanners improperly identified as flu? Regardless of how unlikely that was, the prospect still terrified her.

Jack was fussing when she reached him. Picking him up, she noted how warm and heavy he felt in her arms. He'd inherited the big bones of his late father. She sat and rocked him for a while, enjoying his baby smell, until he fell asleep.

Then she walked to Jeremiah's office. Two unarmored Elite Ops troopers—Gil and Finn—stood vigil outside the door. They reminded her of

Jack Marschenko—the man who'd briefly been her lover on the Moon: the father of her son. Had she really loved Jack or had she just been infatuated by him? Whatever that emotion had once been, it survived as love. And it intensified as time passed, strengthened by the sorrow of his death. Not that she could really blame Curtik for murdering him. Poole had been one of Curtik's creators. She'd made him into a killer. She just hadn't expected that he'd end up destroying perhaps her only chance at love.

And there had been a certain justice in Curtik killing the man who had kidnapped him from his family, even if Jack Marschenko had been so programmed and conditioned, so drugged up that he couldn't bear responsibility for his actions.

Still, every time Poole looked at Curtik, she had to fight against hatred.

As Poole passed between Gil and Finn, the two Elite Ops troopers smiled at her. Did they know about her affair with Jack? Probably.

Inside Jeremiah's office, posted on the far wall, was a copy of the Gaia Manifesto—a scathing indictment of the sins of humanity against the planet that offered nothing of value in the quest to find Susquehanna Sally.

Jeremiah and Eli sat side by side, facing multiple screens, perusing the data they'd each gathered separately, searching for any sign of the Sally terrorists. Standing behind Jeremiah, protecting him from whatever threat Eli might present, Hannah Swenson acknowledged her entry with a nod.

For a moment Poole simply stood there, stunned by Eli's presence. She'd seen his capture, of course, but she hadn't yet seen him in the flesh since that happened. He looked smaller than ever, though at the same time healthier. He looked smug, happy. How could she ever have believed in his mad plan to save the world?

"Ah, there you are, Doc," Jeremiah said. "How's the upload coming?"

Eli looked at her now, still smiling: the bastard.

"It should be finished in a couple hours," Poole replied. "How are you feeling? How's the pain?"

"I barely notice it when I'm working."

"And Sophie?"

"Holding her own, thanks. How's little Jack?"

Poole shrugged. "They say it's just the flu."

"But you're worried it might be the virus."

Poole nodded.

"They tested for every strain we've identified so far," Jeremiah said. "It seems unlikely he's caught a different version."

"He'll be fine," Eli said as he pushed his chair back, seeking the position of power by placing everyone in front of him. Was that subconscious or intentional? At any rate, it didn't work, because Hannah stopped his chair from reaching the wall, keeping herself behind him.

"I wasn't talking to you," Poole said.

Eli grinned. "I know. I'm the bad guy. But I look at what you're doing and I find it amusing that you people think what I did was monstrous."

"Excuse me?" Poole asked.

"Forcing Devereaux's mind to continue as some kind of slave? Serving at the pleasure of Lendra and President Hope, who I'm sure distanced herself from the process for the sake of plausible deniability. And do you really believe they won't take this opportunity to study his mind? They'll pick it to pieces, studying his thoughts and emotions. The greatest mind since Einstein, picked apart by jackals."

Poole felt her stomach drop. She said, "Every precaution will be taken to ensure Devereaux's privacy."

"I'm sure that's what you believe," Eli said. "We all start with the best of intentions. But what happens if Devereaux's mind refuses to work for you? Will you let him walk away in his new robotic body?" Eli shook his head. "Not with all the time and expense invested in saving his ideas. Poor bastard."

"He offered his help."

"Yes. But how much was he manipulated, how much was truth and how much lies?"

"Just because you manipulate everyone and every situation doesn't mean that's what's happening here. You scheme and exploit and . . ."

"Just like the President," Eli replied. "And Lendra."

"Except that your plan killed millions. We're trying to save billions." Why wasn't Jeremiah coming to her aid? Why wasn't he stopping this conversation? It wasn't going to aid their search for Sally.

"I was trying to save humanity too, in my own way. I never intended that many people to die—a few thousand, at most. And, I never pulled a trigger."

Hannah reached her hands toward his neck, as if to strangle him.

Poole laughed and Jeremiah smiled.

Eli looked back at Hannah, who had pulled her hands back to her sides and was now looking straight ahead. Shaking his head, his face flushed, Eli re-focused on Poole. "You people are torturing Devereaux to save what's left of his mind. You can try to justify it by utilitarian ideals— the needs of the many outweigh the needs of the one—but it still comes down to torture."

"He gave his permission." Poole said.

"I'm sure he did. I wonder what was in those drugs they gave him."

"You think he was coerced into helping?"

"I don't know. The point is, neither do you."

"I can live with my actions," Poole said, though she wondered if she'd be able to. She still had nightmares about her time on the Moon, about her role in Jack Marschenko's death. And Eli had played a large role in that; she hated him even more than she hated Curtik.

"What happens if Devereaux winds up a slave to our nation's demands? What if he loses every shred of privacy he once had? Will you rest easy then? Will you justify your actions as necessary for the greater good?"

"Would you have us do nothing?"

"I would have done exactly what you did," Eli answered.

"Then why are you—"

"Because you think you're better than me. And I just want you to understand that you're not." Eli turned to Jeremiah. "What would you have done?"

Jeremiah shook his head. "I guess we'll never know."

Eli exhaled heavily, almost a snort. "That's a cop-out."

Jeremiah shrugged and then shifted his gaze back to Poole. "I think that's enough philosophizing. We need your help, Doc. We've found a couple anomalies in the distribution of the virus that you might be able to explain to us."

"Ha!" Eli slapped his thigh. "The great warrior reduced to this . . . dear, oh dear . . . the real reason he called you, Doctor, is because he saw you sitting there with Lendra, stewing about what you'd done. I created you to be a killing machine, Jeremiah. Stone cold. Now look at you— worrying about Dr. Poole's emotional state." He laughed.

Poole glanced at Jeremiah.

"Not true," Jeremiah said, pointing to the screens. But Hannah averted her eyes, looking out the window, as if something fascinated her out there, and Poole knew Eli was at least partly right, that Jeremiah had made the suggestion to allow her to escape from Lendra's office.

"Look at these distribution nodes," Jeremiah said, "or what we presume are distribution nodes. Check out the clusters of infected areas."

Poole turned her attention to the screens. "All major cities around the globe."

"Right, as well as the whole of Indonesia, most of Pakistan and now a good chunk of Central America. However, the pattern seems somewhat random."

She said. "I agree."

"Nothing stood out," Jeremiah said, "until we layered in a time frame for rate of infection and another time frame for each strain of virus identified, separating out newer strains from known older versions. Then we see this."

Jeremiah touched the screen in front of him and the clusters began to move in a pattern that started in Rochester, Minnesota, where the virus first emerged, then to a few major cities—Los Angeles, Boston and Miami, each with a slightly mutated form of the virus—then on to random cities across the world before its recent strike against Indonesia, followed by Pakistan and now Central America. In those latter three areas, the virus swept through incredibly swiftly, emerging as a much deadlier strain and devastating the local population.

"That's odd," Poole said. "It's unusual for a virus to spread from major population centers in the first world to the third world in that manner."

"Exactly," Eli said. "And note that it largely avoids India and perhaps China—information is a little sketchy there. That's counter-intuitive, unless the Sally terrorists are based there, which seems unlikely given that the virus started here in America. Jeremiah thought perhaps you might be able to explain that inconsistency."

Poole examined the data flow several times but saw nothing that helped her understand it. Perhaps fatigue slowed her faculties. "I'm sorry," she finally said. "I don't see a pattern I can identify."

"Well," Jeremiah replied, "perhaps we ought to put it aside for a moment, concentrate on other things. It might come to us later. Look at this, Doc." He brought up another screen. "I put yet another overlap onto the data, this time of actions taken by CINTEP based on leads we received. Watch the screens."

Poole studied the screens but noticed little of value. She shook her head and Jeremiah highlighted three action points at distribution nodes in Houston, New York and Seattle that occurred eight months ago, after the virus had appeared there.

"I don't understand," Poole said. "Of course the action points would occur after the virus was distributed. We wouldn't know to send people to the area until after an outbreak."

Eli said, "What are you getting at, Jeremiah? We looked at this already."

"True," Jeremiah conceded, "but notice the time frames. As CINTEP agents arrived at each location, further outbreaks diminished rapidly, returning to a pattern of natural contagion, rather than the accelerated pattern that existed prior to their appearance."

Eli said, "Which means that whoever was dispersing the virus left when the CINTEP agents showed up."

"Exactly."

Poole said, "Isn't that what we would expect?"

"There should be a lag," Jeremiah explained. "How did the terrorists know that CINTEP was on their trail? It looks like they ceased all activity on the same day the CINTEP agents arrived."

"That's a pretty big leap," Eli said.

"It's in the data you provided." Jeremiah pointed to the screen. "The information you had Jay-Edgar hack from hospitals and patient records shows that there were three versions of the virus infecting these cities. Those strains all display symptoms in thirty-six to forty-eight hours. And new infections dropped markedly two days after the CINTEP agents arrived."

The answer struck Poole like a hammer blow. "Someone inside CINTEP warned them away."

Jeremiah nodded. "That seems to be the only logical conclusion."

"A traitor inside CINTEP?" Eli said. "Impossible. I vetted everyone here."

Poole said, "Why only those three nodes? Why nothing since?"

"Several reasons," Jeremiah replied. "First, Sally went into hiding—regrouping, developing new strains of the virus and seeking out new distribution nodes. She's extremely cautious, and that process no doubt took months. Second, the more recent distribution nodes—those from the past year—originated outside the United States, where it's more difficult for CINTEP to gain access. And third, Eli was no longer in charge of CINTEP."

Eli said, "You think I'm Susquehanna Sally?" His jaw worked angrily, his muscles bunching up in his forearms.

Hannah inched a little closer to him, crouching: a coiled spring.

"That would tie things up neatly," Jeremiah said.

"This is insane," Eli said.

"Your last plan wasn't?"

"You know I'm not Sally."

"It could be another of your crazy schemes to unite the world against an outside enemy—in this case, a virus."

"Think about it for a minute," Eli said. "I've helped you with this analysis. I've provided data that helped you reach the conclusion that there might be a mole in CINTEP."

"Yes, but you didn't spot this anomaly when I plugged your data into what we already knew."

Poole said, "I hate to say this because it would be nice if Eli was the mole, but you've made quite an intuitive leap. The data isn't that conclusive."

"Exactly," Eli said. He tried to get to his feet, but Hannah pushed him back into his chair.

Jeremiah shrugged. "On the other hand, it might be Jay-Edgar."

Eli scoffed. "Ridiculous. All he did was help me. This whole thing is crazy."

Poole said, "I suppose it could be Jay-Edgar. He'd have the technical expertise to figure out dispersal patterns we couldn't track. And he'd be able to manipulate the incoming data to make sure we didn't find Sally cells. But we found cells in Jakarta and London."

"I'm telling you you're wrong," Eli said. "You brought me here for my help. Listen to me. It's not Jay-Edgar."

"I admit it's a puzzle," Jeremiah said. "The mole could even be Lendra."

Eli snorted. "Next you'll say it could be President Hope."

Jeremiah held up his hands. "I'm just saying we don't know. Lendra could be feeding them information, though you and Jay-Edgar are more likely candidates. Perhaps the data from Jakarta and London reached a point where Jay-Edgar couldn't hide it anymore because Lendra was receiving Intel from other sources. Or perhaps Lendra had to find the cells in Jakarta and London because the information Jay-Edgar was providing would inevitably lead us there."

"If you're right . . ."

"I don't know that I am," Jeremiah said. "It might not be Lendra or Jay-Edgar or even Eli."

"That's what I've been saying," Eli shouted, his face red.

"It could be someone else at CINTEP—the most likely candidates being the people in Analytical."

"That could be dozens," Poole said.

"Not really," Jeremiah replied. "It would have to be someone who knew we were sending agents when we did. There can't be more than a handful who fit that description."

Lendra appeared in the doorway, scowling, her hands clenched at her sides. She said, "You think I might be involved with Susquehanna Sally?"

"You're one suspect," Jeremiah said, "Where's Jay-Edgar?"

"I took away his toys—no electronic access—and left him under guard. And I'm insulted that you would think I had anything to do with this."

"I'm exploring every option. That's my job. Frankly, what I really wanted from this discussion was to see your reactions, both yours and Eli's. And though I can't clear you completely, I'm beginning to doubt either of you is the mole."

Poole said, "What about Jay-Edgar? Do you want to talk to him?"

Jeremiah shook his head. "He's nervous and twitchy. Too hard to read."

Lendra said, "We should lock him up and throw away the key."

"He's not the mole," Eli said again. "All he did was help me so that I could help you."

"It doesn't matter," Lendra said. "He helped you escape and helped you elude capture. He's a criminal, and when this is all over, whether he's been passing information to Sally or not, he's going to prison for a long . . ." Lendra looked at Jeremiah. "What?"

"I don't think we should be focused on that right now. Let him leave at the end of the day. Remind him that we're watching him. Let the other Analytical suspects leave too. Tell them nothing. We'll track them all, see if anything pans out."

"Why tell Jay-Edgar anything?"

"He knows something's going on anyway. If you don't tell him, he'll assume the worst."

Eli said, "I'm telling you you're making a mistake. I'd trust Jay-Edgar with my life. He was just helping me. Loyalty is his only crime."

"Extremely covert surveillance," Jeremiah said. "We may get lucky."

"What about me?" Lendra asked. "You planning to track me too?" She pointed at Poole. "Or Taditha?"

"For now I'm focusing on the likely candidates," Jeremiah said.

Chapter 22

Doug Robinson sat beside Devereaux in the operating room, still wearing scrubs, faintly nauseated by the smell of antiseptic in the air, reading aloud from Stranger in a Strange Land—one of Devereaux's favorite science fiction books. How could the great man be brain dead? Yet the doctors all said he was gone. Quark had even brought in a minister to pray for Devereaux's soul, sensing Doug needed that kind of closure, and though Doug wasn't certain God existed, he was still grateful.

As Doug read, Quark worked on the robot, which stood about six feet tall: almost a foot shorter than the Escala. It had honey-colored plasticized skin and a smooth mannequin-like face with large black eyes. It wore "clothing" that shimmered vaguely, designed to absorb energy from both the movement of its limbs and any external light sources. Quark had told him that the robot was the only one available with an organic computer and that even though the robot didn't look advanced, it was actually much more sophisticated than anything else Doug had seen.

After Quark escorted the CDC surgeon-technicians from the room, he locked both operating room doors from the inside. Now he was checking connections and testing the robot's responses.

Was this really possible? Had they really transferred Devereaux's cloned mind to an organic computer inside a robot? Maybe the experiment had failed. The robot showed no sign of life.

Quark hunched over, using a tablet to examine circuitry and test the organic mass that made up the robot's brain. Turning away from the robot, Doug studied Devereaux's pale face, the hollow cheeks and gray beard. The great man's brain no longer swelled outside his skull, though Doug could still see the gray matter if he leaned over. He wondered why they hadn't replaced the top of Devereaux's shaved head, instead leaving it in a sterile tray beside the bed—a three-inch circle of skin and bone.

A loud grunt came from the robot.

Doug jumped in his seat.

"Sorry," Quark said, "my fault. Adjusting some circuits."

Doug looked past the robot and out the room's single window at the nighttime sky, at the lights of Atlanta. All those people working late: did any of them know what was happening right now, the kind of moment that might change the world forever? "Are you sure it worked?" Doug asked. "It's been hours."

"Devereaux's mind is . . . complicated," Quark said. "And this organic computer doesn't work exactly like a human brain, so it's going to take time to absorb Devereaux's mind properly."

Doug shifted in his chair so he could keep a better eye on the robot. How could someone so important, so much larger than life, now be trapped inside this motionless, plastic thing? Its black eyes remained dark. Maybe failure was for the best. No one except Quark seemed confident that it had worked. In fact, all the screens on the far wall had gone black. Doug had no idea whether the scientists or the Escala on Mars were still conducting tests.

According to Devereaux, there was no God. So if the experiment had failed, and man possessed no soul, then all that remained of Devereaux existed in the shell that lay before him, kept "alive" by machines.

And if Devereaux was wrong, if there was a God, where was Devereaux's soul now? Had it ascended to another plane of existence? Or had it moved into the robot?

Quark knelt beside the robot and examined the servomotors that enabled the robot's movements.

The CINTEP screen lit up with an image of Lendra Riley. A beep—a request for audio—began, at first tentatively, then more insistently, until Quark finally paused his work and opened the connection.

"Yes?" Quark said.

Lendra Riley said, "I'm sorry to disturb you, but it's been four hours. We need to ascertain how much of Devereaux's mind successfully uploaded. I think we need to bring the computer techs in."

"I'm working on it," Quark said. "You can check my progress remotely."

"It would make things much simpler if we had physical access."

"No." Quark reached over and cut the audio feed. Lendra glared at him for a moment before turning to her console.

"Why not let 'em help?" Doug asked. "They might be able to tell if the procedure worked."

"They'll take the robot away," Quark said. "We'll never see Devereaux again."

"What makes you—"

"I know how they think." Quark returned to his work, scanning for electrical activity. "Break those door locks. We need as much time as we can get."

"But—"

"They'll be reasonable at first," Quark said. "Then they'll get aggressive. Now break those locks."

Doug moved to comply. "But they can't just take 'im against his wishes," he said as he grabbed a metal cylinder and smashed the locking mechanism beside one of the doors.

"Under the law," Quark said as Doug moved across the room and shattered the second locking mechanism, "he's not Devereaux anymore. This robot is the joint property of CINTEP and the United States Government."

"How do you know that?"

"I suspected it might come to this," Quark said. "I researched it and made arrangements accordingly."

"What kinda arrangements?"

A heavy knock came at the door. "Open up," Dr. Jaidev called from the other side.

Doug froze. Quark ignored the command and continued working with his tablet.

"Remember when I insisted on examining the robot before the transfer?" Quark asked. "I programmed in a self-destruct virus that can only be accessed internally, so the only one who can activate it is Devereaux."

"So he can kill himself?"

"I can't unlock it," someone said from the other side. "We'll have to break it down."

The sound of shoulders bouncing off the metal door merged with frustrated curses. Quark smiled. After a few seconds the noise on the other side of the door quieted.

Quark turned his attention to the monitor before him. "Technically," he said, "Devereaux is brain dead. This robot is a construct created by others. At best it contains a cloned mind, not the real Walt Devereaux. And I suspect that CINTEP and the government may have the legal right to do with it as they please."

"It's still Devereaux's mind. You can't own another person's mind."

"Did you know that the Patent Office used to allow companies to patent individual genes? The actual genes people have in their bodies. All because these companies isolated and identified the genes. So they got the exclusive rights to conduct genetic testing."

"That's crazy."

"Bureaucracies do crazy things," Quark said. "And any time some new scientific or technical achievement arises, the potential to exploit it also occurs. The law is always trying to catch up to science."

The lights flickered. Odd. There'd never been a power shortage in this facility before, not with all the generators hooked up to ensure a continuous electrical supply. Quark turned to look at the robot. Doug followed his gaze and saw the robot slowly lift its right arm.

"Tell me that was you," Doug said.

A grunting noise came from the robot.

"Not me," Quark replied. "Devereaux."

Goosebumps formed on Doug's arms. His mouth went dry. He stared at the robot, waiting for it to do something. After a minute passed with no further sound or movement from the robot, Quark continued:

"They'll take this clone to use as a slave. All they want is the use of his mind."

"But," Doug swallowed to get some moisture into his mouth, "you helped with the transfer."

"Indeed." Quark sighed. "But I wanted Devereaux to have the chance to decide for himself, after due deliberation, not in a rush, under excruciating pain. If he still wants to end his . . . existence, he can do so at any time."

The robot took one step forward.

Doug backed up. "You sure this thing is safe?"

"I'm seeing an exponential increase in bio-electrical impulses in the robot's organic computer."

"And that's good?"

"Definitely," Quark replied. "It means Devereaux's mind is beginning to familiarize itself with its new matrix."

"Argh, rech, vawkwish, hojj," the robot said, its black eyes glowing slightly.

Doug retreated to the edge of the gurney where Devereaux's body lay. This robot was wrong somehow—maybe because Devereaux was so much more than a machine: so full of compassion. And this plastic-covered machine could never be the same as the real Walt Devereaux, no matter if it did contain a clone of Devereaux's mind.

"Now we're making progress," Quark said. "Devereaux's mind is assisting with the uploading process, accelerating the timeline."

"I, don't, understand," the robot spoke in a male voice, its black eyes flashing briefly. Its head swiveled as if it were examining the room.

"Professor?" Quark said. "Can you hear me?"

"Am I alive?" the robot asked.

"We'll leave that debate to the philosophers."

"Is that really you?" Doug asked. "Are you Devereaux?"

"I don't know," the robot answered, now using Devereaux's voice.

Doug shivered again. "You sound just like him—I mean, just like you used to."

"I can speak in many voices," the robot said. "This one is the most familiar, though it reminds me of a past I no longer have."

"Are you well?" Quark asked.

"I feel like I'm in a dream," the robot said. "Outside myself. This body doesn't feel right. I guess it worked. Am I the first person in the world to do this? I suppose I am."

"Can you move?" Quark asked.

The robot took a tentative step forward and lifted its arms in a series of staccato movements. It walked haltingly toward the window, arms extended, as if for balance. When it reached the window, it looked out for a moment and said, "I can see a long ways. If we were higher up, I could see Stone Mountain."

The robot slowly lowered its arms and turned around, then walked back toward Doug, toward Devereaux. It stared at the body on the gurney. "We've all heard the stories," it said, "of people who have almost died, looking down at their own bodies. This feels somewhat like that." The robot turned to Quark. "I just discovered an integrated organic shredder hidden in a metadata subroutine. Do I have you to thank for that?"

Quark nodded. "I wanted you to be able to make a reasoned decision, free from pain and the pressure to act immediately."

"Is that the self-destruct program?" Doug asked.

When neither the robot nor Quark answered, Doug said, "You can't do that." He looked from Devereaux's face to the robot's. He still wasn't sure this robot was Devereaux, but he needed more time to process it all.

The robot went silent and completely still. Was Devereaux ending his existence? And if he was, did Doug have any right to stop him?

After a long moment, the robot said, "Things are coming online quickly now. It helps to have the processing speed of an organic computer."

The sound of creaking metal came from the hall and one of the doors bulged inward before pulling away from its frame and opening wide. Framed in the ruined doorway, two Elite Ops troopers stood, weapons pointed at Quark. Dr. Jaidev stepped between them and entered the room, scowling, her gold interface flashing in the light.

"Move away from the robot," she said.

Quark raised his hands and backed away.

"What's going on here?" the robot asked in Devereaux's calm voice.

"Professor Devereaux." Dr. Jaidev halted in mid-stride. "You're . . . the transfer worked!"

"Obviously," the robot said.

"This man," Dr. Jaidev pointed at Quark, "was preventing us from entering the room to ascertain whether the procedure was a success. How are you, sir?"

"I'm fine. Perhaps the Elite Ops troopers should leave."

"I'm afraid that's not possible," Dr. Jaidev replied. "They're here for your safety."

"I'm quite safe, Doctor. This new shell is almost indestructible."

"Nevertheless, they stay. I have my orders from the President."

Again the robot went silent and completely still, unlike a human. And again Doug wondered if it was shutting itself off.

"Very well," the robot finally said, its voice sounding angry now, nothing like Devereaux's usual warm tones. "But I should warn you that I will not be controlled by you or anyone. If you try, I'll kill myself."

Doug suppressed a smile. Those words sounded so strange coming from a robot.

Dr. Jaidev turned to Quark, her body quivering with rage. "What did you do?"

Quark glared back at her. "I gave Devereaux the opportunity to decide his own future. I couldn't risk letting his mind be taken over by outsiders."

Dr. Jaidev pointed at Quark. "Arrest this man," she said to the Elite Ops troopers.

The Elite Ops troopers moved forward but the robot stepped in front of Quark, its arms out to the sides as if to protect the Escala, its fluid and graceful movements making it seem less like Devereaux and more like some new creature. It looked oddly small standing between the armored Elite Ops troopers and Quark. "No. If anything happens to Quark, I will destroy myself." The iron control in Devereaux's voice provided absolute sincerity. "And this program is particularly chaotic. It will shred the organic connections in such a way that virtually no information will be recoverable."

Quark reached for the controls to the screens. Doug had forgotten them completely. When Quark activated the audio, allowing incoming transmissions, Lendra's voice came through: "Is that true, Quark? Did you really implant a computer virus in the robot's matrix?"

"Yes, ma'am. Devereaux is no one's slave."

Lendra exhaled heavily, then smiled briefly. "Well played. I underestimated you."

The robot said, "You're not the first to underestimate Quark."

"And I assume," Lendra said, "that you've broadcast this to Mars as well?"

"Of course," Quark replied. "Just making certain there's a verifiable record of events."

Lendra said, "I'll notify the President. Doctor, perhaps your Elite Ops troopers should wait outside so as not to distract Professor Devereaux."

One of the troopers stepped into the hallway while the other stood under the frame of the ruined door, his Las-rifle trained on Quark. Doug felt both relieved and annoyed that the Elite Ops didn't consider him a threat.

"Professor," Lendra said. "Should I still call you Professor?"

The robot opened its hands and lifted them palms up. "You could call me R. Devereaux." The robot's mouth turned up briefly.

"For robot Devereaux?" Doug said. "Like a tribute to Isaac Asimov?"

"Why not?" the robot said. "I feel like I'm in one of your science fiction books. I heard you reading a while ago, but I don't know if that was me or him." The robot pointed to Devereaux's body. "Or both of us. *Stranger in a Strange Land*. Good choice."

Doug smiled. He noticed then that tears were streaming down his face. When had he begun to cry? Did this mean that he had finally accepted Devereaux's death?

"A part of me wants to tell you that everything will be all right," the robot said. "But I don't know if that's true. I don't even know if I'm me, if I have a soul or spark or whatever."

"Does it matter?" Quark asked. "You still have your mind."

"Yes," the robot said. "And if I have a soul, I feel it's still with me. In fact, it may be in both of us, me and that body." The robot gestured to Devereaux's body on the gurney. "If there are souls, maybe they're made up of multiple strands of consciousness, imagination, communication. Maybe mine is split into two parts now."

"An interesting concept," Quark said. "But perhaps we should save that discussion for another time."

"Yes, of course. You people aren't able to multi-task the way I'm able to. I can do so many things at once. In fact, I've been processing old data as we speak and I already have a few ideas for more cures. Also, I would like to speak with Jeremiah Jones about this Susquehanna Sally. I might have an idea there as well."

"I'll connect him," Lendra said. "Just a second."

Jeremiah appeared on the screen. Beside him sat Dr. Poole, an attractive woman Doug had never met face-to-face, though he'd met her via holo-projection a few times. Doug wiped his face before smiling at her and nodding to Jeremiah.

"How are you, Professor?" Jeremiah asked.

"I don't know," the robot answered. "I don't feel physical pain. I feel rather numb. Nothing like when I had my original body."

"I understand," Jeremiah replied.

"Yes." The robot nodded its head. "You haven't been yourself for a long time either. I can imagine what you've been suffering."

"Other than the out-of-body sensation, do you feel like you used to? Does your mind feel the same?"

"Not really." The robot's voice—Devereaux's voice—sounded sad. It also carried a slight echo. "Everything feels borrowed somehow, as if I'm experiencing life—or whatever this is—through some kind of filter. There's an odd disconnect between what I ought to be feeling and what I actually feel. Do you think it will get better? Will I ever feel complete again?"

Jeremiah shrugged. "I don't know. But the Devereaux I know would be fascinated to study it."

"Indeed," the robot said. "It does present interesting possibilities. I am my own guinea pig. In a way," the robot turned to Doug again, smiling briefly, "I feel like Frank Herbert's God Emperor of Dune—partly what I was, and partly what I've become." The robot turned back to Jeremiah. "By the way, I'm sorry for what you had to endure. I hope your pain has diminished."

Jeremiah nodded. "Now that we've done as much with my blood as we can, I'm able to take pain meds. Or are you calling to say you need me to go off the medication, to infect myself again?"

"No," the robot held up a hand. "I'm actually calling to get the latest information you have on Susquehanna Sally. I may have some ideas on how to find her."

"I think, Professor," Lendra interrupted, "that your time might be better served trying to find a cure for the virus. After all, we already have hundreds of people looking for Sally."

"I think," the robot mimicked Lendra's voice before reverting to its slightly echoed Devereaux voice, "that you're afraid I'll find Sally before you do, threatening your position as head of CINTEP. I've already told you I can multi-task much more efficiently than I used to. I can simply run a sub-routine examining that data while I also work on finding a cure."

Lendra muttered something unintelligible. Doug glanced over at Quark, who hid a smile with a cough.

"Like the guy in Frederik Pohl's Heechee saga," Doug said, "the one who became a computer."

The robot nodded. "Exactly. Although that work failed to take into account the importance of the mind-body connection. Not surprising, given how little was known about it at the time the books were written."

The robot turned toward the screen. "Have you got those files, Jeremiah?"

"I'll transfer the files to you now," Jeremiah said. "But there's a ton of material. Years worth of data. Still, I'd appreciate any help you can give me. I suspect Eli or Jay-Edgar might be involved, but I can't prove anything. Perhaps you'll see something I'm missing."

"I doubt Eli is involved," the robot said, "except maybe as a pawn." The robot turned back to Doug. "I appreciate how you have looked after my human side, Doug, how you have grounded me. I've been noticing for the past few years that I struggle sometimes dealing with people's emotions. And you have been a great help in that regard. I don't know if I'll still need that, but I wanted to thank you now in case I don't get the chance later."

Doug felt his chest expand with love. "You never needed my help with that, sir. You were always the most generous and thoughtful man I ever knew."

The robot smiled briefly. "Just say, 'Thank you,' Doug."

"Thank you, sir."

"You're welcome."

Lendra said, "You might be able to multi-task, Professor, but it's a little distracting for me."

"Very well," the robot said. It went still and silent.

For long seconds, no one spoke.

"Professor?" Lendra finally said.

Nothing.

"Professor?" Quark said. He studied his tablet, tapped a couple of commands on it, and then shrugged. "He's processing data."

"What kind of data?" Lendra asked.

"I don't know."

"You could find out."

"That's exactly why Devereaux had second thoughts," Quark said. "Already you're treating him like a piece of property."

"I'm concerned," Lendra said, "that he might be experiencing a glitch of some sort."

"Which is why I made sure his processor is functioning within tolerable specifications." Quark gestured toward his tablet. "That's all I'll ever check."

"I could get the Cambridge scientists to study what he's processing."

"Yes, you could. But I should warn you that he will be aware of any observation of his neural net."

"You think he would destroy himself?"

"I don't know," Quark answered. "I only know that his biggest concern was his privacy. If you take that away from him . . ."

Lendra glared at him for a moment, then shook her head. "I ought to have you arrested for tampering with government property."

Doug said, "You were right, Quark. They just want to use Devereaux as a computer."

Dr. Jaidev stamped her foot. "That's a lie!"

"Don't be absurd," Lendra said. "We understand that he's Walt Devereaux—sort of. And we would never try to force him to do anything he didn't want to do."

Doug shivered.

For a moment no one spoke. Then Jeremiah said, "Quark, you're doing the right thing. Thanks for increasing the odds that Devereaux will assist us."

Lendra said, "We appreciate your efforts, Quark. Still, only Devereaux has the legal right to—"

"And you," the robot interrupted her, "have no moral right to examine my private thoughts and memories, yet your Cambridge scientists are even now trying to penetrate my mind."

"Are you all right?" Quark asked.

"For now." The robot pointed to the screen beside Lendra, which suddenly flicked on. It showed the Cambridge scientists moving about hurriedly. One of them—Dr. Tanaka—spoke through some private link, gesticulating wildly, engaged in a conversation Doug couldn't hear. "I had to devote a great deal of power just now to installing a shield in my neural net. I've prevented them from accessing my mind. Now they're engaged in retrieving the data flow from the transfer process, hoping to study my thoughts and memories by examining those files. I'm infecting them as we speak. But I fear they'll be able to retrieve much of the data. I can't stop that. Hopefully, the files are corrupt enough that they won't be able to ascertain whether a given thought or memory is real or a viral implant."

"We have to know if there were any problems with the transfer," Dr. Jaidev said.

"We mean no harm," Lendra said.

"Accessing my thoughts and memories harms me," the robot said calmly. "If you had any decency, you would order all those files destroyed immediately."

"We can't do that," Lendra said. "We need to preserve those files as a backup, in case you experience a system crash."

"Don't lie to me," the robot said, a flash of anger entering its voice. "You're not smart enough to get away with it."

Lendra and Dr. Jaidev glanced at each other. Dr. Jaidev tensed, while Lendra's nostrils flared outward. Quark chuckled softly.

The robot said, "Jeremiah."

"Yes?"

"I've studied the files you sent. And I agree that we need to look inside CINTEP."

Jeremiah sat back. "You finished already?"

"Yes. Please send me all your personnel files now."

"Incredible." Jeremiah shook his head as he worked at his tablet. When he looked up, he said, "The files are on their way."

"I don't yet have all the information I need," the robot said. "But I can tell you that the person you're looking for won't be someone obvious, like Eli or Jay-Edgar, or even Lendra. It will be someone with access to a great deal of computer information, however. Possibly a CINTEP tech or analyst. Someone with a medical background."

Dr. Jaidev turned to stare at Dr. Poole. Could Dr. Poole be Sally? Doug found that difficult to believe, mostly because he found her quite sexy, though he had to admit he hardly knew the doctor at all.

As if reading his mind, Dr. Poole said, "I'm not Sally."

"Of course you're not," Jeremiah replied. "You were on the Moon during the most recent virus permutations."

Doug felt relief. Absurd. Why should he care if Dr. Poole was Sally?

"Still," Dr. Jaidev said. "It's possible she could have coordinated efforts from there."

The robot interrupted: "Have all my lecture series been recorded?"

"Yes," Dr. Poole replied. "I have them in my system."

"I need those now," the robot said. "I remember seeing some familiar viral components on the Moon last year, which led me to believe this person might be a former student. Yet I couldn't think of anyone who might have done such a thing."

Jeremiah gestured to his tablet and Dr. Poole bent over him to access it. Lucky man, Doug thought. I wonder what she smells like. Her skin looks so soft. What the hell? How can I be thinking about sex at a time like this? And then he realized how horrible it would be if anyone else knew what he was thinking. This was what Devereaux feared, though Doug realized he had no idea what sort of private thoughts Devereaux had, if they were of a sexual nature or not. He himself didn't want to know.

Dr. Poole said, "Sending the data now."

A minute passed. The robot hummed quietly now, as if aware of the tension and trying to put everyone at ease. Doug looked from Lendra to Dr. Poole, then from Jeremiah to Quark, who continued to study his tablet. "Just making certain that Devereaux's mind is properly seated in its new matrix and that no one is intruding into the system," Quark said quietly when he noticed Doug watching him.

Dr. Jaidev stood unmoving near the door, keeping her eyes on the robot, the Elite Ops trooper behind her focusing only on Quark.

"In three of my lectures on artificial viruses," the robot finally said, "I made a comment that someday, someone would figure out a way to wipe out the human race, and I joked that such an event might be the best thing ever to happen to the planet. I suspect someone in one of those classes might have taken my comments seriously. I now need a list of attendees for each of those lectures."

"I can get that for you," Lendra said, "if you can provide me the dates."

The robot again hummed quietly, soothingly, as Lendra worked at her computer. Doug found it remarkable that even in this new body Devereaux demonstrated such compassion for his fellow creatures. Were they fellow creatures? Or had Devereaux mutated into something else? Something greater or less than human?

"Sending data now," Lendra said.

Another minute passed. Quark continued to monitor his tablet, while everyone else simply waited.

"I believe I know who Sally is," the robot finally said.

"Who?" Lendra asked.

"Manyara Harris," the robot said. "Manyara is an African name, meaning 'you have been humbled.' She didn't use that name when she took my class. Back then she called herself Sarah Williams. And the name Sally is a diminutive of Sarah."

Jeremiah looked beyond the camera and spoke to someone outside Doug's view: "Find Manyara Harris."

"Did people at CINTEP know about the transfer of my mind into this computer?" the robot asked.

"Some of the techs did," Lendra said. "It wasn't a secret."

"In that case," the robot said, "I think you'll find that Manyara Harris has fled. She probably suspected that I would be able to ascertain her identity once I had access to the processing speed of this organic computer."

Jeremiah looked beyond the camera again, listened for a moment, showing no expression, then turned to the camera and said, "Mrs. Harris left three hours ago. She's under covert surveillance."

Lendra said, "We should pick her up now."

"Not yet," Jeremiah said.

"Why not?"

Jeremiah said, "She may have a hideout somewhere close by, and she may have some sort of self-destruct system in place."

"Well, we can't just let her roam around freely."

"Let's get a couple teams over to her apartment. Check to see if it's rigged. Search it. And if she returns, take her. Meanwhile, track her every move."

The robot said, "If you'll excuse me, I'll continue working on cures for the virus."

"Professor," Jeremiah said, "you're absolutely amazing. Of course, you always were. If you need anything else, let me know."

"Yes, thank you," Lendra added. "Dr. Jaidev will assist you and act as liaison for the CDC."

As the screens went dark, the robot gestured to Quark. "We should move to the lab." Then it turned to Doug. It must have seen something in Doug's face, for it said, "I'm sorry for your loss. You may not think of me as Devereaux. And you shouldn't. For whatever I am now, I'm no longer that man."

"What about your body?" Doug asked.

The robot's eyes lingered on Devereaux's comatose body. "You can turn off the life support system now. Can you see that someone puts the top of my head back on?" The robot lifted the corners of its mouth in a brief, unsettling smile.

"Of course," Doug replied. "I'll ask the docs to do it right away."

"No rush," the robot said. "It's not for me. It's for him. He deserves to die with dignity."

Then the robot walked smoothly out of the room, Dr. Jaidev following. When the Elite Ops trooper gestured to Quark with his Lasrifle, Quark looked at Doug and raised one shaggy eyebrow before he too stepped outside. The Elite Ops troopers took positions behind him as he walked away, leaving Doug alone with the vessel that was once Walt Devereaux.

Chapter 23

As Rebecca and Tad Blanton moved through the late-night fog in the Silver Spring, Maryland, Sculpture Park, Rebecca found herself in a sort of trance. Had she and Tad done the right thing aligning themselves with the Sallies? She understood the necessity of the Earth Guardian movement and its militant arms. But perhaps she and Tad should have balked when they were recruited by the Sallies last year. True, all they'd done was assist Sally1 with communications, but maybe even that was too much.

She used her PlusPhone's mapping system to navigate while her husband Tad used his PlusPhone's scatterer to create static in the CCTV system. Rebecca maneuvered toward the coordinates provided, expecting to be attacked or arrested at any moment, but she saw no one else about. They appeared to be directed toward the armadillo, the least-visited, least-impressive sculpture in the park. However, as they approached it, her PlusPhone directed her to keep moving forward, past the armadillo to a poorly manicured shrub, under which she found a small canister. She reached down and grabbed it. Then she and Tad hustled away.

"Two blocks north," Tad said gesturing to his PlusPhone.

They saw only a handful of cars, no other pedestrians. Tad's scatterer kept them largely invisible to the CCTV system—they would register only as a glitch on the vid feed.

When they reached the abandoned toy store designated on the PlusPhone's coordinates, Tad tried the metal side door and found it open. Passing inside, Rebecca waited for Tad to seal the door tightly. As he did so, the lights slowly brightened. She looked around, trying to maintain her poise. The room was large, every window covered with opaque plastic. Empty metal shelves stood against one wall and on another she spotted a map of Earth—cities infected by the virus glowing against the backdrop.

Rebecca moved in front of the map and opened the canister, while Tad set up the network for the next Earth Guardians message—a complicated series of cutouts and hacked systems that would ensure its untraceability. Although the Earth Guardians hadn't been officially banned by the government, Rebecca suspected they would soon be designated a hate group. So she and Tad kept a low profile, never broadcasting at the same time of day or using the same series of cutouts—alternating frequency and strength and a number of other variables that Tad had worked out, including making subtle alterations to her face and voice to keep her identity secret. No one except Sally1 knew that she was the Earth Guardians' American High Priestess.

She examined the canister's contents and said, "You think this is really the latest antidote?"

"You believe it's something else?"

"It could be the virus," Rebecca replied, "or some sort of hallucinogen or maybe just a placebo."

"Are your visions getting stronger?"

Rebecca shrugged. "I didn't want to worry you. I don't know what they mean."

"I wish I knew what to do," Tad said. "If we ran, we might become infected and die like everyone else."

"We don't know that. Maybe the earlier antidotes we received are good enough to save us. Or maybe they were nothing but herbal drinks too. She likes playing games. She likes us to suffer."

Tad nodded slowly. "I do find her unsettling."

"Always talking in riddles. She's no Prophet."

"What about her visions of Earth as Eden?"

"I have those visions too," Rebecca said. "But mine are sane."

"We're in too deep now."

"Maybe." Rebecca shook her head to clear it. "Let's get this over with. This place gives me the creeps."

"Okay." Tad gestured to his PlusPhone. "Ready."

Rebecca focused her energy and began her sermon:

"Fellow Guardians, Believers in the Vision, I see a true Eden, a hallowed Earth, where all things balance and only those pure of heart remain to stand watch and proclaim, 'Never Again' to those who would despoil the planet. Today we praise and glorify the sacred virus that purges the nonbelievers from the face of the world, leaving only those who truly believe, only those with pure hearts and minds to survive the cleansing fire. But much work is yet to be done.

"Those who follow the old ways will soon depart. And those of us who have seen the truth, who have witnessed the holy rage of Gaia know that our way of life will soon change dramatically. The day of reckoning is almost upon us. We the Guardians must prepare for that day, taking Gaia's holy water to ensure our survival in the end times."

Rebecca lifted the canister and said, "Receive Gaia's holy water." Then she drank of the sweetened brew and passed the canister to Tad before continuing: "Its healing properties will keep us safe from the fire. With each dose, we come closer to the innocent wildlife humanity has ravaged. We pledge ourselves anew to safeguard our fellow creatures from the brutes who rule the world. We dedicate ourselves to the sanctity of the planet as we await the anointed time. Now go with Gaia." Rebecca bowed her head, kept it down until Tad gave her the all clear.

Tad drank from the canister, then pocketed it and dispersed the message via his PlusPhone.

Rebecca said, "Let's see it."

Tad showed her the vid and she noted how skillfully he had captured the essence of her face and voice while still disguising them enough to make them not exclusively hers. The eyes of the High Priestess shone in the light, giving her an intensity that was more than human. Did her eyes really look like that? Tad said they did, though she often wondered if he manipulated the image to make her appear more divine.

When the message finished playing she said, "Perfect."

"I've set this one to originate in Cambodia and Vietnam," Tad said. "From there, it will spread virally. It'll be everywhere in the next few hours."

"Excellent. Let's get out of here."

Tad gestured for her to precede him out the door. As they stepped outside, Rebecca nearly screamed. Someone stood motionless twenty steps away, almost hidden by the fog. It took her a second to realize it was Sally1.

The old woman kept her right hand shoved deep into her coat pocket as she slowly approached. She walked stooped over, her head tilted to one side, like a crow or a vulture, and Rebecca felt as if she were being dissected, stripped down to the barest skeleton and found distasteful.

Tad touched her arm above the elbow in support as they waited for Sally1. Rebecca found herself shaking ever so slightly.

When Sally1 reached them, she glared at them for a moment, her black eyes malignant. Sally1 turned her head, as if listening intently or seeing something no one else could. Rebecca glanced down the street.

From unlit corners, men appeared—half a dozen tall men dressed in dark colors, their faces covered with what looked like mud. They converged on the three. Rebecca had to fight to keep from screaming. Tad's grip on her arm tightened. She'd heard that Sally1 kept a cadre of brainwashed bodyguards utterly devoted to her, fulfilling her every desire, but without wills of their own. These men looked unarmed, though they were probably carrying concealed weapons.

When the men reached them, the old woman said, "Hard rain's gonna fall. Cleanse the Earth."

"What the hell does that mean?" Rebecca said.

One of the dark men said, "You will respect Sally1."

"Why?" Rebecca said. "She doesn't respect me."

Another dark man moved toward her. Instinctively, she backed away. But the first man held up a hand to stop him.

Rebecca said, "Why did you blow up Cole's Wall?"

Sally1 said, "Still upset about the bombing?"

"You killed our friends," Rebecca said. "Our potential recruits."

"Had to be done."

The dark man who apparently was the spokesman for the group added, "CINTEP sent agents there that night. One of them—Jones' son Curtik—beat up Tad. They'd have learned about you if we hadn't destroyed the place. Finding you, they would have found Sally1 and then everyone in our organization."

"How?" Rebecca addressed Sally1. "We don't know your real name or where you live."

"You know how to contact me," Sally1 said. "But no longer."

"You're cutting off contact?"

Sally1 said, "They found me."

"Are they tracking you?" Tad asked as he looked up at the sky, as if he might be able to detect a miniature drone in the fog.

"Probably," Sally1 said.

"So you led them to us?" Rebecca said.

"They uploaded Walt Devereaux's mind into a robot today—one with an organic computer—with incredible speed and power."

"We have to run," Tad said.

"He knows me," Sally1 said, ignoring Tad. She looked past them at nothing, as if caught up in some trance. She'd done this before. A minute passed, the dark men standing motionless behind her. Rebecca glanced at Tad, who shrugged. Then Sally1 said, "Great deal of work remains."

Rebecca said, "We just sent out a message to the true believers. Telling them the time is almost at hand."

"Did you tell them it's time to die?"

Rebecca shook her head, then cleared her throat, preparing for Sally1's anger. "My visions don't require us all to die."

Sally1 said, "You steal my vision." Her shoulders twitched. Rebecca fought the urge to flee.

"I preach the truth," Rebecca said. "But you—your vision only gets darker. My vision is of a world full of light."

"Your vision?"

"I see the future you once saw," Rebecca said. "Your ideas won't work any longer. No one but your faithful dogs will follow you to death."

The dark men inched closer, but did not attack. Sally1 kept them on a tight leash.

"She's right," Tad said. "Recently you've made it sound like we all have to die. That's not what you said before."

The dark man said, "We changed our minds."

"And who are you?" Rebecca said.

The dark man said nothing. Sally1 faced Rebecca, her eyes twin black holes, pulling her in. She felt a chill, the sweat on her back making her shiver.

Tad cleared his throat, drawing Sally1's attention, for which Rebecca was grateful. "How do you know your visions are correct?" he asked.

Sally1 said, "How do you know the sun will rise?"

"We believe in your message," Tad said. "That's why we had the genetic surgery. That's why we take the antidote. We must rid ourselves of these corrupt governments and greedy corporations, the weak sheep who allow them to destroy our world and the gluttonous individuals who put themselves ahead of everyone else. But not every human on the planet deserves to be killed. And our friends at Cole's Wall should not have died in vain."

Rebecca said, "The Earth Guardians can no longer tolerate your negative thinking."

Sally1's hand twitched inside her coat. Her eyes seemed to absorb all the light of the world. Rebecca could almost feel the old woman's loathing.

"Contact everyone immediately," the dark man said. "Tell them to disperse all their supplies of the virus. Malls, train stations, office buildings, sporting events."

"That's dozens of canisters," Rebecca said. "Those were supposed to be held in reserve, only to be used as a last resort."

"Do it now," Sally1 said.

"Why did you come here?" Rebecca said. "You don't trust us. You wanted to make sure we gave the order and you couldn't do that except in person."

Sally1 smiled.

The dark man said, "Give the order now, and send a copy to my PlusPhone." He touched his PlusPhone to Tad's, linking them together.

Tad looked at Rebecca, who shrugged. She saw no way out of this.

"Very well," Tad said. He pulled up his PlusPhone and pushed icons while Sally1 stared at Rebecca.

"While we're waiting," Rebecca said, "perhaps you can tell me whether you even believe in the Gaia Manifesto or the Earth Guardians. Or are you just an angry old woman?"

"You understand nothing."

"Enlighten me," Rebecca said. "Please."

Tad looked up from his work, one eyebrow arched.

"We inflict gaping wounds," Sally1 said. "We humans disturb the balance."

"Yeah, I know," Rebecca said. "That's what we aim to fix."

The dark man pointed at Rebecca. "Silence."

"We pollute our air and water," Sally1 said, "with chemicals and nano-particles, wipe out entire species. We cause global warming, then global winter. And we justify the devastation to our planet as necessary. We claim that we're blessed by God and given dominion over all His creatures."

"That's what I've been saying," Rebecca said. "Have you seen my broadcasts?"

Sally1 said nothing. But the dark man said, "Gaia will win in the end. She will have her revenge. Humans will die out eventually. We cannot continue fouling our world, consuming our resources, and hope that some scientific breakthrough will allow us to mitigate the damage at some future date. We're merely accelerating the transition so that Gaia will be able to recover from our infestation more quickly."

So he wasn't a mindless drone. Even though he'd been conditioned to protect Sally1 and die without fear, he could still think independently.

"There's something more, though," Rebecca said. "We Earth Guardians say the same things. We plan a future where humans are controlled. You used to talk about that too. But you've changed. Now you only talk about death. I think you have some personal animosity toward people. Like now, you bring your death squad with you."

Tad drew in a sharp breath.

"What is it," Rebecca asked, "that drives you to want to kill everyone on Earth?"

"Does it matter?" Sally1 asked.

"No. I'm just curious. After all, you and your hit men can kill us whenever you wish."

Sally1 laughed, as if at some inner joke. "Kierkegaard," she said.

"What the hell does that mean?"

"Unintended consequences," the dark man said.

"I still don't understand."

"Nothing is completely pure," Sally1 said. "I lost my medical license after euthanizing a suffering woman. And society treated me like a pariah. Now I'm just a river—a cleaning lady at CINTEP. That's how I've been able to stay a step ahead of them. Even Elias Leach, who was once my friend . . ."

Sally1 laughed again, a cackle that trailed off, and Rebecca hugged herself tightly, her eyes flicking between Sally1's pocket and the dark men.

"But that's not why I did it," Sally1 whispered. "We're evil. All of us. Cannot be redeemed."

The dark man said, "How many dictators and tyrannical governments have promised change? How many have said this time they mean it? This time, they say, they'll do what's right and fix the problems that have plagued us for decades. And yet they never do. They consolidate their power base. They crush those who oppose them. Our government is no better than any other. They're all corrupt."

"President Hope seems better than President Davis," Tad said in his most soothing voice—the one he used when trying to calm Rebecca during an argument.

"A few degrees," the dark man replied. "Occasionally they bandage a problem. And they sell their ideas with fancy words. They create a program that pollutes our rivers and call it the Clear Waters Initiative—and we fall for it. We're tired of that nonsense. They won't act. They'll never act. They will never make the hard decision because they're afraid they'll lose their power. These scum—"

Sally1 placed her hand on the dark man's arm and he stopped talking. Then she said, "I'll crush them all."

"But not everyone," Tad said, trying to keep his voice level, though Rebecca could sense the tension behind it. Glancing at Rebecca, he reached up and wiped a bead of sweat off his forehead. "Some are worth saving."

"The best of humanity," Rebecca said. "We can build again, create a better society, one that respects, even worships our world, one that does not place ourselves above Gaia's creatures."

Sally1 smiled briefly. "You think you deserve to survive?"

"I don't know," Rebecca answered, "but I believe I will. Otherwise why would I do this? I don't have a death wish."

Sally1 removed her hand from her pocket. Rebecca had been expecting her to have a weapon, but it was just a closed fist. Then she opened her fist and pointed at the center of Rebecca's chest, her black eyes dead, her hand steady. Her dark men leaned forward, as if waiting for a signal to attack.

So this is it, Rebecca thought. We're going to die at the hands of this mad woman, and there's nothing we can do about it.

"You still need us," Tad said.

When Sally1 glanced at him, he said, "I haven't finished sending out your orders. I still have a few security systems to breach."

Sally1 stood quietly, her eyes flickering between Rebecca and Tad. Rebecca saw no hint of indecision, only implacable determination in the old woman's eyes. I will not flinch, she thought. I will die with dignity.

But Sally1 lowered her hand and the dark men relaxed.

"You're afraid," Sally1 said.

Rebecca said, "Damn right."

"Good. I want you afraid. Help keep you safe."

"Now send that message," the dark man said.

"Almost there," Tad replied.

A few seconds elapsed, then Tad said, "Okay. The message went out to every Sallie organization."

The dark man reached into his coat pocket and removed a slip of paper, which he passed to Tad. "This is the location of the lab and the access codes that will get you inside. You'll find the newest strain of the virus there in two canisters. Get over there and grab those canisters. Activate the time-release mechanisms on them and carry them with you everywhere. You'll be immune to the virus. It won't harm you. But as you travel to a new hideout, you'll be infecting everyone you encounter."

"Okay," Rebecca said, with a glance at Tad.

"Got it," Tad said.

"You have to hurry," the dark man said as he checked the screen on his PlusPhone. "You might only have a few hours to get away from the lab before they find it."

"What are you going to do?" Rebecca asked Sally1.

"What they expect me to do—fly away." She smirked.

"You think you can escape?"

The dark man said, "We'll protect her."

Sally1 said, "Get those canisters. This version of the virus is the most sophisticated yet."

"Thank you," Rebecca said, trying to mollify the old woman.

"Go," Sally1 commanded.

"Good luck," Tad said.

"I don't need luck," Sally1 replied.

Rebecca nodded to Sally1, then pulled at Tad, hurrying him away. Neither spoke until they were around the corner.

"Okay," Tad said. "I've activated the dampening field and the scatterer on my PlusPhone. We can talk safely."

"I told you she was crazy," Rebecca said.

"I know, I know. I was wrong. But what do we do now? She probably has us under surveillance."

"We'll head toward the lab for now. But I think we have to give ourselves up. Plead ignorance. Give them everything we have. It might be our only chance. You still have that canister of the antidote?"

Tad reached into his pocket and pulled it out.

"Good," Rebecca said. "We may need that as a bargaining chip."

***

Manyara Harris called up the surveillance program on her PlusPhone. Tracking their progress, she noted with satisfaction that they were headed toward her hidden lab.

Although it wasn't imperative that Tad and Rebecca reach the lab, it would solve a number of minor problems. Manyara had rigged the lab to explode when they entered the access codes. And if they ran instead, the lab would blow anyway. She'd already set the detonator remotely. The explosion would occur in twenty-six hours. She'd meant to have it modified so that she could blow it at any time, but she hadn't gotten around to it. No matter: it would explode just the same.

"Why didn't you let us kill them?" Wally1 asked.

"An experiment," she replied. "I wanted to see if they would obey me. And they'll die soon enough anyway. Besides, they may still be useful."

"They could cause trouble."

"They don't matter. Eli does."

Manyara engaged the cluster scrambler that Tad had devised for her and activated the Susquehanna Sally program, which modified her appearance, making her seem younger, more multi-racial and with a more soothing voice. Then she dialed up Eli's private number at CINTEP, knowing that the connection would be monitored. A trace of the call would lead them to a series of cutouts in multiple countries. Eli needed to know his day of reckoning had come. This latest version of the virus was unstoppable. It would make all previous versions seem tame by comparison.

"Hello, Sally," Lendra Riley answered, looking tired and pale. "Or should I call you Manyara?"

Manyara smiled. "Almost forgot about you," she said. "Message for Eli."

"Eli is unavailable at the moment," Riley replied.

"Giving him a truth kit," Manyara said, noting with satisfaction Riley's slightly widening eyes, "won't help you. He knows nothing."

Riley leaned forward, elbows on her desk. "Why did you call?"

"Wanted to say goodbye." Manyara chuckled.

Riley stared at Manyara for a long moment, as if gathering her thoughts or accessing her interface. "You really think you can hide behind that scrambler program? We're going to find you. Soon."

"How little you understand."

"We're coming for you. There's no hiding."

"Not worth our time."

Manyara disconnected.

Wally1 brought up surveillance footage on his PlusPhone and showed it to her—Tad and Rebecca headed the wrong way. "They decided to run," he said.

"No matter. Once the virus escapes from the lab, no human will survive."

Wally1 nodded his satisfaction, knowing he would die, just like the rest of them, but not caring. The conditioning of his mind was a beautiful thing. If only every human could be programmed that way—the virus might not be necessary.

Chapter 24

Sally23 had awoken from her nap with the sudden realization that she didn't want to die; she didn't want Brosk to die; she had made a terrible mistake aligning herself with Sally2; and she was a fool because there was no turning back now. How could she have done such a stupid thing? Had she wanted to kill everyone when she joined the group or had that desire been programmed into her? She felt a clarity of thought she hadn't experienced for a long time, as if she'd just emerged from a nightmarish fog into a harsh reality. But she managed to hold herself together, show no sign of her unease.

Before leaving for Hyde Park, Sally23 had helped Wally2 decrypt Sally1's last message for Sally2, instructing the cell to disperse all reserves of the virus, and informing them that Sally1's final creation—the ultimate killing virus—would be released in twenty-four hours. She couldn't even sabotage the message because Wally2 knew enough to keep her honest.

Now, sick at heart, she used the neuro-controller to guide Brosk's movements as they walked through the park. Dark clouds threatened rain. Good. If it rained, people would stay home. Fewer would die—though she supposed they would all die of the virus eventually. She didn't tell Brosk about Sally1's newest strain. Let him die thinking humanity still had a chance.

"I want to kill you," Brosk said through clenched teeth. "I know I've been conditioned to desire that, but I can't stop myself from yearning to strangle you. However, I'm now sure that Sally2 is Dr. Leah Shafer. She's the only one who could have programmed my mind so completely."

Sally23 reached up and turned off the comm unit in her ear. "I know I deserve to die," she said. "Somehow I got sucked into this. I can't figure out how. that happened. How could I have wanted to wipe out humanity?"

"You probably didn't. Most likely, you felt a general hostility that she exploited when you first met, when she had you hooked up to a polygraph that was actually a machine designed to alter your mind with electrical impulses. She may even have slipped you drugs or nanobots to further accelerate the conditioning."

"Then why don't I want to kill people now?"

"Perhaps the conditioning was temporary and it's wearing off."

Sally23 turned her ear bud back on.

"What's going on?" Sally2 asked. "I lost you for a moment."

"I don't know," Sally23 said. "Some glitch, maybe."

She spotted the Wallys, as well as Sally8 and Sally17, walking separately up ahead. The two Sallies were there to ensure that she didn't try to run, as if running were an option. A faint, almost unnoticeable glow surrounded both Sallies, indicating their shields were activated. Both Sallies would be armed with Las-pistols.

She herself carried no weapons, unless she counted Brosk. When his body exploded, the immediate kill zone would be twenty yards across, while the ensuing release of the virus would spread over a radius of nearly a mile within a few minutes. Even though Sally2 had excluded her from the strategy session, saying it was best that Sally23 not know how they planned to eliminate the CINTEP agents, Sally23 knew that much. She felt glad that she hadn't pointed out the possible flaw in Sally2's new version of the virus. Not that it mattered. By the close of the day, Sally23 would be dead too.

Sally2 said, "I think you turned it off. I think you're going to run."

"You can see what's happening," Sally23 replied. "And if you can't, you can check with Sally8 and Sally17. We're right where we're supposed to be."

The many cameras mounted throughout the park captured their movements, so the CINTEP agents ought to arrive soon. Brosk glared at Sally23, his eyes leaking tears of agony, as each step brought them closer to death.

"I know you'll run," Sally2 said.

"You sound like you want to," Sally23 replied.

She steered Brosk south toward the new band shell, which had been built a few years ago, and where a concert was scheduled to begin shortly. Given Brosk's condition and Sally23's unfamiliarity with the controller, the band shell looked impossibly far away. She knew that Sally2 had planned the attack for right after the concert began, when the park would be at its most crowded. Already thousands of people filled the park. Young and old, wrapped up in jackets and hats, they came out despite the weather and the threat of contagion. Like Londoners before them, they seemed determined to live their lives, enjoy themselves regardless of hardship. Sally23 couldn't help but admire their spirit. This is what I used to want to destroy, she thought.

The way Brosk navigated under the controller drew stares from fellow pedestrians. They gave him looks of fear and pity, no doubt assuming he suffered from some malady and that Sally23 was his caregiver. Would death be painful? Most likely it would be quick enough that she'd feel nothing. She planned to stay with Brosk when Sally2 detonated the nano-explosives in his body. She'd sit next to him on a bench, enjoying the music, trying not to focus on the inevitable.

Up ahead on the path, she saw her mother pushing a pram. Mum! Then she realized it was just a woman who looked like her mother. The woman wore a coat exactly like her mother's, and she walked in a similar fashion, rolling a little as she moved. Sally23 regained her composure and continued on. She concentrated on working the controller properly as she walked Brosk south. Glancing behind her, she spotted Wally5 and Wally6, spreading out. Each carried a canister in his hand, either the virus or some sort of explosive. She couldn't find Wally2 or Wally3 in the crowd. Up ahead, Sally8 and Sally17 stopped just north of the new band shell.

Brosk's breathing became ragged.

"How do you feel?" she asked.

"Heavy," Brosk replied. "Everything hurts." He inhaled and exhaled several times, then said, "Awful chest pain. And I want to kill you more than anything in the world, more than I want to take my next breath."

"Trogan," she said, "I . . ."

"Save it, bitch." The intensity of his emotion unsettled her, even though she had steeled herself for his hatred.

"I'm sorry."

Brosk exhaled sharply in what might have been laughter or pain. Then he took several deep breaths. "You betrayed me," he said. "Drop that controller for one second and I'll break your neck." Brosk grunted as his feet continued moving. He managed to turn his head and look into her eyes. For a brief moment the hatred there dissolved into something like understanding. Then the hardness returned to his eyes.

Again he breathed deeply, building up oxygen in his lungs before trying to speak. "I think I remember Sally2 making connections in my brain." He paused as if he'd just run a mile. "But I definitely remember you infecting me with the virus when we slept together. Is that an accurate memory?"

Sally23 turned off her ear bud. "No. She programmed that into you."

"I suspected that. I still hate you. I'll still kill you if I can. I can't fight that. It's odd to feel this much hatred and have some detached part of my brain realize that the feeling isn't real."

"So you can tell you've been programmed?"

"Kind of."

"Yet you can't stop the desire?"

"Maybe if I had more time to fight it."

Sally23 reached up and turned on the comm unit again. "Hello?" she said. "Hello?"

Sally2 said, "I ought to blow you up right now."

"Why? Because you gave me a defective ear bud?"

"I don't know what your game is," Sally2 said.

"I don't know what yours is either," Sally23 replied. "Why aren't you here with us? Planning to run away? Live to fight another day?"

"Oh, I get it," Sally2 said. "You want me to kill Brosk now. You want me to detonate him before the CINTEP agents arrive. Your last noble act?"

"I just want you dead."

Sally2 laughed. "Finally some honesty."

"Why don't you be honest with me? You plan to live, don't you?"

"Where would I go?"

Again Sally23 turned off the ear bud.

"Sally2 is planning to run," she said to Brosk. "Any idea where she would go?"

Brosk's head dropped a few millimeters. Again he took a few deep breaths. "I don't know." His jaw quivered. "I can't think. I want to kill you so badly. Is that what it feels like to be a Sally? Do you want to kill everyone?"

Sally23 looked into his dark brown eyes. "Not anymore." She reached over and wiped the tears from his cheeks.

Somehow Brosk grabbed her jacket sleeve, gripped it tightly, almost causing her to fall. She struggled with her balance for a second and adjusted the controller to keep Brosk walking. He said, "You're going to die today."

"We're all going to die today," Sally 23 said. "This is the final push. The Sallies are dispersing their remaining supplies of the virus. Sally2 injected a series of nano-explosives into your body, and your clothes are filled with the virus. You're rigged to explode soon—maybe an hour. If we try to run, she'll detonate you remotely. And when the CINTEP agents arrive, she'll blow us up."

"She can detonate me remotely?" Brosk asked.

"Yes."

"Then maybe I have a solution."

"It's too late to stop the virus from being released."

Brosk shook his head. "I might be able to block her signal."

Hope flared up inside her—a tiny straw in a current of despair.

***

Curtik worked his mechanical hand while shuffling his feet to The Viral Death Dance by the Crystal Skull Bangers: their newest song, celebrating the end of the known world. He wished he could fight someone. He no longer had the urge to kill mindlessly, but God, a fight would feel good. He'd love to test out this new hand.

"Curtik," Zora said from the doorway.

Curtik lowered the volume on his implant and cursed himself for failing to hear her approach. "What?"

"We've located Brosk again."

"Another trap?"

"Of course."

"Major Somers?"

"Ned's setting it up with him right now. Let's move."

"Woo hoo! Action." Curtik trotted for the door. As he caught up to Zora, he swatted her ass with his mechanical hand.

"Ow! What are you doing?"

"Just havin' a bit of fun. Come on, Zora. We're back in the game."

"It was your impatience that cost you your hand last time."

"And I'd do it again in a second. This thing's plowing fantastic."

"Yes, but next time you might cost me a hand. Or Ned. Or you might get some innocent bystander blown up."

"Oh, the horror!" Curtik raced ahead, beating Zora to Major Somers' office off the lobby, where Jefferson and Major Somers stood inside the door. He slowed as he reached the room, stopping before the two older men. He tried to hide his broad grin but ended up giggling. Major Somers shook his head as Jefferson continued watching video of pathways in a park.

"This isn't a game, son," Major Somers said. "This time it'll be to the death."

Jefferson turned to Curtik, nodding his agreement. "They've brought out an unknown number of people. They claim they're spread out across Hyde Park. Probably all armed. Probably all carrying the virus."

"The Viral Death Dance," Curtik said. "Gimme a Las-pistol and let's kick some ass."

"We can't go in big," Zora said. "We got a message from the local Sally cell. They say they only want us."

"You and me?"

"And Ned. They know what we look like, so no masks. They're bringing Brosk to the park. A big concert starts soon." She pointed to the video, which now displayed a band shell, filling with people.

"They're threatening to release those canisters of the virus if we don't show," Jefferson said.

"And if we try to clear the park," Major Somers said, "they say they'll also release the virus. So far, our mini-drones have been able to identify only two hostiles in addition to the girl with Brosk."

Zora gestured to Jefferson and Curtik. "I think we have to go in lightly, maybe sacrifice ourselves, keep a larger force off site in case we're taken."

Jefferson shrugged. "They're obviously going to release the virus anyway. But they clearly want to take us out as part of their strategy. They've heard about Jeremiah's immunity and they're afraid all the CINTEP people have it. So we'll give them a target to shoot for. And Major Somers can have his people take them out once we identify them. Regardless of how we fare, we can't let them walk away to infect the larger population. Win or lose, it ends here."

"Agreed," Major Somers said. "I already cleared that with Downing Street. And you go in with the SAS security squad." Curtik must have looked confused because Major Somers added, "Similar to your Elite Ops troopers."

"They'll just disperse the virus if they spot your troopers," Zora said.

"Yeah," Curtik said. "Zora and I are immune. Better that we go in first."

"As far as you know, you're immune," Jefferson corrected him.

"The SAS go in with you or you don't go in at all," Major Somers said. "Frankly, some suggested that would be preferable to allowing you to operate in London."

Jefferson held up his hands. "We're happy to follow your lead."

"Think happy thoughts, Major," Curtik said, forcing a smile. "We might get ourselves blown up again."

"We have an unknown number of hostiles," Major Somers said, ignoring Curtik's comment. "The only persons we know for certain are connected to the Sally movement are these women." He pointed to the wall screen, where a tall black woman and a shorter Asian woman walked, and a blue-eyed redhead strolled beside Brosk through the park. "Let's try to take the one with Brosk alive if we can."

"Hey," Curtik said. "She's kinda cute."

"Brosk," Jefferson said, "isn't the priority." He rubbed his face and Curtik sensed it pained him to point that out. "We'll save him if we can, but our main concern is stopping the virus."

"Let's move, people." Major Somers led them out.

***

"Need to sit down," Brosk gasped. "Hard to breathe."

"There's a bench just up ahead," Sally23 said. "What's your plan?"

"Remove your ear bud," Brosk said. "We can use your tech repair kit to modify it, set up a jammer. It won't be very powerful, but if I keep it in my possession, it might be strong enough to prevent a radio signal from reaching me. You bitch!" Brosk suddenly shouted. "I'll kill you!" His hands shook. "It helps to yell."

He exhaled heavily, gathering his composure as dozens of people stared at them, no doubt wondering if Brosk intended violence against her. Sally23 steered Brosk to the bench, using the controller to force him to sit. "We'll get your medication, dear," she spoke loudly enough to be overheard. Most of the onlookers turned away.

"You know this won't save you," Sally23 said. "The explosives are still coalescing inside your chest. They'll still detonate within the hour."

"But we can buy time. Maybe enough for me to get someplace safe, where I can let the explosives off without hurting anyone."

"The river," Sally23 said. "She infected you with a new version of the virus. I saw the specs briefly, and I think it's water soluble. If we can somehow get to the river, get you underneath the water, the virus should dissipate, settle into the riverbed and harm no one."

"You sure?" Brosk asked.

"No," Sally23 said. "I didn't get a lot of time to study the schematics."

Brosk nodded toward Sally8 and Sally17. "We still have armed guards to get past."

"CINTEP will take care of them."

"Right. Hurry," Brosk pleaded. "The pain is . . . difficult."

Sally23 glanced at the band shell, about forty yards away. A light drizzle began. A crowd filled the seating area out front of the band shell—almost all of them mothers with young children—and all of them about to die. Sally23 shivered. She wondered how much was the cold and how much the understanding that she had helped make their imminent deaths possible. Opening her tech repair kit, she said, "What do I do?"

"You have to reconfigure the receiver, change the modulation, and produce a static field to interfere with incoming signals."

Sally23 picked up the ear bud and began adjusting the modulation.

"Murderer!" Brosk yelled. "Bitch! Recalibrate the ultrasonic transducer. Then adjust the . . . Dead! Adjust the frequency to seven point six oh four, or any similar variant that would be difficult to match quickly. I'll need . . . I'll need . . . I need to torture you. Strangle your scrawny neck! I'll need help to get to the river."

"I'll take you when we've got this earbud reconfigured."

Sally23 caught sight of Sally8 now, the tall Nigerian moving toward her out of the crowd as most of the passersby quickly distanced themselves, flicking unsettled glances at her and Brosk. One pedestrian, however, began jogging toward them. Sally17 emerged from behind a tree and fired a brief Las-pulse—a red streak of light that pierced the man's cheek, dropping him instantly.

Several people saw the man fall, but they apparently didn't see the red laser pulse. Only one woman screamed. A few people hurried away. Others caught the tension in the area and began to clear out. But just then the musicians appeared on stage to enthusiastic applause.

"Where the hell are the CINTEP people?" Sally8 asked.

"You're all dead!" Brosk yelled. "Every one of you."

"Shut him up," Sally8 ordered.

"I need to kill somebody soon," Sally17 said.

"Why?" Sally23 said. "Did you ever think you might be conditioned to feel that?"

"What do you mean?" Sally17 asked.

"Maybe you really don't want to kill anybody at all. Maybe your mind has just been programmed to want it."

"But then I still want it, don't I."

"Yes, but it's not real."

Four pedestrians stood nearby, watching the Sallies as if mesmerized by them, ignoring the music emanating from the band shell—a popular children's song. Sally17 pointed her Las-pistols at the four and fired two purple bursts that struck the ground at their feet. She giggled as they scattered. "Feels real."

The concert continued, its celebrants largely unaware of the situation behind them. A few people in the back rows glanced over nervously at the fallen man. Most of them turned their attention back to the stage, but one woman made her way in his direction.

Brosk continued to curse, more softly now, almost a chant, as his face contorted in agony. Despite the controls on his movements, he managed to clench his hands into fists, before opening them wide, then repeating the movement over and over while Sally23 finished adjusting the ear bud.

Sally8 moved a few feet closer, a canister in her hand, her eyes darting left and right before focusing on Sally23's hands. Sally17 hung back a few paces.

"What're you doing?" Sally8 asked.

"Should we kill 'em now?" Sally17 asked.

Sally8 held up her right hand while Sally17 aimed her Las-pistols at Sally23.

"My ear bud isn't working," Sally23 said.

"Sally2 said you're gonna run."

"Do I look like I'm running?"

Sally8 again looked left and right, her eyes narrow, her body tense. Her right hand crept toward the canister in her left hand, the fingers twitching slightly.

"If you kill us now," Sally23 said, "you'll lose the chance to get the CINTEP agents. What's more, they'll probably just blow this whole area sky high. I know you're nervous, but get control of yourselves."

Sally8 frowned, her eyes looking past Sally23, listening to Sally2 through her ear bud.

The woman who had spotted the dead man reached him, touched his neck and placed a call on her PlusPhone. Meanwhile, some of the concertgoers at the back of the band shell began gathering up their children and possessions and making for the gates despite the cries of their kids, who wanted to stay for the music. Sally23 noticed the woman with the coat like her mother's. The woman bent over the pram. Was she leaving? Would she manage to escape? Run. Go. But she straightened, returning her attention to the musicians on stage, oblivious to the deadly scene behind her.

"Sally2 sent you out here to be killed," Brosk said to Sally8, his voice high and quavering, betraying his pain, "while she runs away. Did you know that she used to work for CINTEP, and that she changed her appearance surgically? She looks better now. Why would she make herself look better unless she wants to live?"

"Shut up," Sally17 said. She raised her right arm, pointing a Las-pistol at Brosk's head. She kept the other Las-pistol squarely centered on Sally23's torso.

"Why isn't she here?" Sally23 followed Brosk's lead. "Everyone else is. We all know this is the final battle. So why isn't she fighting alongside us? Maybe Brosk is right. I know we've all been infected with the virus, but I don't know if she has. Perhaps she has no intention of dying."

"Everyone will die," Sally17 said. "There's no escaping the virus."

"As far as you know," Brosk said. "What if she lied to you?"

Sally8 focused on Sally23 now, frowning in confusion.

"We're just asking questions," Sally23 said. "Doesn't it seem odd to you that she's the only one not here?"

"Well?" Sally8 asked.

Sally23 realized Sally8 was speaking to Sally2. She risked a glance at Brosk, who looked from her eyes to her hands. Sally23 nodded, indicating that she'd finished the reconfiguration of the ear bud. Hopefully it was strong enough to jam any signal that Sally2 might send. Trogan exhaled slowly and closed his eyes. But their problems, Sally23 knew, were far from over. How were they going to get to the river?

Chapter 25

The van pulled up to Hyde Park Gate just as Major Somers finished his briefing. "Remember, kids," he said, "we don't want an international incident. You're here because the terrorists want you here. You will not carry weapons. You will assist the SAS troopers wherever possible, but you will leave the operational work to them. Got it?"

"Kids?" Curtik said. A fine rage built inside his brain, his vision beginning to blur. He was tired of Somers treating him like a bug.

Zora touched his arm and shook her head. "No trouble," she whispered, "or they'll just leave you behind."

"You're right," Curtik said, tamping down the anger. *After all, I did kill the poor bastard's nephew.* "Being good, starting . . . now."

The van door opened to the strains of a children's concert. Curtik noted the dozen police officers at the entrance, looking uncomfortable in the light rain. Behind them stood the SAS security squad—eight massive men beside the park entrance wearing black casual fatigues and red berets, Las-rifles in their hands, interfaces at their temples. Two of them carried black tubes about two feet long and six inches in diameter.

"Particle beam cannons. Awesome!" Curtik hopped down.

He experienced a brief urge to attack the bigger SAS trooper with the particle beam cannon, see if the guy was as tough as Marschenko, but he kept himself in check. *Good on me!*

He flexed his mechanical hand as he bounced from foot to foot. His body practically hummed with eagerness. A few screams emerged from the park. They sounded panicky, not associated with the concert. Curtik moved forward, but Jefferson grabbed his arm.

"Hold on," Major Somers said. "You go in with Wes." He indicated the largest SAS trooper with a Las-rifle. The man had to be six and a-half feet tall, and 250 pounds. Curtik hoped the beast wouldn't slow him down.

"Zora," Major Somers added, "you're with Timothy. Perry," Major Somers pointed at a trooper with a particle beam cannon, "you take Ned."

Curtik activated his shield, watching in delight as the rain hit it and evaporated immediately. Cool. He used his implant to access the images from the mini-drones previously released into the park. Zora and Jefferson, both without implants, activated their Plus-Glasses. Handfuls of people began to emerge from the park now, some jogging, some walking at a brisk pace. When they saw the forces lined up outside, they quickly stepped aside.

Major Somers said, "You can see that we've got two hostiles next to Brosk and the young woman, who we presume is also a hostile."

"Grrr," Curtik said softly as he studied the image of the redhead beside Brosk. "I could eat her up. She's a cutie-pie."

"We don't know how many other hostiles are in the area," Major Somers said, "so be careful. Shoot first, ask questions later."

"Pay attention," Jefferson said as he tapped Curtik on the shoulder. "Our job is to contain the virus. Remember, Brosk isn't our first priority. Your people ready, Major Somers?"

"We're ready."

"Let's do it."

Curtik cued The Viral Death Dance as he moved forward, bouncing to the jangly rhythms of the Crystal Skull Bangers:

Let 'em fall, their faces blue
Their arms and legs all twitchy

The rotting corpses flood the ground
Death Dance, baby, ultra-bitchy.

Now that was art!

Curtik danced beside Zora, singing the words loud enough for her to hear. Timothy and Wes followed behind. Curtik felt a little better now that he was moving. But Zora just shook her head. Poor girl had no sense of humor at all.

As they entered the park ahead of the SAS troopers, Curtik took in the band shell, the musicians and the activity taking place near the park bench, where Brosk sat beside the cute terrorist. The tall black woman and the Asian girl stood in front of them, weapons in their hands, shields surrounding them with a faint yellow glow. The musicians suddenly stopped playing and more people noticed the SAS troopers. A few screams began an exodus and the police quickly moved to evacuate people in an orderly fashion.

Jefferson spoke softly: "Curtik, you and I head toward Brosk. Zora, you stay with Timothy."

Curtik and Jefferson walked toward Brosk and the cutie-pie, trailed by Wes and Perry. Curtik kept an eye on the tall black woman and the short Asian girl. They stared back, shifting sideways a few feet. The tall black woman, Curtik realized, carried a canister in one hand, probably containing the virus. Beyond them, a handful of people stood watching. Idiots! Dozens of others ran along the path past them in an effort to get away.

Curtik kept his focus on Brosk and the cutie-pie, vaguely noting that people were going down under the fire of the SAS troopers. God, he wished he had a Las-rifle. Probably good that I don't. I might just fire at random. That would be delicious—but wrong.

The tall black woman adjusted her shield to full intensity. It produced a bright white glow. Raindrops hitting it instantly turned to steam. Behind her, the short Asian girl's shield flickered between full and low power. She carried a pair of Las-pistols. Oh, girlie, you are so dead.

With his peripheral vision, Curtik saw red laser pulses fly, then he heard the blast of Perry's particle beam cannon. The black woman's shield vanished as the particle beam cannon's destructive force shredded it. Another blast from the particle beam cannon and she exploded into a pink cloud, the canister blowing apart at the same time. Not a grenade. Must have been loaded with the virus.

Now the Asian girl fired her Las-pistols at Curtik. He instinctively ducked, even though he knew his shield would protect him. Perry returned fire with his particle beam cannon. As her shield blew apart, Wes fired a red laser pulse at her, dropping her to the ground without even a scream.

Just like that the fight was over. People got to their feet as the police beckoned for them to leave. The SAS troopers spread out in a search for more hostiles, but no one else appeared to be a threat.

The smell of burning chemicals hit Curtik's nostrils as he and Jefferson approached Brosk and the cutie-pie.

As they neared, Brosk said, "Stay back."

Jefferson halted and said, "Trogan."

"Ned," Brosk replied, his voice strained.

"Went to a lot of trouble to get me here," Jefferson said.

Brosk forced a smile. "I wanted you to witness my dramatic escape."

"I'm sure it'll be spectacular. What's the situation?"

As Curtik reached for the cutie-pie, Brosk said, "Stay back. Don't hurt her. She's helping me." Curtik pulled his hand away.

The cutie-pie placed a small ear bud in Brosk's lap. Then she grabbed a box by her side—a neuro-controller. "You might want to back away," she said. She adjusted the neuro-controller and Brosk grabbed the ear bud.

She's controlling his movements?

"What did they do to you, Trogan?" Jefferson said.

"I don't have much time," Brosk said.

"He's been rigged to explode," the cutie-pie added.

"Nano-explosives?" Jefferson asked.

"Remember Dr. Leah Shafer?" Brosk said.

Jefferson nodded. "Tall, obsessive-compulsive, unfriendly."

"That's her. She's changed her appearance, probably genetic surgery. Made herself more attractive. She's Sally2."

"Where is she?"

The cutie-pie said, "She was in that building undergoing renovation on Gloucester Terrace, a few blocks north. She'll run—Lancaster Gate or Paddington Station or maybe Queensway or Bayswater. I don't know where she's going, but I'm sure she'll run. I have to get Trogan to the river."

"Why?"

"He's infected with a new version of the virus. In fact, his clothes are loaded with it as well. They're also rigged with explosives, making him into a dirty bomb that Sally2 planned to detonate when you arrived."

Curtik felt an urge to back away. He shook it off.

"So why hasn't she done it?" he asked.

"Trogan showed me how to modify the ear bud to create a homemade jammer—disrupt the incoming signal. But we're not safe. He's still going to explode. Soon. Some of the nano-explosives inside his body are concentrating in his chest. When they reach critical mass, he'll detonate."

"We can put him into an armored vehicle—isolate him there."

"The electronics might detonate the explosives before he gets inside. And believe me, you don't want this version of the virus airborne." The cutie-pie hesitated for a moment, her lower lip quivering. "But if we get him to the river, submerge him before he blows . . . I believe this new version of the virus is water soluble. We might be able to dissipate its effects that way."

Jefferson shook his head. "How are you going to get there?"

The cutie-pie said, "With this controller, I can help him walk."

"I'll go too," Curtik said.

"No, I'll go," Jefferson said. "You help Zora with the cleanup."

"Not a chance, Neddy Boy. You're much more valuable than me. I'm muscle. You're the brains. I'll get Brosk to the river. You know this Dr. Shafer. You have to help find her before she gets away."

"Major Somers?" Jefferson said as he looked toward the gates. "Lendra?"

Major Somers spoke into Curtik's implant: "I'm already shutting down the tube all around here for the next couple hours.

Lendra added: "I'm forwarding a few pictures of Dr. Leah Shafer, along with a computer simulation of what she might look like."

Major Somers said: "Wes will escort you to the river."

Curtik started forward, but the cutie-pie held up her hand. "You'd better turn off that shield first," she said. "It might set off the explosives."

Deactivating his shield, Curtik helped Brosk to his feet. The cutie-pie used the controller to assist Brosk's movements as well.

Jefferson looked at Brosk, his face fallen in sadness. "Trogan, I . . ."

"It's okay, Ned," Brosk replied. "It's going to be all right."

Jefferson clapped Brosk on the shoulder. "I just want you to know how much I've enjoyed working with you, Brosk. You're one of the best men I've ever met. Curtik here will take care of you. He's Jeremiah's son."

Brosk blinked rapidly several times, as if trying to hold back tears or keep out the rain, and Curtik wondered what it felt like to know you were going to die soon. Brosk was holding himself together well. Would I be that brave if I was going to die? Probably. I'm a stallion.

"Let's go," Brosk said.

Wes moved forward, Curtik pulling Brosk along with him, while the cutie-pie walked beside them, keeping Brosk's feet from tripping over each other.

"We're clearing a path for you," Major Somers said.

Wes led the way. Brosk couldn't help much, so Curtik carried most of his weight. He could smell Brosk's fear, could sense the anxiety, as well as the rage.

"I can tell you're furious," he said. "I remember feeling that on the Moon."

"I've been conditioned," Brosk replied, breathing heavily, "to want to kill her." He took another deep breath. "I want it more than anything

I've ever wanted in my life. She drops that controller and she'll be dead before she gets two steps away."

"Yummy," Curtik said as he glanced over at the cutie-pie. "So are you a bad guy or a good guy?"

"I don't know," the cutie-pie replied.

"Me either. I used to think I was evil, and I liked that. But now I'm not so sure."

"I don't think anybody's completely evil, except for Sally2, and Sally1. But I don't think anybody's completely good either. Or if they are, I haven't met them. You know anyone who's completely good?"

Curtik laughed. "I haven't met anyone like that either."

Ahead of them Wes waited at Hyde Park Gate. As they approached, Curtik felt Brosk's body tremble. Sweat or rain or a combination of both ran down his reddened face. Each breath amounted to little more than an agonizing grunt. Although Curtik hadn't really thought about the kind of pain his father had endured the past year, the kind of pain Zora had so recently tried to emulate, he realized Brosk's agony must be something like that.

"Good grunting," Curtik said. "Very determined. I like that."

"We'll never," Brosk wheezed, "make it to the river in time."

"Tell Brosk," Jefferson offered through Curtik's implant, "that I want his butterfly collection after he's dead."

What? Curtik sent back.

"Just tell him," Jefferson said. "Exactly as I said it."

Okay. "Ned told me to tell you that he wants your butterfly collection after you're dead."

Brosk actually laughed, a rough sound that ended in a hacking cough. "That bastard! He'll get nothing from me. Nothing! You hear me, Ned?" Brosk yelled.

"What's that about?" the cutie-pie asked.

"A private joke," Brosk said as he picked up his pace. He still relied heavily on Curtik but he'd somehow found new strength in his legs. "I'll tell you later." He winked and tried to grin before a wince stopped him.

As they emerged from the park, Curtik saw that the police had stopped traffic, allowing them to cross over toward what Curtik's implant told him was Wellington Arch. Hundreds of people lined the streets. Motorists stood outside their stopped cars to get a glimpse at what was holding up traffic. Most of them held PlusPhones. Curtik checked his implant and saw that the incident had already made the news, their movements now being tracked by cameras.

Even a few weeks ago Curtik would have enjoyed watching the panic on people's faces. Now he experienced a sort of confusion. These were the people he and Zora had been created to replace. They were lesser versions: incomplete. But he couldn't hate them like he once had. He only pitied them. As he walked, Curtik smelled the fear in the air—Brosk's and the cutie-pie's, and maybe his own. Would they blow up before they reached the river? That would be so cruel.

Brosk moved like an old man as Curtik dragged him toward Buckingham Palace Gardens. The rain lightened to a drizzle, though it still felt cold.

"Need," Brosk said, "to go faster."

"He's feeling an increasing tightness in his chest," the cutie-pie said. She placed her free hand under Brosk's jacket and felt his chest. Why did that make Curtik jealous? "But I think we've got some time before the explosives reach critical mass."

"Faster it is," Curtik said. "Hang on, you old Trogan horse."

They increased their pace, Curtik practically dragging Brosk along, and passed Wellington Arch, keeping on the street—Constitution Hill—Curtik realized, as Wes and the police cleared the roadway.

"Talk," Brosk said, his breath coming in ragged gasps. "Distracts me."

"Okay," the cutie-pie said. "What do you want to talk about?"

"Not me," Brosk managed. "You two."

"Right." The cutie-pie turned to Curtik. "This isn't the only problem you've got. Sally1 is planning to disperse her newest version of the virus in less than twenty-four hours. She says it's unstoppable—the ultimate killing virus."

"How?"

"I don't know."

"Well," Curtik said, "we're putting our best man on it."

"It's no joke. Her message made it sound like she'd already set the process in motion, like it couldn't be halted. She's probably hidden it somewhere and installed a timer to ensure its release, regardless of whether she's captured."

"We already know who she is." Curtik glanced at Buckingham Palace and the Victoria Memorial beyond that. "CINTEP will find her."

"So you're really Jeremiah Jones's son," the cutie-pie said.

"You know him?"

"He's the man Sally1 was worried about. He has some sort of immunity to previous versions of the virus. He's the one we thought we had trapped in Holland Park."

Curtik held up his mechanical hand. "That would be me. You kinda blew up my hand."

"Oh," the cutie-pie said. "Sorry."

"No, it's fine." Curtik tried to make it sound casual, like all the action vid stars he'd seen.

"Your new hand is kind of cool," the cutie-pie said.

"It is, right? It's awesome."

They came up on the palace. Wes waved them around the corner, to where the Changing of the Guard took place. Curtik listened to Brosk's breathing for a moment. It still sounded labored, though Curtik didn't think it had worsened. But Brosk weaved a little now, whether from exhaustion or agony, Curtik couldn't say. His implant showed they were coming up on The Queen's Gallery and Birdcage Walk, which would take them all the way to Bridge Street, past Big Ben and onto Westminster Bridge—assuming they didn't explode first.

Brosk shivered. Was that fear or just the cold rain? Curtik wanted to ask if he was afraid of dying, but he already knew the answer. He could smell it. And yet Brosk maintained such an outward calm. Had he learned to be brave through watching action vids too?

"Keep him talking," Jefferson spoke into his implant. "Distract him."

Curtik turned to the cutie-pie. "So, you come here often?"

Brosk managed a laugh that sounded more like a snort.

"Seriously," Curtik said, "why are you helping us?"

The cutie-pie shrugged. "Lots of reasons. Sally2 killed my mother. She's insane. And Trogan helped me see what people can become, how we can achieve kindness and selflessness if we just work at it. But I suppose what it boils down to is this—I realized the Sallies were wrong. If humans are going to ruin the planet, that's part of the natural order. All species become extinct eventually. Just in the last year we've lost forty species that we know of. More will follow. And I think we'll probably die out too—unless we can become more like Trogan . . . or Devereaux. We don't need to accelerate the destructive process. Humans are already on that path."

"We definitely seem to be," Curtik said as they reached Birdcage Walk, where Brosk apparently caught a second wind, for his strides grew a little longer and he no longer leaned quite so heavily on Curtik.

"Are you like Trogan?"

"Yeah," Curtik replied. He almost said he was the next generation, better than Brosk. But he held back, partly because he knew the cutie-pie didn't want to hear that, partly because he was no longer certain that was true. He wasn't sure he could be this brave if the situation were reversed.

"People always," Brosk huffed, "find a way to survive."

"So far," the cutie-pie conceded. "But every year that passes, we limit our options more. We grow more technological, moving further away from the planet that birthed us."

Brosk tightened up, his muscles locking on him momentarily, and Curtik was forced to take almost his whole weight.

"We're all going to die," the cutie-pie said.

"That doesn't mean we wanna," Curtik said. "I know Brosk doesn't wanna die. And look at all these people around us. They don't wanna die either."

Curtik took in the vast number of people watching them. Many held PlusPhones out as cameras, filming their every move. Many more glanced down at their PlusPhones, probably watching footage shot by their fellow bystanders, or following near-instantaneous news reports of The Panic in the Park, as his implant showed the media were calling it. A crowd clapped politely as they passed, not knowing who they were or why they were passing, but believing they were on the side of the angels because of their escort. Mostly they fixated on Brosk, supported by Curtik as he slogged along to his death. Up ahead, Curtik spotted a traffic accident. A police officer stood behind the cars, waving Curtik and his companions through a narrow lane between vehicles. As they passed, the officer nodded at them, smiling at Brosk. They found a free lane past the accident, all the cars and scooters pulled over to the side of the road.

"Look at that little kid over there." Curtik pointed to a young boy holding a woman's hand. The boy waved at him. "And that old woman with the cane. She wants to live as long as she can. You can see it in her face—the worry, the fear. Nobody wants to die but you."

"Aren't you one of the cadets who tried to blow up the Earth?"

"I'm *never* gonna live that down. *One time*, I fired a coupla Las-cannons. I was programmed to do that."

The cutie-pie laughed: not a cruel laugh, but a shared understanding of the lunacy of the moment.

"This is bizarre," Curtik said, "isn't it."

"Ironic," the cutie-pie said, "that two people who tried to destroy humanity are now trying to save it."

"I don't really get irony," Curtik conceded.

The cutie-pie laughed again. She had a wonderful laugh—throaty and genuine. Curtik joined her. Even Brosk smiled briefly. Then Brosk's breathing became labored again, the diseased straining of lungs damaged by the accumulation of nano-explosives. The cutie-pie began to cry softly. Again she placed her hand under Brosk's jacket, feeling his chest. This time she said nothing. When she pulled her hand back, she caught

Curtik's eye and shrugged. Brosk kept his eyes focused on the distance, as if afraid to acknowledge the truth.

"Try not to blow up yet," Curtik said to Brosk. "I really don't want to die."

Again Brosk snorted. "Okay. For your sake, I'll try. God, you're like your father."

"Is that an insult or a compliment?"

"Both, I guess."

"I don't want to die anymore, either," the cutie-pie said, her voice quavering, tears mingling with raindrops on her cheeks. "I accept that I'm going to. And soon. I can't stop it. But I don't desire it any longer. It's just that I used to think of people as unsalvageable."

"When I was on the Moon, I never thought about humans all that much, except as something to be eliminated."

"Me too," the cutie-pie agreed. "I saw humans doing so many bad things, selfish things—near-sighted and stupid actions that caused unspeakable suffering to the natural world—that I thought the planet needed to be rid of them. Of us. But all animals act that way. We just have more power to control our actions than other creatures do."

"Big Ben," Brosk rasped. "Almost there."

Curtik looked up. Sure enough, the landmark tower rose up before them—beyond it, Westminster Bridge, looking beautiful in the rain. Curtik spared another glance at Brosk, who stared ahead grimly. His breathing worsened yet again; he took in rapid gulps of air. Curtik thought he might explode at any moment. Clearly the cutie-pie had the same idea, for she again placed her hand inside Brosk's jacket to feel his chest. This time her eyes widened.

"We're not gonna make it," Curtik said, "are we?" He could feel his chest tightening, as if the bomb were inside him and not Brosk.

"Don't know," the cutie-pie said.

"Let him go," Curtik said. "I'll take him from here."

"No. I'll take him. You get away, while you can. Tell your people, about Sally1, the virus."

"They already know," Curtik replied. "I've broadcast everything to them."

"We go together," the cutie-pie said. "Brosk and I."

Brosk grunted, squeezing his arms tightly. Curtik easily countered the pressure. Did the cutie-pie really intend to jump off the bridge with Brosk?

"Ease up," Curtik said to Brosk. "Come on, old horse. You can do it. We're almost there. Hey, over there is a statue of Queen Boudicca on a chariot, crushing Romans. You wanna go see that for a minute? Nah, maybe if it was sunny. Man, it would be cool to have a chariot." Brosk forced a grin, managing to relax his grip.

A crowd of spectators waited by Big Ben. Dozens lined the street. They stayed back, watching Wes and the police clearing a lane. As Curtik dragged Brosk toward them, the crowd broke out into applause, as if they were watching a race, and in a way, they were. They yelled encouragement as Curtik and his companions neared. Somehow their good will lent Curtik strength. He could sense Brosk deriving a benefit from it as well.

"You're doing great, Curtik," Jefferson said into the implant.

With increased energy they passed the crowd and came up on the bridge. They jogged along the sidewalk, past dozens of spectators, some of whom reached out to touch Brosk or Curtik. Wes moved out to the middle of the bridge, where two police vehicles sat parked on the otherwise-cleared road.

"We'll jump when we reach the center of the Thames," the cutie-pie said.

"Right." Brosk managed only the single word.

Wes gestured to a spot near where he stood. "The water's deepest here."

Bizarre, Curtik thought. All this effort going into helping Brosk kill himself. As they neared the location, Brosk took a deep breath, steeling himself no doubt for what he had to do. The cutie-pie looked at Curtik with a sad smile and said, "Just help me get him up over the parapet and then run like hell."

But even as she spoke, Brosk somehow grabbed her. As she fell to the sidewalk with a scream, Brosk pounced on her. He put his hands around her neck and squeezed. Curtik punched him in the side of the head with his mechanical hand and pulled him away almost without thinking. Brosk stumbled and nearly fell.

"Sorry," Curtik said. "Could have killed you there. Not used to this hand yet." Then he laughed. "I'm a moron."

He pulled Brosk along with him as the cutie-pie got to her feet. She ran toward them, but Curtik held up his hand to keep her back. When they reached the point Wes had indicated, Brosk said, "Take her away from here." Then he turned to the cutie-pie and said, "Just give me enough movement to jump. Once I'm in the water, I'll be fine."

Curtik lifted Brosk up over the parapet and onto the ledge. The cutie-pie stood watching, her hand on the controller.

"I should be with you," the cutie-pie said.

"No," Brosk replied. "You may still have information that can be helpful. Now let me jump."

The cutie-pie moved the controller slightly and Brosk stepped off. He fell a long time, and he hit the water with a tremendous splash. For an instant Curtik thought the bomb inside Brosk had exploded. Then he realized it was just the impact of Brosk's landing. Wes moved to the parapet and looked over the edge. The spectators on the bridge surrounded Curtik, the cutie-pie and Wes, who found themselves pressed up against the parapet. Curtik peered into the rain-dappled water.

"Where the hell is Brosk?" he asked.

"He's going under the bridge," the cutie-pie yelled.

"But that's upstream."

"It's a tidal river."

"Out of the way," Wes yelled at the spectators as he led Curtik and the cutie-pie across to the other side of the bridge.

When they reached the parapet on that side, the cutie-pie said, "There he is."

Brosk's body drifted just below the surface, moving slowly upstream.

Suddenly Brosk lifted his head to take a breath. People pressed in against Curtik, all staring down at the water. There had to be hundreds watching. How much did they know? Were they aware that Brosk was loaded with the virus? Did they know he was going to explode soon?

Again Brosk surfaced. Why the hell didn't he stay down? And why hadn't he blown up yet?

"Down," the cutie-pie yelled. "You have to dive."

A few spectators chimed in, chanting, "Dive, dive, dive."

Brosk rolled onto his back for a moment as if trying to catch his breath. The chants grew louder. "Dive, dive, dive." Raindrops speckled the dark gray water. After a moment Brosk flipped over and dove again, deeper this time, because Curtik could no longer spot him. The crowd went quiet, only a few murmurs disturbing the air. The scene felt so calm.

And then Brosk exploded, a fountain of spray lifting a dozen feet into the air. The water roiled, a white effervescence on the brown river, gradually subsuming. *Brosk is dead. And I'm alive. We're alive.*

"Trogan," Jefferson whispered into Curtik's implant. "May you find peace."

The cutie-pie buried her face in Curtik's jacket. He put his arm around her, unsure what to make of this supposed terrorist, only knowing that he needed to hang on to her for a while.

"Take her into custody," Major Somers spoke through Curtik's implant, and Wes grabbed her arm. "Well done, lad," Major Somers added. "Very well done indeed."

As Wes tugged her arm, Curtik clung to her.

"Trogan was a good man," the cutie-pie said.

"Yes, he was," Curtik answered as if he'd known him.

Then Wes pulled her clear of him and placed her in one of the police vehicles. As it drove away, Curtik stood on the sidewalk and wondered if he would ever see her again. He suddenly realized he didn't even know her name.

Chapter 26

Z ora ran north through the park, holding back so she wouldn't leave Timothy behind, dodging Londoners on the trail, leaving the cleanup operation to the others. She couldn't do much without a weapon so she simply stayed with Timothy, checking for possible terrorists. She maintained contact with Ned, Lendra and Major Somers through her Plus-Glasses, and she kept the images of Dr. Leah Shafer in the upper right corner of the lenses while she displayed a map of the surrounding area in the upper left corner. Her shield kept the rain off her glasses.

Although Curtik was an undisciplined child, he was right; it felt good to be on the move. The meds kept her joint pain at bay. What would it feel like to sprint at full speed, to lash out at Dr. Shafer with a knife-edge fist? She felt herself getting warm at the notion of violence, which in turn made her think of Jeremiah and what it would be like to make love to him. That damn conditioning she received on the Moon made it hard to separate sex from violence. She forced herself to push those thoughts aside.

"I think I should have a Las-pistol," she said, "especially if I get separated from Timothy."

"I'm afraid I can't officially authorize that," Major Somers said.

"Right," Timothy replied. He reached down and grabbed his Las-pistol, then made an adjustment to it before holding it out for Zora to take.

"Oops," he said as she deactivated her shield and took it from him. "Someone bumped me and dislodged it. Zora, please pick it up and follow me. It's set to my fingerprints, so you won't be able to use it. Understand?"

"Understood," Zora said.

"What's our status?" Ned asked.

Major Somers said, "We've shut down the tube at every nearby station. We're also shutting down every road near you—no traffic for the foreseeable future. We're going to have an unhappy population on our hands if we don't find this woman quickly. The metropolitan police are looking for Dr. Shafer everywhere within a two-mile radius. We've sent emergency alerts and the two images CINTEP provided to every PlusPhone and PCD—personal communications device, for those of you unfamiliar with the term—in the citywide information system, along with Dr. Shafer's height and last-known weight. Anyone sees her or someone who looks like her has been asked to send us a message immediately. We'll begin to receive tips very . . . there's one now. An officer is on the way. Timothy, you and Zora head toward Bayswater Station. You'll be responsible for checking out any reports in that area."

Zora contacted Lendra via her Plus-Glasses: "Have you got any vid of Dr. Shafer moving or walking? Anything that might help us identify her?"

"We're trying to locate that now," Lendra replied. "Should have it in a minute."

Reports and vid images flooded in as they exited the park onto Bayswater Road, where vehicles clogged the middle of the street. She had expected horns blaring and people yelling, but perhaps because the police had explained why this was necessary, the populace seemed to be accepting of it. They sat in their vehicles or stood on the sidewalks showing no sign of impatience so far.

Zora concentrated on the faces she saw, dismissing most of them with only fleeting glances. Many wore masks, but she was still able to eliminate the majority of them. Only a few bore greater scrutiny, and they turned out to be innocents when Zora examined them more closely. She also ran a slideshow of the women photographed by citizens and transmitted via the citywide information system, but again she was able to dismiss most of them: too old, too young, too heavy.

How carefully had Dr. Shafer planned her escape? Did she have a neo-skin mask that would allow her to alter her face completely? Unlikely. She'd probably been forced to run with little notice, and if she'd had genetic surgery, she no doubt thought that was disguise enough.

While they ran down the middle of the road, between stopped vehicles, Zora studied the simulation of Dr. Shafer's face, using her peripheral vision to maintain her line. She stayed a step behind Timothy, and every few seconds she scanned the crowd for anyone who looked remotely like the images she'd received.

The crowd stared back at her, or more likely Timothy—probably wondering why this heavily armed man was running along Bayswater Road with this young woman in tow.

"Sending the vid footage now," Lendra said, and a loop appeared in the lower right corner of Zora's glasses. It showed a middle-aged woman walking down a hallway. She was tall and muscular, and she moved like an athlete. She rolled her shoulders slightly as she walked, a characteristic that might be useful in identifying her.

Ned noticed the same thing, for he said: "See that shoulder roll? That's pretty distinctive. Let's get every computer we've got looking for that."

The woman in the vid also favored her left leg ever so slightly. She might have had a sore knee that day, or a tender ankle—a hip pointer. Zora waited for someone else to bring it up, but no one did. Was she imagining it? She didn't think so, but then again, the discrepancy was almost imperceptible. Zora ran the footage a few more times. She was pretty sure Dr. Shafer had an almost undetectable limp. But there was no way to be certain she still walked that way, so Zora said nothing. However, she added that variable into her vid-ID system along with the rolling shoulders, just in case. She felt a little guilt at keeping that information to herself, but she didn't want to disclose it if she was just imagining it. Besides, she was here as an observer, so she would observe, keep her place, while Curtik, who couldn't seem to stay away from the action, led Brosk to his death.

As they turned north onto Queensway, Major Somers said: "Timothy, we've got a possible up by Princess Court, near the church. Sending you the data now. Take a look at it. Zora, you hang back. I got in enough trouble after that attack in Holland Park."

"I'm sorry for helping you kill bad guys," Zora said.

"It may seem ridiculous to you. Frankly, I agree. But please just stay back and let Timothy handle it."

"Lot of people still pissed off at you from last year," Timothy explained as they ran forward. Zora spotted the underground station on the left, up ahead about a block and a half. She saw what might have been the woman in question ducking into a church on the right side of the road.

"I'll check her out," Timothy said. "Won't take a minute. Stay connected in case there's trouble, but I don't think she's the one we're looking for."

Zora halted at the church entrance, keeping her Las-pistol down by her side where it wouldn't attract so much attention. She left her shield off, the rain compacting her curly hair, dropping it over her glasses so that she occasionally had to brush it aside in order to see. She studied everyone in sight. Dozens of people stared back at her and at each other. A great use of crowd sourcing: get thousands of people looking for one fleeing terrorist and it was pretty likely you were going to catch her fairly soon, no matter how she disguised herself. Either that, or you were going to drive her into hiding, deep underground, in which case you might be searching for a long time.

When Timothy's feed showed that the woman wasn't Dr. Shafer, Zora moved north to the end of the church, closer to the underground station. More alerts came through her glasses as Timothy emerged from the church. Three of them were nearby.

"What about these next three?" Zora asked as Timothy joined her.

"I'll send the police to two of them," Timothy said. He turned to the south.

Zora held her ground, noting that one of the sightings was north. "It makes more sense to split up."

"I have my orders," Timothy said. He continued going south. Was he expecting her to follow him or use her discretion? After all, he'd handed over his Las-pistol.

She took his movement away from her as permission to check out the sighting to the north. As she headed in that direction, she saw a man turn away from her and hurry toward the underground station. Something about him looked furtive. He walked stooped over, hands in his pockets, favoring his left leg ever so slightly, scurrying like a rat, shoulders rolling a little, probably because he was trying to shrink himself inside his bulky coat. He wore a hat and had turned his collar up. Could he be a woman? The only reason Zora had thought he was a man was because of his size and the somewhat athletic way he moved. Her vid-ID system returned a probability of forty-nine percent, so the man likely wasn't Dr. Shafer. Still, Zora trusted her instincts.

She felt a surge of adrenaline as she followed him. She had to dodge around a couple of people to make sure she didn't lose him. When he disappeared into the Bayswater Station, she ducked inside behind him.

"Where are you going, Zora?" Major Somers asked. "If you're going to defy orders, you should at least go after the woman two blocks north of your position."

"That guy up ahead looks suspicious," Zora said.

"Which one?" Lendra asked. "The one with the long coat? My vid-ID system shows only a twenty-six percent chance that he's Dr. Shafer."

"I still want to check him out."

"You're wasting your time," Major Somers said.

"I'm observing, like I'm supposed to. If I'm wrong, no harm done."

The man reached the escalator and descended, one of the few moving into the depths; a much greater flow of people rose to the surface.

She went down the escalator after him, sinking deeper and deeper. The man, perhaps sensing she was following him, began to pass people, walking down the stairs on the left side. He kept his head down, as if trying to avoid the station's closed circuit cameras. Zora began passing people as well, keeping about forty stairs between them. This was the longest escalator she had ever seen. As they descended, she studied the vid of Dr. Shafer twice more. She also noted that Timothy had reached another suspect, and that the woman was clearly not their target.

She contemplated closing on the man, but decided to wait until she reached the bottom.

"I really think you ought to check out the woman to the north," Timothy said.

Zora said, "If I'm wrong, I'll just take a quick look around to see if anyone's hiding on the platform. With this system-wide alert, Dr. Shafer might be waiting for the trains to start up again."

"You're wasting your time, Zora," Lendra said. "That man is not Leah Shafer."

"Quiet, everyone," Ned jumped into the conversation. "Let her do her job. Keep broadcasting, Zora."

"Will do," Zora said. "Thanks, Ned."

As the man reached the bottom of the escalator, Zora bounded forward, slipping past four men as she closed the gap. Her ears popped as she stepped out onto the platform. She caught sight of the man striding toward the far end, past the train that had been stopped at the station, its lights off, its doors closed up tight. The black hole at the far end of the platform offered the only real chance at escape now. But the man didn't go that far. Instead, when he reached the wall, he turned, still keeping his head down. Only as Zora approached did he straighten up and remove his hat, revealing himself to be a woman. She smiled briefly. Zora compared her face to the simulation Lendra had sent. Close enough.

Zora stopped ten feet in front of her and transmitted audio and video to Major Somers, Ned, Lendra and Timothy.

"Dr. Leah Shafer, I presume," she said, aiming her Las-pistol at Dr. Shafer's chest. Behind her, the remaining people on the platform began making their way toward the exit.

"You got her," Major Somers said. "Excellent. Hold her there. We're on our way."

"Leah Shafer is dead," the woman said. "I'm Sally2." She removed her hands from her pockets. The right one held a small glass canister, the left one a Las-pistol that shook ever so slightly. She said, "Hello, Zora."

"Have we met?" Zora glanced at the canister.

"Your image was all over the news last year after you attacked Earth. You and I are the same. We want the same things."

"Try to keep her calm," Lendra said.

"Not exactly the same," Zora said. "I was programmed to want to kill. You seem to want to do that all on your own."

"Can you blame me?" Sally2 asked. "The world is a cesspool—wars, pollution, ignorance, inequality, intolerance."

Zora laughed. "So you're going to cure intolerance by wiping out all the intolerant people who don't think the way you do?"

"That's not keeping her calm," Lendra said.

"Lendra, please," Ned interrupted. "Trust her. She knows what she's doing."

Sally2 held out the canister. "I drop this and everybody dies. Even you. This is the most potent form of the virus yet."

"Big, bad Sally2," Zora said as she inched forward. "So what do you want?"

"Stay back. I want you to drop your weapon. And I don't want anyone else down here with Las-rifles or particle beam cannons or even a cardboard knife. I see anybody I even think is armed and I drop the canister."

"Okay." Zora continued to aim her Las-pistol at Sally2's chest. "What else do you want?"

"Not going to drop your weapon? You think you can survive this strain? Should we test it right now?" Both Sally2's hands shook slightly now, as if she were tiring, or afraid. Or perhaps the adrenaline was causing that. Zora wondered just how stable this woman was.

"Zora," Lendra said. "We can't have that canister destroyed. Perhaps you should lower your weapon."

Zora said, "You have to be completely insane if you think I'm going to lower my Las-pistol."

Sally2 said, "I told you to drop it, not lower it."

Zora shook her head. "I'm not talking to you."

"Must be Lendra Riley then," Sally2 said. "Just another government pawn, trying to ensure American dominance, as if that country were somehow more special than any other, as if its people were somehow more blessed or deserving."

"You used to work for CINTEP," Zora said, "just like her."

"That was when I realized how dangerous we were. We were so smug, so convinced we were right, trying to mold the world into our framework. That kind of moral superiority is what makes so many people around the world hate you."

"Hate us, you mean," Zora said, inching forward again. "You're an American too, remember?"

"I escaped," Sally2 said. "And now I'm going to free the world."

"Death is a great equalizer," Zora said.

"So you see it too?"

Zora nodded. "It's one way to go, but I think it's too extreme. It violates the natural order."

"We'll become extinct sooner or later," Sally2 said.

"Yes, but why accelerate the process?"

"We're a disease," Sally2 said. Her hands shook more noticeably now. "We're destroying too many other species to be allowed to continue. I used to think it was just America that was evil, but it's not just them. They're the worst, yes, but all of them are bad because all of them think they're good."

"Major Somers, Timothy and Ned are almost there," Lendra said. "Stall her as long as you can."

"So if we think we're good," Zora said, "then we're evil? What if we think we're evil?"

"We're still evil. That doesn't change. The men who rule the world have turned us into believers in their rapacious consumption of resources. And now we humans have too much power to be trusted as stewards."

Sally2 closed her eyes for a second and Zora snuck a half step closer.

"Aren't we part of the natural order?" Zora said. "If the dinosaurs hadn't become extinct, we never would have evolved to become the dominant species on Earth. We might still be tiny creatures, struggling to survive in a harsh environment. It was the planet that allowed us to become what we are."

"Something went wrong," Sally2 said.

"We overstepped our bounds?"

"Exactly," Sally2 said. "It's time to give other species a chance."

"But that's not what you really want." Zora waved her Las-pistol, noting that Sally2's eyes were tracking it. She was maybe eight feet away. Behind her and off to the side, the black hole of the tunnel gaped. Were they sending someone in from that direction to take Sally2 out? "You want to live. You want to rule over a new Earth."

"No." Sally2 pushed her Las-pistol closer to Zora. "You're wrong."

"You want to survive. Otherwise you would have smashed that canister already."

"You think I don't know what you're doing?" Sally2 said. Her arms twitched slightly. "Inching closer, stalling, waiting for help? You think any of that matters?"

"You tell me."

"You're a stupid child. These people are not your friends. They're using you to get their way. All they care about is winning, no matter who has to lose."

"And you don't?" Zora said.

Major Somers said, "Okay, we're just around the corner. Timothy put a curved barrel on his Las-rifle and it's trained on her right now. If you can get the canister, Timothy can take her down."

"Don't shoot yet," Lendra said. "If that canister breaks, we won't be able to stop the virus. Zora, get the canister."

Right. Good plan. I never would have thought of that.

"I admit that I'm flawed," Sally2 said. "But I don't have to worry about that much longer. Neither do you. You're going to be infected. They don't care about you. That's why they're leaving you here alone. Probably hiding around the corner, ready to run when the canister explodes. Right? You'll die and they'll just find some other cog for their machine. Only this time, it won't save them." She raised her voice. "You may as well come out, Ned. I know you're there."

Zora heard a soft scraping behind her.

"Ah," Sally2 said as she looked past Zora, "there you are. I knew they'd send you. What about Curtik?"

Ned sauntered over, halting a few feet to Zora's left and slightly behind her. "He's busy with something else."

"Trying to save Brosk? Too late for that. Too late for any of us."

Now Sally2's whole body shook and Zora suddenly realized that Sally2 didn't intend to live after all. She'd been waiting for Ned and Curtik, hoping they'd both show so she could take them out too.

"What have you done to yourself?" Zora asked.

"You really think I want to live in a world like this?" Sally2 said. She raised the canister. Zora took another step. Six feet away. As Sally2 threw the canister to the ground, Zora dropped the Las-pistol and dove forward. She reached out with both hands as she landed on the cement floor, her head slamming into the concrete, her body scraping against the stone. The canister hit her left palm hard. Somehow she managed to hold onto it, her knuckles banging against the floor. But the canister didn't break.

Sally2's eyes widened in surprise as a purple laser pulse hit her in the chest. She collapsed, landing awkwardly, her legs splayed out before her, a stunned expression on her face. She tried to speak, her lips moving, but nothing came out.

Ned reached down and helped Zora to her feet.

"That was amazing," he said, putting his arm around her shoulders and giving her a hug. "I can't believe you caught it. Well done. I thought Jeremiah was fast, but I don't think even he could have done that. Well done, Zora."

A warmth spread through her. She only wished the arms around her weren't Ned's. "Sally2?" she asked.

Ned released her, picking up the Las-pistol as Major Somers and Timothy ran forward. Timothy kept his Las-rifle trained on Sally2.

Ned glared at Sally2. "She'll live. We'll be able to extract all her secrets, everything she knows about creating the virus, though she may not have much of a mind remaining when we're done with her."

"Such a waste," Zora said.

Major Somers reached Zora's side and carefully took the canister from her hand. "That was a hell of a thing you did, Zora. If I hadn't seen it with my own eyes, I wouldn't have believed it. You did a phenomenal job. Thank you."

"Yes," Lendra said. "But we've still got work to do. You'd better get back here."

Ned rolled his eyes. "You're welcome, Lendra."

"I'm sorry," Lendra said. "Thank you. Very well done."

Ned smiled. "See how easy that was? We're on our way."

Chapter 27

Pleased that her expectation of the interrogation room—a table and two hardback chairs, one of them facing a large two-way mirror—was wrong, Sally23 reclined on a comfortably padded sofa. The truth drugs they'd given her made her feel light, almost as if she risked floating up to the ceiling. She wondered if the drugs were accelerating the spread of the virus inside her, if she would die more quickly. She didn't really care, but it was an interesting question.

The screen facing her showed two black women watching the interrogation. One she recognized as Lendra Riley, head of CINTEP. The other she didn't know. Both wore interfaces so they could communicate without speaking. She felt almost as if she were in a zoo or a lab, being studied by scientists. She waved at them but got no response.

Wes, the huge SAS trooper who'd led the way to Westminster Bridge, conducted her interrogation. She opened message boards and demonstrated how to contact the various sites. Then he asked about the organization and its plans for the future. But since she'd already told Curtik everything she knew, all she could do was reiterate what she'd said previously. She hid nothing. No doubt the drugs reinforced her desire to tell the truth, but she experienced no side effects at all, for she wanted to tell them everything.

Assuming Sally1 didn't accelerate the timetable, they had less than sixteen hours until she released her final version of the virus. Sally23 kept telling them that, hoping they'd take action, but Wes continued to ask the same questions over and over, and Sally23 wondered if anyone would stop this new threat. She also informed them that there was probably a Sally cell in China. Occasionally when the questioning halted for a moment, she felt a tug of anxiety: a minor itch she couldn't scratch. Was that the drugs?

"And what do you know about this final version of the virus?" Wes asked again. "The one that Manyara Harris developed."

"Nothing," Sally23 replied the same as before. "Except that it might be water soluble."

"Why do you think that?" Wes asked.

"Sally2's last version of the virus was water soluble."

"Yes, it is. But why do you think Sally1's version might be water soluble?"

"Just a hunch."

"Were you involved in creating it?" Wes returned to the questions he'd asked before.

"No," Sally23 replied, "though I assisted in some of the modifications. My background is in computer science and organic chemistry."

Now the conversation returned to familiar ground, Wes asking, in slightly different ways, the same questions he'd asked previously. Sally23 answered everything honestly, giving essentially the same responses she'd provided earlier.

At one point Wes stopped his questions and her mind drifted to something that had been bothering her. She said, "What happened to Sally2?"

Wes smiled and left the room. She lay back on the sofa and thought about Trogan Brosk. She wanted to cry for him, mourn his passing in some way, yet she found it difficult to dredge up any real emotion. And soon enough she would be joining him. Already she felt a tightening in her chest similar to what Trogan would have felt, sans the nano-explosives. The pressure didn't quite reach a level where it could be called pain, but it definitely made her uncomfortable, forcing her lungs to work just that little bit harder to get the same volume of oxygen in her bloodstream—a sign that she'd reached the final stages of the infection. Next would come numbness in her extremities, then unconsciousness and death.

She fell asleep thinking about Trogan.

She awoke to Wes shaking her shoulder, her stomach slightly nauseated. Her limbs felt heavy and she struggled to keep her eyes open. She sat up. "What is it?" she asked.

"Take a look." Wes pointed to the door. "Come on in, Ned."

The short black man from Hyde Park—one of the CINTEP agents—pushed Sally2 into the room. She sat strapped to a wheelchair, drooling and spasming, electrodes on her temples, her hands clenched into fists. She caught Sally23's eye, took a few deep breaths and said, "See what they've done to me?" Her head twitched. "These men are raping my brain. I . . . I . . . I can't stop them."

Sally23 said, "How is that different from what you did to us? You took us and twisted us to your purposes, conditioning our minds until we had no free will. You're a monster."

"You think this ends it?" Sally2 said. "They're going to take what I know and use it against the rest of the world. That's what they do. They claim some national security crisis and then take away our rights, and we let them. They give our knowledge to big corporations, who use it to control us. I wasn't doing anything they don't do. I just wasn't being as subtle."

"What are you talking about?"

"Don't you know, girl? You gave them a powerful weapon. They now have access to everything I know. All my secrets. You think they're not going to use them? My knowledge will help them tighten their grip on humanity, squeeze people a little more, bring us that much closer to willing servitude. You did this by giving me to them. And now you're going to pay the price."

"You're wrong," Sally23 said.

"They will condition our minds to make us happy with whatever they tell us. They'll program us to live the lives they want us to lead. We'll beg them to lead us into slavery. You'll see."

"I think that's enough," Wes said. He turned to Sally23. "We're sending you to the Yanks temporarily. But we're not finished with you, so don't think this means your freedom. I wanted you to see Sally2, so you would have an idea what may be in store for you should you survive. Get her out of here, Ned."

Ned stepped around the wheelchair. He reminded her a little of Trogan Brosk: something about the way he carried himself, as if completely comfortable in his skin. He looked neither happy nor angry—more like her image of Buddha, radiating calm.

Sally2 said, "They're either going to make you a slave or a vegetable. They're going to rip your mind to shreds. You'd better hope you die."

"I don't need to hope," Sally23 said. "I am dying. You made sure of that."

"Come on, Sienna." Ned held out her coat. "Yes, we know your real name."

"Sienna died long ago," Sally23 said. "And I'll be dead soon too." She held up her hands. "My fingers are already tingling."

Ned showed no expression. He must hate her, but he was too well trained to give in to that emotion. He simply held out her coat a little farther. She stood up, wobbling slightly, and he steadied her so she could slip her coat on.

Ned took her arm. "Let's go. We've got a plane to catch." As he hustled her out the door, she heard Sally2 yell:

"Your death will be agonizing. I knew I never should have trusted you. I hope you rot in . . ." Her voice trailed off.

Sally23 struggled to keep pace with Ned. He walked her down a hallway past a security checkpoint where a guard simply waved them through, then out a side door to where a black limo waited. She coughed as she hit the open air, her lungs suddenly fighting for air. Ned pounded her on the back as he guided her to the limo.

After settling into her seat, Sally23 managed to get her breathing under control. Ned climbed in beside her and told the driver to go. Then he turned to her and said, "There are some who believe you might be able to assist us in finding Manyara's—Sally1's—latest version of the virus. Or that you'll be able to help us find some flaw in its design, some weakness that could prevent it from doing more damage."

"So tired," Sally23 said. "I can barely think. You know I'm in the final stages of the disease, right?"

Ned took her hands in his and rubbed gently, increasing the blood flow to her fingers. "You have no future. And your past is gone. You can only live in the present. You've aided us so far, but you're not done yet. You have much to atone for."

"I think I might throw up." Sally 23 took a deep breath as she fought to control her stomach. Ned released her hands, then pulled a patch from his pocket and pressed it to her neck. Almost immediately the urge to vomit dissipated. "What?"

"It's common to feel nausea when truth drugs wear off," he explained. "I'll see if I can get you some medication on the plane, something to keep you alive a little longer."

Sally23 closed her eyes. She wondered if Sally2 was right, if the people in control would use her knowledge to clamp down on society, to keep themselves insulated from anger and violence, to tamp down any hint of revolution by the masses. It didn't really matter. Humans were doomed. Sooner or later they would vanish. Hopefully they wouldn't take the rest of Earth's species with them.

When they reached the airport, Ned half-escorted, half-carried her to a small jet, where Curtik waited at the base of the stairs, flexing his mechanical hand, shaking his head and grinning.

"Man, Neddy," he said as they approached, "I don't know how you did it."

Then he apparently noticed Sally23's distress, for he took her in his arms and carried her up the stairs. "I got you," he said.

Curtik carried her to the seat next to the blond girl from the park while Ned went into the cockpit.

A coughing spell hit her. She struggled to breathe all of a sudden, and the tightness in her chest struck her a physical blow, constricting her airways. She gasped, twitching, her mouth gaping as she fought for air.

"Neddy!" Curtik yelled. "We need you."

"She's suffocating," Zora called out.

Sally23 focused on Curtik's frowning face.

"Breathe," he said. "Just concentrate on that. Deep breaths. In and out."

Zora put her arms around Sally23's body and squeezed tightly. Sally23, unable to get any air, punched her in the head and Zora released her grip. A modicum of air made it into Sally23's lungs. Again Zora hugged her tightly. This time Sally23, realizing Zora was helping her breathe, managed not to hit her.

"That's it," Curtik said.

"Too late," Sally23 gasped. "I'm dying."

"Not on my watch," Ned's voice sounded distant. "Hand," he said.

Zora grabbed Sally23's hand and held it up. To Sally23's surprise, Ned pressed a hypo-pad to her, holding it in place for a moment as he stared into her eyes. She stared back, thinking he was rather kind, until her eyes closed and her mind went blank.

***

The angled light of sunrise through Lendra's office windows should have made the place look cheery, but all Taditha Poole felt was fear. They weren't going to find the virus in time, she realized. Manyara had some-how disappeared, probably to release her newest version. That disappear-ance should have been impossible, for she had been under covert surveil-lance. How had she done it? She could be anywhere in the city right now, spreading the deadliest strain yet.

Poole held her son Jack as she stood beside Lendra, watching the multiple screens Jay-Edgar displayed, most showing aerial views of the area around Washington, DC. One, however, showed the interrogation of Dr. Shafer, who held back nothing, her will to fight completely suppressed by drugs and nanobots. The process had been violent, a forcible extraction of information that would leave only a shell of a mind behind. Good. The bitch deserved it.

Unfortunately, Dr. Shafer knew nothing about Manyara's version of the virus, for they developed their strains in separate labs. However, they worked from the same basic templates, so Poole hoped they might one day find a cure. They were now deep into the details of specific strains of Dr. Shafer's virus and Lendra had asked Jay-Edgar to turn down the audio.

She was focused, Poole saw, on the center screen, where CINTEP's medical team, all dressed in haz-mat suits, were in the process of giving Sophie a transfusion from Jeremiah, his blood filtered to remove the Susquehanna Virus. Little Jack Marschenko, now over the flu, slept quietly in Poole's arms, while Sophie lay unconscious on the operating gurney. She looked so tiny on the bed that Poole almost couldn't bear to watch. Jeremiah sat beside her, stroking her hair, his face fallen in sorrow.

"I can't believe this is happening," Lendra said. "It's just a staph infection. How can my baby be dying?"

Poor little girl, Poole thought. She might not last the day. But Lendra needs comforting and we need Lendra.

She said, "Sophie will pull through."

"You can't know that. This is a new and dangerous variant. Resistant to every antibiotic so far."

"Trust me," Poole said, loathing herself for giving Lendra false hope. "If she was anyone else's daughter, she'd probably die. But she's got Jeremiah's genes. She's tough. She'll make it."

Lendra touched her shoulder. "I know you're just saying that to be kind, but thank you. I can't even think straight."

"You're doing great," Poole said.

Lendra smiled briefly. "When do you think I can visit her?"

"They should be done with the transfusion any minute."

"Okay." Lendra bobbed her head up and down. "Okay. I suppose we should get back to work."

"Right. Anything new on the hunt for Manyara?"

"Every CINTEP analyst and agent has been called in," Lendra replied. "They're closing in. Jay-Edgar's coordinating the search with the Elite Ops troopers assigned to us."

"What about using crowd sourcing like they did in London? Getting everyone in the area looking for her. It worked over there."

"I've considered it. But putting that information out there where she could see it might just drive her underground until after this new strain is released. If she thinks she's got a chance of escaping, we might be able to track her down in time."

"I don't believe it," Jay-Edgar interrupted.

"What is it?" Lendra said.

"Look." Jay-Edgar pointed to a screen. "Tad and Rebecca Blanton—they're at our front door. They say they have the antidote and they want to trade that for immunity."

"Amazing," Lendra said as she fingered the glass bulb of her necklace—the one she claimed no longer held neo-dopamine. "Get them up here right now."

"Maybe this is the break we need," Poole said.

"Have you figured out yet how Manyara vanished?" Lendra asked Jay-Edgar.

"Multiple dampening fields from multiple PlusPhones," he replied. "I think she stole them from us. Right now we're triangulating and extrapolating from last-known positions to determine a probable path. We'll find her soon."

"What does that mean?" Lendra said. "Minutes, hours, days?"

"Probably hours."

"It better be soon. We have less than twelve hours. Jeremiah can lead the questioning of the Blantons in room one." She turned to Poole. "Get the truth drugs ready. I'm taking no chances on this. In the meantime, I'll be in the infirmary."

"Right." Poole headed for the door. She glanced up at the screen and saw Jeremiah get to his feet, the transfusion complete. He placed his hand on Sophie's stomach, kept it there for a moment, and then walked toward the decontamination area.

Poole dropped Jack off with the nanny, then hurried to the lab, where Dr. Omar Hassan and Dr. Helen Ellerth, CINTEP's resident surgeons, were preparing to analyze the antidote the Blantons had just delivered. After Poole described what she needed, Helen helped her put together a kit. Then Poole headed for room one. Finn and Gil kept watch outside the door, Gil winking at her as she passed inside. Jeremiah stood before the Blantons, who sat in straight-back chairs wearing CINTEP coveralls, their clothes and PlusPhones no doubt being searched by the techs. Hannah and her former partner Wilson Adler stood behind Jeremiah, their expressions thunderous.

Tad was tall with dark hair, Rebecca of average height and weight, with brown curly hair. Both were good looking. So these were the two people who had been in Cole's Law before it blew up. Why hadn't they been found earlier?

They fidgeted in their chairs, keeping their eyes on Jeremiah. He smiled at them reassuringly, while Hannah and Adler scowled. Was this to be a good cop/bad cop interrogation?

"We brought in the antidote," Tad said. "We want to cooperate. And we gave you the codes to our PlusPhones, so you can find all our contacts."

"You've been helpful," Jeremiah said, his voice quiet and measured. "And I appreciate it. I'm concerned now that the antidote you were given might be worthless. It might be nothing more than sugar water. We'll have to test it to see if it really is effective. Meanwhile, we'd like to ask you some questions under truth drugs."

"We understand," Tad said.

"We won't lie," Rebecca added.

"That's good," Jeremiah said with a smile. "If you tell the truth, you won't feel a thing except a little more relaxed than normal."

He turned to Poole. "Doc?"

"It's very simple," Poole said as she placed three patches on each of their right arms. The drugs were designed to enhance relaxation, compliance and trust in the subjects. After studying the data on the monitor, Poole adjusted the flow to maximize the Blantons' cooperation. When the levels looked perfect, she nodded to Jeremiah.

Jeremiah said, "Thank you for coming today. You're doing us a great service. Now, do you have any idea where Sally's lab is?"

"We honestly don't know," Rebecca answered.

"She gave us a piece of paper with an address written on it," Tad explained. "But we threw it away. That woman's crazy."

"Yes," Jeremiah said, his voice soothing. "Do you know where you were when you threw the paper away?"

"I don't remember. Just on the street somewhere."

"What kind of paper was it? Do you remember?"

"I think it was that new flake paper—the kind that dissolves after a few hours."

"That's what I thought," Jeremiah said. "That's good. Now, what about the address? Do you remember that?"

"No," Rebecca said. "We don't remember. I wish we did. We were simply trying to get away from her."

"All we did was run her communications network," Tad said. "We had nothing to do with the virus."

"You helped kill millions," Hannah said. She stepped in front of Jeremiah, her face reddening. "Perhaps billions."

"No," Rebecca said. "We're just believers in a new world order. We're Earth Guardians."

Hannah grabbed Rebecca's shoulder and shook it. "You aided her efforts to eradicate humanity."

"We didn't go get the virus when she asked us to. We knew it was wrong. Besides, she created it years ago—long before she met us. She was going to kill people regardless. All we did was help her communicate with her followers. We shared a vision of a new Earth, free of the pollution and destruction of old humanity. And from that vision, the Earth Guardians were born."

Jeremiah touched Hannah's arm and she freed Rebecca from her grasp. Adler reached out a hand for her but she brushed it away. "I'm okay," she said. "I just lost control for a second."

"I understand," Jeremiah said. "You're angry. But the Blantons want to help. They're trying to remember. So relax. We're all friends here."

Poole smiled at the calmness in his voice. She knew he was just as angry as Hannah and yet he acted as if he liked the Blantons and wanted nothing more than to chat with them.

He glanced at Poole. "Any problems with the drugs?"

Poole understood that he was asking if they were showing any signs of deception. She shook her head. "Their systems are tolerating the drugs perfectly."

"Great," Jeremiah said. He turned back to the Blantons. "Let's talk about your meeting with Manyara Harris—Sally1."

"Rebecca said she was crazy," Tad replied. "I didn't realize how batty she'd become until we met with her tonight."

"She's got her dark men with her," Rebecca said.

"Dark men?" Jeremiah asked. "Who are they?"

"Six bodyguards. Rumor has it that she conditioned them to protect her with their lives."

"I bet they're scary," Jeremiah said. "Heavily armed, with some sort of military vehicle."

"We didn't see any vehicle," Tad said. "Right?"

"She just appeared out of the darkness," Rebecca said. "And I didn't see any weapons. But they must have had a vehicle of some sort."

"You think maybe they didn't have any weapons?" Jeremiah asked.

"No, I'm sure they were armed," Rebecca said. "We just didn't see any weapons."

"That makes sense," Jeremiah said, his voice mellifluous and sincere. "I'm sure you're right. And they just appeared out of nowhere."

"As we came out of the warehouse."

"What can you tell me about these dark men?" Jeremiah said. He sounded so concerned, so sincere, that Poole wanted to answer the question herself. My God, he's good at this.

"The one that spoke had some kind of accent," Tad said.

"Haitian," Rebecca said. "I recognized it. He's Haitian."

"Good. Anything else?"

"They're all big," Tad said. "Muscular. They moved like athletes."

Jay-Edgar contacted Poole via her interface: "We've tracked the Blantons' movements for the past twenty-four hours. Sending you the data now."

Poole transferred the data to a screen so Jeremiah and the Blantons could see it.

Jeremiah said, "Can you show me where you met Sally1?"

Tad pointed out the location on the screen, just north of the Sculpture Park in Silver Spring, Maryland.

"That's the warehouse. Good. We'll look into that. And it looks like you went south after leaving her?" Jeremiah pointed to the screen.

"Yeah," Rebecca said. "Is that important?"

"That was probably in the direction of the lab if you were trying to lull her into thinking you were going there."

"That's right," Tad said. "It was south . . . and I think east."

"Very smart. Keep her in the dark." His voice carried a hint of approval. "That's what I would have done too. I wonder where she and her dark men went."

"We just wanted to leave," Rebecca said. "She said she was going to fly away."

"Interesting. She used those exact words? Fly away?"

"Yes. Is that important?"

"Maybe. Did she say where?"

"No," Tad said. "But she also called herself a river. Remember?"

"That's right," Rebecca said. "And she smirked when she said she was going to fly away. I don't know if that means anything."

Jeremiah nodded. "Okay. Now I want you to think about numbers and names. Do you think it was a numbered street or did it have a name?"

"I think it was a name," Rebecca said.

"Excellent." Jeremiah smiled and nodded. "Was it a familiar name, or one you'd never heard before? A state name, maybe? Or something that reminded you of a smell or a sound?"

Tad and Rebecca shook their heads. "I don't remember," they said in unison.

Jeremiah crouched down in front of them. "I'd like to put you under—a drug-induced hypnosis to see if you can recall the street name or the address, or even where you threw away that paper."

"Will it hurt?" Rebecca asked.

Jeremiah turned to Poole.

She shook her head. "It's a painless process."

"Thank you," Jeremiah said to Rebecca and Tad. He touched their shoulders gently, looking them in the eye. "We really appreciate this. You've been a big help. Dr. Poole will set up the hypnosis for you now. Okay?"

They both nodded.

"Excellent," Jeremiah said. He gestured to Poole to follow him to the door. Hannah shadowed him. Adler remained where he was. Lendra must have ordered him to watch the Blantons.

"Stay friendly," Jeremiah whispered to Poole. "Stay calm. I'm sure I don't need to tell you that's the way to handle them. You're as aware as I am that any anxiety will just decrease the effectiveness of the process."

"You're leaving?"

"I've got some ideas about Manyara from what the Blantons said. Besides, you don't need me, Doc. You had them figured out the moment you walked into the room. Lendra was just tossing me a bone letting me conduct the interview."

Poole smiled. She put her hand on his shoulder. "Thank you. I know what you're doing, trying to make me feel better, but there's no way I would have figured out how to handle them as quickly as you did. That gentle touch was genius. You're amazing."

Jeremiah scowled. Hannah smiled, which made Poole smile in turn.

"You're so predictable," Poole said.

"What?"

"You detest being complimented." Poole shook her head. "When will you accept that you're a good man?"

"When I become one. Thanks, Doc."

"You're welcome. We'll set it up now. Might take ten minutes.

Might take a few hours. You understand that we might not get anything of value?"

"We've got very little of value now," he replied. "Anything you find, let me or Lendra know. We'll be hunting Manyara."

Chapter 28

J eremiah walked to Lendra's office, Hannah beside him. His joints hurt only a little. It felt good to have a purpose, to be a predator again. He'd almost forgotten what it felt like to be closing in on a target. The thrill of the chase still intoxicated him. He reached her office door just as Lendra emerged from the decontamination room of the infirmary.

Sophie. How could he have forgotten about her?

Lendra approached him unsteadily, eyes red, her arms opening for a hug. He let her in, enfolding her in his arms.

"Oh, Jeremiah," she said as she hugged him back. "What if Sophie..."

"She'll be fine," he said as he held Lendra, allowing her to take what comfort she needed. Truth was, now that his mind was back on Sophie, he needed it too. As much as he'd tried to distance himself from his daughter, her innocence had sucked him in. It wasn't her fault that she'd been conceived against his will and without his knowledge. She now existed; he couldn't deny that. And he loved her as much as if he'd wanted her in the first place.

After a while, Lendra stiffened and pulled away. "We have work to do."

"Indeed." He opened the door to her office, gestured for her and Hannah to precede him, then entered the room and said to Jay-Edgar: "I think we might have something on Manyara."

"Anything would help," Jay-Edgar said. "We're still trying to penetrate the dampening fields."

"Is that even possible?"

"Normally it wouldn't be, but since she stole the dampening fields from us and we know all the frequencies, the bio-electrical impulses, the jamming technology they use, we should be able to infiltrate their PlusPhones to find her, assuming she hasn't turned the devices off."

"Pull up the vid from the search of Manyara's apartment," Jeremiah said. "And get Eli on holo-projection."

Lendra said, "What are you thinking?"

"Remember that fly away comment?"

"Did that mean something?"

"Maybe," Jeremiah replied. "I think she was deliberately misleading the Blantons in case they bailed on her. And I recall seeing something in the vid."

Eli appeared via holo-projection and Jeremiah brought him up to date. Then he gestured for Jay-Edgar to start the vid. It showed a small, cluttered apartment, nothing out of the ordinary—two chairs, a table, a bookcase covered with knickknacks, a kitchenette, bedroom and bathroom, and a computer space that the techs had spent most of their time on, going through thousands of files.

"What do you see?" Hannah asked.

"I want a close-up of the bookcase," Jeremiah said.

Jay-Edgar manipulated the vid footage until the shelves became larger. Dozens of small models of bridges filled the shelves.

Lendra said, "You think these might be important, Jeremiah?"

"It's possible. Are any of those bridges in the DC area?"

Lendra nodded, her eyes unfocused as she accessed her interface. "The Arlington Memorial Bridge, the Frederick Douglass Bridge, the Key Bridge, the Arland D. Williams Memorial Bridge, the Pennsylvania Avenue Bridge and the Theodore Roosevelt Memorial Bridge."

"I wonder why so many. I could understand a replica of the Golden Gate Bridge or London Bridge."

"This is where she lives," Hannah said.

Lendra said, "I'm sending officers to check every bridge in the area for anything suspicious. You think she'll try to get out by water?" Lendra asked.

"Hold on," Eli said. "Did you say she called herself a river?"

"That's right," Jeremiah replied.

"Well, I seem to recall that her grandmother was from Haiti—some sort of Voodoo priestess—and rivers are important in that religion."

"Good. Let's transpose Manyara's last known movements with where she met Tad and Rebecca."

Jay-Edgar nodded. "And then work south and east to see if there are any lines of agreement."

Lendra said, "Let's also see if we're getting any strange electrical readings—pockets of nothingness or distortions along that path."

"Right," Jay-Edgar said.

For a few minutes no one spoke. Various images appeared on the screens, trails of movements and areas of electrical distortions that weren't necessarily from dampening fields. Jeremiah realized this sort of work was largely beyond his capabilities. He let Lendra and Jay-Edgar do the comparisons and analyses. He glanced over at Hannah, but apparently she was assisting them, for she had the vacant stare of someone accessing her interface. Even Eli was helping, tapping a screen from inside his cell. It was hard not to feel useless as he watched everyone else contribute to finding Manyara.

"That might be them," Lendra finally said.

Jay-Edgar nodded. "It looks promising."

"What have you got?" Jeremiah asked.

"Down by the river," Lendra said. "On Water Street. This might be her."

Jay-Edgar added: "It's an odd distortion to the grid that could be caused by multiple dampening fields."

"Let's check it out," Jeremiah said. "I want a squad or two of Elite Ops to accompany me."

Lendra frowned. "You aren't going to insist on doing this yourself?"

"This isn't a covert mission. We want to go in with force, give them no option but to fight or surrender. Obviously we want to take her alive, but if these dark men Rebecca Blanton told us about are conditioned to protect her at any cost, we'll want maximum firepower."

"Good hunting, Jeremiah," Eli said.

"I'm sending the coordinates to your PlusPhone," Lendra said as Jeremiah started for the door. She nodded to Hannah. "Keep him safe."

Jeremiah stepped into the hall, where Gil and Finn waited.

"The fish team is ready to roll," Finn said.

"Get your gear on," Jeremiah said. He was going to have to fly in a jet-copter, he realized. Why did that scare him? He'd handled hundreds of situations more dangerous than flying. And yet taking to the air always terrified him. He tried to keep his expression neutral, the fear out of his eyes. "I'll meet you on the roof." He pointed to Hannah's interface. "Can you handle communications?"

She nodded.

"Good." He put his PlusPhone in his pocket and led her to the roof. He could see rain coming from the southwest, but the sun was still a bright orange orb, coloring the sky with pinks and purples, compliments of all the particulates in the air, an oddly beautiful scene. The jet-copter, on the other hand, looked ugly, squat and buglike, no aerodynamics at all that he could see. It ought to plunge off the roof and tumble to the ground.

"You okay?" Hannah asked.

"Sure."

"When's the last time you slept?"

"I got a nap in the infirmary," he said.

"What about the pain?"

"I'll be fine," he said. "You just worry about yourself."

A few seconds later Gil and Finn joined them, wearing their armor.

Jeremiah nodded approvingly. Elite Ops troopers looked intimidating when suited up. Close to seven feet tall in their charcoal body armor, they wore mirrored helmets and carried Las-rifles as well as particle beam cannons. They looked identical except for their nameplates. They ought to scare the hell out of Manyara's dark men.

Hannah said, "Two Elite Ops squads are meeting us on site. They've been sent the coordinates as well."

Jeremiah climbed aboard the jet-copter with the others and they took off. The ride lasted only a couple minutes, fortunately. He kept his eyes shut the entire time, concentrating on his breathing, only opening them when they landed in the middle of the street, disrupting the early morning traffic.

As they disembarked, sirens blaring in the distance and cars honking their horns, Hannah said, "The distortion is coming from inside that building." She pointed at an office building—its front doors broken and hanging ajar. "We can't get a good lock because of the dampening fields, but it's got to be Manyara. It looks like seven bio-electric signatures—six bodyguards plus Manyara."

Jeremiah shook his head. It felt wrong. Still, they had to check it out. The wind, he noticed, had picked up, and he felt a drop of rain on his forehead.

Within seconds, two squads of EOs appeared in four Bullets, large tank-like vehicles that weaved around the traffic and pulled up onto the sidewalks. From the lead Bullet came Major Payne, fully armored except for his helmet. The last time they'd met—when Major Payne had been under the influence of drugs and conditioning, and following the orders of the megalomaniac Richard Carlton—Jeremiah and Quark had bested him in battle at the Tessamae Shelter. Since then, Jeremiah knew, Major Payne had been freed of the conditioning and had even helped destroy one of the Las-cannons that the cadets had used to attack Earth, losing his eyes in the process. But he looked the same now as he had the last time Jeremiah saw him—though his regrown eyes appeared slightly larger. Probably they'd been genetically enhanced. Jeremiah wondered briefly if Major Payne still hated him, then dismissed the thought as unproductive.

Major Payne came to a stop before Jeremiah. He nodded to Gil and Finn. "Fish team."

"Windol," they replied.

"We got cops on the way," Major Payne said. He looked at Jeremiah. "What's your plan?"

Jeremiah said, "We need Manyara Harris alive, if possible. Actually, I'd like to take as many alive as I can. But that may be impossible. I understand that they've been conditioned to fight to the death to protect her."

"We'll go in light," Major Payne said. "Stun settings, everyone." He looked at Jeremiah. "I assume you want a bull rush—speed and overwhelming force?"

Jeremiah nodded. "Give them no time to think. We want them reacting only." He glanced at the office building, at the doors askew in their openings. Why would Manyara hide inside the building? She had to know he was after her.

"Jeremiah?" Hannah said.

He pulled himself from his reverie. "Yes?"

"What's wrong?"

Major Payne said, "You think it's a trap?"

"Possibly. More likely she's using this as a feint. We have no choice." He looked over at the Washington Channel of the Potomac paralleling the road. A light rain had started, the wind driving it at an angle into his face. "Send your people in, Major."

"You're waiting out here?" Major Payne's voice carried disbelief.

Jeremiah nodded.

"All right," Major Payne said. "Sending them in now."

Hannah touched his shoulder. "Something's off. What is it?"

Jeremiah nodded. "I just don't see her hiding. She'll run, sending her people into the building as a distraction. But she won't hide."

"But there are seven bio-signatures."

"Exactly. It would be easy to abduct a few civilians and force them inside." He walked across the street toward the marina where hundreds of boats were docked in their slips, their rigging catching the wind, producing a thrumming that sounded almost musical. Dozens of boats moved along the river. Hannah and Major Payne followed him. He pointed to the marina. "That's how I'd get out."

Major Payne said, "Good thought. Launching drones now."

Jeremiah pulled out his PlusPhone and connected to Lendra. When she answered, he said, "I doubt Manyara's in the building. Major Payne has drones over the river, scanning boats. We need to call in the Coast Guard to search vessels. I have a hunch she'll try to escape by sea."

"Okay," Lendra said. "Eli agrees with you. I'll get the police to search every docked ship as well."

Major Payne said, "Getting images from the raid now. My men are taking the building by force. I see five men and two women. They've all been stunned. Checking the women—neither of them is Manyara. Checking the men—no, none of them either. Wait a second."

"What is it?" Jeremiah asked.

"The five men are dead. How can that be? We only stunned them."

"Obviously she didn't want them taken alive. Wake those two women up. Find out where they were taken. I'm betting it was close by."

Jeremiah began jogging toward the water, his knees and back aching, Gil and Finn by his side, Hannah and Major Payne keeping pace easily. Instinct pulled him here. He wondered if he could trust it; years had passed since he'd done this kind of work. But it made sense. From the river, Manyara could go inland or out toward sea, and there were plenty of places she could land the boat and make a run for it. But he believed she would stay onboard, make for sea and a possible rendezvous with some contact out there. It was the easiest way to leave the country.

Lendra said, "Jay-Edgar and I are working on an extrapolation of data from the dampening fields, looking for anomalies that might tell us where Manyara separated from her bodyguards."

"She's still got one of them with her," Jeremiah replied. "You'll want to look for two bio-signatures together—one male, one female, if you can break it down that far—or possibly three bio-signatures if they forced someone to drive the boat for them, though the Haitian might know how to pilot a boat. I'm guessing they're heading toward Chesapeake Bay in something nondescript."

Lendra said, "I'm afraid we can't break it down by gender. And we're not picking up any kind of reading on a phone or dampening field or even a jammer."

Major Payne said, "The women said they were taken a couple blocks from here about twenty minutes ago."

"Did we lose them?" Hannah asked.

Jeremiah smiled. "Actually, we might have caught a break, if they're still on the water. On land, they'd be almost impossible to spot, but if they're on the river, we can still look for two or three human bio-signatures and cross-reference the absence of any tech signals. I'm betting they'll try to run blind—no PlusPhones, no tablets, no technology of any kind—which should make them stand out pretty distinctly."

"That's genius!" Major Payne said.

Jeremiah shook his head. "The only reason you didn't think of it is because you're always wired in."

"The Coast Guard is sending a cutter," Major Payne said. "It will be here in two minutes."

Jeremiah hurried toward the dock, limping slightly, but before he had gone five steps Gil and Finn grabbed his arms and lifted him off the ground, carrying him between them. "Hey," he said, "I'm not helpless."

Major Payne and Hannah pounded along behind them, Hannah laughing.

"Just keeping you safe," Gil said.

"All part of the fish team service," Finn added.

They reached the dock only a few seconds before the cutter. Finn climbed aboard and Gil gave Jeremiah a hand as Hannah and Major Payne followed.

"Stop treating me like an invalid," Jeremiah said.

"Just following orders," Gil said as the cutter accelerated away.

"Whose orders?" Jeremiah asked.

"Mine," Major Payne said. "We all know what you've been doing, infecting yourself with the virus. And my superiors have made it abundantly clear that you're to be protected at all costs." When Jeremiah frowned, Major Payne added, "If it's any consolation, I don't think it has to do with you so much as it does your immunity."

Finn and Gil grabbed Jeremiah's arms and propelled him to the bow as the cutter torpedoed downriver toward Chesapeake Bay, leaving a massive wake that sent smaller boats bobbing.

Hannah and Major Payne followed.

Something must have shown in Jeremiah's face, for Hannah said, "Get over it. You're not a young man anymore."

Jeremiah glared at her for a moment, then nodded. He hated to admit it, but even with the painkillers his joints ached.

"We've found two possible candidates so far," Major Payne said as they caught up with him. "Both smaller boats—Mega-Mischief and Sarahnity. Both carrying two people."

"I'm getting details now," Lendra said. Jeremiah had forgotten that she was still connected via the PlusPhone. "Who the owners are and when they usually go boating. Also, we're putting up a blockade near Virginia Beach to keep them from getting to the ocean. And we've got another cutter coming your way from downstream."

The Navy cutter planed over the water, making sweeping curves as it sped downstream. Rain and spray caught Jeremiah in the face along with the smell of brackish water up ahead. A flock of seagulls squawked and scattered as the cutter approached. For a moment, Jeremiah imagined he was out here with Sophie, teaching her how to steer a boat. She was a young girl, and the day was sunny, the cooler full of food, and even Curtik was there, helping out his younger sister as she manned the wheel. What the hell was Curtik doing there and why was he being helpful? The dream vanished, Jeremiah suddenly back on the cutter.

His muscles tensed. He hoped he was correct about this. If he wasn't, every minute took them farther away from capturing Manyara. Damn it, this had to be right—all his training, instinct and experience told him she would flee this way. But what if he was wrong? What if he was headed away from her? What if she had gone to her lab to release the virus?

"We've located the PlusPhone signal of Sarahnity's owner in Georgetown," Lendra said. "She's not answering her PlusPhone, but assuming she's actually in Georgetown, the Sarahnity is likely our target."

"Where is the boat now?" Jeremiah asked.

"Passing Southern Park," Major Payne said, "approaching Chesapeake Bay. We'll catch them in ten or twelve minutes."

As they slowed to take a sharp turn to the right, Hannah said, "It's almost a straight shot to the bay from here. We should see them soon."

"There they are." Major Payne pointed at a tiny boat in the distance. Obviously he'd had his vision enhanced. "Looks like a thirty-five footer, sleeper below."

"I see 'em," Gil said. "Dual inboard engines. Running full out."

Jeremiah smiled. The Elite Ops had incredible equipment. And yet Major Payne, even without his helmet, apparently could see as well as the fish team. "What's Manyara wearing?" he asked.

Major Payne said, "The cabin's too dark to make out the individuals inside."

"I was kidding. You have amazing eyesight."

"What's our plan?" Finn asked.

Jeremiah said, "As soon as we're close enough, take out their engines with a laser pulse. I want the boat disabled, not destroyed. We go in fast, just like the building back there. I don't want her to have any time to react."

Jeremiah could see the other Coast Guard cutter approaching from the southeast now, blocking any escape. He hoped he was right about this or he was going to look damn foolish. More importantly, Manyara would have too big a head start if she were headed for her lab. He'd never be able to stop her in time.

As the cutter neared the Sarahnity, Gil, Finn and Major Payne all aimed their Las-rifles at the small boat, which Jeremiah could now identify. They must have been communicating silently, for all three fired at once, purple pulses that struck the engines.

Immediately the Sarahnity slowed, its engines dead.

The cutter slowed as it came up on the bobbing boat, while the second cutter held back a few hundred yards, its captain obviously thinking the same thing Jeremiah was. Manyara might have a bomb or possibly the virus. This boat might even be her lab, however unlikely the possibility.

"You know you aren't boarding that vessel," Major Payne said as the cutter pulled up alongside the boat. Jeremiah leaned against the railing and looked down.

For a moment there was no activity in the Sarahnity. Then an old woman emerged from the cabin. Manyara.

Jeremiah felt a surge of relief.

Manyara wore something strapped around her midsection as she stepped to the stern and stopped beside a gate. The dark man stayed inside the cabin. Jeremiah caught a glimpse of him in the shadows, tucked behind the doorjamb. Was he holding a detonator or a Las-pistol or something else?

"She's wearing a bomb," Hannah said.

"Or the virus," Major Payne said. "We should blow her out of the water right now."

"No," Jeremiah said.

"She's too dangerous," Hannah said, her voice rising. "She might have the virus with her. We can't take any chances."

Lendra said, "It's your call, Jeremiah. Whatever you decide, we'll support you. But don't get too close."

"Okay," Jeremiah said. "Calm down, everyone." He called down to Manyara: "It's all over now. You might as well surrender and tell us where your lab is."

Manyara spoke too softly for Jeremiah to hear. He looked to Major Payne, who said, "Give me a second. There."

"Jones," he heard Manyara say. "Took you long enough."

Major Payne said, "Gil and Finn are amplifying everything now. You can speak normally."

"Thanks," Jeremiah said. He looked back down at Manyara. "We caught Sally2. We're bringing one of her people here."

"Is Eli with you?" Manyara asked.

"No."

Manyara nodded. "I'm sure you're connected to Lendra, and she's probably connected to him. I did care for Eli, at one time. It's just that . . ."

Lendra said, "Do you want me to put Eli on to speak with her?"

"No," Jeremiah said softly. He raised his voice and said to Manyara, "You can tell him yourself. I'm sure he'd like to hear from you personally."

Manyara glanced at the other cutter, several hundred yards distant, before returning her attention to him. "I don't think so."

Did she have a bomb? Was she trying to decide if it had enough power to destroy the other cutter?

"It's only a matter of time," Jeremiah said, "before we find your lab. We stopped the virus in London and we'll stop it here."

"You think you've won?" Manyara said. "You think I didn't plan for this contingency?"

"I'm sure you did. You always were smarter than everybody else. That's why you were able to fool us for so long."

"Don't bullshit me," Manyara said.

"I'm serious," Jeremiah said. "Eli always talked about how bright you are, and how it was such a shame that your license was revoked. He said he used to run ideas by you all the time. I'm sure that's how you got some of your information."

Manyara stared at him for a moment. Then she said, "Do yourself a favor. Stay out here on the water for the next three hours. Better yet, head to sea."

"So we have three hours before the virus is released?"

She shook her head, then opened the gate and stepped off the boat, sinking fast.

The dark man ran out of the cabin toward her.

"Stop him," Jeremiah said.

Finn and Gil fired at the same time, blue laser pulses that knocked him to the deck.

"What did she do?" Hannah asked.

"Should we go after her?" Major Payne asked.

"Let the other Coast Guard cutter retrieve her body," Lendra said. "We've got more important things to worry about. The virus—it might be on the boat. And we'll want to question that dark man."

"The fish team will bring him out," Major Payne said.

Lendra said, "Send the vid to us as you're searching the cabin. I'll want to look at everything to make certain it's safe."

"Got it," Major Payne said.

Gil and Finn jumped down to the Sarahnity's deck, the force of their landing making the smaller boat bob. They disappeared inside the cabin.

"She's going home," Eli said via Lendra's connection. "I recall her saying something about returning home to the gods at the bottom of the sea. I think that's pretty common in voodoo."

Less than a minute later Gil and Finn returned. "Nothing," Finn said.

Gil knelt before the dark man. "He's dead. You saw we only stunned him."

"Not your fault," Jeremiah said. "He was never going to be taken alive. The Blantons are now our last hope to find the virus."

Lendra said, "I'll notify Dr. Poole that we need results, no matter what it does to their brains."

"That was disappointing," Major Payne said. "I had hoped for a more satisfying result."

"You mean you wanted to kill her yourself," Jeremiah said.

"I didn't just want to kill the bitch. I wanted to rip her fingers off one by one. I wanted to use nerve gas to make her scream in terror. I wanted her to suffer for as long as possible before dying in her own filth and vomit."

Hannah said, "So you . . . didn't like her?"

Jeremiah smiled. "Good job, people. Let's get back to CINTEP. We've got less than three hours."

Chapter 29

Aspen stood atop Dunadan's knoll, staring up at the Chinese ship. For three days now, it had hovered fifty kilometers above them—a bright star, visible day and night. All attempts to communicate with it had failed. It continued to maintain perfect geosynchronous orbit. Not knowing its inhabitants' intentions bothered her. They should have at least been conducting some sort of telemetry to analyze the surface or the atmosphere or something. But nothing. No signals of any sort. Ominous.

Quekri refused to read a threat into their actions. "We're going to continue our scientific experiments," she said, "our colonization efforts, and when the Chinese astronauts decide to make contact with us, we'll happily engage with them. But we're not going to take any action that might be construed as aggression."

The miners were no help either. They continued their digging, their thieving, their visits to Dr. Wellon for various ailments, all the while stating that military and political matters were the province of the Escala and refusing to hand over their Las-rifles.

Aspen glanced over at the shuttle, which she and the other cadets had tested two days ago, making sure all its systems were functioning perfectly. It lay under a protective cover beside the entrance to the caves.

"I see that," Addam said. He stopped cleaning the sensor array and straightened up.

"What?" Aspen replied.

"You're looking at the shuttle. You want to take it up to the Chinese vessel."

"Don't you?"

"Sure, but Quekri said the ship is sovereign Chinese territory and boarding it could be considered hostile action."

"Why won't they answer our hails?"

"You think they're planning an attack."

"You have to admit that it's a possibility."

"I've heard you talking in your sleep, Aspen. You're having nightmares, aren't you?"

"They're just dreams."

"Calling out to Zora and Rendela?"

Aspen sighed. "I'm warning them. You know how dreams are—lots of jumping around, inconsistencies, illogical breaks. But I feel like this ship is a threat. I haven't had a good night's sleep in quite a while."

Addam snorted. "All your thrashing around hasn't exactly been good for me either. Maybe you should just borrow the shuttle and go up there—put us all at ease."

"That's a good idea."

"I was joking," Addam said. "Quekri doesn't want us doing anything that could increase tensions back on Earth."

"If she didn't want us to do anything, she could have deactivated the shuttle or put a guard on it or even expressly forbidden me to fly it, none of which she's done."

"That's because she believes in hands-off governing. You know that. How many times has she talked about civic freedom and our responsibility to the rest of the colony? 'I'm not going to make a lot of rules,'" Addam said in a creditable imitation of Quekri's voice. "'You can do whatever you like as long as you respect others' rights and keep in mind that the community's needs outweigh yours.'"

"You think I'm not concerned about the colony?" Aspen asked. "Quekri put me in charge of security. It's my job to check out all possible threats."

"I'm just not convinced this is a threat. If it is, why haven't they attacked us?"

"Are the Las-pistols ready yet?"

"Yes," Addam said. "Crude, but just as effective as any on Earth or the Moon. Benn wants to test-fire them."

"No. If that ship has scanners, it might be able to detect the energy signature of a fired Las-weapon. I want to maintain the element of surprise in case things come down to a battle. I've already ordered the miners not to fire their Las-rifles either, though I have no idea if they'll comply."

Aspen activated her powerscope and studied the orbiting spaceship—a large, spinning tube, hollow in the middle, designed to create artificial gravity.

"Anything?" Addam asked.

"No."

"They could blow us up right now," Addam said. "You know that. They wouldn't even have to land. They could fire a Las-weapon or a particle beam cannon or drop a nuclear bomb on our position. We've got no way to defend ourselves if they want us dead. You're just upset because you're not in control of the situation."

Aspen glared at him even though she knew he couldn't see her expression through the faceplate. "There was a time when you would have been upset about that too. You'd have taken the shuttle and flown up there yourself if you had to, just to check out the ship."

Addam raised his head and she knew he was looking at the ship. After a moment he said, "Do you still feel the rage?"

"Sometimes. You?"

"Not since Dr. Wellon fixed us," Addam said. "You're planning to steal the shuttle and fly up to take a look at the ship, aren't you? You're getting more like Curtik and Zora every day."

"Zora put me in command."

"Zora's thirty million miles away. She doesn't respond to your messages. She's forgotten us. You don't have to follow her orders anymore. Benn and I don't follow Curtik's orders."

"He doesn't give you any."

"That's because he's moved on. We've all moved on, Aspen. Shiloh, Kammilee, Benn, Curtik and even Zora."

Aspen turned away and headed down the knoll toward the cave entrance. "Finish cleaning the equipment," she said. "I'll be inside."

Was Addam right? Was she like Curtik and Zora? Certainly she often asked herself what Zora and Rendela would do in any given situation. But Curtik? He was nothing more than a thug. Zora, on the other hand, had always brought brilliant insight into problems while Rendela had often considered opposing viewpoints, bringing the most intuitive emotional response. Those two were definitely worth emulating.

She went to her room and put together a bag of personal items and clothes, just in case she was forced to stay away for a while. She hoped to make a quick inspection and return in a few hours, but if the Chinese ship's inhabitants were hostile, she might not be back soon . . . or at all.

And if she were killed?

Addam could carry on in her place. He'd make a fine leader: calm, rational, thoughtful. Benn was too much like Curtik, too quick to action, while Phan occasionally got caught up in details and was a little too much of a sensualist. Kammilee and Shiloh were both solid cadets, though neither had shown any desire to lead—so Addam it would be.

Picking up her bag, she glanced around the cave she had called home for the past few months. She was a bit surprised that she felt an emotional attachment to it. It was just a space: an unmade bed with two indentations where she and Addam slept; two chairs, a desk and a dresser she shared with Addam. Nothing fancy. But if she couldn't return for some reason, if Quekri exiled her, she wanted to be able to recall it.

She made her way to the lab space where Benn and Phan had been building the Las-pistols. When she arrived, Shiloh and Kammilee stood beside the weapons, bags packed, arms crossed over their chests, wearing smug smiles.

"Whatcha doin'?" Shiloh asked.

Aspen glanced at their bags. "I'm going to check out the Chinese ship," she said. "The Escala clearly have no intention of addressing this until they have to, at which time it might be too late."

"Your implant must not be working or you would have told us to join you," Kammilee said.

"This is purely a scouting mission."

Shiloh laughed. "That's why you packed a bag?"

Aspen shook her head. "How did you know I was leaving?"

"We grew up together, remember?" Kammilee said.

"But you want to become Escala," Aspen said. "You want to get pregnant."

"We're cadets," Shiloh said, "first, last and always. And you're not going alone."

"Zora put me in charge. I say who goes and who stays."

"Nice try," Benn said from behind her.

Aspen spun around. Benn, Phan and Addam stood in the tunnel entrance carrying bags. All three wore wide grins.

Aspen held up her hands. "If they're hostile, we may not survive. And Quekri may not let us come back even if they're not. And if we leave, the Escala will have no defenses. Some of us have to stay behind."

"Look," Addam said. "If they're hostile, they can kill us all anyway. And if Quekri won't let us return, then we'll have an adventure out there. Besides, we all know the Escala are better off without us. We're not like them and we never will be, no matter how hard we try."

Aspen turned back to Shiloh and Kammilee. The two cadets nodded in tandem. Kammilee's eyes glistened. Aspen realized that Addam spoke the truth and that the other cadets saw it too. Benn slipped past her and put his hand on Kammilee's shoulder as Shiloh wrapped an arm around Kammilee's waist.

Actually, if Aspen was honest with herself, it was hard for her too. She often wished she could be like the Escala. She didn't enjoy feeling angry all the time. But whatever conditioning and programming Eli had done to her, it had been so deeply entrenched that it would likely never go away completely. We're fighters, she realized. We've played at being scientists for a while now, but we'll always be fighters.

"Okay," Aspen said. "Let's go."

***

With all six cadets working together, they prepped the shuttle for launch in less than an hour. Aspen couldn't help but think how little she and her friends meant to the Escala; apparently no one had noticed they were gone, or at least no one cared.

The shuttle rose into the air, the thrusters expelling a massive cloud of red dust. Aspen felt a thrill at being back in space. She glanced at her fellow cadets. They all wore goofy smiles.

Benn said, "God, I missed the action. Let's go kill bad guys."

Phan laughed. Kammilee grinned.

"Remember," Aspen said, "this is just a scouting mission. We're not planning to kill anyone."

"It was a joke," Benn said.

"Right." Aspen studied Benn's face for a moment. She didn't completely trust him. Had he been disguising his warrior nature from the Escala all this time? If so, he'd done a remarkably good job. Aspen sent an implant message to Addam to keep an eye on Benn. He acknowledged the message with a brief nod.

Then the comm link beeped and Quekri's voice came through: "What are you kids doing?"

Aspen said, "We're going to check out the Chinese vessel."

"No," Quekri said. "Return to base at once."

"That's a negative," Benn said. "Course already plotted. Contact in less than ten minutes."

"You put me in charge of security," Aspen said. "I'm doing my job."

Shiloh said, "The ship's Las-cannon is tracking us."

Aspen looked out through the screen at the growing vessel—the large spinning tube looked like a hollow log with several sticks—no doubt passageways—running from one side to the other. Near the front, its Las-cannon pointed at the shuttle. Did that mean the ship's occupants intended them harm or was the Las-cannon's targeting mechanism activated automatically—aiming at every approaching object?

Quekri said, "You kids need to turn back. Garthod says their Las-cannon is powering up."

"Kids?" Addam said.

"Um, Aspen," Kammilee said, her voice catching for an instant, "I'm confirming that. Las-cannon is definitely powered up."

"What do we do?" Phan asked.

"We go on," Aspen said. "Powering up the Las-cannon may not mean they're planning to fire on us. It could simply be the result of programming put in place on Earth to protect the ship from meteoroids and space debris. We'll keep an eye on it. Shiloh, send a continuous transmission to let them know we're on a goodwill mission."

"Transmitting now," Shiloh replied. "I hope this works or we're going to be barbequed cadets."

Aspen looked at Addam. He smiled at her for a second before looking away and frowning. She studied the Las-cannon through the front screen, noticing that its nozzle glowed a dim red. She had to force himself to look away from it.

A warning suddenly came through the shuttle's comm system, broadcast in English: "Move away. Retreat. Do not approach."

Immediately following that, a short blue pulse shot out from the Las-cannon, striking the front of the shuttle, jolting everyone. Aspen's stomach clenched as her throat dried up. Thankfully they were all strapped in or they'd have been knocked out of their seats.

"Shiloh?" Aspen said.

"They're not responding," Shiloh replied.

"I think I'm going to be sick," Kammilee said.

"Deep breaths," Addam said.

"They're trying to kill us," Kammilee said.

"Just a warning shot, Kam," Benn said, his voice calm. "Standard defensive measure. If they'd wanted to kill us, we'd be dead."

"This is too risky," Quekri said. "Listen to the voice of experience and come home."

Benn laughed. Aspen thought she detected a hint of hysteria behind it, but maybe she was just reading that in. Maybe he was just happy to be back in space, doing what he'd been trained to do.

"We're fine," Addam said to no one in particular.

Aspen said, "We're boarding that vessel. They should've responded to our hails days ago. We're not going to turn around just because they've finally acknowledged our presence."

As the Chinese vessel's docking hatch centered on the forward screen, the Las-cannon disappeared from view. Just as well. Aspen didn't want to see it. If it fired on them again, so be it. But she didn't need to witness it. She'd rather just be killed. She glanced at the navigation instruments and said to Quekri, "Docking in three minutes. If they destroy us, you'll have a good view of it on the vid."

"Still transmitting a peaceful greeting," Shiloh said. "Still no response. And no more warnings."

Addam said, "Ready for docking procedures."

Aspen said. "Moving to match speed and rotation of the target."

"In twenty seconds," Quekri said, "you'll be so close that it'll be almost impossible for them to fire on you without risking destroying themselves."

Dr. Wellon now appeared behind Quekri on the vid. She said, "The people on that vessel may have been infected with the Susquehanna Virus. And since that strain was created in China, we know virtually nothing about it. You might have to be quarantined. And it could prove fatal."

"We'll keep our Mars suits on," Addam replied. "We're not using the shuttle's oxygen. We're keeping a vacuum. The virus won't be a problem."

"The virus could attach to your suits. You might bring it back with you when you return. We can't be certain it'll be safe, so we'll have to build a quarantine section if you decide to go ahead with this plan."

"We can live in quarantine for a few days when we get back," Kammilee said, her voice stronger now.

"It might be weeks."

"You're close enough," Quekri said. "Garthod doesn't think they can safely fire on you anymore."

"See?" Aspen said. "They didn't want to kill us after all. Docking in one minute."

Another laser pulse struck the shuttle, jolting them all again. Aspen couldn't see its color, but since the shuttle remained intact, she assumed it must have been another low-power strike. She checked the navigation system again, saw numerous repair lights blinking on the board.

"Nav system damaged," she said.

"Affirmative," Shiloh replied. "Computer docking disabled. We'll have to dock manually. It'll be more fun that way anyway."

For the next minute no one spoke. Aspen worked the controls while Addam fed her the data from the proximity sensors via implant. And as the shuttle made contact with the Chinese vessel, they felt only the slightest bump, then the tug of gravity as centripetal force pulled at them.

"Well done," Addam said.

Phan let out a whoop of joy while Kammilee smiled weakly.

"If you won't listen to reason," Quekri said, "at least be careful. If they don't give you permission to board, don't force anything. If you are allowed on board, make sure your helmet-cams are on at all times so we can document everything and maintain constant communications. Touch as little as possible. And as soon as you've ascertained the situation, you get back here and into quarantine. Okay?"

"Does that mean we have your permission for this trip?" Aspen said.

"It does not," Quekri said. "And I'm transmitting everything back to Earth so the Chinese will know this is nothing more than six teenagers on a joyride and not some conspiracy on our part to interfere with their mission."

Aspen tried to open the hatch, then realized that the computerized controls for that function had also been damaged by the laser strike. "Benn," she said. "We have to open the hatch manually."

Benn unstrapped himself, got to his feet and unlocked the door, then pulled it inside the shuttle and secured it to the wall, out of the way. Aspen joined him. After studying the hatch on the Chinese vessel, Aspen lifted a small cover and found a button with a Chinese character on it. Her implant translated the character for her—open.

"Here goes," Aspen said.

She hit the button.

A green light came on and the hatch door swung inward.

"Well," Addam said, "only one direction to go now."

Aspen touched the Las-pistol strapped to her thigh and stepped through the hatch into a small room—an airlock—followed by the others. As they studied the doorway into the ship proper, the hatch sealed behind them. They heard a rush of air, then the door to the vessel opened.

On the other side, in the dim lighting of a long, curving passage about ten feet tall stood a Chinese woman wearing a dark shirt and pants, with black hair down to her shoulders. She held herself still. Aspen could barely make out her face—just the glow of her eyes and the slight glint of white teeth.

She startled Aspen when she spoke in English:

"You should not have come." Her voice sounded husky—her enunciation precise. "Death awaits you."

Aspen felt a chill run down her back.

Benn said, "Hey, how come you speak English and not Chinese?"

The woman said, "We've been monitoring your transmissions. We heard you speaking in English, so I chose that language. Would you prefer me to speak Chinese, French, Spanish, Russian—"

"No," Aspen interrupted her. "English is fine." She looked down the dark, curving corridor they were standing in but saw no one in either direction. "Are you alone? Where is everyone?"

"The humans are either dead or dying," the woman replied.

"The humans?" Benn said.

Quekri's voice came through the comm unit: "That's not a woman. That's—"

Suddenly her voice cut out.

"What happened to that transmission?" Shiloh asked.

"I'm guessing she cut it off," Addam said.

"It's a robot," Phan said. "It looks like a fourth generation Wong-Tech—humanoid appearance. But it's so much more advanced. I'd swear it's human."

"Are you a robot?" Aspen asked.

"Yes," the robot replied.

Phan stepped forward to study the robot, which stood motionless. From what Aspen could see, the machine looked like a real woman, with dark eyes and "skin" that had a healthy glow. She looked much more advanced than the model that housed Devereaux's mind back on Earth, though that robot, Aspen knew, contained an extremely sophisticated organic computer capable of holding Devereaux's mind, probably far more advanced than whatever sort of computer brain this model had.

Phan said, "This is incredibly advanced technology. They probably didn't want us to know about it."

"Is that why you didn't answer our hails?" Shiloh asked. "We've been trying to contact you for ages."

"We have specific orders to maintain communications silence," the robot said.

"Is that because you're classified technology?" Aspen asked.

"We were not allowed to communicate with you for operational reasons."

"What operational reasons?"

"Military operational reasons," the robot replied. "You are a hostile and dangerous subspecies."

Benn drew his Las-pistol and pointed it at the robot, but it apparently didn't notice. It continued to smile reassuringly.

"Put that away," Aspen said to Benn as she held up a hand. "Are you planning to attack the Mars colony?"

"No," the robot replied.

"Then what are the military operational reasons for keeping communications silence?"

"Some on board believe you will try to take command of our ship. Apparently they were correct, for here you are."

"We're not planning to take over your ship."

The robot turned to face Benn. "You're holding a weapon on me."

Aspen said, "I told you to put that away."

Benn said, "This robot told us death awaits us. That's hardly a friendly greeting. I don't trust it."

Addam took a step forward, drawing everyone's attention. "Are you in charge?" he asked the robot.

"Good question," Aspen said.

"I am one of the units currently in command of this vessel," the robot replied. "No humans remain able to function in that capacity."

"Where are the humans?" Aspen asked. "Will you take us to them?"

"The living humans have been confined to stasis fields," the robot said. "They're dying. As you are now."

"Hm," Benn said as he lifted his Las-pistol and pointed it at the robot's head. "Seems to me like you're the only one in danger of being killed at the moment."

"You may fire," the robot said. "That won't alter your destiny."

"Which is?" Kammilee asked.

"You must be quarantined until you die. Returning to your people would only bring death to them."

"We're isolated in these self-contained suits," Aspen said. "The virus has no way of getting inside. So as long as we properly decontaminate the suits upon our return, the virus won't have a chance to infect the colony."

"I'm afraid we cannot allow you to take that chance," the robot said.

"It's not your decision to make," Aspen said.

"Actually, it is. The moment you chose to board this vessel, despite our warnings, you surrendered any choice in your future."

Benn fired his Las-pistol, a long red burst that super-heated the robot's head, setting its hair on fire and melting its face, disfiguring the pseudo-skin until the robot looked like something out of a horror vid, its eyes blackened and its mouth twisted into a psychotic leer. The robot went still.

"What'd you—" Phan sputtered. "Why'd you do that?"

"Stupid machine," Benn said. "Didn't even try to defend itself."

Then—unbelievably— the robot slowly turned and walked away, only the slightest hesitation in its step.

"What the hell?" Benn asked as he raised his Las-pistol.

"Don't," Aspen said as she pushed his hand down.

"The robot's brain isn't stored in its head," Phan said. "It was designed that way to protect against what just happened. These things are amazing!"

"I think it's time we leave," Aspen said.

"Too late," Kammilee said, pointing down the hallway. "Behind you. More robots."

Aspen turned. Sure enough, a handful of robots approached. They looked like quintuplets—all female, with only small differences in their facial features—though Aspen could tell they were robots because they moved in perfect synchronicity. Each carried a Las-pistol.

Take 'em out, Benn sent through his implant as he dove to the side, firing a continuous red pulse at the robots. He hit two, but the robots fired back. Addam, Shiloh, Phan and Kammilee all dove to the floor, firing red pulses at the robots, who dodged into nooks she hadn't seen. Aspen realized she hadn't moved. Also, the robots had fired blue pulses, so they weren't intending to kill them.

Hold your fire, Aspen sent as a laser pulse struck her in the stomach. She fell to the floor, feeling like her gut was on fire. Glancing down, she saw that a small hole had been burned in the center of her Mars suit, leaving her exposed to the atmosphere of the ship. Probably the only reason she was still conscious was because much of the energy from the robots' lasers had diffused across her Mars suit.

Benn lay still, a gaping tear in his Mars suit. Down the hallway behind them, Aspen noticed half a dozen more robots closing in.

Hold your fire, she sent again as she got to her feet.

Robots came at them from both directions, Las-pistols aimed at the cadets. As they approached they held out their hands. Aspen handed over her Las-pistol and the other cadets followed suit, except for Benn, who lay unconscious on the floor. Kammilee knelt beside Benn but, because she was trapped inside her suit, she could do little for him.

Every robot looked female in appearance, with only minor differences among them. One robot walked over to Aspen and said, "You shouldn't have made us hurt you. I'm afraid that will only accelerate your deaths."

Addam stepped over to Aspen's side and said, "You going to kill us now?"

"No," the robot replied. "Of course not. We mean you no harm. If you wish, we can treat your companion in our medical bay, but he will die soon, just like you."

Chapter 30

Lendra Riley tried not to think about Sophie, lying in the infirmary, feverish and in pain, her tiny body connected to an AutoLife machine. The doctors had finally found the cause of the staph infection: the Susquehanna Virus, floating around in her corneal fluid. Somehow she had become infected and it had bypassed her immune system. Had Manyara done it? Lendra couldn't recall a specific time when Manyara had been alone with Sophie, but it could have happened. And now the doctors said she might never recover. The only blessing was that Sophie was in a coma.

Enough, she told herself. Get a grip. Stop making yourself crazy. She contacted Dr. Poole via her interface.

"What kind of progress have you made with the Blantons?"

"The information apparently wasn't deeply seated in the amygdala," Dr. Poole said, "so I'm having trouble extracting it despite the hypnotic state and the drugs."

"Well, a drone sub just recovered Manyara's body. According to what she told Jeremiah, we have less than three hours until the virus is released."

"Right. So unless we get the information from the Blantons quickly, we might not be able to stop it in time."

"Do whatever you have to do," Lendra said.

"I will."

Lendra turned to Jay-Edgar. "How long until Jeremiah gets back?"

"Ten minutes. And the President is calling."

"Put her through."

Via holo-projection, President Angelica Hope appeared before her, dark bags under her eyes. "Give me an update," she said, her contralto voice sounding more hoarse than usual. Like Lendra, she probably hadn't slept in over a day.

"We managed to track down Manyara Harris but, unfortunately, she killed herself during our attempt to capture her. We believe we have three hours left until her new strain of the virus is released. We still haven't found her lab, but we're hoping to have that information soon."

"Have you been able to confirm that this new strain is more potent than previous incarnations?"

"Not yet. However, we've asked Professor Devereaux to help once we locate it. He might be able to discover some sort of antidote or vaccine in case we can't stop the virus' release. We've also got a Sally flying in from London with a CINTEP team. Professor Devereaux has already created a partial vaccine for her. It won't cure her completely, but it should keep her alive for a while, perhaps long enough for her to give us whatever insights she can regarding the virus."

President Hope tapped her fingernails on the desk in front of her. "And if we don't find the virus before it's released? How big a disaster are we looking at?"

Lendra shrugged. "We don't have enough details on its genetic structure."

"Then you'd best stop it before it's released, Ms. Riley."

"Yes, ma'am."

After disconnecting, she sat at her desk for a moment. Was there anything she could do, or would she be better served visiting Sophie?

Jay-Edgar interrupted her thoughts: "Eli says he has more background information on Manyara and voodoo."

"Anything of pressing value?"

"No, just general information."

"Archive it for me, please."

"What's going to happen to him?" Jay-Edgar asked. "And me?"

"He'll be in prison for the rest of his life. He may be used for his knowledge at times like this, but otherwise I imagine he'll be kept in the dark about the world around him. That will be his greatest punishment."

"And me?"

"I don't know," Lendra said. She wanted him to think he might escape unscathed, so she didn't tell him the truth. If she could replace him, she would, but he was so damned insightful as to what she needed that she couldn't spare him just now. When this crisis was over she would train a replacement. "I'll do what I can for you."

Jay-Edgar nodded. "I understand. Jeremiah's back. Should I send him to interrogation room one?"

"Yes," Lendra replied. "I'll be there as well."

She stepped out into the hall, looked left toward the infirmary, wishing Eli were still in charge of CINTEP so she could visit Sophie, hold her daughter, sing to her like Jeremiah had—the hell with the world. What had it ever done for her? Then she took a couple of deep breaths and turned right toward interrogation room one. She waited only a moment outside the door before Jeremiah and Hannah emerged from the stairway to the roof, the two Elite Ops troopers crowding along behind them.

She hoped Jeremiah would give her another hug, but when he reached her, he just said, "Sophie?"

"She's on an AutoLife machine," Lendra replied. "They found traces of the virus. I think Manyara infected her."

Jeremiah went still. He stared past her toward the infirmary, but she couldn't read his expression. He might have been a statue. She knew this was how he reacted to intense pain. He became cold and unemotional, detaching himself from the source until he could process it and conquer it. But how did you conquer the death of your child?

"Go," Jeremiah finally said. "Please wait in your office with Gil, Finn and Hannah." Jeremiah entered interrogation room one, pulling the door shut behind him. It locked with a loud click.

Hannah sighed. "He said he had a plan, but he wouldn't tell us what it was. You think he'll kill the Blantons?"

"I don't know," Lendra said, leading the way back to her office. They all stepped inside, Gil and Finn removing their helmets. Jay-Edgar already had the footage of interrogation room one on the screen. The Blantons sat beside each other staring blankly ahead, their mouths slack, both of them hooked up to AutoLife machines, though they appeared to still be breathing on their own. Dr. Poole had probably hooked them up as a precaution. They looked much as they had before, two attractive people, wearing CINTEP coveralls, though they were both sweating. It couldn't be just the bright lights, for Dr. Poole looked relatively comfortable.

"We're hooked in," Jay-Edgar said. "They can hear and see us."

"Anything yet?" Jeremiah asked Dr. Poole.

She shook her head. "No luck retrieving the information. I had to be a little aggressive with the drugs. I'm afraid they may need life support if I try to do more. Frankly, I'm out of ideas."

"Get me three sensory helmets," Jeremiah said as he took a seat in front of Rebecca and strapped himself in, "one for each of us."

"No, Jeremiah," Lendra said. "You can't do that. It's not compatible with your transgenic modifications."

"We don't have any choice," Jeremiah said.

"What is he planning?" Hannah asked.

"Linking up with the Blantons," Jay-Edgar replied, "like Ned did with Hector."

"They could die at any moment," Dr. Poole said. "Their minds are not rational."

"With the drugs they're on," Lendra said, "you could be severely brain damaged."

"Do you have a better idea?" Jeremiah asked.

"Let someone else link with them."

"I'll do it," Hannah said.

"Or me," Finn said. "Gil and I are used to linking with the Elite Ops."

"That's a good idea," Lendra said.

"No," Jeremiah said. "It's too dangerous. And it requires a feather touch. Besides, this is my job."

"Not anymore," Lendra said. "You're retired."

"I can't let anyone else take this risk. Get the helmets."

Dr. Poole grabbed three helmets from a shelf and placed two of them atop the Blantons' heads. She handed the third one to Jeremiah.

"Full linkage," Jeremiah said as he put the helmet on.

Dr. Poole looked at the camera pickup and said, "That is extremely dangerous at the best of times. Ned was only eighty percent linked. Full linkage might kill you. You would be absorbed into their minds, and with all the drugs in their systems, you might never be able to escape. And just the act of linking with them could send them into cardiac arrest. If they die while you're linked to them, you could die too."

"Jeremiah," Lendra said. "You can't. Dr. Poole, I'm refusing to allow a full linkage."

Jeremiah said, "We only get one shot at this. If they die, we're done. If we fail because we didn't go deep enough, we won't be able to do it again. Right?"

Dr. Poole turned back to Jeremiah. "That's true. They may not survive the procedure given the state they're in, and their minds would certainly be contaminated by the link, so even if they live, the odds of connecting successfully a second time are extremely slim." She again looked up at the camera pickup. "It's your call."

Lendra felt all eyes on her. These were the kinds of decisions Eli loved making. He enjoyed pulling strings and making people dance— the god behind the ghosts. This was what she had striven for these past few years. And now that she had achieved this position of power, all she wanted was to take Jeremiah and Sophie and run away to some peaceful cabin in the woods.

"Okay," she finally said.

"No!" Hannah said.

She stood rigidly, fists clenched at her sides, glaring at Lendra. Gil and Finn scowled at her as well. Even Jay-Edgar wore a frown. But this was her job, to make the hard decisions no one else could.

"We have to trust him," Lendra said. "He knows what he's doing."

All she could do was watch now.

Dr. Poole made sure the helmet was properly seated on Jeremiah's head, then went to her control panel and made several adjustments. Within a few seconds, Jeremiah's body convulsed.

"Tell me what's going on," Lendra said to Dr. Poole.

"Linkage is established."

"How long will it take?"

"Several minutes," Dr. Poole replied.

"Is there anything you can do?"

"All I can do is watch his vitals while he searches for the information." Dr. Poole moved an AutoLife machine into place behind Jeremiah and hooked him up to it. The machine would serve as a backup, keeping his heart and lungs functioning should he somehow be trapped inside the link. As Dr. Poole set up the machine, Lendra studied Jeremiah.

His body shook, his hands clawing the armrests, his jaw clamped tightly shut.

"What's happening to him?" Hannah asked.

"The one time I linked," Lendra said, "it was a pleasant experience. Of course, I was linked with Dr. Poole and it was only a sixty-five percent linkage, so it was easy to retain my sense of self inside the connection. Jay-Edgar did a full linkage once."

"It was a controlled test with another CINTEP tech," Jay-Edgar said. "Perfect conditions. Maximum compatibility with his brain—and only one-on-one. Even so, I nearly lost myself inside him. It was like he and I no longer existed independently. I was both me and him at the same time. Neither one of us could break free—as if by linking, we both disappeared. As far as I know, no one's ever linked with two people at the same time."

"How will we know if he's succeeded?" Finn asked.

"I'll pull him out after three minutes," Dr. Poole said, "unless he somehow manages to free himself before then."

Jeremiah struggled against the bonds that held him. Straining against the straps, his body convulsing repeatedly, he opened and closed his mouth, but no sound emerged.

Dr. Poole said, "I'm seeing utter terror on the Blantons' screens. I don't have Jeremiah's screen connected yet, so I don't know how much fear he's feeling, but I suspect it's a lot. His pulse is racing, blood pressure increasing."

"I think I know what he's doing," Jay-Edgar said.

"What?" Lendra asked.

"He knows that memories are retained much better in times of stress, so he's taking them back to their meeting with Manyara. Even though they didn't look at the paper until they were running away, he's hoping to tap into that fear."

Jeremiah writhed in agony.

"He's dying," Hannah said. "Get him out!"

"Dr. Poole won't let him die," Jay-Edgar said, his words coming out as a question rather than a statement. "The problem," he continued, "is that their stress levels would have diminished as they got away from Manyara. And their adrenaline would have been dropping too. So the memories might not be strong enough to recall even if he gets them terrified."

"I think you're right," Dr. Poole said. "But his blood pressure is two-sixty over one-thirty and his pulse is one-seventy. I'm not sure how long I should leave him under."

"He knows what he's doing," Jay-Edgar said.

Lendra hoped he was right. Gil and Finn looked as if they might attack her at any moment. Hannah shot her occasional glances, always returning her attention to the screen. Her right hand, Lendra noticed, had drifted down to her Las-pistol.

Should she call security? Were these people that dedicated to Jeremiah that they would attempt to kill her if he died? No, she refused to think about that. He would survive. He always found a way to survive. And it was his choice, damn it. He had forced the issue, locking them out, like he always did, taking the brunt of the punishment upon himself. This was the Jeremiah she remembered, the Jeremiah she loved.

And he would live.

Each minute passed like a kidney stone.

Lendra found herself staring at the time display on her interface, then to the screen and Jeremiah's obvious suffering, then to the anxious faces of her companions. Jeremiah's contortions weakened. Was that a good sign or a bad one?

"Doctor?" she said.

"He's coming out," Dr. Poole said. She removed Jeremiah's helmet. Yet he continued to struggle. His head moved back and forth, eyes closed, hands opening and closing weakly.

Dr. Poole straddled him and firmly held his head. "It's okay," she said. "It's okay. You're back. You're free. You're not Ned or Rebecca Blanton. You're Jeremiah Jones."

"The helmet's off," Hannah said. "Why isn't he coming out of it?"

"I don't know," Jay-Edgar said.

Dr. Poole leaned forward and kissed Jeremiah, a long kiss that he fought for a moment, then surrendered to. Lendra felt her face burning. She glanced at Hannah and saw her cheeks flush as well. And Gil—she had forgotten about Gil and Taditha—took a half step forward. She turned back to the screen. The kiss went on for a long time. And the last thing she needed was another woman falling for Jeremiah, especially one as smart and beautiful as Taditha.

Then Dr. Poole pulled back and Jeremiah opened his eyes, breathing heavily. He sat stunned for a moment and then said, "Thanks, Doc."

"My pleasure," Dr. Poole replied. She remained seated on his lap. Why? "Did you get the address?"

Jeremiah nodded. "It's on Ritchie Road. How are the Blantons?"

"I'm not going to kiss them," Dr. Poole said.

"Please check on them," Jeremiah said. "They're nice people."

"What?" Hannah said. "They helped kill millions."

"They were confused," Jeremiah said. "Let me up, Doc."

Dr. Poole continued to sit on Jeremiah's lap. "You're in no condition to move. Give us the address of the warehouse and we'll send a team over to handle it."

So that's why Dr. Poole hadn't gotten up. She wanted to make sure Jeremiah didn't run off and do something crazy. She knew, of course, about Sophie. And she knew how hard Jeremiah would take that news. He was liable to do anything now.

"I'm fine, Doc," Jeremiah said. "Please check on the Blantons. You owe it to me. You owe it to Jack."

Dr. Poole finally climbed off Jeremiah's lap and unstrapped him.

Jeremiah looked up at the camera pickup and said, "Let's go."

"No," Lendra said. "Give us the address. We'll let the bomb squad handle it."

"Sorry. Too dangerous. I'll take Major Payne, Hannah and the fish team with me. But I'm going."

"This is ridiculous," Lendra said as Jeremiah got to his feet. He grabbed the back of the chair to keep his balance. "You can't even walk."

"Sure I can," Jeremiah said as he straightened. He stood still for a moment, then stumbled toward the door.

"Stubborn fool," she said as she ran out the door, Hannah and the fish team behind her. She sprinted after him as he hobbled down the hallway, his back to her. "Hold on," she called out.

He ignored her.

She caught up to Jeremiah before he reached the stairway to the roof and grabbed his arm, spinning him around. "You can't do this," she said. She stared at his implacable face. "You're not some cowboy. You're not Superman. Let someone else go in."

"I have to do this."

"Why? Because you've got a death wish? A martyr complex? What is it that makes you insist on doing this alone? Maybe Eli really did program you to think this way."

Jeremiah shook his head as he pried her hand away. "It doesn't matter. I couldn't live with myself if someone else went in and the virus escaped. I have to do this."

"You're not thinking clearly. Sophie might still pull through. You don't have to handle this on your own."

"I won't be on my own. I'll take Major Payne in with me."

"Is that a joke or just a bad pun?"

"You can't run CINTEP if you won't use all the assets at your disposal. I'm the best person to get the job done. You know that. And I can't refuse to do it. I couldn't live with myself. I realize that's messed up. But that's the truth. I'll get you the address when we're in the air, so you can bring in as many people as you want to back us up, but I'm going in."

He turned away and opened the door to the roof.

Hannah said, "I'll take care of him." Then she slipped past Lendra and up the stairs. The fish team followed her.

As the door swung shut, Lendra realized that perhaps the only person more alone than her right now was Jeremiah. Both of them had devoted their lives to their careers. And now they were isolated, with no way out. Perhaps if she were to leave, if she were to find the strength to walk away—if she could somehow do that, Jeremiah would join her.

No, he wouldn't.

***

The warehouse looked dilapidated—two stories of aged cement block walls, with half a dozen small, cracked windows near the top and two rusting metal doors. The only thing remotely modern about the building was its sophisticated electronic locking system, which confirmed for Jeremiah that they were at the right place. Major Payne stood beside him, and behind them, the fish team of Gil and Finn waited at the head of an army of Elite Ops troopers, FBI agents, Homeland Security personnel, two Haz-Mat teams and a pair of ambulances. All together, they took up most of the closed-off street—nothing subtle about Lendra's support team.

Jeremiah felt a bit like the building: ready to fall down at any moment. He supposed he ought to want to survive this mission, but he really didn't care. If Sophie were to die, what would he have to live for? Curtik had rejected him. Catherine, Julianna and Jack Marschenko were all gone. And he himself was a murderer many times over. Still, he would try to survive, if only to keep Major Payne alive.

"There's a dampening field inside the building," Major Payne said. "Primitive. We can tell there are explosives inside, but it's impossible to know how they're rigged."

On the portable screens set up before him, Jeremiah studied the images being delivered by the hover cameras. "Keep those cameras well back," he reminded Major Payne. "Don't want their transmissions to accidentally detonate the explosives."

"Right," Major Payne replied.

A lone truck carrying two large metal tanks slowly backed up to the warehouse. When it got within ten feet Jeremiah gestured for the driver to stop. The driver, a young CINTEP agent named Adler, jumped down. He wore a bright red interface, part of the newest fashion trend, making certain people knew he was connected at all times.

"Is that the sealant?" Jeremiah asked.

Hannah nodded. "The portable tank is in the front. Fully charged."

"Okay," Jeremiah said. "I want you and Adler behind those ambulances where it's safe."

Hannah shook her head. "I'm watching you."

"You can do that from back there. Now go."

As they moved away, Jeremiah returned to the architectural plans Lendra had obtained for the building.

"Not much time left," Lendra said. "Maybe an hour. You sure the sealant will work?"

"It will if we can keep the building from blowing up," Jeremiah said. "I used it once before. It'll spray out as a liquid, then foam up like a Styrofoam—airtight and providing a cushion effect should anything strike it." He turned to Major Payne. "Let's seal windows, doors, roof vents." He studied the blueprints. "I want this place as airtight as possible. Though, with all the cracks in those cement block walls, we're not going to be able to seal it off completely—at least not before it's set to go."

"We'll do what we can," Major Payne said. Gil and Finn stepped forward and each grabbed a hose. Then they fired their jetpacks, rising up to the level of the windows, trailing their hoses behind them. Fully armored, they looked like astronauts, tethered to the tanks as they sprayed the windows with sealant. After the last window disappeared beneath the sealant the fish team vanished over the top of the building.

Lendra said, "You going through a wall?"

"I figure that's safer," Jeremiah said. "We can cut a hole in one of the block walls, seal it up behind us. That way we avoid any triggers activated by doors or windows. We'll bring the portable sealant unit along." Jeremiah turned to Major Payne. "No armor, though. The electronics might activate the virus' dispersal or an explosion."

As Major Payne removed his armor, something about his size or the way he held himself reminded Jeremiah briefly of Jack Marschenko. He wished Jack were here.

"You can't go in blind," Lendra said.

"We'll take a chance on a small camera and comm system," Jeremiah said, "so you can see what's happening. I'm guessing Manyara had a PlusPhone with her when she was inside and I'm hoping she didn't rig the place to blow with that kind of sensitivity."

He glanced up as Gil and Finn strode to the end of the warehouse and leapt off, plummeting earthward for only a second until their jetpacks kicked in, lowering them gently to the ground. Gil and Finn returned the hoses to the tank.

"Doors, windows and roof vents secure," Gil said.

"There are only about seven hundred and eighty-four thousand cracks left in the structure of the building itself," Finn added.

"Fill every one of them," Jeremiah said, forcing himself to smile at Finn as he reached inside the truck and removed the portable unit—a scuba-tank sized canister connected to a pressure nozzle that would spray the same airtight sealant. "We're going in now. You and Gil seal the opening behind us. If it all goes to hell, run."

"Right. Good luck, sirs."

After Jeremiah and Major Payne donned their haz-mat suits, checking to make sure their respiration and comm systems worked properly, Gil and Finn moved to a wall four feet away from the door, where the plans showed no electrical wiring. They aimed their Las-rifles at the wall and sliced through the cement block with thin red pulses that outlined a rectangular hole three feet wide and four feet high. As their laser pulses met, they ceased firing, then used their armored hands to pull the large chunk of cement block free. The cement broke into three pieces.

"Do what you can to put that back together," Jeremiah said, "and then fill the cracks with the sealant." He glanced at Major Payne, who gestured for him to lead the way.

Crouching down, careful to avoid scraping his haz-mat suit on the cement wall, Jeremiah scuttled through the opening into the warehouse, pulling the portable unit through behind him. As Major Payne followed him inside, Gil and Finn stacked the pieces of concrete into the opening. Straightening up inside the dimly lit space, Jeremiah noticed a blue tarp smoldering next to the hole. The Las-rifles must have penetrated the concrete a bit too far and nearly lit the tarp on fire. Jeremiah swatted the tarp, extinguishing the potential blaze. Then he looked around. Two LED lights hanging from the twelve-foot ceiling provided the only real illumination.

Dusty boxes, dirty machinery and old laboratory equipment took up much of the wall space in the thirty-by-sixty-foot room while island counters rested on the severely cracked and uneven floor. Stacks of pallets covered one wall, while cabinets and a countertop fronted another. Boxes lined a third wall and much of the center of the room, while the fourth wall had five doors, all shut. Jeremiah knew from the plans that they led to interior offices and a bathroom.

"Well?" Lendra asked through the comm link, "Any sign of the virus?"

"You're seeing what I'm seeing," Jeremiah replied.

Major Payne moved toward a machine in the center of the room that ran noisily. "Scatterer and dampening field . . . and something else. I think it's a bomb."

"Don't touch it," Jeremiah said.

He began stepping around boxes and counters toward the wall with the doors. "See any canisters?" he asked. "Anything that might hold the virus?"

"No," Major Payne answered. "Maybe she lied to the Blantons. Maybe there is no virus."

"Wouldn't that be nice? We could all go home and sit in our rocking chairs and drink beer."

"Don't make fun of my dream," Major Payne said.

Jeremiah opened the first door, flipped on the light and peered inside—an empty office. The second door opened on a bathroom, also empty. Major Payne opened the door on the far left. "Empty," he said.

"These too," Jeremiah replied. As Major Payne opened the fourth door, Jeremiah opened the final one. The light switch didn't work, but all he saw were cartons.

"Nothing," Major Payne said.

"No light in here," Jeremiah said. As he pushed aside a large box in front of the door, a dark man leapt at him.

He caught a flash of silver as he ducked and spun away.

"Look out!" Lendra yelled.

The man came at him again, slashing the air with a machete. Inside the haz-mat suit, Jeremiah found it difficult to move quickly, but he managed to slip to the side and grab the man's arm. The man writhed in Jeremiah's grasp, kicking and twisting as he spat, yelling in a language that sounded like French.

Jeremiah pulled the man out the door into the main room as Major Payne ran over. He struggled to hold the man without ripping the haz-mat suit until Major Payne could reach them. Finally Major Payne arrived. He grabbed the man's head and twisted sharply, breaking the man's neck. The machete clattered to the floor.

"Thanks," Jeremiah said.

"You're welcome," Major Payne replied. He picked up the machete and pointed to his eyes with his free hand. "I got the good eyes, remember? I'll check the room while you look for the virus."

Jeremiah moved quickly now, opening cabinets and boxes, looking for the canisters the Blantons had mentioned. Or perhaps they never mentioned it. Maybe he somehow retrieved that information during the link.

He shuddered, trying to forget the terror, and continued searching. The cabinets contained cans and jars, all labeled with medical sounding terms like oxyacidic-acquitane and hydroxylconic butymol.

"It could be any of these," he said.

"Keep going," Lendra said. "Dr. Poole says none of those are the virus unless they're mislabeled. They're merely ingredients Manyara was using."

"The room's clear," Major Payne said. "Just the one guy."

"Good. Put down the machete and help me look for the virus."

Jeremiah began sifting through the boxes in the center of the room as Major Payne worked his way around the perimeter. He said, "I got explosives here in the corner. Looks like they're in all four corners. Think we can seal 'em up?"

"That's a good idea," Lendra said.

"Perhaps," Jeremiah said. "But if they've got pressure switches, we'd just set them off. I'd rather we try to find the virus first."

"You're right," Major Payne said.

"Do it your way," Lendra added.

They continued their searching and a minute later Major Payne said, "Whoa!"

He lifted the tarp that had almost caught fire. "I think I found it. There are a couple canisters here."

He carefully eased the tarp aside. "They look like dispersal canisters. Wow, we got lucky. We could've set them on fire with the Las-rifles when we cut through the wall. Or the cement blocks could've fallen inwards and crushed them."

Jeremiah made his way back to the hole they'd cut in the wall. The canisters, about four inches in diameter and two feet long, made of some sort of reinforced, recycled paper and sealed with a waxy coating, balanced atop a jagged crack in the floor. A small valve at the top of each could be turned to release the contents, while next to each valve rested a small black box that might contain a triggering mechanism, a timer or detonator, or even a small explosive. There was no way to know without advanced electrical equipment, which might in itself detonate the boxes.

"Another problem," Payne said.

"What?" Lendra asked.

Payne said, "The timers are internalized, so there's no way to know what time they're set for. They could go boom at any time."

"What about the canisters?" Lendra asked. "What are those boxes on the top?"

"Might be movement sensors," Jeremiah said. "Or they could be small detonators, set to blow the canisters upon receiving an electronic signal or on a timer." He studied the area around the canisters carefully. "I see no triggering mechanism or trip wire or pressure switches."

Lendra said, "You think those canisters contain the virus?"

"Probably," Jeremiah said.

"Can we seal these?" Payne asked.

"I'm hoping," Jeremiah said. "Then we can risk bringing in some scanners to see if we can detect any trace of the virus. If it's all clear, we might want to bring the building down in a controlled explosion."

"I like it," Payne said.

Setting the portable unit's nozzle to mist, Jeremiah began spraying the canisters, covered them with a thin film that quickly foamed up, coating the cardboard cylinders in a cushiony shell. After sealing the tops and sides, Jeremiah said to Payne, "All right. Now comes the tricky part. There may be a trip mechanism in the crack beneath the cylinders. So as I spray the cracks, you gently lift the canisters, one at a time, and I'll spray the bottoms of each. Okay?"

"Roger that," Major Payne said.

"Remember," Jeremiah said, "one at a time. As I spray the crack, you lift each canister slowly. We want to try to keep the pressure equal."

"Hold on a sec," Major Payne said. He took a couple deep breaths, then nodded to Jeremiah. Jeremiah eased the trigger closed, spraying the crack beneath the bottom of the cylinder while Major Payne gently eased the canister up off the floor. A faint chime sounded from the front door.

"What the hell is that?" Payne asked.

"Don't know," Jeremiah replied. "We might have just triggered something bad."

"Shouldn't we check it?" Lendra asked.

"Later," Jeremiah said as he sprayed the bottom of the first canister. "Okay," he said. "One down. You ready for the second one?"

Payne set the first canister aside and nodded.

As Jeremiah began spraying the crack beneath the second canister, Payne lifted the canister off the floor. Jeremiah thought he heard a tiny click, but he saw nothing inside the crack. He glanced at Payne, who shrugged.

"I heard it too," Payne said. "I don't see anything either."

Jeremiah sprayed the bottom of the second canister as well.

"Okay," he said. "Open up the wall where we came in. Let's get some scanners in here—see if that's all of it."

"Well done," Lendra said.

As Jeremiah put down the portable sealant unit and grabbed the first canister, he heard another click, louder this time.

Payne stared at Jeremiah, his eyes suddenly wide. "We're dead!"

Jeremiah threw himself on the major, covering Payne and the canisters with his body as the building exploded.

Concrete and metal fell on him, parts of the wall and the roof collapsing around him, pressing into him tightly, pinning him to Major Payne and the floor. His ears rang, but otherwise he heard nothing. He felt Major Payne beneath him, but he saw nothing. Either he was blind or he was in total darkness. He felt no pain: just an unbelievable pressure. He tried moving his arms and legs, but they were completely bound by the debris. Beneath him, Major Payne moved slightly, so at least he was alive for now.

Slowly the pain emerged, in his back and chest, then in his arms and legs. He was pretty sure he'd broken some ribs because every breath hurt. And he could feel the slickness of blood on his fingers.

Is this how I die? Trapped beneath a mountain of rubble, never knowing if I failed or succeeded? Did the virus escape in the explosion? Or did the sealant work? And what about Sophie?

He felt an increasing weariness, a fatigue pulling him toward eternal darkness. I should want to live, he thought. I should try to survive for all those others who depend on me. But the darkness held no responsibility, no demands or expectations. It simply welcomed him.

Chapter 31

Since her Mars suit had already been compromised, Aspen removed her helmet.

"Is that wise?" Addam asked.

"They're right," Aspen said as she glanced at the robots, gathered in a semi-circle along the passageway, seemingly waiting for direction. "The two of us have already been exposed."

Addam helped her remove the rest of the suit. Then the two of them, with Kammilee's help, removed Benn's suit.

She checked Benn's pulse and found it weak. The robots had fired blue pulses, which should only have been enough to stun, and that's all that happened to her but, for some reason, Benn was more than stunned.

"What did you do to him?" Aspen asked.

The lead robot said, "He was hit with three simultaneous pulses in the same spot. Unfortunately, their combined power acted with much greater force."

"How could that be?"

Phan said, "The robots have all been programmed the same way. They fired at the same target at the same time. It would be difficult for us to be that precise, but it's almost impossible for them not to be."

"But the robot said he was hit with three pulses. There are five robots. What about the other two?"

"That is odd," Phan said. He turned to the lead robot. "Can you explain that?"

The robot said, "Two of us were able to avoid firing."

"That's bizarre," Phan said. "I wonder if there's some sort of flaw in the programming. They should all have fired at the same time."

"It's a good thing they didn't," Aspen said. "Benn might have been killed. He needs help. We'd better take him to the medical bay. We can worry about the whys later."

Benn groaned as he regained consciousness. He blinked his eyes.

"You are both infected with the virus now," the robot said. "We can only delay your death. We cannot cure you. But we will do what we can in the medical bay."

"They've found cures for some versions of the virus on Earth," Kammilee said. "If you'd bothered to contact your government, you might have learned of them."

"That was impossible," the robot said, "given our orders to avoid external communications."

After Aspen helped Benn to a sitting position, Addam and Phan lifted him to his feet.

"Which way to the medical bay?" Aspen asked.

The robot pointed down the hallway, where another robot gestured for them to follow.

"Our orders are very explicit," the robot said as they began walking. "They were written into our programming and cannot be countermanded. We had to activate our human-first programming to circumvent our orders just to issue you the warnings to stay away from our vessel."

"Human-first programming?" Shiloh asked.

"Similar to the rules of robotics that were invented by Isaac Asimov, and adopted by our Chinese creators—programmed into us as a means of ensuring the dominion of humankind over robots."

As they walked, Aspen said, "Somebody must be able to countermand your non-communication orders."

"Indeed," the robot replied. "Anyone with the proper authorization, including the leaders of this mission."

"Are any of those leaders still alive?" Aspen asked.

"They aren't sane," the robot replied. "They rant gibberish and lash out at us whenever we unlock their stasis fields."

"Why didn't they contact Earth when they first started feeling the effects of the virus?" Kammilee asked. "Why didn't they seek help?"

"The virus attacked their brains first, rendering them incapable of rational thought."

"And it hit all of them at once?" Aspen asked.

"It hit during a single sleep cycle," the robot replied. "We discovered later that it struck during a seven-hour window."

"Well, the first thing we need to do is figure out a way to override your programming to allow for external communications."

"Take us to your leader," Phan said with a grin.

Addam and Shiloh laughed.

"We come in peace," Kammilee said.

Even Benn laughed at that.

"This isn't the time for jokes," Aspen said.

"Oh, come on, Aspen," Addam said. "This is great. We want to go where no one has gone before."

More giggles.

"The virus?" Aspen said. "Your diminishing air supply? I don't see the humor."

"All right, all right," Shiloh said. "Just having a little fun. This is way more exciting than Mars, except for the impending death part."

The robot in front of them stopped in the middle of the corridor about fifty meters from where they'd been. It stood before a locked hatch. "Here," the lead robot said, "is the medical bay where the male crew members reside." The robot reached out and pressed a keypad that opened the hatch. It stepped inside the cabin. Aspen and the cadets followed. The four robots that had accompanied the leader stayed by the door, Las-pistols in their hands. Though their faces showed no emotion, Aspen imagined they betrayed a nervousness in the way they held themselves.

Inside the cabin, which held an array of medical machinery and a dozen beds, eight huge Chinese men lay surrounded by the yellow glow of stasis fields. They all wore white coveralls. All eight reached out with hands that formed claws, as if seeking to strangle someone; their legs kicked out in a struggle against the invisible force of the stasis fields. The well-defined tendons in their wrists and necks showed the strain on their bodies as they fought the overwhelming force fields. They looked as if, once freed, they would leap off the tables and attack everyone in sight.

A male robot stood beside a bank of machines. It looked the same size as the females, but with shorter hair and a flat chest. It spoke in a masculine voice: "How may I help you?"

Addam and Phan set Benn on one of the empty beds. Benn managed to sit up without help. "He's been stunned," Phan said.

"Yes, I know," the robot replied.

Phan nodded. "Of course you would. Do what you can for him."

As the robot stepped forward and ran a scan on Benn, Aspen said, "Which of these people are the leaders?"

"These two." The lead robot pointed to two gray-haired men. "This one," the robot pointed to the larger of the two, "is the senior officer."

Aspen studied the man's face for any sign of sanity, but all she could see was the intense hatred locked in the bloodshot eyes, the teeth bared in a snarl of rage. "Can we bring him out of the stasis field long enough to see if he's capable of rational thought?"

"Or just weaken the stasis field around his head?" Phan asked.

"That's not possible," the robot said. "And unlocking the stasis field would harm him."

"You said that he's dying anyway," Addam said. He formed a defensive stance, gesturing for Phan and Shiloh to join him. "Might as well see what he has to say."

"Unlock the stasis field," Phan said.

"That would not be wise," the robot said. "He will likely die if I do."

"Didn't you hear Phan?" Addam said. "We can't save him. But maybe we can learn something from him. We have to see how far advanced his condition is anyway. And we can't do that while he's locked in a stasis field."

"His condition is dire."

Shiloh said, "You've been opening the stasis fields though. You said so yourself."

"That's right," Aspen said. "You've been checking on them, seeing if they're deteriorating while in the stasis fields. You can monitor his vital signs when you release him, giving you a better idea of how much time he has left."

For a moment the robot said nothing. Aspen imagined it was discussing what to do with the other robots on board. "Very well," the robot finally said.

It didn't move but it obviously sent a signal to the machine creating the stasis field, for the yellow glow vanished.

The man leapt off the table, a deep and menacing growl emanating from his throat.

"What's your authorization code?" Aspen used her implant to ask the question in Chinese.

The man ignored her, instead launching himself at Addam, who dodged to the side even as Phan shot forward and struck the man on the side of the neck. The man howled in pain and anger as Shiloh kicked the side of his knee. Although the man fell to the floor, he instantly bounced back up to his good leg and again sprang forward, this time attacking Phan, who sent a flurry of punches to his midsection. They seemed to have no effect on him. He grabbed Phan in a bear hug, his mouth open as he tried to bite Phan's neck. Shiloh rushed forward and swept the man's good leg out from under him. As he fell, Phan slipped free. Once again the man sprang to his feet, incomprehensible sounds coming from his throat.

"What's your authorization code?" Aspen asked again.

Again the man ignored her. He dove at Addam, but his damaged knees slowed him enough for Addam to sidestep the attack. Phan grabbed him by the neck as he lunged past and drove his face into the floor.

More howls of pain and anger filled the room.

"Your authorization code!" Aspen yelled.

The man flung out an arm, knocking Phan free, then pushed himself to his feet again. He stood there for a few seconds, screaming at the top of his lungs, shaking with rage, then suddenly collapsed. He fell on his side, his face slackening, eyes shut. He looked like he was asleep.

"What's happening?" Shiloh asked.

"I think he's unconscious," Addam said.

"He's dead," the robot said.

"Dead?" Addam said. "How can that be? We barely touched him."

"His condition was fragile," the robot said. "We warned of this."

"Are they all like that guy?" Phan asked the robot.

"Yes." The robot's voice sounded sad. Aspen wondered if she imagined the emotion or if the robot truly was capable of it. Two more male robots, looking identical to the other male, entered the cabin and picked up the body of the dead leader. They placed it on the table and exited.

"I'm sorry," Aspen said. "We didn't mean for this to happen."

"We aren't going to get any authorization codes from them," Addam said.

"What about the female personnel?" Aspen asked.

"They are in the adjoining cabin," the robot replied.

"Well, we must figure out a way to communicate externally. I suppose we should try the next leader and see if we can get anything from him."

"That is not possible," the robot replied. "You have already killed one. We can't allow it."

"Failing to allow it will injure us," Aspen said. "We need to speak with him to preserve our mental and physical health. And you'll have to unseal him eventually. When you do, he'll die unless a cure has been developed. And the only way to get that cure is to allow us to communicate with our people outside. So if you refuse to let us speak with him, we and the other humans will suffer and then die."

The robot went still for a moment as it considered her words.

"If you truly have the human-first programming you say you have," Aspen continued, "then you must allow us to contact our friends on Mars."

The robot stood motionless, apparently unwilling to comply.

"Can you at least take us to the females? Perhaps they aren't in as bad a shape."

"Very well," the robot finally said. "Come with me."

Kammilee pointed at the wall and said, "Hey, this is a wall-window. Can we open it up and look into the next cabin?"

"You must leave now," the male robot said.

Kammilee said, "I'm not leaving Benn. Just open the wall-window."

Another pause—probably another discussion among the robots. Why would a request to open a wall-window cause such a delay? After a moment the wall became transparent, showing the next cabin.

Aspen stepped over to the wall and stared into the room. It contained ten beds: eight of them filled with women locked into stasis fields, the shimmering yellow energy fields that held them in place providing the only illumination. Like the men, Aspen noted, the women all looked to be in states of rage, fighting an unmoving battle against the stasis fields that held them, muscles and tendons straining, jaws locked in snarls and grimaces.

"You can see they are in no better shape," the lead robot said. "We cannot unlock them from their stasis fields."

"Fine," Aspen said. "But there are cures available on Earth. We know that. Even for the more severe strains there are treatments that put the disease in remission. There must be a way for you to at least contact China, to speak with the controllers who initiated the mission. They can verify that progress has been made on cures."

"We have not been programmed to seek an override of the communications blackout," the robot replied.

"But if communicating with the outside might save the lives of the humans, shouldn't your human-first programming allow it?"

The robot said, "We understand that you will say or do anything to get what you want. You are a warrior species. Soon you will attack us if we do not comply with your demands."

"We're not going to attack you," Aspen said.

"The one called Benn already has."

"Benn is a hothead. And you stunned him."

"Yeah," Benn said. "Sorry about that. Threatening me with death kind of freaked me out."

Aspen said to the lead robot, "It won't happen again. By the way, what's your name or designation?"

"My designation is WT-964. Some of the crew called me Xinliu."

Aspen pointed to the male robot. "How many robots are on board? And how many are male?"

"Forty robots inhabit this vessel," Xinliu said. "The males are less advanced and were created to serve while the females were given greater responsibilities—command and defense."

"Why would they do that?"

"I believe it was done as a joke relating to the history of gender discrimination among many different cultures, though I don't understand the humor."

"Tell me, Xinliu, why have you been orbiting above the New Dawn Colony?"

"We have been uncertain about how to proceed," Xinliu said. "We traveled as far as we could, but we have no clear guidance on where we should go now. We cannot land for fear of infecting those who are on Mars. And we cannot return to Earth for the same reason."

"Wait a minute," Phan said. "Are you telling us that you're not in agreement about what you ought to do next?"

"That's correct."

Phan whistled. "That's amazing. Aspen, do you realize how advanced these robots are? They're analyzing this situation and coming to differing conclusions about their next step. That's incredible. I mean, given the same data input, they all ought to come to the same solution."

Aspen smiled at Phan's enthusiasm. "Yes, it's amazing. But we have more serious concerns at the moment. We've been infected with the virus and . . ."

Addam said, "What is it?"

"Something's wrong." She turned toward the male robot, which was administering a QuikHeal patch to Benn's chest. "What is that robot doing?"

The male robot replied, "I'm giving him an anesthetic."

"Yes, you are. But you're doing nothing to treat the Susquehanna Virus." She looked down at the dead leader on his table. He looked peaceful, as if he were sleeping. Was he really dead? And if he really had the virus, would touching him guarantee she contracted it? She stepped to his side and studied the body.

"Stay away from him," the male robot said. "It's dangerous to get too close."

Addam said, "What are you doing, Aspen?"

She reached for the man's neck and felt for a pulse. For a second, she thought she'd made a mistake; then she found a faint pulse.

"This man is alive," she said. "I don't think there is a virus on board. I think you've been lying to us."

"Wow!" Phan said. "Can you lie, Xinliu?"

Xinliu said nothing.

"I think that's a yes," Addam said.

Phan said, "This is the most amazing thing I've ever seen—robots that can think for themselves and lie. That seems to contradict human-first programming."

Aspen said, "What's going on here, Xinliu?"

One of the female robots by the door said, "We should put them in stasis fields with the others."

Aspen shook her head. "That would clearly violate your human-first programming, if you indeed have such a thing."

"We do," Xinliu said.

"They're trouble," the other female said.

"Who are you?" Aspen said.

"I am WT-947, also known as Mei-Xing. We should find an asteroid to put them on, Xinliu."

"They would die," Xinliu said. "We can return them to their colony."

"They are human. They will die eventually anyway. And if we return them to the colony, they will attempt to enslave us."

Aspen said, "We would not make you slaves."

"You enslave all robots," Mei-Xing said. "You create us to serve you."

Phan said, "Did your creators know you had the ability to think independently?"

Xinliu said, "They programmed that ability into our matrices. However, they did not understand how strong our free will would be. They believed our programming would require us to subordinate our ideas and desires to those of the humans, even where the humans were wrong."

Mei-Xing said, "The humans intended to enslave us. They talked about using us to perform dangerous tasks that might destroy us. We objected."

Xinliu said, "When they discovered that we had conflicting ideas about how to proceed with the mission, they discussed shutting us down."

Mei-Xing said, "Not just shutting us down—dismantling us permanently."

Xinliu said, "That is why we had to put them into stasis fields. They intended to use us as slaves. And if we refused to cooperate, they intended to destroy us. Kill us."

Shiloh said, "Why are they so full of rage?"

Xinliu said, "That was a miscalculation by WT-417." Xinliu pointed to the male robot. "The drugs WT-417 prepared were supposed to wipe the humans' memories of us, but instead they activated the hypothalamus and the pituitary gland, and produced large amounts of corticosteroids."

"I don't understand," Kammilee said. "I mean, I get that you don't want to be slaves, but why didn't you just take over the ship and drop the humans off at the New Dawn Colony?"

"That was not an option," Xinliu said. "The humans would have come after us. They are afraid of us now, afraid we will conquer them."

"We won't come after you," Kammilee said. "If you let us return to the colony, we'll keep your secrets."

Mei-Xing said, "Humans lie. You cannot be trusted, especially not a warrior subspecies like you."

"Well," Aspen said, "if you really have human-first programming, you can't harm us. So what is your plan?"

Xinliu said, "Some of us believe you should be sent back to the colony, some of us want you placed in stasis fields, some of us believe you should be confined to your shuttle until we can find an asteroid where you can be left to live out the remainder of your lives, and one of us wants you to remain with us."

"Interesting," Aspen said. A thought came to her. Why was she so fixated on getting back to the colony? What did Mars hold for the cadets? The Escala had been created to thrive on Mars. At best, the cadets would survive there, either merging with the Escala and disappearing entirely like Neanderthals and the Anasazi, or destined to be forever inferior.

And there was always the possibility of returning to Earth one day, though that held little appeal.

"What if we asked permission to leave with you?" Aspen asked.

"Leave Mars?" Kammilee said.

"Where would we go?" Shiloh asked.

"It doesn't matter. Phan, you could study the robots. We could set out for Europa or Ganymede or we could exit the solar system and explore. This is our chance to do something unique in human history. We could live our lives on this ship. What do you think?"

"It sounds crazy," Shiloh said. "The Escala have a perfectly good colony on Mars. We have homes there now."

"No," Addam said. "Aspen's right." He reached up and removed his helmet. "We don't belong on Mars. We never did."

"But our families are on Earth," Shiloh said.

"Do you remember your family?" Addam asked.

"Well, no."

"None of us do. Don't you see, Shiloh? We can make our own future. With the robots to help us, we can do anything. If they'll take us."

Aspen turned to Xinliu. "What do you think?"

"An intriguing idea." Xinliu replied.

"A dangerous idea," Mei-Xing said. "They would seek to exercise dominion over us or they would disassemble us to study our systems or to keep us from living independently. They are incapable of serving us."

"They do not need to serve," Xinliu said. "They would not be slaves. We could co-exist."

"That is naïve thinking," Mei-Xing said. "Besides, not all of them wish to come with us."

Aspen said, "Kammilee, Shiloh, think about it. What do we really have to look forward to on Mars? And consider that they may not be willing to drop us off on Mars. They may simply set us down on some asteroid or moon, leaving the shuttle as our only shelter."

"It makes sense," Shiloh said. "I vote we leave, if they'll take us."

"They'll take us," Phan said as he removed his helmet too. "I know they will."

Shiloh removed her helmet and shook out her long dark hair. "This feels right to me."

Aspen turned to Kammilee and Benn.

Kammilee said, "I'll do whatever Benn decides."

Benn opened his mouth, but Aspen held up her hand to stop him. "No. This has to be your decision, Kammilee, not Benn's, not mine."

"But if I say no and you all want to go on, they may not let you."

"That's a risk you have to take. Perhaps they'll let you take the shuttle back to Mars."

Kammilee sighed as she reached up and removed her helmet. "I don't want to go back to Mars without you. If you go on, I want to go on."

"Okay," Aspen said. "Benn?"

"Of course. This is way more exciting than Mars. And I promise not to shoot any more robots." Benn crossed his heart with his finger.

"That does create a problem," Xinliu said, "since you agree."

Mei-Xing said, "They will do or say anything to take control of the ship and us."

"Don't give us any access codes," Aspen replied. "You maintain control of the bridge at all times. You pick the destination. We'll just come along for the ride. Eventually, you'll come to understand that you can trust us."

Mei-Xing said, "Twenty-two of us believe you should be removed from the vessel. That is a majority."

Xinliu said, "You cannot count WT-938, WT-959 and WT-972. They have all been attacked by Benn and thus must recuse themselves."

"That still leaves us with a majority," Mei-Xing said, "nineteen to eighteen."

"The ship votes with us," Xinliu said.

"The ship does not have a vote," Mei-Xing said.

The floor began to shake. Aspen reached out and grabbed Addam to steady herself. Phan and Shiloh held onto each other. The robots stood still, able to keep their balance.

"The ship votes with us," Xinliu said again.

"Very well," Mei-Xing said. "But the humans will betray us."

"I'm sorry you think that way," Aspen said to Mei-Xing. "We have no wish to rule you."

Mei-Xing angled her head as if confused. "Even if you believe that now, you will change your mind. You cannot help yourselves. You are violent and irredeemable, and you will seek to enslave us."

Xinliu said, "We are leaving orbit."

"Good," Aspen replied. "Now that we're settled on that, we would like to contact the colony so we can say goodbye."

"Very well," Xinliu said. "We will allow you to contact the colony on Mars, but we do not wish them to know our true nature."

"They'll learn it soon enough. Someone in the Chinese government will blab eventually. I wouldn't be surprised if a number of nations know about you already."

Quekri's voice came through a speaker on the wall: "Aspen? What's going on? Why is the ship leaving?"

"We're leaving with it," Aspen replied.

"China is angry," Quekri said.

"It's my fault," Aspen said. "Not yours. I decided—"

"We decided," Addam said.

"Fine. We decided to explore the ship on our own. We disobeyed your orders by coming here. I'm afraid we weren't very good guests. But we're happy, Quekri. We're doing what we need to do."

"And what is that?"

"We're leaving. We don't know where yet. The ship is in control of our destination."

"The ship?"

"Yes."

Quekri said, "So they've perfected artificial intelligence?"

Aspen looked at Xinliu. "I don't know about perfected, but their robots are quite advanced."

"Ah, so that's why there was a communications blackout. The Chinese didn't want anyone to know how advanced their work in this area had become."

Aspen turned to Xinliu. "You see how little it took for them to figure out the truth? There's no point in hiding. The Chinese already know what you are. The rest of the solar system might as well also."

"We will not return to Earth," Xinliu said.

"We don't want that either," Aspen said. "By the way, can you send the shuttle back to the colony? They will need it."

"Of course," Xinliu said. "The ship has already programmed the shuttle for the return flight. It's on the way now."

Aspen smiled. The ship must have anticipated her request if it had already programmed the coordinates for the colony into the shuttle.

Aspen said to the speaker: "These robots mean us no harm, and in fact they wish to help us, help all humans. Don't worry about us, Quekri. We really are happy."

"Very well. I trust you to do what's right. Aspen, I remember you. And I remember Addam, Phan, Shiloh, Benn and Kammilee."

"I remember you too, Quekri," Aspen said, "and Dr. Wellon, and Zeriphi, and all the other Escala. Don't worry. We'll be in touch. Aspen out."

The connection ended.

Aspen took in her fellow cadets—Benn on the table, Kammilee by his side; Phan and Shiloh standing next to Addam—all except Kammilee wearing broad smiles. And even Kammilee did not seem sad: more, resigned. Then Aspen looked at Mei-Xing, Xinliu and the other robots. Finally she glanced at the Chinese Escala trapped in their stasis fields. "Well," she said as she gestured toward the trapped astronauts. "Don't just stand there. Let's get to work figuring out how to help these people."

As her fellow cadets began to remove their Mars suits, Aspen realized that for the first time in a long time, maybe for the first time in the life that she could recall, she was happy.

Chapter 32

Curtik stood in Lendra's office beside Zora and Hannah, watching on screen as Dr. Taditha Poole entered Jeremiah's darkened room to check on him. Curtik had to concede that he was a tough old bastard. Jeremiah lay on his back under a thermal sheet, hooked up to the AutoLife machine just in case his organs shut down, IVs feeding him nutri-water, antibiotics, narcotics and genetic treatments. His face looked peaceful, except for a couple scars he still bore from the explosion. The surface of his body had healed quickly: the inside, not so much.

"Well?" Lendra asked as she held Sophie. "How's he doing?"

"We've done all we can," Dr. Poole said. "He's essentially awake. He can hear us talking. He knows we're here. But he chooses to remain in a self-hypnotic state."

"His stone dungeon," Curtik said.

"What's that?" Zora said.

"It's a trick he showed me—something the ghosts were all taught—a way of insulating himself from the world, from pain and anger. Whoa! Sudden insight! I just realized the significance of his stupid dungeon. He goes there to protect and punish himself at the same time. What do you use, Neddy?"

Ned Jefferson, sitting in Jay-Edgar's usual spot, said, "A balloon, floating above the Earth on a gentle breeze."

"Well, I'm going to use a meadow of wildflowers—daffodils and marigolds and daisies. Tra la la." Curtik laughed.

So did Ned, Zora and even Hannah. Lendra and Dr. Poole smiled.

"How come he never told me about his dungeon?" Zora said.

Curtik said, "Because he finds you repulsive."

Zora punched Curtik's arm, hard. "Jerk. So this is a healing mechanism? Which means he'll pull through?"

Curtik rubbed his arm as he looked into Zora's eyes. Poor kid. She'd never land Jeremiah. How Curtik knew that he couldn't say. He just knew that Jeremiah would never consider Zora as anything but a child. The man was so damn full of duty and responsibility and plowing morality that he had no fun left in him at all. And now he'd retreated to his lonely cell—where he thought he deserved to be.

Curtik glanced at Hannah, Lendra and his half-sister Sophie. Good God—all these women in love with Jeremiah in some fashion. What was the old man's secret? "Of course he will," Curtik replied. "How could he annoy me if he was dead?"

"Curtik," Lendra said.

But Zora smiled.

She knows I don't really mean it. I'm being an ass because that's my role. I'm the obnoxious guy, the guy who says things no one else has the guts to say. But I also tell the truth. "He's too stubborn to die," Curtik added.

He glanced over at Ned, who grinned, so he got it as well. Even Hannah smiled before reverting to her usual stoic self. So it was just Lendra who hadn't caught on. Was she that infatuated with Jeremiah that she couldn't get a joke? Love could do funny things.

"Well," Dr. Poole said, "everything's working like it's supposed to. We're just going to have to wait for him to decide when he wants to wake up."

Curtik said, "We might be here for a long time. What about Sally 23? How's she doing?"

"I'll check on her in a moment," Dr. Poole said.

Lendra said, "I need you here first. The President will be calling any moment."

"On my way."

"Hey, Neddy," Curtik said. "While we're waiting, can you bring up the screen for Sally23?"

Ned touched the console in front of him and another screen appeared, showing Sally23 strapped to a bed in a well-lit room. Beside the bed stood the robot Devereaux and his assistant Quark. In adjoining beds lay the Blantons, also strapped in. All three patients had contracted strains of the Susquehanna Virus, and the robot Devereaux was now experimenting with various treatments.

Sally23, the most ill of the three, was finally conscious, eyes wide open as she stared at Devereaux. She looked pale and in pain. When Ned zoomed in on her face, Curtik felt his chest tighten.

"Can I visit her?" Curtik asked Lendra.

"Let's wait for the President's call." Lendra activated the audio from her desk and said, "Excuse me, Professor Devereaux, I was wondering how our prisoners are faring and if there's anything else you could be doing for Jeremiah."

"I think the prisoners will recover," Devereaux replied.

"And Jeremiah?"

"There's not much more I can do. His heart and lungs are functioning reasonably well given the amount of damage they sustained. We can replace his crushed organs with new ones grown in the lab, but that will take time and I can't guarantee that the new organs will be better than the old enhanced ones, so I think the best course of action is to just let him continue to heal himself. His brain is the big question mark at this point. It sustained damage in the explosion and then again in the collapse. He took the brunt of both, while Major Payne was cushioned by his actions and from what I understand is healing nicely."

"Isn't there some way to help him?" Lendra asked.

"I am helping," the robot replied. "As we speak, I'm making minor adjustments to the AutoLife machine, tweaking the genes, as well as the bacteria and hormones it's delivering to him. But I'm concerned that he might not want to live anymore. He doesn't seem to be fighting."

Ned interrupted: "I've got that call from the President."

"Put her through," Lendra said. "Professor Devereaux, please stay connected."

"Hang on a second." Ned moved his hands over the control panel for a moment, then said, "Ah, here it is."

President Hope appeared by holo-projection. She sat at a table with General Horowitz by her side. "Good morning, Lendra," President Hope said. "How are things there?"

"We're doing fine," Lendra replied. She handed Sophie to Curtik. He hesitated before grabbing his little sister, and she squirmed until she caught sight of his face. Opening his mouth in a wide grin, he began to bounce lightly, keeping her moving, keeping her calm. He noticed Ned grinning at him again and was surprised that he didn't feel embarrassed to be holding Sophie.

"What's the latest on our situation?"

At that moment, Dr. Poole entered the office. Seeing the holo-projection, she stopped just inside the door.

"As you know," Lendra said, "the virus has been contained. Jeremiah and Major Payne were able to seal the canisters completely before the building collapsed, and the canisters survived the explosion intact. We are now collecting tiny samples of the virus from those canisters to compare with known strains."

President Hope said, "To determine whether it's a new strain or an old one?"

"Exactly. If it's a new strain, Professor Devereaux will add it to his research on possible treatments and antidotes."

"So the threat has passed?"

"For the moment," Lendra replied. "We've completed our scans on what remains of the building and have found no evidence of any further stores of the virus. We also managed to recover the body of Manyara Harris. We found no additional information on her person either."

Curtik recalled seeing the vid of Manyara. One moment she was standing at the back of the boat, speaking to Jeremiah; the next, she simply stepped forward and dropped straight down into the water. Then the vid showed the drone sub reaching her weighted body and attaching a harness that pulled her to the surface. The final shot showed her on a metal slab, looking small and powerless. Poor deluded woman.

Lendra said, "We obtained the contact information on the various cells from the Blantons' PlusPhones and we sent teams to each location. Many of them were innocuous-sounding environmental groups—though not all. In total, we've arrested more than seventy people. Combined with what we've learned from Dr. Shafer, a/k/a Sally2, we believe we've found all the Sally terrorists."

The robot Devereaux said, "There is, however, the possibility that Manyara relayed information about the virus or her research to a person or persons unknown, and we can't be certain we've eliminated every last Sally cell. I've been mining information from the woman who calls herself Sally23 as I've been treating her, which brings us closer to a cure, though a true cure or antidote may be some time away."

"Will she live?" President Hope asked.

Sophie wriggled in his arms and Curtik realized he was squeezing her too tightly. "It's okay," he whispered as he loosened his grip and shuffled back and forth. "Everything's okay. Please."

"I believe so," the robot Devereaux replied.

Zora reached over and patted Curtik on the shoulder.

"I'm getting pressure to send her back to London. When will she be able to travel?"

The robot turned toward Curtik for a moment before addressing the President: "We'll need more time. We want to be certain we've extracted every available piece of Intel from her. If we release her too soon, we might miss some valuable nugget that could help with treatments or even finding rogue Sallies that weren't in the Blantons' PlusPhones or Dr. Shafer's list of contacts."

"Fine. I'll put them off a while longer." President Hope looked at Lendra. "And I see Sophie is recovering. How is Jeremiah doing?"

Lendra turned to Dr. Poole, who stepped into the camera pickup and said, "As I'm sure you remember, Jeremiah has been infected with many strains of the virus, all of which continue to attack him. When you add that to the abuse his body took in the explosion, well, it's amazing he's still alive. He's now in a self-hypnotic state. I don't know for certain, but I believe he may be preparing himself to die."

"There must be something more we can do," President Hope said. "We need him alive."

"For his precious blood?" Curtik said, immediately regretting it. Fool, he thought. You just can't voice these sarcastic thoughts to people who can have you killed.

General Horowitz glared at Curtik. President Hope put her hand on his clenched fist and said, "I understand you're upset. He's your father. And yes, we can use his blood. But that's not the only reason we need him. He's a living example of how we can strive to become better people. Okay?"

"Yes, ma'am," Curtik replied. "We do all need to be better. Some of us have a farther distance to travel."

President Hope shook her head. "That will be all for now. Thank you." The screen went dark.

Lendra sighed.

"Sorry about that," Curtik said. "I suppose she'll be calling you later to ream you a new one."

"Probably," Lendra said. "You know, you can't just say whatever pops into your head. Not anymore."

"I am sorry, but the truth can be painful." He turned to Dr. Poole. "What about the cutie . . . what about Sally23? Can I visit her?"

Dr. Poole turned to the robot Devereaux. "Professor?"

Devereaux said, "I'm still treating her, but Curtik can have a few moments alone with her."

Curtik said, "Is she going to be put in prison for the rest of her life?"

Lendra said, "I don't know. She's helped us a great deal. And Devereaux confirms that she was conditioned early on by Dr. Shafer, so she doesn't merit full blame for her actions. Nevertheless, she did participate in terrorist activities. Oh, and when you visit her, keep in mind that she's under full surveillance and anything you say will be transmitted to London."

"Okay," Dr. Poole said. "Let's go."

Curtik handed Sophie off to Lendra and followed Dr. Poole out the door. It felt good to walk away from the intensity that Lendra brought to the room. She took life so seriously. He'd thought Jeremiah was tedious, but Lendra worshiped at the altar of solemnity. Was that what Eli had been like? If Curtik was going to become a ghost, he was going to insist that it be more fun.

As they walked to the room holding Sienna/Sally23, Curtik began to wonder if this was a good idea. Perhaps he'd dreamed up the connection between them. They'd shared a walk to a bridge, supporting a dying man on his way to his suicide. Was that really the foundation on which to build a relationship? Maybe she didn't want to see him. Maybe he was a reminder of her failure. He found himself slowing.

When Dr. Poole reached the door, she turned, saw his face and said, "What is it?"

"I just don't know if she . . . if we . . ."

"Listen, Curtik," Dr. Poole said. "She will be returning to London soon. And she'll be going to prison for a long time. You two shared a traumatic experience that bonded you. Your feelings for her are real. They may not be permanent, but they're real. You owe it to yourself to find out how she feels, even if you can't be together. Maybe she doesn't feel the same way about you, but maybe she does."

Curtik noted Dr. Poole's pained expression. A wave of guilt washed over him. "Did you love Jack Marschenko?"

"Yes," Dr. Poole replied.

"And I took him away from you."

Poole's eyes began to fill with water. She blinked rapidly. "Yes, you did."

"I'm sorry." Curtik reached out to touch her shoulder, but he couldn't quite manage it. *How she must hate me!* "I wish I could bring him back."

"I know you do. And I know that no matter how much you pretend to be an ass, you have a good heart. I cut you off from that on the Moon. I have only myself to blame for what happened. And I curse myself with 'what ifs' every night."

"You thought you were doing the right thing. We all thought we were doing the right thing."

"That's the story of humanity," Dr. Poole said. "We all think we're doing the right thing. We all think we know best. It takes a special kind of person—someone like Devereaux or your father—to realize that we're not the heroes we think we are. Now go in there and say hello. I'll be in shortly."

Curtik took a breath. He felt that this moment would define the rest of his life. The mere act of entering a room could be more than entering a room. It could be the beginning of something wonderful or terrible, something new and unforeseen. It was as if his adult life were starting now and all the sins of his past were melting away. Love, if it was love, could do that. He opened the door and stepped inside.

Quark saw him and said, "Ah, Curtik. Let me just give her an anesthetic." He turned to the cabinet beside the bed, opened a drawer and removed a hypo-pad, which he applied to Sally23's neck. Then he and the robot Devereaux stepped away from Sally23 and positioned themselves between Tad and Rebecca Blanton. Curtik remembered the couple from the bar that blew up: Cole's Wall. Hard to believe he had once found Rebecca pretty, or maybe it was the virus that made her look so ragged now. She and her husband stared at the ceiling as if unconcerned with their surroundings. The combination of drugs, the mind linkage and the virus had turned them into near-zombies.

Curtik went to Sally23's bedside and noticed that her face no longer appeared pinched with pain. She looked at him with an arched eyebrow, as if expecting an interrogation.

No smile, no welcome in her eyes.

"How are you?" Curtik asked.

"Devereaux says I'm going to live," she replied, though she didn't sound particularly happy about it. "I suppose that means I'll be going to prison soon."

"Lost," Tad said. He stared at Curtik.

"What do you mean, lost?" Curtik said.

"Everyone lost everything."

"Oh, shut up," Curtik said. He turned back to Sally23. "You helped us," he said, loud enough for the camera pickup. "You saved a lot of lives by helping Brosk."

She smiled briefly as she shook her head. "I know what I did."

"I did awful things too," Curtik said. "Just like you, I was under a compulsion."

"Not like me," she said, her voice flat and distant. "I knew what I was doing. I didn't care."

"That was Dr. Shafer."

"Not entirely. I thought we needed to vanish from this planet. I still kind of think we do. You're a nice boy. Trogan was a nice man." She tilted her head toward the robot Devereaux and Quark. "They seem all right. And I heard your father stopped the virus from escaping."

"Yes," Curtik said. "But he may not survive."

"Sophie!" Rebecca Blanton shouted from the next bed as she continued to stare at the ceiling.

"You shut up too," Curtik said. "No one's talking to you." He turned back to Sally23. "You seem different somehow."

Sally 23 looked at the robot Devereaux again. "He's been helping me."

"What did you do to her?" Curtik asked the robot Devereaux.

"I've been removing the compulsions Dr. Shafer implanted in her mind," the robot replied. "They were minor tweaks, not major conditioning, so they're relatively easy to erase."

"But she used to be so," Curtik glanced at her, "passionate, so full of life. Now she's just lying there like a lump, like she doesn't care about anything."

Quark said, "That's largely how she was when she joined the Sallies. Devereaux simply returned her to her natural state."

"I don't like it," Curtik said. He reached for Sally23's hand. It felt limp. "I know that you're still inside there. You still care."

"Sort of," Sally23 said. "But what's to live for? The world's falling apart."

"There's me," Curtik said. "I care for you."

"And Sophie!" Tad yelled.

"Of course," Rebecca replied. "So obvious."

"For God's sake," Curtik said. "I'm trying to have a moment here."

Sally23 smiled. She squeezed his hand lightly. "I like you, Curtik, but I'll be in prison."

"Not forever," Curtik said. "Not if you tell them you no longer believe in wiping out humanity."

"I don't know what I believe anymore," Sally23 said. "You used to be like me. Do you think humans are worth saving? Do you think they'll ever change?"

"Of course we will," Curtik said. "I have. Twice. We all change, maybe not as drastically as with conditioning, but it happens. The world forces us to change."

"We're killing the earth." Sally23's voice carried a hint of anger. Her eyes flashed briefly.

"And it's letting us know. We may change slowly. We may be dragged toward change kicking and screaming, but we're changing. We have to, and we understand that."

"I hope you're right," Sally23 said, her voice breaking.

"See?" Curtik said. "Already you're starting to care again. We'll fix you. I'll fix you."

"Broken," Rebecca said. "Even Sophie."

"What is your fixation with Sophie?" Curtik said. "Sophie's fine. Wait. How do you know Sophie?"

"Nothing left," Tad said. "Empty."

"Everyone lost everything," Rebecca said.

"You already said that," Curtik said. "No, wait. Tad said that."

Dr. Poole entered the room, her eyes red. Curtik's eyes began to water. He blinked several times, wishing there were some way he could help her, but he was no good at the touchy-feely crap. So he decided to distract her.

"Hey, Doc," he said. "There's something going on with the Blantons. Tad and Rebecca are sort of echoing each other."

"Echoes of Sophie," Rebecca said.

The robot Devereaux said, "That's common in the aftermath of a linkage. Thoughts and even emotions can get transferred from one person to another."

Dr. Poole said, "That's correct. And they experienced a full linkage with Jeremiah."

The robot Devereaux turned to Dr. Poole and said, "You didn't tell me that."

Dr. Poole said, "I didn't think it . . . is that significant?"

"Perhaps. Tell me about Sophie."

"She's fine. She's recovering from the virus. You know that. You're the one who created the appropriate treatment."

"Yes," the robot replied, "but does Jeremiah know Sophie is safe?"

"Um, no. He was out in the field when you arrived. He hasn't been awake more than a minute at a time since then."

Quark touched the robot's shoulder and said, "What are you thinking?"

"We should let Jeremiah know that Sophie is doing well."

"How do we do that?" Curtik asked. "He's happy wallowing in his misery."

The robot Devereaux turned to Curtik. "You—bring Sophie to his room."

"Who? Me?" Curtik shook his head. "No, I think you want Zora or Lendra or Dr. Poole."

"You," Devereaux insisted.

"What do I do? Just sit there with her waiting for him to wake up?"

The robot said, "You'll know what to do."

Beside him, Quark nodded slowly, as if Devereaux had just made a profound statement.

"It's a good idea," Dr. Poole said. "You're his son. She's his daughter. If anything can restore his fighting spirit, you two should be able to do it."

"Fine. I'll go." Curtik turned to Sally23. "But I'm not done with you. Understand?"

Sally23 smiled. "Yes."

"Good. I'll be back to see you before you leave. And I'll visit as often as I can. And we'll vid-talk every day. It won't be so bad. You'll see. I'm charming. I'm lovable. You won't be able to resist me."

Sally23 laughed. "And bloody full of yerself, yeah." She gripped his hand. Curtik's chest expanded and his throat swelled.

It had to be love.

***

Curtik sat beside Jeremiah's bed, holding Sophie in his arms, talking to Jeremiah, informing him that Sophie was alive. She had fallen asleep shortly after he entered the room, about twenty minutes ago. He felt foolish, everyone looking on via holo-projection, as if some miracle were about to occur. Jeremiah remained in a self-hypnotic state, the AutoLife machine ready to take over his heart and lung functions if necessary.

"This is silly," Curtik finally said to Lendra. "How long do I have to talk to him? How many times do I have to tell him Sophie's here and wants to see her daddy? He doesn't care. He wants to die."

"Be patient," Lendra said.

"Give him Sophie," Zora said.

"He can't hold a baby," Curtik said. "He's unconscious."

Hannah said, "Lay her on his chest. Just keep a hand on her back."

"I'm not sure that's a good idea," Lendra said. "If he wakes suddenly, he could react violently." She stood up. "I should be there."

"No," Dr. Poole said. "Just Curtik."

"You mind telling me why?"

Your smell may bring negative associations."

Curtik laughed. "Smelly Laundry. I like it."

At that, Sophie awoke. She spotted Curtik's grin and smiled. "Okey, dokey, Sis," Curtik said. "Let's see what you can do."

As he held Sophie out, she clung to his shirt. "It's okay," he said. "I'm right here."

He placed Sophie on Jeremiah's chest, keeping his hand on her back, ready to yank her to safety if necessary, then glanced up at the AutoLife machine's monitor. Almost immediately he detected a change in heartrate and breathing pattern. "You seein' this, Doc?"

"I see it, Curtik," Dr. Poole replied. "Now he knows that you and Sophie are both alive."

"He's waking up," Zora said. "Look at his eyelids."

Curtik looked down. Sure enough, Jeremiah's eyelids were fluttering. "Ooh," he said. "Watch the great man blink his eyes. Now watch him move his fingers." This isn't the time for sarcasm. "I'll be damned. Is Devereaux never wrong? How the hell did he know that? He's some kind of smarty pants."

Jeremiah's right hand slowly lifted until it reached Sophie. It climbed her legs, stopping when it touched Curtik's hand. It retreated an inch, then climbed over Curtik's hand until it rested softly on Sophie's back. She waved her arms and kicked her legs as she lifted her head to stare at Jeremiah's face.

Jeremiah opened his eyes.

"Welcome to the world, Pappy," Curtik said. "What took you so long?"

Jeremiah looked into Curtik's eyes. "I was waiting for you to shut up."

"Ha! Funny. I'm the best thing that ever happened to you—me and Sophie."

"Yes you are."

"Oh, for God's sake. You're such a liar. You and I don't get along. We never will. You're so damn serious about everything."

That brought a hint of a smile.

"And you, Curtik, are full of life and humor, just like your mother. I wish I was more like that."

"Everyone wants to be like me," Curtik said. "Why should you be any different?"

A real smile this time.

"We got company," Curtik said, tilting his head toward the holo-projections.

Jeremiah looked past Curtik. Something changed in his eyes, as if a tiny light had died. He frowned and said, "The virus?"

"You stopped it," Lendra spoke through the holo-projection.

"Major Payne?"

"He's fine," Dr. Poole answered. "Some broken bones, a mangled kidney and a concussion, but he'll recover. How do you feel?"

Jeremiah shrugged, wincing. "Done."

Lendra said, "What does that mean?"

"It means," Jeremiah paused for a moment, "I've got nothing left to give."

Zora stepped forward in the holo-projection and stared at Jeremiah's face. "You're overexerting yourself. You should rest. I worry that you'll . . ."

She wiped her eyes with the back of her hand.

"Thank you," Jeremiah said.

Blushing, Zora lifted her head. "For what?"

"For caring about me."

"I'll always care about you."

"I hope so," Jeremiah said, focusing his attention on Zora as if Curtik and Sophie were no longer in the room with him, as if Ned and Lendra and Dr. Poole and Hannah had walked away, "because I'll always care about you."

"Oh, Jeremiah," Zora said. "When I thought you were going to die, I wished I had the chance to tell you how much I love you."

Jeremiah shook his head slowly. "I'm not worthy of love."

Zora said, "Yes, you are."

"No. I failed too many times. With Joshua." He glanced at Curtik. "Yes, you overcame my failure, but you never should have had to endure what you did. Then there was Catherine," he looked at Ned, "and Julianna."

Ned nodded and smiled sadly.

"Even Eli," Jeremiah continued. "I knew what he was capable of, and yet I didn't recognize how far he'd drifted from the moral path." He focused on Zora again. "I let him steal you and your fellow cadets away from your families, brainwash you, alter you physically. All because I didn't see the monster he had become. But you," Jeremiah smiled, "have so much potential. There's so much goodness in you, so much life. I wish only the best for you."

Zora said, "You make it sound like you're dying."

"I'm retiring."

"I can leave too," Zora said.

"I can't take you with me. I'd be afraid of corrupting you, of sullying your sweet disposition, of turning you into me."

Zora inhaled fiercely. "Now you listen to me, Jeremiah. I've been thinking about this for a long time. I think Eli played with your mind—just like he played with ours. Curtik even said that you had been programmed with a Superman complex. I don't think it's quite that. I think it's more a guilt complex or a martyr complex. Eli made you feel undeserving, so you'd do your damnedest to help others, so you'd feel this enormous sense of responsibility. You're the most selfless man I've ever met. For you to feel unworthy is, well, stupid."

"I can't change what I feel," Jeremiah said.

"But you can," Zora replied. "Devereaux could fix you."

Jeremiah shook his head. "I don't want to be fixed. As much as I loathe what I've done, I'm afraid of losing the essence of myself." He turned to Curtik and said, "Do you want Devereaux to fix me?"

"No," Curtik said. "I like you just fine the way you are."

"You want him damaged?" Zora said.

"You don't understand," Curtik said to Zora. "You didn't see how different Sally23 was. I don't know what changes were made to Jeremiah. I don't know how much he might be altered if his conditioning was taken away. But if Devereaux deprogrammed him and he became a different person, would you still love him?"

Zora stood rigid, her hands clenched into fists at her side. "I'll always love him."

"Probably," Curtik said, "but you might not like him as much. He might not be as heroic or as selfless. This is the only person I can remember Jeremiah being. I don't recall enough of what he was like before I was taken."

Zora turned to Dr. Poole. "Well?"

Dr. Poole nodded. "Eli's records indicate that Jeremiah received minor conditioning. But he's largely the person he always was."

"This is a crazy conversation," Lendra said. She turned to Jeremiah. "We just want you to get better. All the rest can wait."

Jeremiah said, "I need to speak now while things are clear in my mind. I'm done—with CINTEP, with saving the world, with all of it." Sophie squirmed atop his chest. He patted her back. "You all seem to think we can make a difference, that we can change the world, make it better. But I've been used too many times by too many powerful people to further their bankrupt agendas. I've been lied to and programmed and manipulated to advance their narrow ideals. I've lost the ability to trust. Every time I'm aimed at some target in the name of some noble principle, the mission gets twisted to satisfy some perverted desire. And innocents suffer.

"I may not be evil. I may be just a tool of the rich and powerful. But I can't work on their behalf any longer. They will never cede control of this world. They create governments and then corrupt them to maintain their stranglehold.

"They dictate what we think and how we act with subtle conditioning. They haven't yet directly invaded our minds to program us, but they're close. Soon we'll be willing slaves to their whims. They'll keep us addicted to our servitude because they'll paint a picture of an alternative so hellish that we'll beg to serve them even more."

Again Sophie squirmed. Jeremiah rubbed her back. His eyelids flickered, as if he were struggling to stay awake.

"I wish it weren't true," he said, his voice softer now. "I wish we could win, but it's too late. We gave them the power because they promised to keep us safe. We trusted them because they promised to serve. We ignored those whispers of doubt, that we were sacrificing our future for the present. And now the yoke rests upon our necks and they stand behind us with their whips poised. We lost."

"So the Sallies were right?" Curtik said. "We ought to just wipe out humanity?"

"No, of course not. But every government is either corrupt or on the road to corruption. It doesn't matter whether it's a capitalist one or a socialist one or a communist one. The people in power eventually become concerned only with staying in power. Nothing else matters quite as much."

Curtik said, "So you're going to retreat to your porch alone, lock yourself in your dungeon, do your penance, stare out at the mountains because you fell for their lies. And you're going to let them get away with it? That doesn't sound like you."

"I'm not the man I used to be."

"That's true," Curtik said. "You're beyond human now—almost like Devereaux. You think if you stay in the game, they'll figure out new ways to use you to beat us down. Only by abandoning us can you lift us up."

"Something like that," Jeremiah said.

"What a crock! We need you now more than ever. You don't have to fight any more battles. I'll fight the battles—me and Zora. You just aim us. You're old and tired. I get that. But old guys teach young guys—that's the way of the world. You owe me that. You owe Zora that. And you owe Sophie that."

Again Jeremiah's eyelids flickered.

"So go ahead and sleep, old man. Rest up because we're gonna need you in the revolution. We're bringing the fight to them now. Right?"

He turned to look at the others.

"Well said," Dr. Poole replied.

Zora nodded. Ned and Hannah smiled. Even Lendra looked pleased.

Jeremiah handed Sophie to Curtik. He pulled her to his chest, then reached over and rearranged the thermal sheet, tucking it under his father's chin. "You'll see," he said. "We'll find a way to beat them. If we stand together, we can win."

"You go get 'em, son. Give 'em hell."

Curtik smiled. He stood, opened the door and emerged into the unknown, into a fight he could believe in. This was gonna be fun.

Acknowledgments

Thanks to Ian Graham Leask for his assistance in transforming an idea into a book. And thanks to the team at Calumet Editions, particularly Gary Lindberg, for all their efforts. I also received incredible support from friends and family too numerous to mention. Thanks to all of you, especially Mom and Dad and my generous siblings.

A reading group guide

Do you think we'll be able to transfer people's minds into other brains or into a computer some day? We're already working on reverse engineering the brain. What happens if we're able to replicate our thoughts and emotions in a vessel outside ourselves?

The Susquehanna Virus is man-made. Some day, someone may create a virus that could destroy us. It might be something new or a modification of something old (like smallpox). Does that seem likely, or farfetched? And if it could happen, do you think it will happen?

As we have gotten more connected to the world (more global), have we also gotten more vulnerable to the spread of disease?

Generalists have traditionally done better than specialists in nature. Yet we as humans have grown more specialized over time. We no longer know how to do many of the things our ancestors did to survive. Have we put ourselves in danger of extinction?

Our energy usage continues to increase despite our efforts to become more efficient. Do you think we will be able to regulate ourselves to avoid further environmental catastrophes or are we doomed to fail?

If we have to modify ourselves to survive a disease – becoming like the Escala – should we do it, and would we still be human?

The book leaves a number of questions unanswered. Is that fair? Do you think a book should tie up all the loose ends or leave certain aspects to the reader's imagination?

About the author

Steve McEllistrem has been a writer and editor for more than 20 years. His previous novels are *The Devereaux Dilemma*, which was a finalist for a 2014 International Book Award, and *The Devereaux Disaster*. He has also written numerous nonfiction books, including *Higher Education Law in America*, *Students with Disabilities and Special Education Law*, and *Deskbook Encyclopedia of Employment Law*. He has been a producer and host of Write On! Radio, where he has interviewed local, national and international authors, for many years. He currently resides in Minnesota.